Praise for *A June of Ordinary Murders*

'A vivid and crafty whodunit … Fans of mysteries that capture the flavour of the past will hope that Swallow has a long literary life.' – *Publishers Weekly, Starred Review*

'Brady's powerful first mystery novel is evocative of the period. The many aspects of life in 19th-century Dublin are cleverly woven through a baffling mystery.' – *Kirkus Reviews*

'Swallow is an increasingly interesting protagonist who is left to face the realities of his professional future and his closest personal relationship; readers will want to see more of him.' – *Booklist*

'Making his mystery debut, former *Irish Times* editor Brady presents a fascinating and in-depth historical peek at crime solving in a bygone era when it took more than a few keystrokes and a phone call to catch a perp. Swallow is a complicated, earnest hero with just enough flaws to make him endearingly sympathetic.' – *Library Journal*

'Conor Brady's debut novel is a slice of history about Dublin, Ireland, and the Dublin Metropolitan police, intertwined with a first-rate murder mystery, and peopled by characters both complex and realistic.' – *NY Journal of Books*

'Like all great historical fiction, *A June of Ordinary Murders* stuns us into fresh recognition of a period we thought we knew – and as if that weren't enough, hides all of its meticulous research inside a superbly engaging mystery. Get in on the ground floor. Conor Brady is the real deal.' – *Charles Finch*, bestselling author of *The Laws of Murder*

'Brady weaves a police procedural that does full justice to the complex nature of the social, political and criminal labyrinth that was Dublin in the summer of 1887. He paints a vivid picture of the city … Swallow himself is very much in the mould of the classic fictional policeman, a man ostensibly dedicated to upholding law and order and seeking out justice …' – *The Irish Times*

'As in the best crime fiction, the city itself is here a kind of character – and it's a Dublin we haven't seen a great deal of in recent fiction … An absorbing read, cleanly written, beautifully structured and thrillingly vivid … Brady has done an excellent job of conjuring the febrile atmosphere of the city as it lurches and stumbles its way towards the War of Independence.' – *Sunday Business Post*

'Delivers a thrilling sense of the familiar, lit with the profane … the pace raises the novel above the period pastiche.' – *Sunday Independent*

'Brady handles the political atmosphere of the time with aplomb. *A June Of Ordinary Murders* pulsates with a vivid sense of a country on edge as the land wars rage and preparations get under way for a royal visit.' – *Irish Independent*

Praise for *The Eloquence of the Dead*

'In Brady's stellar second whodunit set in Victorian Dublin … the astute Swallow is a particularly well-rounded lead, and he's matched with a complex, but logical, page-turner of a plot.' – *Publishers Weekly*

'The second case for the talented, complicated Swallow again spins a fine mystery out of political corruption in 1880s Dublin.' – *Kirkus Reviews*

'If intricate plotting and journalistic descriptions of time and place pique your fancy, Brady is your man.' – Historical Novel Society

'He has given us a compelling and memorable central character in the shape of Detective Swallow … If the RTÉ drama department are looking for something to fill a *Love/Hate*-sized hole in next year's schedule, they could do worse than look at the continuing development, and adventures, of Detective Joe Swallow.' – *Irish Independent*

'Swallow, a keen amateur painter, brings a sharp eye to bear on his surroundings, which in turn allows Brady to give us a vivid account of late Victorian Dublin in all its squalid glory. The result is a very satisfying police procedural/mystery and an equally fine historical novel.' – *The Irish Times*

A HUNT IN WINTER

A HUNT IN WINTER

Conor Brady

NEW ISLAND

A HUNT IN WINTER
First published in 2016 by
New Island Books
16 Priory Hall Office Park
Stillorgan
County Dublin
Republic of Ireland

www.newisland.ie

PRINT ISBN: 978-1-84840-528-8
ePUB ISBN: 978-1-84840-529-5
Mobi ISBN: 978-1-84840-530-1

Typeset by POLAND, PUP Introkar, www.introkar.com
Cover design by Nina Lyons

New Island received financial assistance from The Arts Council (*An Chomhairle Ealaíon*), 70 Merrion Square, Dublin 2, Ireland.

10 9 8 7 6 5 4 3 2 1

For my beloved Ann,
I shall face the stars and greet you there.

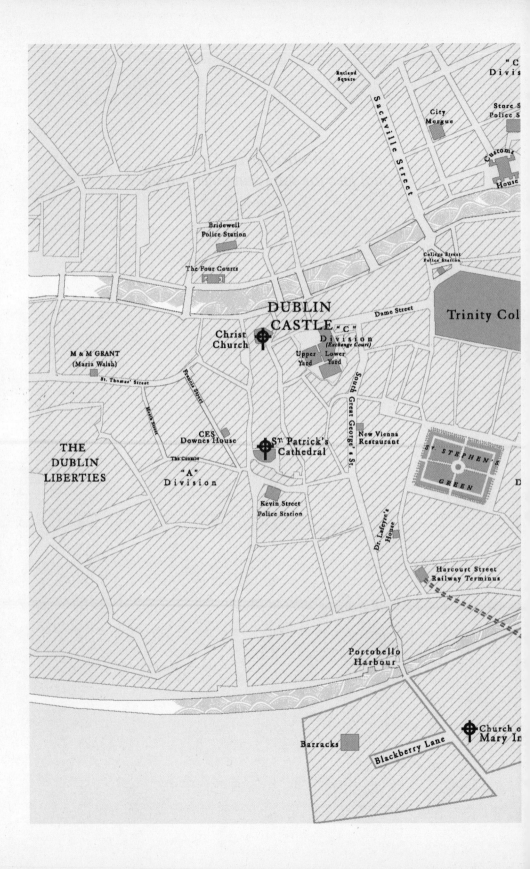

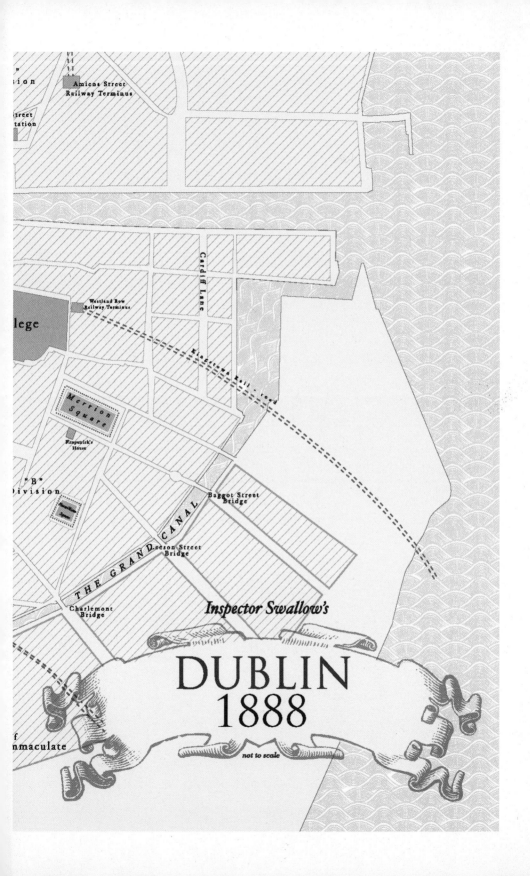

Amiens Street
Railway Terminus

Cardiff Lane

Westland Row
Railway Terminus

lege

Kingstown Rail - road

Merrion
Square

Fitzpatrick's
House

"B"
Division

Baggot Street
Bridge

THE GRAND CANAL

Leeson Street
Bridge

Charlemont
Bridge

Inspector Swallow's

DUBLIN
1888

not to scale

nmaculate

INTRODUCTION AND ACKNOWLEDGEMENTS

As with its two predecessor volumes, chronicling the life and times of Detective Sergeant Joe Swallow (now promoted to detective inspector), the backdrop to *A Hunt in Winter* is drawn from social and political conditions in 1880s Dublin. And as with *A June of Ordinary Murders* (2012) and *The Eloquence of the Dead* (2013), the narrative blends fact with fiction, while real life characters of the era mingle with others of my own creation. It is hardly necessary to state that *A Hunt in Winter* is a novel, not a history book.

I would like to acknowledge the many readers who have furnished me with additional information on some of the locations, institutions and individuals that feature here as they did in the earlier books. The store of local history of late-nineteenth-century Dublin appears to grow incrementally, as does that of Irish policing history.

As with the first two Joe Swallow books, I would like to acknowledge the support and professionalism of the team at New Island Books, in particular Dan Bolger and Justin Corfield, in bringing *A Hunt in Winter* to fruition. In an interval in my life during which circumstances made it difficult to write creatively, Dan was patient and indulgent. Justin was, as ever, a scrupulous, exacting and supportive editor.

I would also like to acknowledge the support and enthusiasm of my literary agent, Maria White, who has succeeded in bringing the Swallow books to a wider readership abroad, arranging North American publication with Minotaur Books, an associate imprint of St Martin's Press, New York.

– Conor Brady
Dublin, September 2016

Dublin

Friday November 2nd, 1888

PROLOGUE

The girl clutched her shawl tightly around her shoulders against the night chill. But once she had crossed the Portobello Bridge to the Rathmines Road the walkway was firm and reassuring. The smooth surface helped to ease the discomfort in her leg. The rate-payers of the new affluent suburbs to the south of the city could afford good roads, which contrasted with the broken, uneven pavements within the old City Corporation area.

The ground here is hollow and low. When the wind is still and the night is moist, the mist that rises from the Grand Canal lingers and thickens. Tonight it had quite overwhelmed the gas lamps' feeble efforts at illumination. But she knew her route well. She could see the faint glow from the Portobello Cavalry Barracks that lay beyond Blackberry Lane, where she lived. To her left she could faintly make out the darkened bulk of the Roman Catholic Church of St Mary Immaculate.

There was no sound of any other person on the footpath, but she was accustomed to the silence of the road at this late hour. The public houses that she had passed on Camden Street and South Richmond Street had been noisy and filled with loud-voiced men and women bawling and shouting. Out here it was as quiet as the countryside. A new terrace of lawn-fronted red-brick houses was hidden across the road in the fog. The southern side, along which she now made her way, was still bounded by meadow fields.

She sensed the pressure of the cold air pushing behind her a moment before she heard the hissing of the steam tram on its outward run from the city. When she glanced over her shoulder she saw it forming out of the mist behind her, its bull's-eye lamps deploying a meagre illumination over the cobbles. She caught a momentary glimpse of passengers in the dimly lit interior. Men with hats, huddled in overcoats, drawn in tight against the November air. Two or three tired-looking women, probably making their way back to the houses where they worked in service. It would be the last tram from the city for the night. She heard the church clock strike the half-hour after eleven as the vehicle disappeared into mist.

There was no street light where Blackberry Lane rose from the fields to meet the road, but she knew the bramble hedges that grew at the place where she would turn. She could make her way blindfolded to the cottage at the end of the rutted laneway. Even in the darkness, she knew how to navigate the cart tracks, ankle-deep with rainwater. She knew how to avoid the thorns and the nettles on either side. She could not afford to destroy her boots or muddy her waitress uniform.

Perhaps ten yards up the lane, she knew, a wooden gate gave entry to the meadow field. The children of Blackberry Lane were in and out through it, winter and summer, tolerated by the farmer who accepted the futility of trying to keep them out in the first place. Now it was invisible, obscured by the mist. But she knew that something was wrong when she heard the scrape of its iron bolt being drawn back.

She had walked the lane many times in darkness. She was not frightened by its night sounds. Foxes, rats, badgers, sometimes a wandering cow pushing its head through the bramble. But she knew that none of these creatures could draw a gate bolt. She froze, straining to see through the fog.

The first blow came out of the darkness, taking her across the mouth and nose. It was solid and hard, not a fist or a hand. She felt teeth splinter in her mouth. The second blow came to the side of her head, setting off an explosion of red and yellow stars behind her eyes. Immediately she felt the warm blood flowing into her mouth and down her face. She tried to scream, but the sound caught in her throat. Her legs buckled and she pitched forwards, face downwards, into the mud.

Now the man was on her from behind. One hand came around her cheek and clamped across her mouth. The other pushed a rough rope down over her head and around her neck. The noose bit deep into her skin, and she heard him grunt as he dragged her towards where the gateway opened to the field. Once in there, she knew, it would be hopeless. She gasped for breath, scrabbling at the hand clamped across her mouth, but he was too strong and his grip too tight.

She felt mud and stones against her face as she tried to clutch at the reedy grass on the laneway's edge. Then, a foot or two from where she knew the gate opened into the meadow, her hand found a jagged stone, perhaps the size of an apple. She fastened her fingers around it, pushed herself upwards as best she could and swung the stone with all her strength. She felt it connect with his head, and the hand across her mouth flew away. She heard him scream in pain. The rope slackened as he fell back. She drew in air, rolling, squirming away into the thorny ditch.

Now she found herself in a space of earth where the brambles had thinned. Perhaps a fox's run or a badger trail. She tried to undo the rope that was still knotted around her neck, but her fingers were slippery with the blood from her head and face. Somewhere in the laneway she heard a shouted call. Then another. Men's voices. Running footsteps in the fog. She started to feel a shivering warmth that travelled from her legs and then ran upwards through her body. She felt a weightlessness. Her hiding place seemed to darken, and there were no more sounds.

Saturday November 3rd, 1888

ONE

Swallow disliked Saturdays. Most policemen felt that way, he reckoned. Perhaps more precisely, Swallow disliked the day that followed Friday night. Friday was payday for those citizens of Dublin fortunate enough to have employment, however poorly rewarded it might be. By late Friday night a sizeable proportion of men's meagre wages would be on the way back to the breweries and distilleries—Arthur Guinness, John Jameson and John Power. There was always trouble on Friday nights: street fights, brawls in public houses, misadventures of every variety, with broken bodies in the hospitals and sometimes dead ones in the mortuary.

Because the Dublin Magistrates' Courts did not sit on Saturdays, the police cells were invariably filled to capacity. And with the growing trend for businesses to give employees a half-day off on Saturday afternoon, it was often impossible to advance police inquiries after noontime. Many commercial offices closed for the afternoon. Schools closed at noon, releasing their charges to engage in whatever mischief might present itself. Invariably, the latter part of the day was forfeit.

Swallow's strategy to offset Saturday's adversities was to start the day earlier. The morning crime conference at Exchange Court, the headquarters of G-Division at Dublin Castle, was ordinarily timed for nine o'clock. The night's crime tallies would be set out and the day's tasks allocated. But on Saturdays he brought it forward to half past eight. That way he could ensure that all available detectives were at their posts or out on their inquiries for the full duration of the morning.

Since his promotion to detective inspector, Swallow had sharpened up procedures at Exchange Court. His predecessor, Maurice ('Duck') Boyle, since elevated to superintendent and posted to take charge of the E-district, headquartered in leafy Rathmines, had been notoriously lazy and undemanding. Swallow, on the other hand, insisted on punctuality and a strict adherence to procedure. Report-writing had to be accurate, clear and up-to-date. Cash drawn for informants had to be accounted for in full and not frittered away on unnamed and often fictitious informants in public houses. There was grumbling from some, but the greater number among the G-men, as the detectives short-handed their designation, supported his approach.

The bedroom on the top floor above M & M Grant's public house on Thomas Street, in the old city quarter known as the Liberties, was cold when he woke. He looked past Maria's sleeping form beside him to the window and saw that the glass was fern-patterned with the first frost of winter. He rose, then washed and shaved quietly across the corridor in the room which, for the sake of decorum, was always referred to as 'Mr Swallow's room'. As far as outward appearances were concerned, the young, widowed Mrs Walsh and the detective inspector were simply landlady and tenant. Maria's servants knew differently, of course, as did many of the patrons of M & M Grant's, Maria's public house below. So too did most of Swallow's senior colleagues in G-Division, even though it was against police regulations to board on licensed premises, much less to share a bed with the licensee.

The servants observed the fiction of attending to the tenant's room in accordance with respectability and convention. Each morning Swallow would leave his soiled clothing in the linen basket in his room to be collected for laundering later in the day by Tess, Maria's housemaid. Every evening Tess carefully laid out a clean collar and shirt at the foot of the bed and changed the water in the glazed pitcher on the washstand.

It required concentration to work with the razor, soap and cold water in the dim morning light. Although most of the G-men followed the fashion of the time with moustaches or beards, Swallow preferred to go clean-shaven. It made him look younger than his forty-three years, he reckoned. Maria said she thought so too.

The morning darkness had not fully dissipated when he stepped out into Thomas Street through the side door that gave private access to the living quarters above the public house.

At St Catherine's Church, where the rebel Robert Emmet had been executed after the abortive insurrection of 1803, he saw that the November frost had whitened the classical pediment and the black roof slates. He passed the Municipal Art School where on Thursday afternoons, duty permitting, he indulged his sole diversion from police work in the painting class led by Maria's sister, Lily. Then he crossed High Street and Corn Market before flanking Christ Church Cathedral towards the Castle.

The streets were quiet. Dubliners were neither early to bed nor early risers. The city's trams did not stir until eight o'clock, when they started from their depots. Shops did not open their doors until half past nine. Many professional men considered it unseemly to be at their rooms before ten. The only sign of life at this hour was a uniformed constable, motionless and solid, surveying the silent thoroughfare from Lamb Alley.

He caught the tang of hops from Guinness's brewery at St James's Gate, and a couple of hundred yards farther on the husky smell of barley wafted in the air from Power's distillery on John's Lane. It was telling, he sometimes reflected, that while other cities might smell of coal or food or human sweat, Dublin smelled primarily of alcoholic drink in the making.

He quickened his pace so that he would be at his desk by eight o'clock to review the night's crime reports from the Dublin Metropolitan Police's seven divisions. Any serious business, he knew, would very likely come from A, B, C or D, which served the city within the canals. E-Division and F-Division, covering the affluent suburbs to the south as far as Dalkey, rarely saw much crime or outrage.

Swallow was more at ease living back in the Liberties. During the previous year he rented a small house near Portobello, sharing it with his sister, Harriet. It suited her because it was close to the school in which she taught on the South Circular Road. But at the start of the new school year, and with his promotion confirmed, he had returned to live with Maria over Grant's.

The public house had come down in the female line, but it kept the name of Maria's grandfather Michael, who ran the business with his brother, Matthew. When Maria married Thomas Walsh in 1882 she saw no need to change it. The marriage had been happy but tragically short. Thomas drowned with his fellow crew members when the small cargo ship of which he was first officer went down in a gale off the Welsh coast five years later.

From Grant's, it was just a ten-minute walk to the detective office at Exchange Court, beside the City Hall. On a sharp, clear morning like this the exercise was stimulating. It loosened the muscles and cleared the head for the tasks of the day. He listed them mentally as he walked. At least those he could predict. Nobody could guess what the night's crime reports might bring in.

G-Division's fifty-odd detectives investigated crime across the city, and were also the administration's first and principal bulwark against political subversion. Their responsibilities ran from protecting the chief men who governed Ireland for the Crown to keeping watch on Fenians, Land Leaguers and the ever-multiplying groups that wanted, for one reason or another, to overthrow the established order.

The uniformed men who patrolled the divisions were unarmed, indistinguishable to all intents and purposes from the helmeted bobbies of any other city of the United Kingdom. But in addition to the standard police accoutrements of baton, whistle and handcuffs, every man of G-Division carried a .44 Webley Bulldog revolver.

Swallow considered what the day might bring. There was to be a public rally at the Mansion House in the afternoon. It would be addressed by the founder of the Land League, the charismatic one-armed militant Michael Davitt. Davitt was a powerful orator and would always draw a crowd. It would require half a dozen G-men, spread across the great Round Room of the Mansion House, to record the presence of suspected persons and to take down an account of what was said from the platform.

The leader of the Irish Party at Westminster, Charles Stewart Parnell, was travelling from London and would arrive at Kingstown on the four o'clock mailboat. Two G-men would be on hand. Officially they would be on protection duty, but there would be as much surveillance and intelligence-gathering involved as protecting Parnell from possible threats. They would carefully record who accompanied him, who greeted him at Kingstown and where they went.

The government's principal civil servant for Ireland, Chief Secretary Sir Arthur Balfour, and his wife would be attending a luncheon at the Royal Dublin Society at Ballsbridge. The ultra-loyal RDS was the least likely location for trouble, but since the murders five years previously in the Phoenix Park of the chief secretary's predecessor in office, Sir Frederick Cavendish, along with his under-secretary, no chances could be taken. The protection detail would require the presence in concealment of two armed detectives and a sergeant.

Three G-men were engaged in watching the movements of two Irish-American gentlemen staying at the Imperial Hotel. The word from a helpful porter was that they were former Union Army officers with guns to sell. So far their principal focus appeared to be on drinking whiskey and making passes at the barmaids, but they had left word with the porter that they were expecting visitors. G-men would be required to take shifts sitting in the hotel bar, watching for someone to make a rendezvous.

Swallow also needed two men to operate the public office and the cells at Exchange Court. That should leave him with a paltry strength of three or four to cope with whatever the crime reports might bring in.

The moment he stepped into Exchange Court he knew from the face of the young G-man at the public counter that things were not good.

'Bad story out in the E, sir.' He jerked his head towards the stairs. 'Sergeant Mossop's above. He's just ahead of you.' Pat Mossop had been duty sergeant for the night shift that had just ended. Swallow took the stairs to the crime office two at a time.

Mossop, recently promoted to detective sergeant, was hunched at his desk. Detective Johnny Vizzard, newly arrived in G-Division on promotion from uniform, was perched beside him, his fingers poised over the typewriter. Mossop looked tired, as he always did now. A year ago the diminutive Belfast man had taken a bullet in the upper torso as G-men closed on an armed suspect on Ormond Quay. Strictly speaking, Pat Mossop should have been dead. Had his colleagues not got him swiftly to the infirmary on Jervis Street, he would have been.

'Something big, Pat?'

'Big enough, boss. E-district. Rathmines Road. A bad assault. Could be more than that. I thought I'd have the report done before you came in.'

'Tell me.'

'I'm just back with the lads from the Baggot Street Hospital. A young girl was attacked in Blackberry Lane off the Rathmines Road some time towards midnight. She's in a bad state. The doctor says she mightn't come through it.'

'How much do we know?'

'A fair bit. But there's no idea yet who might have done it or why.' He flipped his official notebook open. 'Aged eighteen, name of Alice Flannery, lives with her mother and a gaggle of brothers and sisters in a cottage at the end of the laneway. The mother's widowed, makes a few bob as a cleaner at the big church on the Rathmines Road. Seems Alice helps her on the cleaning job, but mostly she works as a waitress at the New Vienna restaurant down in South Great George's Street.'

Swallow knew the New Vienna. It was a short walk from the Castle.

'What do we know of her movements last night?'

'She left the New Vienna to walk home around quarter past eleven after they'd cleaned up and shut for the night. Sometime before midnight a couple of cavalrymen tried to use the lane to slip into the barracks after lights. They heard a commotion and literally stumbled across her.'

'Robbery? She'd have likely been paid her wages, finishing up on Friday?'

'Maybe. She had no money on her when she was got to the hospital. No bag or anything. But it was so damned dark her things could be anywhere around the laneway.'

'What're the injuries?'

14

'No sexual attack, though that doesn't mean it wasn't the motive. Her skull is badly fractured on the right side. Nose broken. Cheek-bone broken on the other side. Doctor reckons about six teeth splintered. Mouth and lips lacerated. There's what looks like a bad rope burn or something such on the neck. Lots of scratches and cuts. It looks as if she got away into the brambles and then crawled out again. The doctor says she was beaten with a blunt weapon, maybe a heavy bar or a club of some kind. She's lost a lot of blood.'

'Is she conscious? Could she tell you anything?'

'Not a lot that's coherent. They put her under with a good dose of laudanum. The doctor was afraid that her heart would fail. Johnny took a note of what little she did say.'

Vizzard shrugged. 'She just said "dark", "noise" and then "the pain, the pain". Then she said, "Me uniform's ruined." But she won't be going waitressing again for a long time.'

Swallow drew up a chair.

'She might have been doing a bit of amateur whoring on the side? Maybe the two soldiers were doing business in the laneway with her? What did they have they to say?'

Mossop grimaced.

'That was my first thought too. But I don't think so. They were well soused after a night in McCabe's tavern. One of them ran out onto the Rathmines Road, roaring for a bobby. There was a beat man, Jack Caviston, at Leinster Road. He judged that the young fella was hysterical. If they'd done it, they wouldn't have come running for a polisman.'

Swallow knew Caviston. A senior man. Reliable. He silently acknowledged Mossop's logic.

'I interviewed them separately,' Mossop continued. 'Two young fellas from Yorkshire. They tell the same story: drinking late in the town, they decided to try to slip back to barracks over the back wall. It's just fifty yards across the field from the end of Blackberry Lane. But I've had them jugged in separate cells by their CO in the barracks. Drunkenness, indiscipline, absent without leave. He can hold them as long as we need.'

'Did they see anyone in the lane?'

'It was so damned foggy they could hardly see each other. They say they heard the girl scream two or three times, and they say they heard someone running. But they saw nothing. Like I said, one of them literally stumbled over the poor girl.'

'Who got her to hospital?'

'Caviston sent one of the young lads to hail a cab at Portobello,' Mossop resumed. 'They had no idea who she was until two in the morning, when a young brother turned up at Rathmines Station to say his sister hadn't come home. They sent him down to Baggot Street and he identified her to Jack Caviston. The mother came down too. We've got a couple of G-men there with her.'

'And Caviston?'

'He finished his shift at six.'

Swallow knew that with Pat Mossop he didn't have to ask the next question, but he asked it anyway.

'The scene's preserved?'

'Laneway's closed off. They put up a barrier with two bobbies. It was too dark for a full search of the ground. The station sergeant at Rathmines says he'll turn out half a dozen men when we want to start.'

In the day room below, Swallow could hear voices and movement as the day shift assembled. The Lower Castle Yard below the windows was filling with a thin morning light.

'Good work,' he nodded. 'I'll take the conference below and get out to Blackberry Lane myself for the search. Just sit in with me and brief the shift, then go on home and get some sleep. Come back when you're rested.'

The crime conference was short. Mossop rehearsed what was known about the attack at Blackberry Lane. The rest of the night's business was routine. Two housebreakings in Kingstown. Some broken windows along Dorset Street. An assault on a publican in Ringsend. Details of each incident would be transmitted after the conference to all DMP stations through the ABC telegraph system. Uniformed men across the city would be on the alert for anything they might encounter that could be related to any of the reported incidents.

'I'm going out to direct the search at Blackberry Lane,' Swallow announced when Mossop had finished. I want Mick Feore with me as book man and Martin Shanahan as assistant. Send to Kevin Street for Sergeant Doolan to join us out there. We'll do a conference here at four o'clock.'

Mick Feore was an experienced crime detective who had worked with Swallow as far back as the Phoenix Park murders in 1882. Martin Shanahan had been transferred from uniform duties to assist them. They were part of the team assembled by the legendary Inspector John Mallon that brought five members of the 'Invincibles' to the gallows after the assassinations of Britain's two most senior civil servants.

The role of book man was key in any serious crime investigation. He had to be meticulous in recording every scrap of information. He had to cherish every detail. And he had to have the gift of being able to make connections between what could seem to be unrelated facts or events. Mick Feore was the best book man in G-Division after Pat Mossop, Swallow reckoned. Shanahan was without ambition, but worked conscientiously and loyally under direction.

Stephen Doolan was a veteran of twenty years in service, and the best search organiser Swallow knew in the force. He was in A-Division, based at Kevin Street, but what the G-Division detectives at Exchange Court wanted by way of resources they invariably got.

There was noisy talk as the G-men started to disperse. Swallow noticed a middle-aged constable at the door of the room. He recognised Jack Caviston, the Rathmines beat man who had been called by the young soldiers when Alice Flannery had been found. Swallow surmised that he had slipped into the day room while the conference was in progress.

Caviston saluted. 'Mornin', sir.'

'Bad business you had earlier,' Swallow said. He could see that the man was exhausted. 'I thought you'd finished your shift.'

'I did, sir,' Caviston seemed uneasy. 'I was on my way home when I remembered somethin' strange from the scene. In all that was goin' on I didn't say it to Sergeant Mossop or Johnny Vizzard.' He hesitated. 'So I thought I'd come back in, knowin' you'd be doin' the conference.'

'Go on,' Swallow said.

'It mightn't be anythin' at all, but it was somethin' I think the girl said when I got up to the laneway. The two young lads were strikin' lucifers to give a bit o' light, so I could see she was in a terrible state, covered in blood. I asked her what her name was, but she didn't answer. I said "Who done this, love?" Then she started to shake and a couple of words came out.'

'What did she say?'

'She said, "I didn't." She repeated it. "I didn't." That's what she said, sir.'

TWO

Swallow did not spend much time thinking about the mysteries of religion. But as a Roman Catholic policeman in a force where his co-religionists rarely made it to senior rank, he thought a lot about its influence. Had he been born into the Protestant faith, he reckoned, he would have enrolled in the Trinity College medical school rather than that of the Catholic University on Cecilia Street. Cecilia Street was his undoing. It all seemed a long time ago now, before he had joined the police.

Trinity medicals were no saints. Their exploits in taverns across the city and in particular in the red-light district around Montgomery Street—'Monto', to knowledgeable Dubliners—were notorious. But perhaps, he reasoned, had he enrolled to study among those of a different religious background he might have been more concerned to put up a show of better behaviour. He might have been careful, more cautious.

He might not so readily have succumbed to the delights of the alehouses, as he did, within days of enrolment in Cecilia Street. His fellow students there were not angels either, but most of them seemed to know when to stop carousing and start putting in the bookwork that was necessary to pass their examinations.

Swallow's inability to identify that point had cost him his hoped-for medical career. And his three years of roistering dissipated the hard-earned money his parents had put aside for it. If blasting away their savings was bad, then shattering their hopes and ambitions was infinitely worse. When his father succumbed to a brain haemorrhage while working in the family bar at Suncroft in rural Kildare on an August evening, Swallow knew that his child's betrayal, as he saw it, had played some part in it.

It had taken years for his mother to forgive him. She had been if anything more ambitious than her husband for her only son. An uneasy peace had eventually been brokered by his younger sister, Harriet, but the bond between mother and son was never the same again. Had he offered to return to Suncroft to help her run the business it might have laid the foundations for a fuller reconciliation, but it was not something that either of them wanted.

He saw himself with three choices after repeatedly failing his examinations: America, Australia or the Dublin Metropolitan Police. Somewhat to his surprise, he managed to control his drinking in order to complete the police educational examination. And he succeeded in masking his drinking habits from the examining surgeon at the Kevin Street depot. His drinking was long in check. He could take alcohol, often quite a lot of it, but it did not control him as before. He took drink—and he liked having it, mellow Tullamore whiskey, porter from Guinness's, good red wine from France—but drink did not take him.

Yet he was under no illusions about his prospects. The bulk of the DMP's rank and file were Roman Catholics. They were country lads, sons of farmers, tradesmen or, as in his own case, small publicans or shopkeepers. Almost all of the top ranks of the force were preserved for Protestants and Freemasons. In the uniformed ranks, he might get to be a sergeant or inspector at best. When he transferred to G-Division he knew his chances of advancement were reduced further, although paradoxically the chief superintendent of G-Division, John Mallon, was a Roman Catholic. But Mallon, the son of a small Catholic farmer from near Crossmaglen in County Armagh, with an outstandingly successful record in the service of the Crown, was the exception that proved the rule. One or two Catholics had gone through to superintendent rank in the aftermath of the 1867 Fenian rising when the authorities came to a greater appreciation of the loyalty of the Irish police forces. But the majority of those in command of the divisions were members of the Church of Ireland.

Sometimes Swallow thought he had been born too soon. The late Cardinal Cullen, Catholic Primate of All Ireland, had denounced the new 'Queen's Colleges', established in 1850, as 'Godless institutions', so the Englishman John Henry Cardinal Newman established the new 'Catholic University' in Dublin. It had proven itself an effective vehicle for the social and economic advancement of young men whose faith or political inclinations were incompatible with the Protestant ethos at Trinity College. Catholics were beginning to make it to the higher levels in business and in the professions. There were even a few Catholic judges now. And the Catholic hierarchy was finding new ways of demonstrating its growing power, even with the country gripped in political turmoil and violence.

Little more than a generation after Daniel O'Connell had secured emancipation, and with the Great Famine within living memory, the Catholic bishops were putting up cathedral-scale buildings, right in the faces of the Protestant classes that still led commerce, business and the administration.

He had spent some time in the summer trying to do a panoramic sketch of the city skyline, using the Castle's Bedford Tower as a viewing point. It had been a not-very-successful project for the course he attended weekly at the Municipal School of Art. It dawned on him that outside the immediate city centre all the significant landmarks on both sides of the river were new Roman Catholic domes and spires. The great copper dome of the Church of Mary Immaculate, Refuge of Sinners, dominated the Rathmines Road. Its Corinthian columns and high pediment, studded with golden lettering and topped with statues of Mary, St Patrick and St Laurence O'Toole, loomed out onto the thoroughfare. It embodied the new confidence and wealth of middle-class, Catholic Ireland.

The magnificence of the church contrasted sharply with the living conditions of its parishioners in Blackberry Lane, just 100 paces away from its gates, facing onto the Rathmines Road. As the police side-car came to the scene, Swallow tried to visualise the widow Flannery and her young daughter cleaning and polishing the altar rails and the pews under the magnificent dome. When he and Mick Feore descended from the side-car, the morning light had strengthened to show the open sewer running down the middle of the lane and the rotten green of the cottages' thatched roofs. Somewhere on the air he got the scent of animal waste. Not the customary smell of horse droppings on city streets. More pungent. Pigs, he guessed. He was grateful for the coldness of the morning. In any warmth the stench would be unbearable.

A second open car clattered up behind them, the horse snorting and steaming from its exertions. It was the police photographic technician with his assistant. The two men climbed down from the car and started to lift the cumbersome camera equipment to the ground.

The uniformed sergeant guarding the crime scene saluted and led him into the laneway. Swallow's first thought was to reprimand him. G-men were never saluted in public as a precaution against identification. But he let it pass. The man had probably been there all night.

'Just a few steps up here, sir.'

He gestured to the ground. The bloodstains were dark brown, almost dry in the morning air. The muddy ground showed a jigsaw of footprints. Three, maybe four men's boots or shoes, and the distinctive smaller imprints probably made by the victim. To his right Swallow could see an indentation in the brambles. A little farther on, he saw the gate leading to the meadow. The metal bolt was undone. Beyond the gate the grass was white with hoar frost.

'Mornin', Joe. Mornin', Mick.'

Sergeant Stephen Doolan came up the lane followed by half a dozen E-Division constables from Rathmines. Each man was equipped with a long, wooden-shafted pike. Swallow surmised the implements were army issue from the cavalry barracks.

He nodded.

'You know the story here, Stephen?'

Doolan nodded. 'Yes, I caught up with it on the routes before I left Kevin Street.'

The 'routes', or 'routines', were the crime reports that circulated to all city police stations on the ABC telegraph from DMP headquarters in the Castle's Lower Yard.

'That's where he waited.' Swallow pointed to the gate. 'Probably got away through the field when the two soldier-boys arrived. So when you've done the laneway you'll have to search the field too, end to end. There's no winter growth so the grass is short. If he's left anything to be found it won't be difficult.'

Doolan deployed his men on both sides of the laneway, starting from the intersection with the main roadway. They moved slowly along the poor thoroughfare, eyes scanning the grass and mud, probing the brambles with their long pikes. Within less than a minute a searcher had located a small handbag off the track beside the gate. The cheap imitation velvet was damp, but the metal clasp was secure. When Doolan opened it he counted five shilling coins—a waitress's Friday pay.

'Have a look at this, skipper.'

A constable by the gate tapped with his foot at a heavy wooden stake lying in the grass. Measuring perhaps four feet and sharpened at one end, it might have come from a farm fence or enclosure. Half of its length was spattered with darkened blood.

'Don't touch it until the photographic technician has taken pictures,' Doolan ordered. 'We'll want pictures of the lane itself, the gateway and those footprints too.'

He turned to Feore.

'Get the plaster kit from the car. I want casts of all the footmarks once the photographs are taken.'

The scene was telling Swallow little so far. The assailant might have known the gateway to the meadow as a place of concealment. Or he might have just come upon it. The bloodied stake might have been brought to the scene as a weapon, or it might simply have been a convenience. The fact that the girl's bag and her wages were still at the scene suggested that the motive was not robbery. But equally it was possible that the attacker had been unable to locate them in the dark.

The photographer had got his tripod up and was busy at his work when a third open car drew to a halt at the end of the laneway. The constable-driver came down from his seat to assist the uniformed passenger to the ground. It was 'Duck' Boyle, Swallow's former superior at Exchange Court, lately promoted to superintendent and placed in command of the E-Division. 'Duck' Boyle's generously cut uniform with its silver braid was moderately effective in disguising its wearer's advanced corpulence, but it could not remedy the distinctive waddle that had earned him his nickname among his former colleagues at G-Division.

Regulations required that the divisional superintendent should attend personally at the scenes of serious crimes. Swallow was not surprised by Boyle's arrival, but he knew from the expression on the fat superintendent's face that this was more than a routine compliance with regulation.

'Good mornin', Inspector Swalla'.' Boyle greeted him formally for the benefit of the constables and sergeants gathered around. He took Swallow conspiratorially by the arm and walked him a few paces to the edge of the lane. 'I'm afraid that things have taken a turn for the worse,' Boyle intoned solemnly. 'The victim o' this outrage, Miss Alice Flannery, died at the Baggot Street Hospital at 9.15 this mornin'. Ye're dealin' now with a murder.'

THREE

'You should come to the meeting, Maria. If we go early we can get good seats. I promise you it will be very interesting, and you can be back here by six o'clock to take care of business for the night.'

Harriet Swallow enjoyed the company of her brother's fiancée and landlady. True, there was no formal engagement between Swallow and Maria Walsh as such, but fiancée was a convenient term in an arrangement that went well beyond that of landlady and lodger but fell short of matrimony.

The relationship had not been smooth. Swallow had rented the room over M & M Grant's for two years. It was, of course, contrary to police regulations to lodge on licensed premises. He squared his conscience on that score by telling himself that his accommodation was located over, rather than in, M & M Grant's. It might be an interesting legal point, he sometimes reflected, if it came to an issue. Grant's had the added advantage that it was convenient to Exchange Court and the Castle.

What started as a simple lodging arrangement had gradually blossomed. At first, he started to help Maria in the business in his off-duty hours. Because had grown up in a public house he understood its routines. The customers at Grant's were different in many ways from the country folk who patronised Swallow's of Newcroft, but dealing with them required much the same qualities he had seen his parents exercise. A publican had to be cheerful without being too fulsome; tolerant but firm on behaviour within the house; understanding of human frailty but not indulgent of excess. Grant's was a well-ordered house, and few troublemakers crossed the threshold. The presence of a G-man sent a clear message to those that did: they would misbehave at their peril.

In time, the relationship developed into intimacy. It was at once private and discreet, as well as being apparent to anyone with eyes to see. But when Maria, five years widowed, had pressed Swallow for a commitment, he had funked it. She would have liked him to finish with the police and come into Grant's as her husband and business partner. It was a generous and tempting offer, but he was unwilling to relinquish being a G-man. Instead, when his promotion to inspector came through, with an enhanced lodging allowance to match his new rank, he had moved out to share a rented house on Heytesbury Street with his sister.

It was not as convenient for Swallow, but it suited Harriet. She enjoyed the freedom of having her own home after two years in the confined routine of teacher training college, with fixed mealtimes, early curfews and a strict ban on visitors outside appointed hours, and even then within the stifling formality of the parlour.

At the same time, she liked the sense of security that came from living with her policeman brother. Dublin was a safe city unless one went looking for trouble. But Dubliners had been made nervous, as had the citizens of every other city across the kingdom, with the terrifying reports of murders from London's East End.

'Four poor women, done to death in the most brutal way since August. It's absolutely horrible. And the police in London don't seem to be doing anything to stop it.'

Harriet had thrown the statement at Swallow across the breakfast table after the murders of Catherine Eddowes and Elizabeth Stride in Whitechapel in September.

He had waved a hand in what was intended to be reassurance.

'London isn't Dublin, Harriet. Heytesbury Street isn't Whitechapel. And the dangers that face unfortunate women of their class aren't going to trouble you. Scotland Yard will have these cases cleared up fairly quickly.'

She misinterpreted his hand-wave as dismissive.

'Well they don't seem to be making much progress so far,' she retorted. 'The London newspapers have a name for the killer, you know. "Jack the Ripper" they call him.'

26

'The London newspapers are much like our own,' he sighed. 'When they have no information, they make it up.'

She poured more tea, filling both their cups.

'It isn't just in London.' she snorted. 'There are murders in other cities too. And it could happen in Dublin. This "Ripper" might even be Irish. There's lots of Irish people, it seems, in the East End of London.'

'Yes, there are.' She caught a tone of exasperation in his voice. 'And there are lots of Russians, Jews and Poles. God knows, there's even a few English, I'm told. As for murders elsewhere, yes there are murders every week. There always are. But if some barmaid gets killed in Dundee it doesn't mean this "Ripper" is going up and down the country attacking all and sundry.'

'It's easy for men to take that position,' she said sharply, gathering the books she needed for the school day from the sideboard. 'Men aren't being murdered by some maniac. They don't have to worry, do they?'

A few days later, when Swallow told her he was going to go back to live at Maria's, she was initially distressed. But she had moved quickly, identifying a colleague now teaching at the Loreto Girls' School on St Stephen's Green and seeking shared accommodation. Harriet still felt nervous for a time without Joe coming and going around the house, but as time went by it seemed to work out quite well, she told herself.

In the ordinary course, Harriet would have asked her new co-tenant to accompany her to the National Land League meeting at the Mansion House. But the Loreto sisters were running a sale of work, and the teaching staff were expected to help at the stalls. Harriet had decided that she would call on Maria to persuade her to abandon the public house during the quiet hours of the afternoon.

'Mr Davitt will speak,' Harriet pressed her. 'It will be a big meeting. In the Round Room. It will be a wonderful experience.'

Maria was still hesitant.

'He doesn't make many appearances now,' Harriet enthused. 'His health is poor. But people have travelled hundreds of miles to hear him in the United States, in Australia, in Africa, even in Russia. He's a world figure, you know. I think he'll probably speak on Mr Parnell's difficulties too. Come on, a few hours away from the business will do you good. And you'll have Joe here in the evening to help out.'

That was true, Maria conceded privately. He had told her he would finish work no later than six o'clock.

'All right. I'll come with you,' she agreed without enthusiasm. 'I'll leave Tom in charge until Joe gets here.'

Tom was the senior barman at Grant's. After more than thirty years in the trade he knew his business, and there were few situations he could not handle. The house would be in good hands for the afternoon.

Maria Walsh was first and last a businesswoman. She had no interest in Michael Davitt's efforts on behalf of the dispossessed, whether in Ireland or anywhere else. She was equally unmoved by Mr Parnell's current difficulties. A special commission had been sitting in London since September probing allegations that he was in league with the violent leaders of the Fenian organisation. Each day's newspapers carried columns of the proceedings, faithfully reporting the cross-examination of witnesses by some of the most able members of the English Bar. Parnell's supporters, who included most of nationalist Ireland, followed the accounts assiduously. Some thought their hero was on the rack. Others held that his evidence was so strong and clear that his enemies were confounded.

Harriet was fervently political and nationalist. She was a member of the Gaelic Union and the Society for the Preservation of the Irish Language. In reality, Maria told herself, she would go along with Harriet to make sure she did not get into trouble.

It had happened before. Her G-man brother had to engage in some unorthodox tactics to disentangle her from the malign influence of a young man whom she said she loved. He happened to be a leading member of a revolutionary group that sometimes called itself the Hibernian League and at other times the Hibernian Brotherhood. It took an amount of clever footwork to prevent her name going on the Castle's intelligence files as a subversive to be watched.

Harriet and Maria caught one of the new steam trams that were gradually replacing the horse-drawn vehicles that had served the city for twenty years. It took them along Thomas Street, across Cornmarket, past the two churches named for St Audoen, the little Norman saint who was the patron of the city walls, past Christ Church Cathedral and down to the city centre.

The November afternoon was dry and mild with a watery sun slanting over the rooftops as it dropped away to the west of the city. When the tram clanked past the City Hall, Maria strained to peer into Exchange Court, where the detective office was located. As often as she had passed the building where Swallow worked, she had never seen him enter or leave it.

The vehicle circumnavigated the curtilage of Trinity College. They dismounted at the first stop on Nassau Street and made their way through the afternoon crowd along Dawson Street towards the Mansion House.

The Round Room, where it was said the acoustics were so perfect that even those in the back rows could hear a speaker whisper on the stage, was filling rapidly. A Land League steward, wearing a green sash, recognised Harriet and came forward, beckoning her and Maria to two seats by the alcove. '*Míle buíochas, a Sheathrúin,*' she smiled at the young man. Maria thought he blushed. He smiled back. '*Fáilte romhat, Harriet. Agus fáilte roimh do chara álainn.*'

Maria grimaced as they sat. 'The only bit I understood was "Harriet". What did he say?'

Harriet laughed. 'Actually, he was paying you a compliment. Sean trained at Carysfort too. He called you my "beautiful companion".'

'Hmm, maybe I'll try and learn a bit of the Gaelic then, if it'll get me that sort of comment.'

'You should.'

'What's his name?' Maria asked. 'He seemed to know you well.'

'Oh, don't draw any unwarranted conclusions,' Harriet laughed. 'He's Seathrún Ó Brolcháin. He was in training at Marino College while I was in Carysfort. He's very active in nationalist activities. I admire him.'

By the time the meeting was to open, the Round Room was packed. Scores of latecomers found only standing room, while stewards argued with people trying to hold empty seats for friends. A fug of smoke was already beginning to fill the hall, rising to the high ceiling. The body heat generated from the crowd was starting to draw out smells of sweat and damp clothing.

Maria surveyed the audience as she might the customers on a busy night in Grant's, sizing up possible troublemakers, noting where the louder voices were coming from. But this was an orderly if unusual congregation. Rough country men with strong accents sat side by side with others whose softer, pale features marked them as city dwellers. Cloth caps and soft hats mixed with bowlers. There were smart, well-cut overcoats and bulky friezes in coarse tweed. She was surprised to see that maybe one in five or six of those present were women.

Three pipers in kilts marched on to the stage. A stout man with a megaphone commanded the audience to silence, and the pipers played 'A Nation Once Again'. The crowd burst into applause and cheering as they squeezed out the last notes.

After 'A Nation Once Again', the pipers struck up 'Let Erin Remember' and then 'The West's Awake', followed by 'The Lament for Owen Roe O'Neill'. The applause rose to a crescendo, accompanied by stamping of boots and clapping of hands. In spite of her detachment Maria felt herself being lifted with the mood of the crowd.

A thin young man stepped to centre stage, and introduced himself using an Irish name that Maria could not understand. Then in a surprisingly strong voice he started to recount details of evictions in Galway, in Roscommon, in Mayo, in Sligo.

'These attacks on Irish farms and Irish families are taking place even as we gather here today,' he announced angrily. 'But we will not be slaves or serfs. Nor will Irishmen turn and run at the sight of a policeman's carbine or a soldier's bayonet. We are the race that has withstood the might of England, from Cromwell to Balfour, and we will not yield in this struggle.'

The harangue lasted perhaps twenty minutes. Then the young man was followed by another. And another. With each successive speech the atmosphere in the hall grew more fervid. Finally, the stout man stepped forwards again. Harriet cupped her hands to Maria's ear. 'That's Mr Andrew Kettle. He's one of Davitt's most senior men,' she told her.

Kettle spread his arms in a gesture to quiet the crowd. '*A chairde Gael* ... Irishmen and Irishwomen ... *fáilte, fáilte agus fáilte arís* ... welcome on this great occasion. You have heard at first hand now of the state of our brothers and sisters and our children across the country and of their struggles to hold on to their birthright. Now we have the privilege of hearing the words of the man who has inspired and led that struggle—the struggle to give the land of Ireland back to the people of Ireland.

'This great Irishman who has suffered at the hands of England and her lackeys is no stranger to us. He is flesh of our flesh and blood of our blood. We have heard him speak across the length and breadth of this island, in fair weather and foul, threatened and harried by police and military and by the mercenaries of the landlords. But he has taken your cause, your just and undeniable cause, around the world. And now the world knows that the Irish race will not be kept down or denied what is theirs by right. Now he is back amongst us. *A chairde Gael*, it is my privilege to make way for a man who has given us back our birthright and our pride, that noble son of Mayo, Michael Davitt.'

Maria had expected an imposing presence, but the man in his forties who came forward as the crowd roared its approval was gaunt, with thinning hair and a slight stoop, the sort of man that one would pass without noticing in the street or on the tram. He waved his one arm in a gesture of greeting to the crowd. The other arm of his jacket, empty of the limb he had lost as a child factory worker, was pinned neatly at the pocket.

'My good friends, Irishmen and Irishwomen, I thank you for the warmth of your welcome. And I salute you for the courage and the constancy you have shown in your great struggle.'

There was an extraordinary projection in Davitt's voice. His words were as clear in Maria's ears as if he were standing beside her. The accent was a curious blend of Irish with the north of England and a touch of something else thrown in. Maria recalled she had read somewhere that his wife was American. But the crowd hushed and was still for this seemingly unexceptional man. Not a foot stirred now. Not a cough was heard. Although he carried no notes, he spoke steadily and without hesitation for well over three quarters of an hour. Extraordinarily, he appeared to know where everybody in the great hall had come from. He broke his address at intervals to welcome one group or another.

'I recognise the Wexford branches of the league. "The Boys of Wexford, who fought with heart and hand." There they are.' He gestured with his one arm to a far corner of the hall. By the time he had finished, Maria reckoned, he had identified every Irish county she knew as well as a few that she had never heard of.

When his oratory was drawing to its climax, he drew a watch from a breast pocket. 'I'll not detain you much longer, good people. I know that you have made great sacrifices and you have been required to show great courage. But I also tell you that you have made great progress in your struggle. Each day we hear of once-powerful landlords agreeing to the terms you have forced from the government in London and returning the estates they have robbed from the Irish people back to their rightful owners. But much remains to be achieved. Too many of the thieves and robbers are still in possession. Even yet, we know of evictions, in Donegal, in Kerry, in my own native Mayo. The struggle is far from over.

'There is one other matter that I want to raise with you, my friends. Mr Parnell … that great Irishman … Charles Stewart Parnell … is currently facing an evil inquisition in London. It is part of an abominable campaign by *The Times* newspaper in collaboration with a corrupt government and supported by those who believe they can continue to hold Ireland as a private estate, a pleasure ground for hunting and fishing, with its people as serfs.'

He paused momentarily. 'I would say to you, maintain your support for Mr Parnell. Stand with him in his time of trial, as he stands with the people of Ireland. It is no secret that I have my differences with him, although even in these differences I believe him to be well-intentioned. He is a powerful enemy to your enemies, and as such he is your ally and your prince of men. Do not allow him to be dragged down.'

Davitt bowed and turned as Kettle emerged from the wings to escort him off the stage. As he disappeared from view, the Round Room broke into a thunder of applause, accompanied by further stamping of feet. From somewhere behind them, Maria and Harriet heard a section of the crowd take up 'A Nation Once Again' even as the seats nearest the doors started to empty.

The November evening was turning to darkness, with the gas lights along Dawson Street flaring into yellow as they left the meeting.

A handful of uniformed DMP men stood watchfully under a sergeant, lining the pavement opposite the Mansion House. Somewhere too, Maria knew from what she had learned of Swallow's work, there would be G-men, measuring the strength of the crowd, noting the presence or otherwise of prominent Leaguers or activists. The Round Room would not have fully emptied before police agents would be delivering an account of who had been on the platform and what had been said by the speakers.

'Wasn't that stimulating?' Harriet clutched at Maria's arm. 'Mr Davitt is a powerful orator. And it's important that he stands shoulder to shoulder with Mr Parnell when he needs support.'

Maria did not answer. The crowd was dispersing up and down Dawson Street with groups making for the public houses or the tram stops. But a knot of people had gathered around the news vendor's stand at the corner of Duke Street. There were raised voices and impatient shouts. A middle-aged lady whom Maria had seen earlier in the meeting emerged from the group clutching a copy of the *Evening Mail*. She waved the newspaper at her companions from the meeting, displaying an open page.

'Dear God,' she called. 'Murder. Here on the streets of Dublin. I knew it would happen. We're none of us safe.'

Maria saw the column headlines.

'BRUTAL DEATH OF WOMAN IN RATHMINES'
'POLICE SAY SHE FOUGHT FOR HER LIFE'
'INSPECTOR SWALLOW AT THE SCENE'

She knew she would have no help from Swallow in Grant's this evening.

FOUR

It started to rain heavily later in the morning, taking the edge off the November chill but darkening the day. By then, Stephen Doolan's constables had searched the ditches and hedges that bounded Blackberry Lane. In a patch of clay behind the farm gate, Doolan had spotted the imprint of a shoe or boot. He had succeeded in capturing its details in a plaster cast just before it was washed away by the downpour.

'We'll need every man you can give us for door-to-door inquiries,' Swallow told 'Duck' Boyle. 'I want to know the names and movements of everybody living up the lane. All the details to go to Mick Feore for the murder book. Then I need door-to-door, all the way back to the New Vienna restaurant. Everyone who lives or works along the route that she came home has to be interviewed and listed. I want to know about anyone who might have seen her or met her after she left the New Vienna last night. I'm going down to the hospital with Shanahan.'

'Oh Jaysus,' Boyle groaned. 'Wasn't I well off when I had your soft job in the Castle instead of bein' out here in the drownin' rain, leadin' a crowd of bobbies like a football team. But it'll be done. If I have to, I'll draw strength in from t'other divisions.'

'I appreciate the assistance, super,' Swallow muttered through gritted teeth. He did not particularly care if Boyle picked up the undertone of sarcasm. This was his division, and as its superintendent the murder of Alice Flannery was first and foremost his responsibility. Technically, Swallow and the G-men were there to assist.

Dr Harry Lafeyre was already at the Royal Hospital on Upper Baggot Street as Swallow and Shanahan arrived. Swallow recognised the city medical examiner's brougham carriage outside the main entrance. Earlier, a constable had been sent to Lafeyre's house on Harcourt Street asking him to attend.

The post of Dublin city medical examiner was part-time and proportionately paid, obliging Lafeyre to juggle the workload with his private practice. He had served six years in Africa with the Natal Mounted Police, and he retained the investigator's instincts developed there. That, together with his qualifications in medical jurisprudence from Edinburgh, made him an invaluable resource in any criminal inquiry.

The city had, nonetheless, invested money in building and fitting out a state-of-the-art morgue on Marlborough Street, just off Sackville Street, and Lafeyre had been invited to choose his preferred equipment and fixtures for its operation. He had sought specifications from modern morgues in England and Scotland, and these had been faithfully honoured. In addition, he was provided with a small office and storeroom in the Lower Yard of the Castle, close to the Army Pay Office.

He had finished his examination and was washing up when Swallow and Shanahan reached the hospital's small morgue. His driver and general assistant, Scollan, was gathering his surgical instruments. A uniformed constable stood by the door.

'I haven't a lot for you,' Lafeyre shrugged apologetically. He led the way to the examination table and drew back the covering sheet to show Swallow and Shanahan the small body. He nodded towards the uniformed officer. 'The child's mother was here to identify the remains. The constable took her statement.' The constable stepped forward to hand a foolscap document to Shanahan. The G-man initialled it and placed it in his file.

'She just didn't have the strength to survive the assault,' Lafeyre said, glancing through his notes. 'Well enough nourished, but a slight girl. No signs of sexual activity or venereal disease. She took a terrible beating around the head and face. An extensive fracture on the left side of the skull. Cause of death was massive clotting on the left cerebral hemisphere. The *corpus callosum* was almost severed at one point. I'd guess there were at least three heavy blows from a club or something such.'

Lafeyre did not need to translate the Latin term for the fibrous material that links the two sides of the brain. If the *corpus callosum* was destroyed, the amount of force must have been considerable. Although Swallow had drunk his way through two years of medical school, he sometimes surprised Lafeyre with the amount of knowledge he had picked up. 'You must have been sober in at least one or two anatomy lectures,' he had once ribbed Swallow. 'Yeah, one or two,' Swallow answered, not untruthfully.

'Could that club be a wooden fence post?' he asked.

'Very possibly. Certainly a blunt weapon, swung hard, applied with very great force, repeatedly. This was no quick blow struck in anger; the intent was deadly.'

'Any other marks or wounds?'

'Nothing too significant that's recent. Bad bruising and skin cuts across the fingers of the right hand. Probably defensive injuries after the first blow was struck.' He gestured to the corpse, 'But there's an old injury there on the left leg, running all the way from the hip to the knee and around to the buttock and thigh.'

Swallow could see an area of discolouration where the skin looked scaly and hard. 'What do you think happened to her?'

'I don't know,' Lafeyre shrugged. 'It could be a burn or a scald mark. It's not new, but it's not from early childhood either. Anything from a year to three years old I'd guess. It would have been very painful and uncomfortable I'd have thought. It probably hasn't been treated as it ought.'

Shanahan scribbled details in his notebook as Lafeyre continued.

'She's still in rigor mortis.' He glanced at the death certificate. 'The hospital staff are giving me time of death here as 9.15 this morning.'

'What time does that condition set in, doctor?' Shanahan asked.

'Usually three to four hours after death. But it can vary according to conditions. It can be affected by temperature, for example.'

A sudden gust of November wind drove the rain hard against the mortuary windows.

'That's about all I can tell you at this stage,' Lafeyre said. 'Have you much to go on?'

'Very little just now, doctor,' Shanahan told him. 'Her name is Alice Flannery. She's eighteen years old, the eldest of a family of six. Worked part-time as a waitress at the New Vienna on South Great George's Street. The father's deceased.'

'I know the New Vienna,' Lafeyre nodded. 'It's owned by a fellow called Karl Werner. An Austrian, as you'd expect. I think he claims some aristocratic connection back in Vienna. The place is very popular with the bankers and businessmen around the area. Then they get a late evening trade when the theatres close. They'd be fairly particular about their staff.'

Swallow nodded.

'She probably did well to get a placement there.'

'I'd say so,' Lafeyre answered. 'At least you won't have to deal with newspaper reporters linking it to these Ripper murders in London. He's after ladies of the street, not people like this. And I don't believe anyone would think of Blackberry Lane as a haunt of prostitutes.'

'A little detail like that won't stop some of the hacks from speculating.' Swallow's tone was cynical. 'If they can find words to frighten people, they'll do it. It all sells newspapers.'

Lafeyre gestured to his assistant, Scollan, and started to move to the door.

'If it's all right with you I'll release the remains to the family. They want to notify the undertakers. I've got a busy afternoon at my rooms. I'll ask Scollan to take care of the details. Would you like to travel with me to the Castle?'

There was nothing more Swallow could learn at the hospital. Later in the day, he reckoned, he would visit the dead girl's home and extend official condolences. By then the door-to-door and other standard inquiries would have been completed. He had arranged a crime conference at Exchange Court for five o'clock. Before that he had to brief his boss, John Mallon, chief superintendent of G-Division.

It was early days in the investigation, he told himself. He knew very little about the victim's circumstances. Usually, in his experience, when one got to know even a little about a victim's life, a motive and a suspect would appear fairly quickly. But he had a feeling that this was not going to be an easy process in this case. Murder was often a relatively easy crime to solve, but so far nothing was clear about the ending of Alice Flannery's life.

FIVE

Swallow decided to treat himself to a large Tullamore and a steak and kidney pie in Deegan's of Parliament Street before presenting himself to John Mallon at his office in the Lower Yard. He and Shanahan had gratefully accepted Lafeyre's offer of a lift in the comfort of his brougham as an alternative to a drenching ride across the city on the open police car.

One of the perquisites of office for the chief superintendent of G-Division was the provision of a house in the Lower Castle Yard. It hardly competed with the splendour of the State Apartments in the Upper Yard, occupied by the Lord Lieutenant and his entourage in 'the season', when the Castle hosted balls, 'drawing rooms' and receptions. There was a world of distinction in rank and status between the Upper and the Lower Yards. Apart from housing the State Apartments, the Upper Yard also accommodated working offices of the powerful civil servants who ran the administration of Ireland for the Crown. Nonetheless, the chief superintendent's house was well-appointed and spacious, and it had recently been redecorated to Mrs Mallon's taste.

After breaking the 'Invincibles' conspiracy in the wake of the Phoenix Park murders of Chief Secretary Cavendish and Under-Secretary Burke five years previously, John Mallon could do no wrong in the eyes of the Castle authorities. If Elizabeth Mallon wanted new wallpaper in her parlour, she could have it.

In providing for their chief of detectives to have his home within the Castle walls, the authorities got excellent value for their money. Whether at his office or in his house, John Mallon received a constant inflow of information on crime and security matters from all over the country, but particularly from across Dublin city. He insisted upon it. Woe betide the duty detective manning the public office at Exchange Court who delayed the transmission of any important intelligence to him in his parlour, or even in his bedroom.

A sheet of icy rain swept across the Lower Yard as Mallon opened the door in response to Swallow's tug on the bell-chain. The chief of detectives put a warning finger to his lips, gesturing him to be silent.

'Detective Inspector, come in. I have two gentlemen inside who were just leaving.'

He led him into the parlour at the front of the house. It was pleasantly warm, in contrast with the outdoor chill, and it smelled of whiskey and tobacco smoke. A good turf fire burned cheerily in the grate. Swallow saw two empty glass tumblers on a low table.

Two men were standing by the fireplace, evidently preparing to leave. Swallow knew immediately that they were from the office of the assistant under-secretary for security, Howard Smith Berry, in the Castle's Upper Yard. Smith Berry's background was in military intelligence in India, and since his appointment to Dublin he had built a separate and supposedly secret security unit, perhaps a score of men, to act under his personal direction. The detectives of G-Division detested them. Most of the secret service men were ex-military, unfamiliar with police work. The G-men regarded them as blunderers and spies. And every G-man believed that they too were being spied upon by Smith Berry's men.

Swallow knew the younger of the men now standing in John Mallon's parlour. Perhaps thirty-five years of age, he was clean-shaven, of average height and athletic build. He was Major Nigel Kelly. At least that was the name by which he had introduced himself. He was an unknown quantity. Swallow had found it impossible to identify his previous posting from the army list when he consulted it. Their paths had crossed unpleasantly, and they had clashed more than once in the past. Kelly had openly voiced his contempt for the way G-Division did its work. Swallow thought him a fraud and a *poseur*. Military men were usually open about their regimental background, but Kelly never spoke of his. Swallow was good on accents. He could always tell a speaker's county, and often what part of that county, but Kelly's eluded him. It was English, but overlaid with something Irish, probably Antrim or Down, he reckoned. And a touch of colonial as well.

'You know Major Kelly,' Mallon said. 'You probably haven't met former County Inspector Waters of the Royal Irish Constabulary. Mr Waters has been assigned as a special investigator to work with Major Kelly on behalf of Mr Smith Berry.'

Waters had a policeman's sharp eyes but an easy expression. Swallow knew him by reputation. He had led the RIC's crime department through the early violent years of the land war.

'The celebrated Inspector Swallow.' The older man held out his hand in greeting. His smile seemed genuine. 'I've heard a lot about your work.'

'Thank you, sir. I appreciate that.'

Kelly's mouth tightened in displeasure, forming an unmistakable sneer. Leading the way out of the room, he made no attempt to acknowledge Swallow.

Mallon indicated towards an easy chair once they had gone.

'Sit down, Swallow. You haven't advanced very much in Major Kelly's affections I'm afraid. A sour bastard, and a dangerous one. He's got a face like a wolf, and the instincts of one too. Unfortunately, he hasn't got its intelligence.'

Mallon had not been so outspoken before about any of Smith Berry's squad. Swallow knew that he had protested to the under-secretary when the new secret service men had begun to make their presence felt. Mallon felt it was an implied slur on G-Division. The secret service men understood little of the complexities of Irish political crime, and they had subverted Mallon's own intelligence network on more than one occasion. But the under-secretary had stood firm. Mallon told Swallow his conclusion: that the orders to establish the unit had come from the chief secretary, Arthur Balfour, who had taken over as head of the British administration in Ireland almost two years previously.

The chief looked stressed; more so than he normally would have, even with the news of an overnight murder, Swallow reckoned. Mallon stood and took a tumbler from the sideboard. Without asking he poured Swallow a heavy Bushmills. Then he poured a shot into his own glass, adding an equal measure of water.

'I'll talk to you about what those two bloody fellows were after,' Mallon said tersely. 'But first tell me about the murder out at Rathmines. Any progress?'

'It's not looking the best, sir.'

Swallow sipped at his Bushmills. It was not a taste he particularly appreciated, but he would never offend Mallon over his own favourite tipple.

'No witnesses worth talking about. No motive. Dr Lafeyre tells us she wasn't sexually active. It probably wasn't robbery because her week's wages were left at the scene, although it's possible someone could have missed her bag in the dark. As of now, I've nothing to go on. I'm going out to meet the mother and the rest of the family later. Superintendent Boyle has turned out his fellows in numbers, so the usual searches, door-to-door and all that, are in hand.'

Mallon scratched his beard.

'With all these London murders the newspapers will raise a racket. Any dead female has to be linked to this Jack the Ripper business in London. I had a query from Commissioner Harrel this morning.'

In the normal course, Swallow knew, the commissioner would only concern himself with 'special' crimes that had a political dimension. The security of the realm was paramount in the thinking of the Castle's senior mandarins. It was G-Division's primary task. An 'ordinary' murder, like that of Alice Flannery, would hardly merit attention. But Mallon was right: the so-called Ripper crimes were causing nerves to fray far from London's East End.

'You can tell him we're pursuing every avenue, chief. Right now we don't have a suspect, but we've just started on the investigation.'

Mallon nodded.

'I know you're "pursuing every avenue". It's at once a useful and a useless phrase. But I understand you've just started. And at least there isn't anything political about it. Just keep me well informed.'

He paused, and indicated with his thumb towards the door through which Kelly and Waters had departed. 'I told you I'd explain what those two wanted.'

Commonality of religion, background and career experience more often than not brought Mallon and Swallow to similar thinking without the need for discussion. He guessed that whatever the secret service men wanted, it had to do with politics.

'I imagine they've got some plan afoot that's likely to inflame passions, give us more work and yield no profit. And they think it's a great idea,' he said.

Mallon's grin was without humour.

'Precisely. They're working flat out to cut the ground from under Parnell at the commission in London,' he said. 'They're desperately looking for ways to blacken him.'

Swallow knew that as soon as the prime minister, Lord Salisbury, had announced the setting up of the inquiry to investigate the allegations that Parnell was encouraging the Fenians to violence, Smith Berry's secret service unit had been further augmented by security detectives, including some drawn from the Special Irish Branch at New Scotland Yard. Some retired RIC men with security experience had been quietly drawn in too. Waters was one that he knew about. They kept to themselves, working out of private offices in the Upper Yard with a military guard outside, but most G-men had got to know some of them by sight. He had encountered them coming and going along Castle Street or Palace Street. They avoided the common police canteen behind Exchange Court that served both RIC men and DMP members. They drank separately too, avoiding the public houses around the Castle habituated by policemen.

'They're digging deep to get any dirt there is on Parnell,' Mallon said. 'The government is supposed to be disinterested and impartial, of course, but it's clear they're doing all they can to support *The Times*'s charge that he's working hand in glove with the Fenians, and that the more violence there is, the more political leverage it gives him.'

'But we know that's not true, chief. We've never got a shred of evidence to support it. If it wasn't for Parnell there'd be a lot more young men enrolling with the Fenians.'

'Of course.' Mallon's tone was exasperated. 'It's their bloody stupidity that angers me. They think they have to destroy Parnell. I've tried to explain, again and again, that he's the best buffer we have between order and chaos, just as you're saying. As long as we have him in position, moderate opinion has a place to express itself. If he's brought down, the extremists will move in to fill the vacuum.'

Swallow drank from his Bushmills. It was good, but he still preferred the mellow Tullamore.

'So what do Kelly and Waters want of us?'

'They want the originals of the protection logs.'

G-men were assigned to Parnell's protection every time he came through Dublin. They monitored his movements from the moment he would step ashore from the cross-channel steamer, returning from Westminster. They watched his house on Merrion Square, logging the people who came and went and the times they did so. When he visited elsewhere, they logged the address and the arrival and departure and any visitors. Swallow had done his share of it before promotion, carefully copying details into the logbooks at Exchange Court at the end of each shift. But every G-man knew that what was officially designated as protection was also surveillance. Every detail of Parnell's life was recorded and passed up the security chain to the officials in Smith Berry's office. And every G-man who did the Parnell 'protection' shifts with any regularity knew that he was frequently accompanied by Mrs Katharine O'Shea, the estranged wife of his parliamentary colleague, Captain William O'Shea. Her home was at Eltham, in Kent, which she shared with Parnell and two of the three children they had together. Their first, it was known, had died in infancy.

'They're going to try to bring him down over the relationship with Mrs O'Shea,' Mallon said. 'They're a married couple to all intents and purposes. She and Captain O'Shea have lived apart for years, but she's legally his wife and the relationship with Parnell is adulterous. He'll be hard pressed to deny it. But Smith Berry believes that our protection logs would be irrefutable evidence.'

'Why can't they get their evidence in England?' Swallow asked. 'As I understand it they live together with their children fairly openly at Eltham.'

Mallon scoffed. 'Oh, they think it'll be far more devastating for him if the adultery is revealed in Dublin. Desecration of the soil of Holy Catholic Ireland and all that.' He grimaced. 'That kind of thing isn't as much a novelty in England, you understand. 'And then the bishops and the priests will rise up and denounce him as a godless sinner, of course. Not everyone will follow their lead, but it'll be the end of him politically. His own followers will split. As you and I know, there's quite a few who'd like to have his place as party leader. McCarthy would love it. So would Healy or Dillon.'

'So they want our protection logs...' Swallow mused. 'What did you tell them?'

'I wasted a good glass of whiskey on each of them before they said what they were after.' Mallon's face reddened with anger. 'I told them that any significant information gathered by G-Division was sent to Smith Berry's office as a matter of routine. Then I told them to go and take a shite for themselves.'

Swallow grimaced. John Mallon rarely used profanities or coarse language.

'That won't go down too well, chief, when Kelly reports to Smith Berry. They'll have the commissioner down on us.'

'They'll try, but Commissioner Harrel understands politics, and he understands about keeping Parnell in power. He won't see his force misused to suit the purposes of the bloody *Times* of London. I don't think he'll buckle to Kelly and his type.'

Swallow was silent for a moment. He sipped again at his whiskey.

'I'd make a suggestion, chief, if you don't mind,' he said slowly. 'I think if I were you I'd make sure the protection logs were put someplace safe. There's about ten or twelve books relating to the Parnell detail. They've always been stored in the crime inspector's office. They're in the filing cabinets where we can get easy access to them if needed. If they're left there, Kelly's men will go in and take them, at gunpoint if necessary.'

He paused.

'Now that I come to think of it, that particular cabinet is nearly full to capacity. If the logs were removed for storage, sure you wouldn't even be certain where they are.'

Mallon reached for the Bushmills and poured again for both of them. He added his customary dash of water and pushed the jug across to Swallow.

'Detective Inspector, you know that I couldn't approve of the removal of official papers from G-Division. But I understand the problem about storage. And I'd be sympathetic to an overworked clerical staff that simply can't keep track of every damned sheet of paper, wouldn't I?'

Swallow drained the last of his whiskey.

'You would, chief. That'd be your style all right.'

The rain cut across his cheeks as he made his way up the Lower Yard to the back entrance to Exchange Court. He climbed the stairs to the inspector's office. It was empty, as he had hoped. He took the key to the storage cabinet from the wall-rack and brought the heavy logs out onto the table, almost a dozen in all. Then he used a pair of canvas straps with metal buckles, standard issue from Her Majesty's Stationery Office for binding heavy files, to make two bundles. He retraced his steps down the Lower Yard to the office of the city medical examiner, the two bundles clasped against his chest to protect them from the rain.

Lafeyre did most of his official work from the city morgue at Marlborough Street. But the authorities had also provided him with a small, secure room in the Lower Castle Yard, close to the Army Pay Office, to store evidence and files. A duplicate key, for convenience of access, was held in the crime inspector's office.

Even though the November evening was closing in, Swallow needed no light to navigate the room. He unbundled the books and inserted them one by one into the space behind a storage cupboard that stood immediately inside the door. Stacked flat against the wall, they would be invisible to anyone coming or going through the doorway. He stepped out into the yard and quietly turned the key in the lock.

SIX

The Exchange Court crime conference on the murder of Alice Flannery was depressingly brief. Pat Mossop and Johnny Vizzard had taken a few hours' rest in the dormitory above the public office before resuming duty. Mick Feore had travelled in from Rathmines with Superintendent 'Duck' Boyle and Sergeant Stephen Doolan in a closed cab that protected them from the freezing rain.

A dozen uniformed constables from the search teams sat on wooden forms, smoking and drinking hot tea. Their sodden capes dripped icy water from coat-hooks along the side of the parade room.

'No suspect in the area,' Feore summarised gloomily, gesturing to the pages of the murder book. 'No motive that we know of. No witnesses worth talking about. We've got a likely murder weapon though, and plaster casts of a pair of shoes.'

'Who's talked to the family? Immediate neighbours?' Swallow asked

'I did that,' Stephen Doolan answered. 'The mother is Bridget. Works part-time as a cleaner at the church across the Rathmines Road. Jack, the husband, died two years ago. Hit by a load of timber at Grand Canal Dock. One boy, Dan, aged seventeen. He's apprenticed as a cellar man at Coyle's public house in Rathmines. The others are just kids, twelve, ten, six and four. The neighbours say they're a very devout family. If the mother isn't cleaning the church, she's praying in it. Young Dan attends Mass every morning and goes to confession every week, it seems.'

'And the neighbours? What do we know about their movements?'

'All accounted for. They're what you'd expect: labouring men, or unemployed. A couple of the women run fruit and vegetable barrows on Camden Street. One or two of the working men were out and about, but they all gave alibis. We're cross-checking them, but so far they seem solid.'

Duck Boyle made a loud harrumph. Swallow had become well-accustomed to this signalling of an impending pronouncement in the years when Boyle was crime inspector in Exchange Court.

'It is me own experience, an' I speak with rank and seniority,' he intoned, 'that a crime like this is rarely a random act. There's a motive somewhere but we're just not seein' it yet.'

'Very true, superintendent.' Swallow could not fully conceal his sarcasm. 'The truth is,' he added in a more conciliatory tone, 'we're seeing very little.'

Boyle shrugged. 'All I can do is put every man I have out on the beats tonight. Question everyone they encounter. I'll get the off-duty lads out buckshee in plain clothes. They're bloody keen, all of them. We don't know if this killer could strike agin', do we? If nothin' else we'll do our damnedest to ensure there's no repeat.'

Swallow nodded. In fairness to Boyle, his instinct was protective. Not every superintendent always put the care of the community ahead of administrative police convenience. The 'buckshees' were young uniformed men who aspired to detective work. Given an opportunity, they would often work in plain clothes to prove their mettle. Putting them out on the street in numbers was a wise move.

'Fair enough,' he responded. 'Mr Mallon's already had Commissioner Harrel on to him. If he can tell him we're doing everything we can to keep the streets safe, that's at least better than nothing.'

The conference broke up with nods of agreement, but Swallow could sense the air of dejection. The atmosphere would be very different if there was a clear line of inquiry or if there were solid clues to be followed up.

'What's next, boss?' Pat Mossop asked.

'I'll go to visit the Widow Flannery and her kids out at Blackberry Lane,' Swallow said. 'I can't say I'm looking forward to it.'

SEVEN

The murmur of prayers carried the length of the darkened Blackberry Lane as Swallow and Mossop made their way slowly through the throng of neighbours gathered outside the small cottage. Mercifully, the rain had eased off and men and women knelt bare-headed around the door, picking up the responses to the Rosary.

They stepped into the room where Bridget Flannery knelt beside her daughter's body. Two candles flickered on a makeshift trestle, scenting the low-ceilinged space with oily smoke. A heavy-set priest of perhaps fifty years, in surplice and stole, stood beside the sobbing woman, giving out the prayers in a solemn recitation.

Police business had brought Swallow to poor homes like this on many occasions. Flannery's rented cottage would not be classified among the lowest grade of Dublin housing, but it was far from palatial. The earthen-floored room in which the dead girl was laid out served as kitchen and living space. To left and right of the open fireplace, rough wooden doors led to two small rooms that comprised sleeping quarters. Ideally, one would be for males and one for females. There would probably be a small yard behind with a dry privy. Less fortunate families living in the city's courts and lanes might have to share such a facility among forty people.

He took in the sparse furnishings. A deal table, covered with a cheap oil-cloth. A wooden dresser with some simple crockery. A few boxwood chairs. A wicker basket, laden with turf sods taken down from the boggy hills behind the city. A crucifix hung on the wall over the fire. On the opposite wall there was a faded paper portrait of the young patriot Robert Emmet, executed in Thomas Street for his abortive rebellion against the Crown. Swallow smiled inwardly at the familiar image: it was one of a series published some years earlier in the pages of *The Nation* newspaper, edited by Thomas Davis, who had initiated the Young Ireland movement. His mother had another in the series, depicting the rebel pikemen of 1798, which she hung behind the bar of Swallow's public house in Newcroft.

His mother's father and two of her uncles had been 'out' in the rising of '98, fighting the redcoat yeomanry in the flat countryside where Kildare borders on Queen's County. Only one of the three brothers, Swallow's grandfather, had survived.

Swallow's mother remained staunchly rebellious even as she advanced in years. But notwithstanding her insurrectionary instincts, she had no qualms about selling drink to the soldiery of the nearby Curragh camp, said to be the largest military installation in the empire. Swallow's of Newcroft had the reputation of being a good house, frequented by senior NCOs as well as private soldiers. Payday at the Curragh was also payday for the adjacent public houses.

He looked around the room. Half a dozen or so books occupied a small shelving space built into the wall beside the fireplace. He strained to see the titles. The Holy Bible. A copy of Butler's *Lives of the Saints*. A heavy volume telling the story of the supposed apparitions of the Blessed Virgin at Knock in County Mayo. Two cookery books. A compilation of *Moore's Melodies*. Incongruously, there was a battered copy of Blackstone's *Discourse on the Study of Law*.

Swallow fell into the rhythm of the prayers, answering the *Aves*, *Paters* and *Glorias* easily and naturally, as in his childhood. Mossop, being Church of Ireland, maintained an awkward silence at his side, rocking slightly on his feet and staring at the ceiling. When the last responses had finished, Swallow stepped forward to the dead girl's mother and introduced himself and Mossop.

'We're truly sorry about this, Mrs Flannery. The G-Division will do all we can to bring whoever did this to justice. We've got every available policeman in Dublin on the case now. Do you understand?'

Bridget Flannery nodded. For a moment she attempted to speak, but the words did not get beyond a sob. Swallow guessed she might be forty, though she looked two decades older. Grey-streaked hair and a deeply lined face spoke of a life of want and struggle.

'Thank you, sir,' she finally managed. 'Thank you indeed. She was a very good girl. A very good girl, sir. She was always in the state of grace, and she's in heaven tonight with God and his saints.'

Swallow was momentarily unsure how to respond to Bridget Flannery's fervour. He found it disquieting, but it seemed to give her strength. He decided to ignore it.

'Have you any idea who might have been responsible for what happened to her? Is there anyone who might have wished her harm?' he asked.

The priest stepped forward, folding his stole.

'You can see that this poor woman isn't in any fit state to answer your questions, constable,' he said sharply. 'Shouldn't you have found the brute that did this already?'

Swallow disliked him instantly. 'And you are, Father…?'

'Monsignor, actually. Monsignor Feehan. I am in charge of this parish of Mary Immaculate.'

Swallow raised an eyebrow. 'Oh, a monsignor. Very good. I'm Swallow. Detective Inspector, G-Division … actually. And I'm in charge of this investigation.'

Bridget Flannery placed a hand on Swallow's arm. 'There's nothing I can say, sir. And it's hard to talk here, what with poor Alice and all the neighbours. Monsignor Feehan is a good man. And all I know is that my lovely daughter is dead. If you'd like to talk to the monsignor about this … terrible thing … he's willing to help you in any way he can. He knew poor Alice very well. All the priests across in the parish church did.'

Swallow was a little surprised by Bridget Flannery's coherence and delivery. Once she found her voice, she spoke with the confidence and tone of a woman somewhat above her station in life.

The priest's tone was marginally more conciliatory. 'If you'd care to come across to the parochial house, Detective Inspector Swallow, I'll try to tell you whatever you may need to know. If I can help the police in any way, of course I will.'

Swallow caught the slightest wink from Pat Mossop's eye. The little Belfast man notoriously hated pomposity and condescension.

Swallow's invocation of his own rank had clearly improved the monsignor's manners.

They followed the priest, moving out through the mourners to cross Rathmines Road. It was dark now and cold, with evening setting in.

The parochial house was generously illuminated with gas lights in the hallway and in the front rooms. The interior smelled of food and beeswax polish. Feehan showed them to a large, comfortably furnished parlour on the ground floor. He sat first and then gestured them to straight chairs around a solid oak table. A coal fire burned in the grate, making the room pleasantly warm.

'You may remove your overcoats if you wish,' Feehan said. It was something between an invitation and an instruction.

'Thank you, no,' Swallow answered. 'We won't detain you any longer than we have to.'

If Feehan picked up Swallow's implicit assertion of his authority, he let it pass.

'This is a shocking thing,' he said slowly, his expression solemn. 'Within yards of this church, the house of God. A very pious young woman from a good-living family. What do you think can have happened?'

Pat Mossop opened his notebook on table and sat, his pencil poised. The monsignor's eyes registered displeasure. 'Is your sergeant taking notes of what I am saying, Mr Swallow?' The tone was hostile again now. 'I am under no obligation to speak to you. The law of the Church is above the law of man. And you should understand that I am personally known to the new superintendent at Rathmines, Mr Boyle. A fine, upstanding Catholic gentleman, if I may say so.'

'Absolutely,' Swallow said. 'Superintendent Boyle is all of those things. But this is standard procedure, Monsignor.'

Mossop grimaced. 'That's correct, sir. Any detail may be important in a serious case like this, and has to be committed to paper. That's my job. I'm sure that if Superintendent Boyle were here he'd confirm that to you.'

Before Feehan could respond, the door opened without a knock. A tall young priest with neatly parted blond hair, perhaps in his late twenties, looked into the room. 'Pardon me, Monsignor,' he said, glancing at Swallow and Mossop. 'I heard you had visitors. Is there anything the housekeeper can get you before she finishes up? Some tea perhaps?'

Feehan waved a hand. 'Thank you, no, Father Cavendish. That won't be necessary.' He made no pretence of introducing the two G-men or offering them refreshment.

'How well did you know the dead girl, Monsignor?' Swallow asked when the young priest had left.

'It would be more correct to say that I know the family rather than … the deceased. They are poor people, as you can see, but decent, hard-working and loyal to their faith. The sort of family our church is built on, gentlemen.'

'Well, actually my own church has the same sort of foundations,' Mossop remarked conversationally.

'Oh,' Feehan was clearly embarrassed. 'I assumed …'

'Yes,' Swallow said, quietly relishing the advantage, 'Detective Sergeant Mossop is a member of the Church of Ireland. Now, if we could get back to my questions. I understand that Alice worked here in the church as a cleaner?'

Feehan seemed relieved to pick up Swallow's questioning as a means of getting away from his faux pas. 'Oh, yes. Occasionally, yes. It was more as an assistant to her mother, who has been one of our regular cleaners for quite a few years. She was a good worker and never had to be told anything more than once.'

'So you would have known her quite well?'

'No. I could only say I knew her slightly. As the parish priest … as a monsignor … one would have little to do with that aspect of parish business. We would have the occasional short conversation if we met in the church. She was very respectful. She would have dealt with the sacristan for practical matters, pay, cleaning materials and so on.'

'How would you describe her, sir?' Mossop asked.

Swallow saw a flicker of irritation in the priest's eyes. He knew why. 'I've already explained that Detective Sergeant Mossop is not of the Catholic faith, Monsignor,' he interjected. 'He's not accustomed to our usages of ecclesiastical titles.'

Mossop nodded apologetically. 'It's true, sir. I'm sorry.'

'As far as I know she was a very ordinary girl,' Feehan said. 'Respectful, as I say. Intelligent, I'm told. Hard-working. After the father died she took on all the work she could to help feed the family. I believe she also worked in a restaurant somewhere in town. I believe she wanted to advance in that area of work.'

'She was anxious to improve her lot?' Swallow put the question.

'Yes, I would say so. From our occasional conversations I gathered that she was ambitious. She liked to read, she told me once. She'd sometimes take the newspapers home when the priests had read them and finished with them.'

'Were there ... any young men in her life?' Mossop asked.

'If you're asking me was she keeping company, I cannot answer that, Mr Mossop. Our Church, whatever about yours, takes a very strict view on such matters. If she was, it could in certain circumstances have been an occasion of sin and she would have been obliged to reveal it in confession. Since I was her confessor, I cannot break the seal of confession, as you'll understand, I'm sure.'

'You were her confessor?' Swallow said. 'Surely then you must know a lot about her circumstances that could help us, without breaking any seal. It can hardly apply once a person is deceased, I assume.'

The priest shook his head. 'I'm sorry. The fact that an individual may be deceased does not alter a priest's obligation to honour the seal of the confessional. But I don't know anything that might be of help. And if I did, I couldn't tell you.'

'I don't know if you understand what we are dealing with here, Monsignor.' Swallow's tone hardened just a little. 'We have a young girl murdered in the most savage way. We have no witnesses, no significant clues, no motive. Whoever did this could strike again on another innocent victim. It's essential that we find out anything in Alice's background or life that could shed light on why this happened.'

Feehan snapped back. 'If the police were more energetic in protecting the citizens of Dublin instead of helping to evict people from their farms perhaps this monster would have been apprehended on the spot. Were there no policemen on duty last night?'

Swallow's irritation was rising. He steadied himself to reply. He would be courteous to a fault when the police were being denigrated or provoked. 'The Dublin Metropolitan Police are not engaged in any evictions, Monsignor. Our task is to prevent crime in this city, and if we cannot always succeed in that then it is to make criminals amenable to the law. But without assistance I am left hunting for a needle in a haystack.'

'Then hunt you must, Mr Swallow. And I sincerely hope that you're good at it.'

Mossop looked up from his notes. 'If I could make an observation, sir, perhaps you'd comment on it. It seemed to me that Mrs Flannery is very well-spoken, very articulate for a woman in her financial circumstances.'

Feehan permitted himself a thin smile. 'Your observation is astute, Sergeant. One might say that Bridget Flannery married somewhat beneath her. Her people owned a small shop, groceries, that kind of thing, in the village of Ranelagh. She had a good education if not an extended one with the Loreto sisters on St Stephen's Green. Her late husband, John or Jack, was a labouring man without education or a trade. You probably know that he died tragically some years ago. An accident at the docks.'

'Might she not then have secured better employment than cleaning in the church?' Mossop followed up.

The priest shrugged. 'That is not for me to say. Tending to the house of God is not menial. She has proven very suitable to the parish. As did her daughter. And as you know, Alice continued to develop her work in the restaurant trade, as I understand it.'

'What can you tell us about the rest of the family?' Mossop asked. 'There are brothers and sisters. It was her younger brother, Daniel, who reported her missing last night.'

'They are but children. The eldest boy is Daniel. Dan. He is apprenticed as a barman. About seventeen I'd say. A fine young man. Extremely devoted to his faith. Perhaps unusually so, compared to most young men of his age and circumstances. He attends Mass daily. His mother would have wished him to have gone on for further education. The Christian Brothers at Synge Street would have taken him without any requirement for fees. He would have made a fine brother himself, or even gone forwards to the priesthood perhaps. He served as an altar boy here at Mary Immaculate.

Indeed, he served my Mass many times, and his devotion to his faith was manifest. But the household needed his income.'

Swallow stood. 'Thank you for your time, Monsignor Feehan. It's very helpful to have an understanding of the poor girl's circumstances. If you think of anything else you'd like to tell me, please send word to the G-Division office at Exchange Court.'

He moved to the door. 'There's one other detail I should mention. The city medical examiner, Dr Lafeyre, found an extensive area of injury on the girl's left leg. A burning or scalding perhaps. It would appear to have been relatively recent. Certainly not an injury from childhood. Would you have any knowledge, perhaps from conversation with her mother, what might have caused it?'

Feehan's face flushed. 'Mr Swallow, it is presumptuous almost to the point of obscenity to suggest that I would have any such … anatomical knowledge of a young female parishioner. You may consider yourself fortunate if I do not report your effrontery to your authorities.' He gestured to the door. 'Please, let yourselves out.'

They crossed the darkened roadway and hailed a cab at Portobello Bridge. It stopped short of the Castle at The Long Hall on South Great George's Street, where Swallow ordered a large Tullamore, and a pint of Guinness's stout for Mossop. Mossop kept a tactful silence while the head settled on the porter.

'They're not all quite as obnoxious as that monsignor, Pat,' Swallow told him, downing half of his Tullamore.

'Ah, sure, I know, boss. Your friend Father Lawrence down there with the Franciscans on Merchants' Quay is a gentleman. This monsignor is a fella with a high opinion of himself.'

Swallow allowed himself a grin. 'Other than his manners, what did you think?'

Mossop took a gulp from his pint. 'Manipulative. Guarded. Nervous behind the bluster. Odd how the mother told us that he knew the girl well. I think she said "all the priests knew her", but your monsignor acts as if he'd only ever seen her occasionally. You could say there's a bit of an inconsistency there.'

Swallow nodded.

'It was almost as if she saw him as a spokesman for the family. But he doesn't see it that way, does he?'

'No. He's definitely trying to put distance between himself and the Flannerys. Maybe it's a matter of class or something like that.'

'Maybe. And speaking of distance, it's time to visit the New Vienna restaurant. It's only across the street. We'll need to have a word with Mr Stefan Werner.'

EIGHT

The New Vienna was rich in mahogany and brass, with an exquisite mosaic floor in the lobby, laid out to depict a variety of exotic vines, game, fowl and fishes. The warm interior was heavy with the aromas of rich food, cognac and cigars.

The G-men showed their warrant cards to a man in a swallow-tailed suit who had emerged through heavy glass doors from the dining room. A buzz of conversation and laughter escaped momentarily into the lobby as the doors swung shut. Through the half-frosted panels Swallow could see that the restaurant was filled to capacity. Harry Lafeyre was not mistaken in his description of its popularity.

The man in the swallow-tailed suit scrutinised the warrant cards and then gave them back. His hand was scented with cologne. Swallow guessed he might be around forty. He smiled politely.

'You have an unusual name. Like the little bird, yes?'

The English was precise but heavily accented.

'And you are?' Mossop asked.

'I am Stefan Werner. I imagine that you must be here in connection with this terrible tragedy concerning our little kitchen waitress.'

'Yes,' Swallow said. 'We are investigating the murder of Alice Flannery last night. What is your position here, Mr Werner?'

Stefan Werner clasped his hands behind his back as if to make a formal announcement.

'I am the maître d'hôtel. My family are the owners of the New Vienna.'

'Oh, so you have you a hotel here too?' Mossop said. 'I don't think we knew that.'

Werner smiled tolerantly. 'It has nothing to do with a hotel. It is a title used in the restaurant business.'

'It's a family business?' Swallow asked.

'Our family is well established in the restaurant business in Berlin,' Werner said. 'I came to operate this restaurant five years ago.'

'Did you move directly here from Berlin?' Swallow asked.

'No. I have worked in London. For some years I was restaurant manager at the Savoy Hotel in the Strand. Perhaps you know it?'

'Unhappily not,' Swallow answered. 'My billets in London on the only occasion of my visiting that city were a little less salubrious.'

'You said Berlin?' Mossop asked. 'So you're not from Vienna?'

Werner smiled. 'Which do you think has the greater appeal to customers, a restaurant called New Vienna or one called New Berlin? Berlin is a dull, ugly place, populated by dull, ugly people. So we dull Berliners present ourselves as ... how do you say ... slightly more romantic Viennese. We bring a sense of the city of Haydn, Beethoven, Mozart, Schubert to our business.'

'Is that legal?' Mossop asked in a puzzled tone. 'I mean, you couldn't pass Tullamore whiskey off under that name if it wasn't from Tullamore.'

Werner blinked uncomprehendingly. 'I'm sorry. I don't see the comparison.'

'Never mind,' Swallow said wearily. 'We need to ask a few questions about the victim, Miss Flannery.'

'I am extremely busy at this time. The restaurant, as you can see, is full. I supervise everything, the kitchens, the wine, the table service. I would wish to be of assistance to the *Polizei* of course, but I can be of little help with your questions. In fact, I did not know the girl other than to see her. She was a casual employee, you understand. We can go to the office for privacy.'

'Thank you. That would be helpful,' Swallow told him.

Werner led them down a corridor into a spacious oak-panelled office, illuminated by four gas mantles set in ornate wall brackets. He waved them to two leather armchairs and opened a glass-fronted cupboard built into one panelled wall.

'May I offer you something to drink, gentlemen? A good cognac perhaps on a winter night like this?'

Swallow was tempted. He saw Mossop lick his lips in anticipation too. But it was better to be prudent.

'No thank you, Mr Werner. Not while we're on duty.'

Werner shut the cabinet door and eased himself into a seat behind the desk.

'As you wish, gentlemen. Now, how may I help you?'

In the light, Swallow saw that Werner's features seemed tanned, yet his hands were pale. Then he caught a gleam of oil on his cheeks. He realised the man was wearing some sort of make-up. Perhaps it was a continental thing. Swallow had never actually met a Prussian until now.

'Did you know the girl well, Mr Werner?' he asked.

'Not so very well, as I have said. But she worked under my supervision, yes.'

'Did you know her family? Anything about her background or circumstances?'

'No, of course not. She was, as I say, casual labour. These people usually come in off the street looking for work. It's rarely necessary for us to run a newspaper advertisement. We interview them, and if they are suitable we will give them work by the day, sometimes by the hour.'

'You don't look for references?'

Werner laughed. 'References mean very little in this business. People will forge them. It's easily done. Sometimes employers will write a good reference just to get rid of a troublemaker. No, we do not seek references when someone wants to start work in the still-room, scraping pots and saucepans.'

'What did she do precisely? What were her duties?'

'Just that, at first. She started here in the still-room. That is, washing and cleaning the equipment and the tableware. She was quite … *ehrgeizig* … ambitious … is that the word? She wanted to be a waitress. But she needed much training. She was a long way off being able to serve the tables.'

'But you said she was a waitress?'

'A kitchen waitress. She would have a uniform, but her job was to bring the prepared dishes from the kitchen to the sideboard tables on the restaurant floor. Then the waiters, our fully trained staff, serve the guests. This is a very efficient system, in use in most of the great restaurants in Europe. This is associated with *service à la russe*, as we call it.'

'Sorry ... *à la* what?' Mossop asked.

'*Service à la russe*. It's the Russian way of serving dinner, with each course put up in succession. It's generally used in restaurants across Europe now. In the older way, *service à la française*, the French way, all the dishes would be served together.'

Swallow saw Mossop struggling to get the narrative down in his notebook. Nor would he be able to grapple with Werner's French. It hardly mattered.

'How long was she working here?'

'I would say about a year.'

'Your employment records should be able to tell us precisely.'

Werner shrugged. 'We do not keep records for casual workers. Our sommeliers, our chefs and our professional waiters, yes, but not for what is, as I have said, casual labour.'

'So there is no record of her working here?'

'I don't imagine so.'

'Not even in the wages book?'

'She'd have been paid out of petty cash. I paid her myself.'

'Did you pay her on Friday?'

'As well as I can remember, yes, I would have.'

'Was she a good worker?'

Werner hesitated for a moment. 'She was ... diligent, never late for work. She was respectful. But she was clumsy. We had breakages, spillages ... more than the average I would say.'

'But you kept her on?'

Werner smiled. 'I am, I think, a kind man. Ask any of the employees, they will say so too. But in fact I had decided to terminate her work here. Her attitude had become, shall I say, resentful, *übelnehmerisch*? And she had learned the basics of kitchen work. It was time for her to move on.'

'Did she have any particular friends on the staff here? Or any enemies?' Swallow asked. 'Can you think of any reason why anybody would wish to harm her?'

'No,' Werner shook his head. 'She did not … how do you say … socialise. The employees will go to the public houses if we close a little early sometimes, but not her. And I have no reason to think she had any enemies here.'

'Who would have been the last person to see her leave here last night, Mr Werner?' Swallow asked.

Werner grimaced. 'I believe it would have been me, Inspector. I recall now that I paid the girl her wages and I saw her leave through the kitchen doorway. I remember thinking to myself that she would be cold going home, walking out to Rathmines, since she had no coat, just a light shawl.'

'That was thoughtful of you,' Swallow said. 'She was fortunate to have encountered that sort of kindness in you. And you have a good memory for detail,' he added.

'Thank you, Inspector.'

Swallow stood. He was tired, and he could see that Mossop was wilting too.

'I'm not sure that it will be necessary to speak further this evening, Mr Werner. I understand that you're busy with many things to attend to here. We can call back at a more convenient time. And we will need to interview other employees. You've been very helpful with your information. It's getting late. Detective Sergeant Mossop and I have reports to write up and we'd best be going.'

Werner spread his hands in a gesture to indicate a willingness to assist.

'I am very happy to assist, Inspector. If there is anything further I can help on, please let me know. It is important that you should catch whoever is responsible for this … *Verbrechen* … this dreadful crime.'

They walked the couple of hundred yards along South Great George's Street to the Castle Lane. The streets were quiet now and the pavements were sparkling with the night frost.

'What did you think?' Swallow asked.

Mossop wrinkled his brow in concentration. 'A smooth operator, boss. But maybe not as open as he wants to appear. He claimed to know nothing of her family or background, yet he knew she had to walk home to Rathmines.'

'Fair point,' Swallow acknowledged. 'He put on a big show of wanting to be helpful, but every question we asked was simply deflected.'

They were at the junction of Dame Street and South Great George's Street.

'Go on home, Pat. Get a night's rest and we'll resume in the morning. We've done what we can for the day.'

He turned into Dame Street to make his way home to Maria.

NINE

By the time Swallow reached Grant's it was closing time. The walk from Exchange Court through the wintry air was invigorating, but it also made him realise he was hungry. He had eaten nothing since he had taken the steak and kidney pie in the early afternoon.

The additional beat men on street patrol that Boyle had promised were visible. Two stood under the shadowy bulk of Christ Church. Another was at old St Audoen's on High Street, his blackened night helmet barely discernible in the darkness. A sergeant and a constable stood half-hidden in a shop doorway at the junction of Francis Street and Thomas Street. In theory at least, Swallow reckoned, the streets should be safer.

Tom, the head barman at Grant's, was dousing the last of the oil lamps around the bar as the laggard clients of the night shuffled out for home. His expression was sympathetic when Swallow walked in. He knew that Maria had expected him to be there from the end of his shift at six o'clock.

'Bloody cold out there, sir.'

'It is that, Tom. Busy night?'

'Much the usual, sir. Brisk, but nothin' unmanageable. I think people are savin' up whatever few bob they have for Christmas. Mrs Walsh is gone up. She's fairly tired what with bein' off listenin' to that fella Davitt and his friends all afternoon down at the Mansion House. You've had a busy day yourself I'd say with that business out at Rathmines.'

Swallow consciously evidenced no surprise at how Maria had spent her afternoon.

'I have, Tom. A busy day. And not much to show for it.'

Maria's parlour, above the bar, was their private retreat after closing time. When he climbed the stairs, she was in her usual easy chair by the turf fire. A small supper table, set for one, stood to the side of the fireplace. 'I heard you coming up,' she smiled. Swallow could see that she was indeed tired. She gestured to the table.

'You're not too late for supper. When I read in the *Evening Mail* about the murder I guessed you wouldn't be home until late, so I had Carrie put some Irish stew in a hot box.'

The stew was good. Chunks of tender mutton with carrots and parsley for flavour. Maria's cook and housekeeper, Carrie, knew Swallow's preferences. There was a bowl of boiled floury potatoes too. He crossed to the sideboard and poured himself a bottle of Guinness's stout.

'Would you like something? A glass of port wine?'

She shook her head. 'No thanks. I'm very tired. I doubt I'd rise tomorrow morning if I took anything at this hour.'

'I'm sorry I couldn't be here,' he said. 'You probably heard about the murder out at Rathmines. This is a bad one. A young girl's head battered in. No clues or witnesses.'

'Dreadful. The newspaper said it might be connected with these murders in London.'

'No. Not at all, for God's sake. That's just the journalists trying to sensationalise things.'

He sounded irritated, and regretted it instantly.

'What I mean is that it's an easy line for a lazy reporter to peddle. Linking it in with these London murders is absolute nonsense. This is a respectable girl. Good family in poor circumstances.'

'That's some comfort, I suppose,' she said quietly. 'Do you know what happened to her?'

'What, yes, but not why,' he answered. 'She was attacked just a few yards from her home. It might have been for any reason. We'll find out in time.'

'How terrible,' Maria said. 'May the Lord have mercy on her.'

He forked a mouthful of mutton and washed it down with the porter.

'Tom tells me you were off at the Mansion House rally to hear Davitt. I didn't know you were planning to do that.'

'I wasn't. Harriet insisted I should go. And I thought you might want me to keep an eye on her anyway. She gets carried away on these issues.'

That was certainly true of his young sister, he knew.

'Did Davitt say anything significant?' he asked unnecessarily. In the morning, at Exchange Court, he would read the G-men's report of the meeting.

'Mostly the usual things one reads about in the newspapers. You know I don't have a lot of interest. But he's a very powerful speaker. He seemed to be very upset about the authorities' attempts to undermine Mr Parnell.'

Swallow's mind flashed back to the set of protection logs that he had earlier secreted away in Harry Lafeyre's room in the Lower Castle Yard.

'He's not wrong,' he said. 'They're out to do him down. A terrible mistake, I think. If Parnell falls, what comes behind him will be more violent and ugly than anything we've seen so far. In one way that would suit Davitt. But I think he understands that Parnell could secure the bigger prize—Home Rule for Ireland.'

She was silent for a long moment.

'Is it not time to get out of it, Joe? All this intrigue and politics and danger. I have a good business here, but it needs a man's hand in it too. You and I could build it into a really prosperous enterprise.'

She sounded weary.

'You know I don't reject the idea, Maria. We've talked about this.'

'I do. We've talked before, of course. But things have changed.'

She looked him fully and deliberately in the eyes.

'I'm pregnant. I'm expecting our child.'

Sunday November 4th, 1888

TEN

Swallow had fixed the crime conference for ten o'clock. That gave tired G-men and their uniformed colleagues a chance to have a lie-in at home or to get to an early Mass, or service, depending on their inclinations and their confessional affiliations. But when he arrived at Exchange Court five minutes before the hour, every man was present. Pat Mossop and Mick Feore were cross-checking details in the murder book. Johnny Vizzard and Stephen Doolan were examining the plaster cast of the boot recovered from the field beside Blackberry Lane. A dozen G-men and a few of Doolan's constables sat around on forms and chairs.

Swallow took a chair at the top of the parade room. The policemen fell silent.

'Any developments?'

Stephen Doolan tapped the reports from the telegraph room on his desk.

'The night was quiet. We had double beats out, as you know. No suspicious activity beyond a couple of fellows found with crowbars outside a shop in Stoneybatter. The cold probably kept the anti-social elements indoors.'

Swallow gestured to the plaster cast taken in the mud at Blackberry Lane.

'What do you make of the shoe?'

Doolan held the cast up and turned it.

'Size nine. Adult. Almost certainly male. Smooth sole without any hobnails. Not a working man's or a farmer's boot. Not an army boot either.'

'Any gaps in the alibis from the neighbours?'

Feore glanced up from the murder book.

'Nothing from the neighbours, but we found a hole in young Dan Flannery's story.'

There was a murmur of interest around the room.

'The brother?'

'Yes. He said in his statement that he worked in Coyle's of Rathmines until after midnight, stacking crates in the cellar and bringing fresh stock upstairs to the bar. Then he turned up at the station in Rathmines at two o'clock in the morning to say his sister hadn't come home.'

He turned a page in the murder book.

'But Constable Caviston checked with Tom Coyle, the publican. He says it was earlier, more like half past eleven, when Dan left. Coyle's senior barman says the same thing. Coyle says that young Dan took off fast as soon as he started calling last drinks. He says he'd been doing that for the past few nights. Coyle had ticked him off and he offered to come in earlier the next day to get the stocks right.'

Another murmur passed around the room.

'We'd better have a few words with young Dan then,' Swallow said. 'There might be an innocent explanation for it, but there's a discrepancy of half an hour between what he's telling us about his movements and what his boss is saying. He could easily have been at Blackberry Lane at the time of the attack.'

'Will we go out or have him brought in?' Mossop asked. 'They've still got the girl laid out in the house. Whatever the story, it wouldn't be decent to have a squad of bobbies descend on a household in mourning.'

Swallow nodded.

'You're right. Just go out to the house on your own and tell him to come in here with you. Don't bring any uniformed men with you. We'll not arrest him unless he makes us. Tell him he's coming in to help with inquiries, but put a couple of men along the Rathmines Road in case he tries to make a run for it. Bring him in here for, say, one o'clock. I'll do the interview with you. In the meantime, I'll go across and bring Chief Mallon up to date.'

'What do I say to the mother?'

70

'As little as possible. There's no need to have her upset any more than she is. Just tell her that he's going to help us put some information together.'

When the conference broke up, Swallow retreated to his office. It was John Mallon's custom with his family on Sunday mornings to attend ten o'clock Mass in the Church of Saint Nicholas of Myra on Francis Street. He would not be at his house until eleven o'clock. Swallow was glad of a little time on his own to reflect on last night's conversation with Maria.

'You're sure about what you've told me?' he had asked her when she had given him her news.

He knew the question was unnecessary, but it was his policeman's instinct to want corroboration.

'Yes. Dr Morrow up on Meath Street confirmed it this afternoon. I'm more than a month past my menstruation. He wants me to see a specialist at the Rotunda Lying-In Hospital. But I know it myself, Joe. I can sense the change in my body. And I'm nowhere near the change of life.'

'Morrow's a very good doctor, I believe. Why would he want a specialist? Is there a problem? Some complication?'

'No. Nothing that he could find. I'm very healthy. But I won't be a very young mother. He says this man is very skilled and I should be seen by him … just as an extra precaution.'

They had spoken in the past about marriage and children. He could envisage marriage, but children had been no more than a theoretical consideration. Maria had said she would want a boy and a girl. They had even talked about children's' names. But it was all in the abstract. This was a conversation he had never seriously thought to have.

She laughed lightly.

'I'm thirty-five. Dr Morrow says I'm fine and all seems normal. But it's early days. He's not too concerned about my age, he says, even though it's not common for a first child.'

'Thank God for that.'

'Well?'

'Well what?'

'What do you think?'

He fumbled for words, reckoning he might be slightly in shock.

'I never imagined … never thought … of course I should have.'

He laughed.

'These things happen, don't they? So we'll have to make arrangements, won't we?'

'Arrangements?'

'Yes. I mean … we'll have to get married. Straight away. Put a respectable face on it all.'

'Is that what you think?' she asked.

He thought he saw relief in her eyes. Perhaps she thought he would suggest getting rid of the pregnancy. There were people who could do that for her. Perhaps she feared he would deny the child. When he saw tears in her eyes he could not be sure if they indicated relief or disappointment at the lack of emotion in his response.

'Look, I know I'm not handling this very well, Maria. It's just a bit of a shock to me too. When you get to my age … of course this is very good for us. It's the right thing for you and for me. A little one will change our lives very much for the better.'

'Are you sure?'

'I'm certain.'

He got to his feet and opened another bottle of Guinness. Now he understood why Maria had refused her customary glass of port wine earlier. He began to feel better. There were too many uncertainties in his life and in Maria's. And he had held off on making decisions for too long.

He walked across to her chair and knelt beside her, placing his right hand over hers.

'Maria Walsh, I know I'm not the greatest catch in Dublin. I'm the wrong side of forty. I'm twenty years a "polisman" and I've just made it to detective inspector. But I'll be loyal and true to you and our child. Would you do me the honour of agreeing to marry me?'

He grinned.

'And sure, isn't there a grand pension for us to look forward to when I finish my service?'

Her face darkened slightly.

'You mean you wouldn't want to come into the business with me? Full time? Equal partners? Like we spoke of before?'

He sighed.

'I know we did. But that was before I got the promotion. I can't just abandon my responsibilities with things the way they are. There's serious crime to be dealt with. You know, this murder. And now I'm told by Mallon that the English are out to destroy Parnell whatever way they can. Besides, you're more than well able to manage the business here.'

'How could I do it with a child to rear?'

'We'll get help. A nurse to mind the child and maybe an extra man in the bar. You've been saying that Tom needs more help there. He's getting on too.'

It was not what she wanted to hear, he knew. He tried to change tack.

'Look, we don't have to decide on this now, do we? What I need to do is to go down to Friar Lawrence tomorrow and make arrangements for the marriage. Are you happy to have the wedding at Merchants' Quay?'

She nodded and smiled.

'So can I take it that you're accepting my proposal?'

'Yes, of course I'll marry you, Joe. And Merchants' Quay would be perfect. A small wedding would be nice.'

Her expression clouded a little.

'Remember, I've walked up the aisle once already. I've been through this before. And it's the responsibility of the bride's family to take care of the hospitality. I'm my own family, so I'm looking after the wedding breakfast.'

He kissed her lightly on the forehead.

'I'm not going to argue with the future Mrs Joseph Swallow.'

ELEVEN

John Mallon always turned himself out impeccably for Sunday Mass. He wore a top hat and a perfectly tailored coat in fine charcoal grey. His invariable accoutrements were a silver-topped ebony cane, silk gloves and a leather-bound missal. Elizabeth Mallon, also clasping a fat missal, invariably wore a fashionably demure ensemble. Their procession to their seats in the forward pew in the Church of St Nicholas of Myra on Francis Street had become a sort of weekly pageant for the parishioners. That the chief of Dublin's detectives, the head of G-Division, the powerful master of Exchange Court would come to worship among them was at once a source of wonder and some pride.

Swallow crossed the Lower Yard to Mallon's house at twelve noon. By now he knew his boss and his wife would have returned from divine worship. The aroma of roasting beef told him that the Mallon family's Sunday routine was in hand. Mallon answered the door and led him into the parlour.

'What news, Swallow? Some progress I hope.'

'We're bringing in the dead girl's brother, sir. There's a hole in his alibi. The lads are gone out to get him now.'

'Her brother? Is there a big hole in the story?'

'Big enough to enable him to be at Blackberry Lane when the girl was attacked.'

'Tell me about him.'

'Dan Flannery. He's twenty. Two years older than her. Works as a cellar man and trainee barman in Coyle's of Rathmines. Very religious and pious. It seems to run in the family.'

Mallon grimaced.

'A religious exterior can hide a lot about a man. Anything else?'

'Not much. We interviewed the monsignor at the church in Rathmines where she worked part-time as a cleaner. And we interviewed her boss at the New Vienna restaurant on South Great George's Street. The place is run by a German fellow, name of Werner. I interviewed him with Mossop. A very smooth character. All charm, but giving very little actual co-operation. There's no immediate suspect. No motivation. She seems to have been a hard-working girl. No romantic associations. No enemies. No motive so far.'

Mallon nodded.

'I know the New Vienna. An expensive place to dine. Much favoured by some of our frock-coated colleagues from the Upper Yard and their friends from the banks along College Green and Dame Street. There's got to be a motive. It's unlikely that it was just a random attack.'

'I agree,' Swallow nodded. 'We might get somewhere with the brother. He said he worked in Coyle's until midnight, but the word there is that he was away by half past eleven. He could have been down at Blackberry Lane as she came home.'

Mallon raised an eyebrow.

'Some domestic issue between brother and sister? Some falling out?'

'The monsignor speaks highly of him. He says he might have gone for the religious life if the family didn't need his wages. Beyond that I don't know, chief. We'll have him in shortly and I'll be better able to get the measure of him.'

Mallon stood from his chair.

'Like I said, in my experience piety and intelligence aren't incompatible with the criminal mind. Indeed, they can sometimes be complementary to it.'

He glanced at his pocket watch.

'My domestic obligations press on me. Time for Sunday dinner with Mrs Mallon. But just so you should know, I've been summoned to the office of the assistant under-secretary for security in the morning. They want to know why I haven't provided the protection logs on Mr Parnell.'

Swallow nodded.

'That's not giving you much time, chief.' He spread his hands in a gesture of mock-sincerity. 'But it's a bit unfortunate, I'd say. You've asked me to locate them, and of course we've searched; they're just not to hand. I suppose they'll be found in due course. But right now they're not easily located. I'm sure Mr Smith Berry will understand.'

'I want you with me at that meeting, Swallow. I think it could be a difficult encounter. And I'll need corroboration that we're doing all we can to find these damned logs. Be at my office at half past nine.'

In the afternoon, still trying to absorb the impact of what Maria had told him, Swallow walked down from the Castle to the Franciscan monastery by the river on Merchants' Quay. The water was high, pushed up against the quay walls by a rising tide from the bay. A flotilla of swans made its stately way along the icy surface downriver towards Queen Street Bridge.

Father Lawrence ushered his visitor to the small private parlour overlooking the quay. In contrast with the public areas of the church and monastery it was comfortably warm and furnished, with a fire glowing in the grate. Upon hearing Swallow's news, the old friar's eyes lit up with delight.

'Oh, this is splendid. Splendid indeed.'

He crossed the parlour and reached into the oak sideboard to produce a bottle of Tullamore.

'This is a little indulgence you introduced me to, Joe. But I keep it for special occasions.' He winked at Swallow as he poured two sizeable tots. 'And if ever there was one, this is it.'

He raised his glass.

'Here's to Mr and Mrs Swallow and the health of their child—their children, we hope.'

Swallow had not until that moment thought beyond the possibility of one child. The old friar was right, of course. Marriage could mean the coming into the world not just of this child but possibly others as well. It was an arresting thought. He was glad of the whiskey.

Lawrence would marry them immediately. It had to be done swiftly, he agreed, in order to preserve both Maria's good name and Swallow's too.

'There's a few fellows in the Castle who'd no doubt use the situation to blacken your name,' Lawrence said. 'Bringing the force into discredit or something such.'

It would be manna from heaven for Kelly and his masters in the Upper Yard, Swallow reflected silently. Even John Mallon's influence would not outweigh the disciplinary charges they could lay against him: lodging on licenced premises, involvement in the business of a public house, cohabiting with a woman other than his wife, bringing the force into disrepute....

They fixed on the following Saturday for the ceremony.

'I won't deny I'm nervous,' Swallow said. 'It's all been a bit sudden.'

'But sure, Joe, the whole world can see that you're cut out for each other,' Lawrence laughed. 'You should have made a decent woman of her long before now. You're doing the right thing, and if both of you make a good confession before the marriage you'll have God's blessing. You just get your two witnesses for the ceremony. Who have you in mind for that?'

'I'll ask Harry Lafeyre to be my best man,' Swallow said. 'Maria will want her sister, Lily, I assume, as her bridesmaid. Is that the correct term?'

Lawrence knew both Lafeyre and Lily Grant from many social visits to Thomas Street. He chuckled.

'A strange pass, isn't it? Harry and Lily are due to be married when? Sometime in the spring? And here you are with Maria, sprinting up the aisle ahead of them. Well, even if the notice is short we'll do this the right way too. Full nuptial Mass, and then solemnisation of the marriage vows.'

He downed the last of his Tullamore.

'I suppose there'll be a bit of a celebration—a hooley—after the event?'

Swallow grinned. Lawrence liked nothing better than good company over a meal, or a few drinks, or both.

'That's Maria's department. But she's at work on it already. You can be sure that end of things will be taken care of.'

Lawrence clapped his hands.

'Ah, sure it'll be a great day. A great day.'

The friar's brow suddenly furrowed.

'Will you be all right to get the time off? You've got that murder out in Rathmines to deal with, haven't you?'

Swallow nodded.

'I have. And the truth is that it's not looking very promising in terms of any early arrest.'

'A terrible, terrible business. It'll be a fearful winter for many a young woman who has to go about the streets if you don't get to the bottom of it.'

'I'd be less than honest if I told you we're going to be able to do that, Father,' Swallow said. 'Usually there's a fairly clear motive, and that can point us towards the perpetrator, but as of now we don't have any idea why it happened. She was just a young waitress on her way home from work.'

'According to the newspaper she worked in the church on Rathmines Road,' Lawrence said. 'It must be a terrible shock to the community out there.'

'She worked part-time as a cleaner out at the Church of Mary Immaculate. I went out to talk to the parish priest there, Monsignor Feehan. Do you know him?'

The old friar frowned.

'No. Only by repute. But I'm told he's a very difficult man. A terrible snob too, by all accounts. There was talk that he would be assigned to the Pro-Cathedral, but I think the priests there objected to the appointment and persuaded Archbishop Walsh to send him elsewhere. I'd say he'd be straight enough though.'

'That's what I was afraid of,' Swallow said. 'He told me we'd get nowhere. He hoped I was a good hunter.'

He finished his whiskey and stood.

'Winter isn't a great time for hunting, though. I think I need a miracle, Father,' he laughed. 'Can you do anything about that?'

Lawrence was solemn.

'Miracles are reserved to the Lord, Joe. And I don't know if he's that much in favour of hunting anyway.'

TWELVE

Young Daniel Flannery gave no trouble to the G-men who picked him up at the cottage in Blackberry Lane. His employer, Tom Coyle, had given him time off work in the circumstances of his sister's tragic death. On Sunday in particular, the trade at Coyle's would be light, and he could manage without the services of his young cellar man.

'You told us you worked until midnight on Friday,' Swallow said after he had introduced himself. 'But our information is that you were gone from Coyle's by half past eleven.'

Flannery sat opposite in a straight chair in the crime inspector's office. He was well composed, Swallow reckoned, and not visibly distressed by being asked to come in to Exchange Court. He was neatly turned out, in a suit that was pressed and clean, albeit of cheap cloth and indifferent cut. Swallow could not decide at first whether it was confidence or defiance he saw in the young man's face.

'Can you explain that?'

Flannery's features seemed to harden.

'First, Mr Swallow, you should understand that I am an Irish nationalist. I like to be known as Domhnal Ó Flanbharra. I'm a proud member of the Gaelic Union. I'm tellin' you now that I have no enmity agin' you, but I reject your authority as an agent of the English Crown.'

He paused.

'Secondly, I'm a truthful person, committed to me religion. The Commandments say "thou shalt not bear false witness". You can believe what you're hearin' from me.'

Swallow silently bit his lip. Few subjects were as difficult at interview as religious enthusiasts. Their indignation threshold was always low, and they were always quick to invoke the deity to confirm their innocence.

Nor had any of the G-men made a link between the Flannery family and any of the nationalist organisations that proliferated around the city. The Gaelic Union, established by Canon Ulick Bourke of Tuam archdiocese, was one of the more inoffensive groups. Yet Swallow felt he knew the name 'Domhnal Ó Flanbharra' from somewhere.

'That hardly matters here,' he countered cautiously. 'I'm interested to know why you told my men you were at your place of employment at the time your sister was attacked when you had, in fact, left much earlier.'

'There might have been a misunderstandin',' Flannery said. 'I told Mr Coyle I needed to leave a bit early. I had things to do and I needed a bit o' time off on Saturday afternoon.'

Pat Mossop's pencil noisily scratched the responses into his notebook.

'Why did you want Saturday afternoon off?' Swallow asked.

Flannery snorted derisively.

'Not for any reason that you or your kind would understand.'

'Try me,' Swallow said patiently.

'I'm an active supporter of the Irish Land League. No doubt you had your spies at the meetin' at the Mansion House yesterday afternoon for Mr Davitt's address. I was goin' there to be a steward.'

'I can understand that, Dan, or Domhnal if you prefer it. But would you not consider it somewhat disrespectful to your dead sister to be out at a political meeting while she was being waked at home in Blackberry Lane?'

'Me sister's death is for our family to deal with. I'm fortified in that loss by me Catholic faith. An' me sister's death doesn't come between me and me duty as an Irishman who wants to free his country. I'd hardly expect you to understand.'

Swallow groaned inwardly. Someone had rehearsed the young man very thoroughly in the rhetoric of the nationalist movement.

'You might be surprised at what I understand. You're entitled to hold your point of view, but I need to know why you lied to the officers who interviewed you. Let me put it bluntly. You could have been at Blackberry Lane when your sister was attacked.'

Flannery raised his head to look him in the eye. His expression seemed anxious now.

'I couldn't have been. I did go to the Portobello Bridge to wait for her, but either I missed her in the fog or she started for home a bit earlier.'

'Why would you go to Portobello to wait for her? That's a bit unusual.'

'You won't believe me, so what's the point?'

Swallow smiled. 'I'm a man used to surprises.'

Flannery started to knead his fingers. It was perhaps the first sign of stress, Swallow reckoned.

'It was that priest,' Flannery said. 'She told me he was botherin' her. Every night as she walked home he'd appear alongside her, and he'd want to walk her along the Rathmines Road. It wasn't right. I wanted to see him off. He's unfitted to wear the holy cloth.'

'What priest?'

'Cavendish. He was botherin' her.'

'Father Cavendish from the parish church? Was there some incident, an event?'

'No, not as such. But there was a lot a' small things that were wrong. He was too much interested in her. I wanted to let him know that I knew that. To warn him off. So I wanted to be there for her as she came home. To see her all right. She was a good girl. She shouldn't have had to resist occasions of sin.'

'Occasions of sin?' Swallow asked.

'Yes.' Flannery became momentarily agitated. 'That's an occasion where sin might be committed. But even if it isn't, placin' oneself in that situation is itself a sin.'

Swallow's mind went back to some catechism diktat he remembered from school days.

'So what happened on Friday night?'

'I left work and went to Portobello Bridge, waitin' for her. But I must have missed her in the fog. I never saw her. So I went for a good walk along the canal. I do that sometimes after work for relaxation. I met a friend at Huband Bridge, and we talked for a bit, then I went home. When Alice wasn't home and me mother was gettin' upset, I went to the police station in Rathmines and said she was missin'. They said she was in Baggot Street Hospital. So I went down there and found her.'

'Did you meet anyone else along Rathmines Road or Blackberry Lane? Anyone who might have been the attacker?'

'No. The priest never appeared. I saw the last tram from the city go by, but nobody else.'

Swallow and Mossop exchanged glances. If Dan Flannery was telling the truth about being on Huband Bridge, a good mile away from the crime scene, it was likely that the rest of his story was true. The alibi would have to be checked.

'Who did you meet?' Mossop asked. 'And an address for that person please.'

'It was Mr Bradley. Geoffrey Bradley. He's a teacher at the Christian Brothers in Synge Street. He taught me while I was there. I don't know his address, but you'll get him at the school and he'll confirm that he saw me.'

'We'll look into that,' Swallow said cautiously. 'Tell me about your sister. What sort of girl was she? Did you get on well with her?'

Flannery's eyes moistened slightly.

'She was … a good sister…. After my father was killed she … she was a pillar to the whole family. To me mam especially. She worked every hour of the day and most of the night to help keep a roof over our heads and food on the table. And she feared the lord. She prayed every mornin' and every night.'

'She cleaned the church and worked at the restaurant. Is that what you mean when you say she worked all those hours?' Swallow asked.

Flannery nodded.

'She wanted to make the most of herself. She was getting trainin' and experience in the restaurant. She said she'd go on to be a cook, maybe in a big house or some place. She'd have been a good cook. She was always readin' about cooking and new sorts of food in bits she'd get out of the *Freeman's Journal*.'

That explained the cookery books on the fireside shelf in the Flannery cottage, Swallow reckoned.

'She was an intelligent girl. A good reader?'

'The Loreto sisters said she was at top o' the class and she should stay with the schoolin'. The brothers over at Synge Street said the same of me, you know. They said I could get into the university or even be a priest if I wanted.'

He laughed bitterly.

'To think o' me as a priest. Imagine. Just pipe dreams for people like us, Mr Swallow. Pipe dreams. That's why, after the triumph of the Lord's kingdom on earth, I want a new Ireland, where people like Alice and me can get our chances.'

'Sometimes people throw their chances away too, Dan,' Swallow said. 'You've a chance to help Alice in the only way you can now. That's by telling us anything you know about who might have harmed her. You can start by telling us about this Father Cavendish.'

Flannery frowned.

'He wasn't like a priest should be to her, if you ask me. When she started working with me mam, cleanin' the church, he started takin' her aside for private conversations. I saw them once sittin' on a bench in the church grounds. An hour later when I passed by again they were still there. I asked her later what they were talkin' about and she said Father Cavendish was tellin' her he could help her to get on in life. I think he might have fixed her up with the job in the New Vienna. He lives well does Father Cavendish. Fancy restaurants wouldn't be any novelty to him.'

'That isn't anything to be upset about. Priests have powerful connections,' Swallow said. 'Maybe he was being genuinely helpful.'

Flannery shook his head.

'Then he started buyin' her books. He bought a few books about cookery for her. But then he'd have novels, and he'd ask her to read these out loud for him in the parlour at the parochial house. He said it was to help her improve her speakin' manner.'

'Seems fair enough,' Mossop observed. 'Your sister was an ambitious girl.'

Flannery shook his head again.

'No. He told her he wanted to work on her voice projection. He told her she had to loosen her clothin'. He had to put his hands on her, holdin' in her stomach, pressin' her back and all that. But it was just an excuse. She knew it was wrong and made him stop. That's when she told me about it.'

'What did you do?' Swallow asked.

'I told her that what was happenin' was displeasing to God. I told her to stop the visits and to warn him that she'd complain to the monsignor, Feehan, if there was any more of it. It seemed to work for a while. Then a couple of weeks ago he started turnin' up on the Rathmines Road at night when she'd be comin' home from work.'

'So what would happen on those occasions?'

'He'd just be there, usually around the bridge, and he'd walk with her to the top of the laneway. She said he told her he was protectin' her.'

'But you suspected his motives?' Swallow said. 'You went out to intercept him?'

'Yes. She said that he was going on about the evils of sin, the importance for a girl to maintain purity and so on. She didn't need that guidance. She was a good girl from a good home. He was usin' her to get his own bad thoughts out into words.'

'But you never actually spoke to him or met him about all this? Not even on Friday night?'

'No.'

'So what do you think happened to Alice? Who killed her?'

'I won't point a finger,' Flannery raised his voice and brought his hands crashing down on the tabletop, 'but you must be blind if you can't see it! Or is it that the police are afraid to take on a priest?'

'No,' Swallow said. 'The police will do their duty. But we need something more than assertion. We need evidence.'

'Well, you have my information for a start. And I'll stand over it.'

'That's a start,' Swallow told him, 'but we'll need a formal statement. But I have other questions.'

'Such as?'

'The medical examiner found a mark, perhaps a burn or a scald, on her left side. He estimated that it might be a year old, maybe two. Do you know how she got that?'

Flannery nodded.

'She tried to lift a kettle o' hot soup or hot water off the fire at the New Vienna, where she worked. It spilled over her. She took herself down to the infirmary to have it tended to.'

'When was that?'

'Sometime after Christmas last. Maybe January.'

Flannery turned to look at the wall-clock.

'I think I should be gettin' home now. Me mother needs me there with Alice bein' waked an' all the neighbours in.'

Swallow stood.

'I understand that. You're free to go home, Dan. Sergeant Mossop and I will be going to see Father Cavendish very shortly.'

'He'll deny everythin',' Flannery said wearily. 'Don't believe him.'

'We'll see,' Swallow said, keeping what he hoped was a neutral tone. 'There's just one thing more. Can you let me see the soles of your shoes? I'd like you to take them off.'

Flannery leaned down and unlaced the shoes. They were polished, but cracked and patched on the uppers. The soles were smooth and without any pattern.

'Are they what you'd wear to work, Dan?' Swallow asked.

Flannery's laugh was bitter.

'I only have the wan pair o' shoes.'

Swallow handed the shoes back to him.

'And they're not a bad pair at all, Dan, even though they've seen a lot of service. Size nine. Would I be right?'

Monday November 5th, 1888

THIRTEEN

Winter tightened its grip on the city. The morning was cold but dry with a white frost on the footpaths and the cobbles as Swallow made his way to the Castle. He was at Mallon's office in the Lower Yard just before half past nine. Jack Burton, the chief's clerk, had a feeble turf fire starting in the grate in the outer office.

'It'll build up nicely now in half an hour,' Burton told Swallow apologetically. 'When you come back from your meeting above you'll get a good warming out of it.'

A few minutes later John Mallon emerged from his inner office. By this hour, Swallow knew, the chief of detectives would have gone through the night's crime reports from around the city, noting any significant occurrences, mentally storing details and adding instructions to the file margins for action during the day.

It was a minute's walk to the office of the assistant under-secretary for security in the Georgian block across from the Bedford Tower in the Upper Yard. Its windows looked directly out at the statue of Lady Justice, complete with weighing scales and a sword, which topped the pediment of the Castle's Cork Hill gate. Cynical Dubliners were wont to make derogatory comments about the fact that the statue's back was turned to the city so that only the denizens of the Castle could look upon her face.

The assistant under-secretary's office, as befitted his rank, was spacious, comfortably carpeted and well-appointed with impressive furniture. A set of vivid watercolours depicting scenes of Indian wild-life, tigers and elephants, adorned the walls, evoking Smith Berry's earlier career as a security specialist in the colonies. Two coal fires burned cheerily, one at either side of the room.

'Good morning, Mr Mallon, Mr Swallow. Please sit down.'

Smith Berry's tone was polite, but as icy as the morning outside. Swallow knew him slightly. He had been at conferences where the assistant under-secretary spoke of the challenges and responsibilities facing the Irish police forces. Swallow was familiar with the man who sat at the apex of the security network that controlled, or sought to control, Ireland, and their paths had crossed before.

He was probably fifty, Swallow reckoned, about the same age as Mallon. He looked fit and trim and was clean-shaven, with greying hair carefully brushed back in two wings above his ears. His spare frame seemed to fit perfectly into the morning suit and starched white shirt that were the prescribed mode of dress for very senior officials in the Upper Yard. He might have been born into it, Swallow thought. Now he sat grim-faced behind his desk, flanked on one side by Major Kelly, on the other by Waters, the former RIC man.

'Thank you, sir,' Mallon said. 'Good morning to you.'

He nodded an acknowledgment to Kelly and Waters.

There was a long, awkward silence. The only sound in the room was the ticking of a glass-domed Ormolu clock over the carved mantle.

'Well?' Smith Berry eventually released the syllable.

'Sir?'

'Don't "Sir" me, Mr Mallon.' Smith Berry's voice was, if anything, icier than his earlier greeting. 'You know why I asked you to be here.'

'I'm not sure what you mean, Mr Smith Berry.' Mallon sounded earnest. 'Why did you want to see me?'

'You know very well indeed why I wanted you. On Friday I asked that you furnish this office with certain records from G-Division. I expected them on my desk on Saturday. It is a very short distance from Exchange Court to here. At the very least I had expected to have them delivered to me this morning.'

Mallon raised his hands in a gesture of comprehension.

'I'm very sorry, Mr Smith Berry. I hadn't appreciated the absolute urgency of the matter. In fact, I requested Detective Inspector Swallow to locate the logs after we spoke on Friday. Regrettably, he hasn't yet been able to do so.'

Smith Berry arched backwards in his chair, his jaw dropping as if to convey incredulity.

'Mr Mallon … this is … unacceptable.'

Kelly angrily slapped the tabletop in front of him.

'I might have known. Are you telling us you can't locate the basic daily records that every police office in the kingdom is obliged to keep and maintain?'

'It's not that, Major Kelly,' Swallow said in a tone that he hoped was not too respectful. 'You wouldn't be aware, but there's been a lot of change recently at the detective office. I've just taken over from former Inspector Boyle who's gone on promotion to E-Division. There's a vast amount of paperwork, as you might expect, at Exchange Court. It's just a question of going through it all.'

'How long?' Smith Berry asked wearily.

Swallow shrugged.

'I don't know, sir. We've got a particularly unpleasant murder on our hands, plus all the usual tasks. It's not easy to find men to give time to the job.'

Kelly's pitched laugh was furious.

'Sweet Jesus Christ, do you take us for fools? I've got to give it to you for nerve, Swallow. You're asking us to believe that basic records of the section you're supposed to run have gone missing, and you don't regard it as sufficiently urgent to put a couple of men on the job of locating them?'

Mallon intervened before Swallow could reply.

'Major Kelly, we are practical people in G-Division. We place a higher value on action and inquiry than on maintaining paperwork. I could keep a very neat office if I held all my men indoors shifting files, but I believe we'd solve very few crimes and glean very little intelligence from the streets. It isn't always possible to keep track of every scrap of paper that passes through a busy crime office. Keeping records may be your priority; it isn't necessarily mine.'

'No, it's clear than running an efficient office isn't a priority for you, Mr Mallon,' Kelly hissed. 'You seem to think you can dictate your own priorities and set aside the requirements of your superiors.'

'That isn't so,' Mallon said calmly, 'and I very much resent what you are suggesting. G-Division does its work and discharges its duties. If you feel we have not done so, I'll bear in mind what you have to say. But my line of report is to my superior, the commissioner of the Metropolitan Police, Sir David Harrel, in the first instance.'

'I hope you'll be able to answer to Sir David very quickly as to who murdered that unfortunate girl in Rathmines on Friday night,' Kelly sneered. 'I foolishly thought you'd have made an arrest by now.'

'Oh, for God's sake,' Smith Berry snorted. 'Let's end this charade. Mallon, you know the government wants all the information it can get on Parnell. You're the people, G-Division, who should have that. So let me be blunt: if you haven't got it, you are in dereliction. And if you have it, and you refuse to pass it to me, you're lending your support to the subversion of lawful authority. So make up your mind.'

Swallow saw Mallon tense himself.

'Sir, it's not my function to engage in political issues. But as I understand it, the objective of the government is to bring down Mr Parnell. I feel it incumbent upon me however to tell you that, in my informed opinion, if he falls, the space left vacant will be filled by some very dangerous people.'

'You're right on one thing at least, Mr Mallon,' Smith Berry snapped. 'It is not your place to question the objectives of Her Majesty's government. Nor indeed is it mine. But since you have opened up a political discussion, let me offer you another perspective, one that goes beyond a policeman's short-term objective of keeping law and order.'

He paused to draw breath, as if about to embark on some marathon task or break vital confidences.

'Mr Mallon, if Parnell has his way, if he succeeds in securing what he calls "Home Rule" for Ireland, the unity of the kingdom will be ended. This great United Kingdom, which has built the most powerful empire that the world has known, will be sundered. If Ireland is lost, what territories will be next? India? Africa? Hong Kong? The Antipodes? A civilisation and an order that spans the globe will be threatened with decline and fall. That, Mr Mallon, is the threat of Parnellism, not whether a few landlords' houses get burned down in Galway or Roscommon.'

Mallon was silent.

'That's a viewpoint, sir,' he said after a pause. 'All I can tell you is that if Parnell is displaced, people will die here in Ireland. And preventing that is my responsibility, not saving the empire.'

Smith Berry sat back and extended his arms as if to illustrate a point.

'And there's the difference between your task and mine, Detective Chief Superintendent. So, can we go back to the instant matter?' he asked rhetorically. 'Lord Salisbury and his colleagues in cabinet, our superiors, know Parnell for a man of double standards and dishonesty, and they are within their rights, indeed they are doing their duty, in exposing it. The details of his private life testify to his dishonesty and double standards. And the records of the men under your command constitute firm evidence of it.'

'I doubt they do, sir,' Mallon answered. 'They may record certain events and details. However, I know Mr Parnell. I know him very well, and I believe him to be a man of honour. But this is beside the point. I do not know where the protection logs are.'

Swallow kept his gaze fixed on the wall behind Smith Berry, trying not to think of the volumes stacked in the space behind the storage cupboard in Harry Lafeyre's office.

Waters spoke for the first time.

'As I told you when last we met, I have a great deal of respect for you and your colleagues, Mr Mallon, and for the work you do.'

His tone was conciliatory.

'Having had responsibility for busy police offices in my time, I can sympathise on the problem of tracking paperwork and files. I hope that your present … ah … difficulties in that respect can be overcome very quickly. But I doubt if Captain Willie O'Shea would agree with you in your estimate of Mr Parnell as an honourable man. He certainly isn't very honourable insofar as his relationship with Captain O'Shea's wife is concerned.'

'Whatever the facts of that relationship, Mr Waters, it appears to be an arrangement that suits everyone, including Captain O'Shea,' Mallon countered. 'And I suggest that it suits us too. As I have said, in my view Mr Parnell stands as a bulwark between us and chaos. And his domestic situation, vulnerable as it appears to be, may actually serve to prevent him becoming too powerful. I'm not totally insensitive to the wider political issues of which Mr Smith Berry has spoken.'

'Absolute tosh,' Kelly interjected. 'You're out of your depth, Mallon. Stick to your backstreet informers and cultivate your touts. You simply don't understand that Parnell is a greater threat to the system than any Fenians or dynamiters.'

Swallow silently acknowledged that Kelly was probably right about Parnell. G-Division, the police forces and if necessary the army could keep violence in check. It was not nearly so certain that the Salisbury government could hold the line at Westminster. If there was a threat to the unity of the kingdom, and by extension to the empire, it was political rather than military.

Smith Berry was growing impatient. 'So, Detective Inspector Swallow, how long do you estimate it will be before you have your man for the Rathmines murder? Might we then expect some attention to be given to the priorities of the government that pays your salary?'

'With respect, sir, the government does not pay my salary. It is raised in taxes and rates from the householders and the businesses of this city,' Swallow answered calmly. 'They're entitled to the protection of the police that they pay for. I'm doing what I can to put order on the paperwork at Exchange Court, but it won't be done in a day.'

Smith Berry seemed unable to find words. The colour drained from his face. Out of the corner of his eye Swallow saw John Mallon take a sharp intake of breath.

To respond in these terms to the assistant under-secretary for security was probably somewhere between insolence and mutiny, he knew. But the facts were on his side. Unlike the paramilitary RIC that policed the country outside of Dublin, and which was funded directly from the exchequer, the Dublin police system was funded primarily by the city ratepayers.

Smith Berry pushed his chair back and came to his feet.

'Please leave my office, both of you,' he said coldly. 'The under-secretary will hear of this. So will Commissioner Harrel. I don't believe that in almost thirty years of Crown service I've ever encountered such wilful obstruction of superior authority. When word of this reaches the cabinet in London, as it will, you will be lucky to retain your posts.'

Mallon was equally cold.

'Mr Smith Berry, Detective Inspector Swallow and I are doing our duty to the best of our abilities. We have both taken an oath to preserve Her Majesty's peace in Ireland. Irishmen do not make that solemn undertaking lightly, and we are obliged to honour it. I don't especially worry who you report to about what has transpired here today, and if it displeases important people at Westminster that cannot be helped, although it is to be regretted. But I would ask you please to bear in mind that I myself am not without influence in the highest political circles.' He paused. 'And in the press.'

Smith Berry's jaw dropped. For a moment, he struggled for speech. Then he pointed to the door, his hand trembling in anger.

'Out,' he whispered hoarsely. 'Get out ... get out.'

They made their way through the outer office and down the staircase. A blast of chilly air coming up from the river swept across the Upper Yard.

'Jesus, Swallow,' Mallon said quietly once they were in the open space. 'You believe in living dangerously.'

'You're doing a bit of risk-taking yourself, chief. Threatening Smith Berry with the press is fairly raising the stakes, I'd have thought.'

'A bit, I suppose. But it's one thing the frocks are terrified of. You know, a line of adverse comment in any of the newspapers, especially the London ones, sends them into total panic.'

Mallon stopped in his stride.

'It's true though about the risks, Swallow. We live dangerously in G-Division. We're Irishmen reporting to Englishmen who don't understand the difference between the two races. It's too late for me to do anything else with my life, even if I wanted to. But you're younger and you have choices. I told you before. Marry that good woman with her fine public house in Thomas Street. The way things are going you might never see your pension.'

They descended to the Lower Yard and found the entrance into Exchequer Court. Swallow wondered if what Mallon had just said gave him an opportunity to tell him that he was, indeed, going to marry Maria. In fact, police regulations required that he should seek permission and have his superintendent's approval to enter into matrimony. But it might turn into a longer conversation than he needed now. He decided to leave it for another time.

'How's the murder inquiry coming along?' Mallon asked.

'If you don't mind, chief, could I brief you on that a bit later? I've got to pick up Pat Mossop inside and we need to talk to a potential suspect.'

'A suspect? Good. Is he in custody?'

'No, chief. But he might be after Alice Flannery's funeral Mass.'

FOURTEEN

Alice Flannery was buried at Mount Jerome cemetery, near Harold's Cross, south of Dublin city, on Monday morning after requiem Mass in the Church of Mary Immaculate at Rathmines.

Swallow and Mossop came into the church at the back of the nave and moved up to the transept, selecting a viewing point from which to survey the mourners. 'Duck' Boyle and an inspector from the E-district, both uniformed in fulfilment of regulations, solemnly took seats in a pew to the front, behind the row that was customarily reserved for next-of-kin.

The congregation, as Swallow expected, was comprised largely of local people, denizens of Blackberry Lane and the poorer cottages scattered behind the newly developed streets and avenues of the Rathmines township. They crowded deferentially in the middle and back pews, leaving the forward seating for the bereaved family and any important people that might be in attendance.

From his vantage point in the transept, Swallow recognised the figure of Stefan Werner from the New Vienna, seated in the same pew as Boyle and his inspector. His fine Crombie coat contrasted with the poor jackets and shawls that predominated among the mourners in the farther pews.

The coffin containing Alice Flannery's remains had already been brought from the mortuary chapel and placed on trestles facing the high altar. Bridget Flannery sat, huddled with her children in the front pew. Daniel sat next to his mother, a protective arm around her shoulders, his siblings ranged on his other side. The pews behind the immediate family were filled, according to custom, by the extended family, aunts, uncles and cousins.

The church bell tolled above the dome of St Mary Immaculate at the moment the doors from the sacristy were opened, as by an invisible hand.

'Father Cavendish, a grand young man, God bless him, Father James,' an elderly woman in the pew behind the G-men whispered aloud to her neighbour as the celebrant came out to the altar, preceded by two acolytes.

Swallow recognised the young priest who had briefly appeared when he and Mossop had interviewed Monsignor Feehan in the parlour of the parochial house on Saturday.

Swallow saw Mossop pencil the detail into his notebook. There was no sign of Monsignor Feehan, or indeed of any other priests. That was odd, he reasoned, given the involvement of both the dead girl and her mother, however humbly, in the work of the parish. If it were a requiem Mass in his native rural Kildare, Swallow knew, there would be multiple celebrants.

When the Communion had concluded, Father Cavendish's homily was clinical and formulaic, the predictable promises of eternal life and resurrection. Formal condolences were extended to the bereaved family. There was an exhortation to anyone with information concerning the crime to come forward and to confess. Curiously, Swallow thought, there was no reference to the dead girl's work in the very place of worship in which she now lay. Everything about the obsequies and Father James Cavendish's manner reinforced his unease. There was no sense of warmth or compassion in the service, rather a cold compliance with necessary formality. Swallow often found himself disquieted at the growing opulence and sense of privilege that he sensed in many of the pastors of his own church. The church's new and growing wealth was given physical form in the magnificence of St Mary Immaculate's rich interior. Yet he thought he detected something else here. It was as if Father Cavendish's Mass and homily were no more than a show, performed to a carefully prepared script.

After the final blessing, the coffin was wheeled down the nave, followed by the dead girl's immediate family and other relatives.

Swallow and Mossop moved swiftly to the back of the church in order to observe the congregation as it emptied out into the concourse at the building's front. There was nothing of any significance to note. Swallow recognised one or two middle-aged men who in earlier years would have figured as minor criminals in police reports.

They followed the funeral cortège in a police side-car through Rathmines and Harold's Cross to Mount Jerome. Along the route, shops temporarily drew down their blinds as a mark of respect. Men on the footpaths removed their headgear and women blessed themselves as the hearse came by. A light flurry of snow came out of the leaden grey sky as the coffin was taken from the hearse at Mount Jerome. Swallow felt cold flecks on his face as it was lowered into the ground.

The priest said the final prayers and led the mourners in a decade of the Rosary, finishing hurriedly with the traditional prayer for the deceased. '*May her soul and the souls of all the faithful departed rest in peace, Amen.*'

There had been nothing of investigational value to be gleaned. No suspicious behaviour. No confidential whispers from any of the mourners. No giveaway comments that might give the G-men a possible line of inquiry. As the gravediggers came forward to start shovelling the earth onto Alice Flannery's coffin, the priest stepped back, removed the purple stole from around his neck and began to make his way to his waiting cab. Swallow stepped forwards, holding out his warrant card as the priest stepped up to the footplate.

'Father Cavendish, I'm Detective Inspector Swallow. This is Detective Sergeant Mossop. We're investigating the murder of Alice Flannery. I'd appreciate a few minutes of your time to help us in our inquiries.'

Close up, James Cavendish had sharp blue eyes. For a moment Swallow thought he was about to protest that he had other things to do or that he had to be away urgently for some reason, but then he smiled confidently and stepped down from the footplate. He might be thirty, Swallow estimated, but he could pass for younger. Women would find this priest attractive, he reckoned.

'Of course, if I can help I will. I'm going back to the parochial house. We can talk there. Would you like to share my carriage? Or have you got your own transport?'

'Thank you, Father. We have our own car here. We'll follow you to the parochial house.'

It was curious, he reflected, this priestly preference for retreating to their own redoubt for any conversation where they might be put under any pressure. Monsignor Feehan had expressed the same preference two days earlier.

Cavendish's carriage covered the distance back to Rathmines at a trot. The police driver pulled in behind it when they reached the parochial house, and Swallow and Mossop dismounted swiftly. Cavendish dropped lithely to the ground once his driver had opened the carriage door. He led them into the house and took them to the same parlour where they had interviewed Monsignor Feehan.

A housekeeper appeared at the door as they were about to sit on the same hard-backed chairs they had occupied two days previously.

'Will you want your dinner soon, Father?'

'Thank you, Mrs O'Reilly. If you'd just keep it warm for me, I'll be with these gentlemen for a short while. Perhaps they might like some tea? It's been a bitterly cold morning.'

'I don't think so, Father,' Swallow responded, against his inclinations. The idea of hot tea with sweet sugar was tempting after the cold of the cemetery at Mount Jerome, but something told him that it was wiser to be strictly formal with Father James Cavendish in spite of his veneer of congeniality.

'Just for myself then, please,' Cavendish told her. 'A shocking thing, the murder of young Alice, and so close to her own home. So close to this church. Now, tell me how I can be of assistance.'

Swallow was direct.

'I need to tell you, Father, that I am interviewing you under caution because certain evidence has come to light in the course of our inquiries. I am advising you that you could be suspected of involvement in a criminal matter, and that while you are not obliged to say anything, what you do say will be recorded and may be used in evidence. Do you understand this?'

The young priest paled. He blinked rapidly. It seemed as if he wanted to speak, but was unable to.

At that moment, the housekeeper came through the door carrying a small tray with the priest's tea.

'Pardon me now, Father.'

She laid it on the table and left.

It was as if her intervention had shaken the priest out of a stupor. Now his eyes filled with anger.

'Mr Swallow, you cannot believe you have authority to question a priest? Do you not realise that I am answerable to canon law, not the criminal law? Your suggestion that I might be guilty of a criminal act is utterly outrageous, but even if it were true you are acting beyond your remit.'

'I haven't suggested that you are guilty of anything,' Swallow said. 'I said that certain evidence has come to light which requires that I caution you, as I have done. As to your status under canon law and the criminal law, you are answerable to both. Canon law has its own strictures, but I represent the Crown and its laws, including the criminal law. I'm sure you understand that.'

Cavendish laughed lightly.

'I think the failure of understanding is on your part, Mr Swallow. I am beyond your jurisdiction.'

Swallow reached into his pocket for his handcuffs. He sensed Mossop stiffen with tension beside him as he clanked them noisily between his hands.

'Now, Father, there's something that you have to accept, difficult as it may be in your calling. These will fit around a priest's wrists, if they have to, just as easily as any other man's. I don't want matters to go in that direction. So can we get on with our questions? The sooner we can be on our way, the better it will be for everyone.'

Cavendish's eyes flickered from Swallow's face to the handcuffs, then back again. There was a long, silent interval before he ceded ground.

'I have no wish to cause an incident either, Mr Swallow. I will try to answer any reasonable questions you may have. But I warn you, you will hear more about this ... exceeding of your authority. Do you understand me?'

Swallow ignored both the threat and the question. He put the handcuffs back in his pocket, silently giving thanks that he and Mossop did not have to grapple physically with the young priest.

'Father Cavendish,' he began, 'I have reason to believe that you had an unusual relationship with Alice Flannery, to the degree that you were in the habit of accompanying her home late at night after she had finished work.'

Cavendish shifted in his chair.

'Don't you dare to make any suggestion of impropriety, Mr Swallow. I was concerned for her safety. She was … vulnerable … if you like. I was exercising pastoral care over a young woman I judged to be at risk.'

'At risk from whom, Father Cavendish?'

'Well, at general risk. With these London murders, decent women are in great fear.'

'It's a long way from London to here, Father. And the victims in London aren't what you'd call "decent women".'

'I understand that, of course. What I mean is that Miss Flannery … Alice … was, as I have said, vulnerable.'

'So would you wait around Portobello Bridge for other supposedly vulnerable young women to see them safely home?' Swallow asked with more than a hint of sarcasm.

'No, of course not. Miss Flannery was special.'

'The truth is that you had an interest in her that would be, shall we say, rather unpriestly, didn't you?' Swallow said.

The air of confidence seemed to dissipate from young Father James Cavendish. His shoulders slumped. The easy grin was replaced with a deep frown.

'I cared for her, yes. But strictly in a spiritual way … a pastoral way. She was so full of promise, of ambition, from such a difficult background. I wanted to protect her, to see her safe and see her take hold of the bright future that might have been hers.'

'Do you take a similar interest in other young girls in the parish? Would you be solicitous of others too?'

Cavendish's face flushed with anger again.

'I resent the implication of what you are saying there, Detective Inspector. I try to help young people where I can, Mr Swallow. That is part of my vocation. Jesus said "suffer the little children to come unto me", as you'll know from your catechism.'

'I don't think Jesus had in mind the kind of close attention you were paying to Alice Flannery.' Swallow hardened his voice. 'We know that she resented it too. So did members of her family.'

Cavendish spread his hands in a gesture of emphasis.

'So that's it then? That's what you call evidence? That's why you tell me I'm a suspect? Members of her family indeed. It's that young man Daniel Flannery, isn't it? Well, I can tell you, Inspector, he's a very strange young man indeed. And I can tell you furthermore that absolutely nothing improper ever occurred or was in contemplation in my contacts with his sister, Inspector. I can assure you of that.'

Swallow could see Pat Mossop struggling to keep up with his note-taking. He paused for a few moments.

'You describe Daniel Flannery as a "strange young man". Would you care to elaborate on that for us?'

Cavendish shrugged.

'I'm always pleased to see a young man who is committed to his faith. But Daniel Flannery is almost fanatical in his Catholicism. He will often stop me and quote to me from spiritual books he has read but for which he has had no training.'

'Are you saying he is something of an extremist?' Swallow asked.

'That would not be an inappropriate term.'

'Can you tell us where you were on Friday night last between half past eleven and midnight?' Swallow asked after an interval. 'And I'm reminding you again that while you're not obliged to say anything, anything you do say will be recorded and may be used in evidence.'

'Yes, I can answer your question, Inspector. I was on duty in the parish that night. As the priest on duty, I was on a sick call. I went to administer the Last Rites to a parishioner at Belgrave Square. And you will find that all of this is recorded here in the pastoral diary in this house.'

If the priest was telling the truth about being at Belgrave Square, Swallow calculated, he would have been at most a ten-minute walk from Blackberry Lane. But diaries only reflect what people write into them.

'I presume, Father Cavendish, apart from the parish books, that someone else can corroborate that? In particular, I'd be glad to have someone confirm the times at which you arrived at Belgrave Square and when you left.'

'Yes, the elderly lady in question has lingered, although her condition is very frail. I stayed with the family and we prayed by the bedside until well after midnight. The other members of her family were present, and they will confirm what I say if you doubt me.'

'In my work, Father Cavendish, one doubts everyone and everything. I'll ask you later to give details of the address and the family to Sergeant Mossop and we will make inquiries. If your account is verified, so much the better.'

The priest smiled, a little too comfortably for Swallow's liking.

'Is there anything else I can help on, Inspector? I've told you what I can. I cared deeply for Alice, in the pastoral sense, of course. Her brother appears to have had a very warped view of that. It's regrettable, but I can't alter his thinking.'

'Of course,' Swallow said non-committedly. 'What would you say was his relationship with his sister?'

'I think that relationship was … well … obsessive. He seemed to think he needed to protect her from some unspecified threat.'

'That's not so different from what you've told us about your own relationship with the girl,' Swallow said.

Cavendish seemed genuinely puzzled.

'Do you not understand, Inspector? I am a priest of God; my motives and intentions can only be the purest.'

Swallow grimaced.

'I meet many people, not all of them priests, who would describe their motives in a great many circumstances as pure. So let me ask you, Father Cavendish, can you think of anyone who would have wanted to harm Alice Flannery? We don't think this was a random attack.'

Cavendish shrugged.

'Frankly, no. But are you ruling out a random act of violence? As far as I am aware she was not keeping company, so there would not have been issues of jealousies or any crime of passion.'

'But she had told you she didn't want you paying so much attention to her?' Swallow said.

'That wasn't Alice's own thinking; it was her brother's. As I told you, he's very religious. But like a lot of these young revolutionary types, he's hostile to the clergy. They have this notion that we're supporting English rule and siding with the landlords in the country.'

'He says you bought her books.'

'Yes, cookery books. She wanted to be a cook, to work in the kitchen of some big house or a hotel or a restaurant. It was a laudable ambition, wouldn't you agree? And anything I could do to further it was quite proper. She was very happy to have them. She asked me for money to buy a couple of law books too.'

'Law books? You mean the ones on the shelf in the kitchen at her home?'

'I cannot say, Inspector. I was never in that house. So I can only surmise that if you saw books there that they were the ones I paid for. She said she wanted to know her rights. She said it was important for a woman in particular to know her entitlements.'

'I think, Father, we're going just a little beyond pastoral care here,' Swallow said slowly. 'You were taking more than a general interest in the girl, weren't you?'

Swallow saw him blushing.

'Mr Swallow, I wish to be true to my priestly vocation, and I will be. But I won't deny, I can't, that there are times when the simple beauty of a young woman, the exquisite formation of such a creature, physically and intellectually, can be a challenge to one's vows. Sometimes one wonders how it might have been had one chosen a different pathway.'

Swallow answered slowly.

'Well, we've all had choices to make in life, Father Cavendish. And we have to live with those choices and maybe answer to God for it in the end.'

'I understand that very well, Mr Swallow. I don't believe a policeman needs to lecture me in moral theology. I studied it for three years in the course of my formation as a priest. So let me assure you that I am fully seized of the relationship between actions and consequences.'

Swallow smiled.

'Do you know anything about the French writer Balzac?'

'Honoré de Balzac? Of course.'

'Well, Father, Balzac writes that the policeman, the priest and the artist have all got to be seized of the same moral values. Now that's rather compacting his argument but it's a fair summary. So maybe it's not entirely inappropriate for a policeman to be able to point out some moral principles to a priest.'

He got to his feet and nodded to Mossop.

'I think that will be all for the present. Detective Sergeant Mossop and I have some other inquiries to make. We'll also need some time to consider the information that you've given us here today. I appreciate that some of what we have discussed may not be very easy for you, but we may ask you to facilitate us again.'

Mossop stood too.

'Before we go, there are two further questions, I'd like to ask you,' Swallow said.

'Please, go ahead.'

'May I ask what size do you take in footwear, and what sort of shoes would you have been wearing on Friday night when you left here to attend to the sick call?'

Cavendish became agitated again.

'It appears in spite of my willingness to co-operate and my openness with you, Mr Swallow, that you insist on treating me as a criminal suspect. Why should I consider myself obliged to answer these ridiculous questions?'

'I'll give you two good reasons, Father,' Swallow said. 'First, along with other evidence from the scene of the assault on Miss Flannery, we have taken plaster impressions of footprints left in the mud. Second, if you don't answer the questions I will procure a warrant to search this house and seize the footwear of all the occupants to enable us to determine the answers anyway. So, to be blunt about it, we can do this the easy way or the hard way. I'd hope you'll choose the easy way.'

'Your behaviour is outrageous,' Cavendish spat out the words. 'And believe me, there will be consequences. For what it's worth I would have worn my heavy outdoor shoes on Friday night. The ones I have on me now. It's a good walk from the parochial house to Belgrave Square. And the weather, as you know, has been very inclement. As to my shoe size, I take size nine.'

Wednesday November 7th, 1888

FIFTEEN

The complaint from Archbishop's House to Sir David Harrel, the commissioner of the Dublin Metropolitan Police, came forty-eight hours later. Swallow was surprised it had taken so long.

'It doesn't worry me.' Mallon dropped the commissioner's minute onto the desk. 'And don't let it worry you either. Willie has to make a stink about one of his priests being questioned. But I have to go through the motions for the commissioner.'

Dublin's new Roman Catholic archbishop, William Walsh, just three years in the post, had already shown himself to be fiercely assertive of the rights of his Church and his clergy.

He had given the go-ahead for the construction of a palatial residence at Drumcondra to replace the four-storey Georgian house on Rutland Square, which his predecessors had found adequate as a base from which to direct their flock. Scores of acres of land were being bought up by the Catholic Church close to the location of the new episcopal palace. There would be colleges, seminaries and training centres for priests and teachers. And it was common knowledge that he was seeking a site upon which to construct a new cathedral that would put the city's two Protestant cathedrals, Christ Church and St Patrick's, in the shade.

Swallow sat opposite Mallon's desk in the Lower Yard office.

'I understand that, chief. What does Commissioner Harrel say?'

Mallon picked up the minute. He grinned mirthlessly.

'He's had a strong note from the archbishop. Willie claims that any Crown officer questioning one of his priests is acting outside the law.

And he's outraged that the slightest suspicion should be attached by "low-ranking detectives from Dublin Castle" to one of God's anointed ministers. Scandal and innuendo. You can imagine the rest. So tell me, Swallow, what were you doing interviewing this Father Cavendish?'

Swallow recounted his interview with the dead girl's brother and his suspicions about the priest.

'You might have told me you were going to interview him under caution,' Mallon grumbled.

'Actually, I did tell you I was going to interview a suspect, chief,' Swallow answered. 'But I must have forgotten to say who it was.'

Mallon's eyes narrowed.

'You mean you didn't tell me because you thought it better I didn't know.'

'Ah, you've enough on your mind, chief. So how are you going to reply?'

'I know what I'd like to say, but first I'd like to hear what you have to tell me. At all events, I need a full briefing on the investigation.'

'There isn't much progress, I'm afraid. No new witnesses. Nothing coming in from the usual informants around the city. The footprints at the scene show a size nine shoe or boot. No nails or studs, so probably a city dweller. We've interviewed her employer at the New Vienna. The German fellow, Werner. Can't say I warmed to him. He says she had become troublesome at work, but there doesn't seem to have been anything that could have led to violence. The investigating team is interviewing the employees one by one, of course.'

He flicked to the next page of his notebook.

'The girl's brother, Dan, is telling us the story that led me to Father Cavendish. Dan left work half an hour before she was attacked, but he said he was still at work at midnight. He's not a bad lad, just twenty, very intense. He seems to be some sort of a religious enthusiast. He keeps quoting scripture and God's laws. He's political too. He says he's a member of the Gaelic Union. Uses his Irish name, Domhnal Ó Flanbharra. I know it from the surveillance reports. He turns up at Land League meetings too. Low-level stuff, but active. He says he left work to walk Alice home, but missed her in the fog, and that he met a friend at Huband Bridge. We're checking on that one, and if his version is confirmed it makes it unlikely that he would have been in the vicinity of Blackberry Lane when the attack took place.'

'Hmmm … why would he want to walk the sister home? Was that usual?'

'That goes to the issue, chief. He says that Alice was being bothered by this Father Cavendish. He says he wanted to protect Alice from him. He says there was some sort of unhealthy relationship between the priest and the girl.'

Mallon cocked his head.

'Go on.'

'But then Father Cavendish tells us that he was worried about Dan having some sort of obsession about the girl. He says he tried to place himself as some sort of a guardian or saviour to her. Dan says he bought her books and took her to the parochial house for lessons in voice projection, as he called it. It involved a degree of physical contact. She eventually realised it wasn't innocent and told him she wouldn't visit any more. Then he started intercepting her on her way home from work. He more or less persecuted her, if the brother is to be believed. Eventually the brother decided to confront him. He says he believes the priest attacked the girl.'

Mallon nodded.

'He gave a statement?'

'For what it's worth, yes.'

'A brave enough stand for a young man to take against his local priest. But it's a long way from making Father Cavendish a murderer. You interviewed him under caution, I gather.'

'Yes, sir. There's nothing positively linking Father Cavendish to the killing. But there could be motive, and there was opportunity.'

'Explain.'

'When Mossop and I interviewed him he said he was absent from the parochial house answering a sick call around the time Alice Flannery was attacked. He says he was at a house on Belgrave Square. Mossop has checked with the family. He was there all right, administering the Last Rites to an elderly lady. But they gave Mossop contradictory versions of what time he came and went. He could have been at Blackberry Lane around midnight.'

Mallon scratched pensively at his beard.

'Hmm. He wouldn't be the first young man in the priesthood to find that the vow of chastity isn't so easy to keep. It's led more than a few of them into trouble. What do you make of him?'

'He's intelligent, as you'd expect. A handsome young man. I could see him breaking young ladies' hearts if he weren't wearing a clerical collar. Maybe even if he was. He's confident too, as you'd expect. Strong on his priestly privileges. He told me he wasn't answerable to any law other than canon law. So I came back on him fairly sharply on that. I got the sense though that behind the bluster and the confidence he's not keen on having trouble with us. When I pushed him, he gave ground.'

'You pushed him?' Mallon raised an eyebrow, tapping the archbishop's letter. 'Is that what I'm to take from His Grace's note here? How exactly did you "push" him, Swallow?'

There was no point in dissembling.

'I, ah, gave him sight of my accoutrements, chief.'

Mallon drew a breath.

'You're telling me you threatened him with handcuffs?'

'In a manner of speaking, sir, yes.'

Mallon raised his hands to his forehead and leaned forward on his desk, his fingers massaging his temples for perhaps a minute in silence.

'Please, Swallow ... in the very unlikely event that you're ever interviewing Archbishop Walsh or the Pope or anyone like that, could I ask that you'd tell me first? And that you'd leave your handcuffs behind.'

'Yes, chief. Of course, chief.'

'Now, tell me,' Mallon fingered the commissioner's note, 'how you intend to move forward on this.'

'We're doing a full review of evidence tomorrow after the crime conference. But to be honest we haven't got a lot in hand. It's possible but unlikely, I think, that it was a random attack. We've eliminated the two soldiers that found her. The priest's a possible suspect. So is the brother. But we don't have a clear motive. Either of them could have been close to the scene. They both take a size nine in shoes, so either of them could have left the imprint at the scene. So unless we get something else, I think we'll have to re-interview and increase the pressure if necessary.'

Mallon nodded.

'I agree. I'll advise the commissioner accordingly. And he'll have to tell His Grace the archbishop that there may be more unpleasantness ahead for Father Cavendish.'

Swallow stood.

'Two other things, sir. One relating to the job; the other totally personal and unrelated to the case. If I may, sir.'

Mallon looked puzzled for a moment.

'Yes, go ahead, Swallow. What's the job issue?'

'Just to say that we're continuing to search around the offices for the protection logs but so far we haven't had a lot of luck. I wanted you to know that we're doing all we can.'

Mallon looked him in the eye.

'Yes, Swallow, thank you. I understand exactly what you're saying to me. I've already had a further query this morning from the office of the assistant under-secretary. I've assured him that no stone is being left unturned in the search. And what's the other matter you want to raise?'

Swallow grinned.

'You've told me often enough that I should, ah … pop the question to Mrs Walsh. So I've done it. And we're tying the knot down at Merchants' Quay on Saturday. Maria, the soon to be Mrs Swallow, and I would be honoured if you and Mrs Mallon might be in attendance.'

Mallon's face broke into a smile that Swallow rarely associated with the man who headed G-Division.

'Swallow, my friend, I knew that underneath all that Kildare bone-headedness there was a spark of intelligence. I'm glad to hear of this. She's a fine woman, and I can tell you that you're making no mistake. Mrs Mallon and I'll be there with the greatest of pleasure.'

Thursday November 8th, 1888

SIXTEEN

Swallow's painting class was on Thursday afternoons at the Municipal Art School. Before his promotion he had juggled his leave every week, taking on extra shifts to wheedle the half-day off duty from his then boss at Exchange Court, Inspector 'Duck' Boyle. He had thought initially that it would be easier to plot his week's work at his new rank, but in fact, as he realised quickly, it put him under more pressure to stay with the job. Nonetheless, he rarely missed the class. The Municipal Art School was on Thomas Street, just a few minutes' walk from Exchange Court.

He took a pork chop with potatoes and parsnip for his midday meal at the police canteen in the Lower Yard. Another blast of chilly November rain, driven before a sharp northern wind, hit him full in the face as he stepped through the Palace Street gate. He turned his coat collar up, jammed his bowler down on his head and set off towards Thomas Street.

He had always been a sketcher, drawing birds, animals, trees and buildings around the scenes of his childhood in rural Kildare. The family finances did not allow for the purchase of sketch pads, but his pencil and charcoal drawings filled the pages of innumerable school copybooks. He had never painted, and it was Maria's sister, Lily, who taught a weekly painting class at the Art School who had suggested that he should enrol with her.

'You'd enjoy it, Joe,' she enthused one evening as she and Harry Lafeyre were having dinner with Joe and Maria at Harry's club, the United Services, on St Stephen's Green. 'If you've worked only in pencil or charcoal, you should try out your hand with watercolours. I'll help you.'

'All I did as a boy every day was to draw what I saw,' Swallow had explained. 'I wanted to record things, reduce them if you like, to images on paper. I've always done that. Even still, I want to frame the reality that I see within … some sort of medium of my own.'

'Hmmph,' Lafeyre had grumbled, forking sole *bonne femme* into his mouth. 'Sounds as if you should have been a photographic technician. Cameras are very good at that sort of thing; far better than people scratching away with pencils. Painters can lie. Flatter to deceive. But the camera doesn't lie.'

Lily rolled her eyes.

'Oh dear, I'm afraid I'm going to marry a complete philistine.'

Despite being more than a year into the course, he felt that he had learned only of his limitations. Lily was a good teacher, patient and tolerant, but even getting him to understand primary colours was a challenge. He had thought initially that using watercolours looked easy, but he learned quickly that if one got something wrong it almost always required a completely fresh start. Moreover, there were some talented people in the class whose work was so superior to his efforts that he sometimes felt embarrassed.

'Good afternoon, Joe.'

Catherine Greenberg greeted him as she set up her easel next to his in the art room. She was one of those talents. Catherine could infuse a still-life—a silver bowl with fruit or a lamp draped in satin—with colour and vitality that seemed to give it an existence beyond its mundane reality.

It was in the blood, Swallow reckoned. Catherine's father, Ephram, operated one of Dublin's finest dealerships in *objets d'art* and antiques from his premises in Capel Street. Unusually among the Jewish community, Catherine had not married, and at thirty or so she was was probably considered beyond marriageable age among her own people. She was now in the business as a partner with her father. As well as an aesthete and an artist, Swallow knew her to be a competent businesswoman.

He had known the Greenbergs, as he knew all of the Jewish

community around Capel Street, from his days as a constable on the beat from the D-Division's Bridewell Station. Miriam Greenberg, Catherine's mother, would give him poppy-seed bread and strong coffee when he would slip into the Greenbergs' kitchen off his beat. She had died in a local influenza outbreak ten years ago. Catherine had inherited her mother's dark good looks, deep eyes, and a slight tendency to plumpness.

The Greenbergs had recently come back dramatically into Swallow's professional life when two London criminals set out to rob the Capel Street shop. When he came on the scene with a uniformed constable, investigating the appearance of stolen gold coins in a number of city shops, Swallow had disabled one of them with a shot from his Webley Bulldog while the other fled.

The investigation into the attempted robbery at Greenberg's of Capel Street had uncovered evidence relating to an earlier murder, that of Ambrose Pollock, a pawnbroker and furniture dealer, done to death in his shop at Lamb Alley, off Cornmarket. In turn, that had revealed the existence of a large-scale embezzlement of exchequer funds in the administration of the Land Acts that enabled Irish tenant farmers to buy out their holdings from their landlords. It was the success of that investigation, John Mallon had told Swallow, which ensured his promotion to the rank of detective inspector.

Catherine made no secret of her affections for Joe Swallow. It had been there even as a young girl, when the handsome, uniformed constable would sit, drinking coffee in her mother's kitchen, his Roman-style helmet on the table. Later, when Swallow had become a G-Division detective, he would come to visit her father. They would drink Lebanese wine from the Bekaa Valley in Ephram's upstairs study, looking down into Capel Street. If there was stolen property on the move around the city's art shops or galleries, Ephram Greenberg knew about it, and usually who was behind it. And as young Catherine became more involved in the business she would sit in on the conversations that ranged beyond the provenance of stolen silverware into politics, philosophy, religion and more.

She was probably seventeen when Swallow realised he was an object of her romantic interest. He was flattered, but nothing could come of it. He was thirteen years her senior. Their faiths divided them, although she made it precociously clear that she was not interested in practising the Jewish faith or any other. And there was an economic divide. The Greenbergs were a wealthy family with an established business. Whatever about the G-Division inspector that he now was, he would have been a poor catch for her as the young uniformed constable he had been then.

He delighted in the painting class, for all the self-doubt about his talent. When he stepped through the doors of the college he entered a different world. Crime, intrigue, dark corridors and dark minds were left behind for a blissful two hours in the company of creative, energetic people. And so it was this afternoon. He felt a lightness in his step and his spirits lifted as he settled to his customary place.

'Hello, Catherine,' he grinned. 'I suppose you're going to dazzle us all with your homework as usual.'

She smiled.

'I wish you wouldn't make fun of me, Joe. I'm just a muddler and I know it.'

'Go on,' he laughed. 'If there's a real artist, as distinct from the ambitious amateurs, in the class, that's you.'

'You haven't been down to Capel Street to see us for a while,' she said, affecting a reproving frown. 'My father isn't as young as he used to be. He's really confined to the shop and the house. He needs friends to come to see him. You know there's always a welcome there for you. From both of us, if you understand my meaning.'

'I'll be in to him tomorrow,' Swallow answered. He fully understood her meaning but he was not going to respond to it. 'I need to make a purchase.'

He had been mentally grappling with what to do about a ring for Maria. She had continued to wear her wedding ring on her left fourth finger, a silent but unmistakable memorial to her late husband. He would not ask her to displace it. At the same time, he knew it would be necessary to mark their nuptials with a gesture. He had raised the question with Harry Lafeyre over a drink at the Burlington Hotel on St Andrew's Street.

'Simple,' Lafeyre answered. 'Go for what they're calling an

"engagement ring". I got one for Lily. You've seen it, I'm sure. Often they're made up around a diamond, but they're available with other precious stones as well. They're expensive, but they're very fashionable among the moneyed classes in London.'

Swallow had indeed noticed the solitaire diamond ring glittering on Lily's hand on social occasions.

'It would be a pretty costly item,' Lafeyre told him, 'but it would be a nice investment too. The De Beers company has brought a big supply of diamonds into the market straight out of the Kimberley mines in South Africa, so the prices are reasonable, and the stones will go up in value over time. You'll see them advertised in the newspapers.'

Later he bought a copy of the London *Daily Telegraph* and found half a dozen display advertisements for 'engagement rings' among the classifieds. He did some financial calculations. The *Telegraph*'s advertisers were mainly London-based, but he guessed that Irish prices should be comparable and certainly not higher. And he remembered that Greenberg's displayed trays of rings under its glass showcase counters. He would see what was on offer. Ephram was sure to see him right both on quality and price.

'A purchase?' Catherine looked surprised. 'Don't tell me you're going to start investing in fine art.'

Before he could answer, Lily Grant took her place at the top of the classroom and clapped her hands, bringing the class of perhaps a dozen students to silence.

'Good afternoon, everybody. It's encouraging to see the loyal few who've braved it through the terrible weather.'

She smiled.

'Now before we get to work, we have some good news. First, I think you'll be delighted to know that Miss Greenberg's still life, *Silver Plate on Marble*, has been accepted by the Royal Dublin Society for inclusion in their December exhibition.'

A spontaneous round of applause spread across the room. There were calls of 'well done' and 'congratulations'. Catherine smiled and nodded in acknowledgment.

'And,' Lily added, beaming, 'we have some romantic news. I've heard from a little bird, no pun intended, that Mr Swallow is to make the big step into matrimony this week. In fact, he is to marry my sister, Maria. So it's congratulations all round!'

There was more applause. Somebody clapped Swallow on the back and wished him well. Lily's face shone with delight. But Catherine Greenberg had gone as pale as chalk. Swallow heard her gasp as she absorbed Lily's words. Then with knuckled hands clasped in front of her face, she ran to the door and into the corridor outside. Lily looked after her with an expression of mock horror.

'Oh dear. Poor Miss Greenberg. The shock of having her painting accepted for the RDS exhibition next month must have been too much.'

SEVENTEEN

Swallow was still in Lily Grant's painting class when the men from the office of the assistant under-secretary for security arrived at Exchange Court.

Major Kelly led four of them through the front door into the public office, where Pat Mossop was working as duty officer. Another four came through the door that opened into the back of the detective office from the Lower Yard. Mossop looked up from the duty roster he was working on to find Kelly dangling a sheet of official foolscap, topped with the royal coat of arms, in front of his face.

'Major Kelly, office of the assistant under-secretary for security,' he barked at Mossop. 'Your name and rank please.'

If Kelly thought that bawling at the scrawny G-man would intimidate him, he had miscalculated. Mossop yawned lazily, scratched under his armpit and leaned across the counter without rising from the high stool on which he was perched.

'Was somebody expecting you, Major ... what did you say the name was? I wasn't told anything about it.'

Kelly responded with a cold smile.

'No, you wouldn't have been told anything about me. Read this please; it's a warrant to search these premises. My men are armed and they will shoot anyone who resists their lawful authority.'

Mossop affected an air of bewilderment.

'Oh Jesus, now we've never had anything like this here before. Let there be no talk of shooting or the like. Will you let me read that, sir?'

Kelly dropped the sheet of foolscap onto the counter. Mossop took his time turning it about so he could read it. The gas mantles were already burning, and he held the sheet at various angles, giving the impression of seeking maximum illumination. Then he started to read the warrant out loud, slowly stumbling through the lawyerly jargon.

'By Jesus,' he said after a long interval, 'that's impressive stuff. A warrant signed by the assistant under-secretary in his capacity as a Justice of the Peace, no less … authorising Major Nigel Frederick Kelly to enter and search the premises known as Exchange Court … otherwise the detective office of the Dublin Metropolitan Police….' He turned the angle of the paper again. '… and to seize and take away from the said premises … any papers, documents … or things … that may seem material to the said Major Nigel Frederick Kelly in connection with … felonies and crimes, et cetera, et cetera, et cetera.'

He folded the sheet and handed it back to Kelly.

'So … what's this all about, sir? These documents … or things? Are we in trouble here?'

'I'm here to take possession of G-Division's recent protection logs. They are required in the interests of Crown security.'

'Well, you're in the right place, sure enough, sir,' Mossop said agreeably, endeavouring to convey the continuing sense of being a fool. 'This is G-Division, not a doubt about that. You're in the right place, sure enough. Sure enough.'

He dropped his hands as if to slide off the stool, and then brought them up swiftly, holding the double-barrelled Remington shotgun that always sat, loaded, under the counter in the public office. He thrust the weapon hard against Kelly's chest, pushing him back momentarily on his feet.

Kelly's men reached into their coats to produce short Webley revolvers. All four guns were levelled on Pat Mossop.

'Now, Charlie,' Mossop said slowly. 'I don't know who the hell you are, or why you think you can walk in here and walk out with official police records. But as you say, this is G-Division. We're very careful with our records, and we're careful about who we let in here. So without authority from my direct superiors, you're not going to get beyond this desk. Some of your four pals might get in all right, the one or two who might … just might … not get their eyes blown out with my buckshot. But if you try to get past me, you'll just be a big, red hole with a lot of lead in the middle.'

Kelly's eyes narrowed as he flushed to an angry crimson.

'You stupid little Paddy. Take a look behind you. Then put that damned thing down, and you can thank your lucky stars if I don't have your job and your pension.'

Mossop's eyes flickered to his right. Half a dozen G-men men who had been in the back offices or in the dormitory filed into the public office with their hands held over their heads. The other half of Kelly's detachment came behind them, their guns pointed at the G-men's backs. One carried a shotgun similar to the weapon in Mossop's hands.

'Get them up against the wall there,' Kelly instructed. 'Keep them covered. Then take their weapons.'

Everyone in the room heard the double-click as Mossop engaged the hammers on the Remington.

'Don't move, lads. Stay where you are,' Mossop called to his colleagues, his eyes never wavering from Kelly's face. 'We're calling this fella's bluff. Let them take your guns and we're done for. And take your hands down. G-men don't give way to anyone.'

Slowly, one after another, the G-men lowered their arms. Then they followed each other to cross the room, joining Mossop at the desk.

'You obstinate bastard.' Kelly spat the words. 'Do you realise you're being given a direct instruction from the office of Her Majesty's Permanent Under-Secretary?'

'And do you realise that you're getting a direct instruction from the Remington Firearms Company of Connecticut to piss off now and get out of this room along with your English pals?'

Kelly's frame shook with anger.

'Stupid bastard … you stupid Paddy.'

Mossop grinned.

'My first name is Patrick, true enough. Patrick Edgar Mossop, Detective Sergeant, since you asked my rank. But I'm no Paddy in the sense that you use the word. I'm a Belfast Protestant, a King Billy man, through and through. True to the Crown. A bit like yourself, Charlie, only more so.'

Kelly glared. For a moment Mossop thought he would try to grab the barrel of the Remington, but instead he took a step back. He gestured to his men to lower their guns. One after another the Webleys went back into their shoulder-holsters. Kelly nodded towards the door. The men nearest to it started towards the street outside.

'You'll live to regret this I promise you, Detective Sergeant Mossop,' Kelly hissed. 'I won't be responsible for a bloodbath here, and I won't let you provoke one either. But I will be back. And when I come, you'll learn to respect rank, and you'll understand your duty to those in authority.'

Mossop grinned.

'You don't hold any rank in this department, Charlie, me chum. And I know my duty, never you fear. So if you do come back, maybe you'll remember to bring your manners with you. Then we can a nice chat without my having to bring out this fellow to make you behave yourself.'

He tapped the Remington's wooden stock, and gently eased the twin hammers to safety. Then his whole body started to tremble.

When they had gone, he turned to the G-man standing nearest.

'You'd better go down the yard and tell the chief what's after happening here,' he said slowly.

He fumbled in his pocket and handed the man a half-crown.

'And before you come back, slip across the street to Brogan's and get me a naggin of whiskey to save me life.'

Friday November 9th, 1888

EIGHTEEN

The night shifts at the Dublin Gas Company's furnaces on Sir John Rogerson's Quay were timed so that the men who had been labouring in the burning heat since the afternoon could have time to cool themselves with drink before the public houses shut down. It was an arrangement that suited the company, the men and most of all the proprietors of the public houses in the streets around the great industrial complex that stretched back to Hanover Quay on the Grand Canal Dock. This was said to be the unhealthiest square mile in Dublin. The air was heavy with sulphur. The canal water was the colour of rust from the chemicals that leached from the plant. It was popularly believed that a scientist from Trinity College had lowered a cage with three salmon into the dock water some years previously. They all died within five minutes.

At ten o'clock, 200 stokers, pump men, loaders, furnace attendants and miscellaneous general labourers handed over their tasks to the incoming shift. Tired, dehydrated and stinking of coke, they dispersed to the rough but functional licensed premises along the Liffey quayside or in the maze of streets behind.

Two furnace men whose tenement homes were situated close together on Great Brunswick Street habitually made their way to Duggan's on the corner of Misery Hill and Cardiff Lane to slake their thirst. The cold of the November night had quickly sucked the heat of the gasworks from their hands and faces and they eagerly anticipated the comfort of high stools at Duggan's counter and the yeasty sustenance of their pints.

'Oh, Jesus, Jesus help me … help me.'

They both heard the faint cry from a darkened corner of the junction where the gas light scarcely penetrated the darkness. One, then the other, saw a movement, dark stirring upon dark, a shadow moving on a shadow where the pavement met the street. Then a hand raised, faint and weak, and another cry.

'Jesus, help me someone … for pity's sake.'

They stepped past the pool of light and saw a bundle lying against the wall that bounded Cardiff Lane. It moved, just a little, then shuddered in the half-darkness. One of the men struck a match that showed a woman on the ground, her face striped with blood, eyes open in terror. She was young, maybe in her twenties. Dark unkempt hair fell loosely over the cheap shawl around her shoulders. She was barefoot.

'Can … you … help me?'

One of the furnace men took off his jacket, leaned down and placed it around her upper body. She shuddered.

'What happened, miss? Are you hurt?'

'Is he … gone?' There was terror in the whispered question.

'There's no one here but us, miss. We're no harm to you. Can you stand now?'

They raised her slowly from the ground, each holding a trembling arm. Then they walked her slowly to the doorway of Duggan's and into the warmth of the public bar. The line of men at the counter turned almost as one and the hubbub of conversation tailed off.

'Drag over a couple of forms,' one of the furnace men shouted at the startled barkeeper. 'We've a woman here … she's hurt, hurt bad.'

Two benches were put together to form a makeshift trestle. The score or so patrons, mainly dockers and labourers, gathered around. The first furnace man took off his jacket and placed it under her head. Her face contorted in pain.

'Oh Jesus … I'm hurted … I'm hurted terrible.'

One elderly patron put his pint glass onto the counter and stepped forward.

'I did me time as a surgeon's orderly in Crimea. Let me see.'

He leaned over the trestle and gently traced the lacerations on her face. Then he probed her torso. When he touched her ribs, she

130

grimaced. When he sought to straighten her right arm, which seemed out of place, she screamed.

'She's been beaten bad,' he said. 'There's broken bones in the face and in the ribs. A broken arm too, I'd say. She needs the hospital. We can get an ambulance from Baggot Street. And someone needs to call the polis.'

The barman indicated to his assistant.

'Get up to the fire brigade station on Brunswick Street and tell them to get an ambulance down here quick. And go into the police station or find a bobby on the beat. Tell them what's after happenin' here.'

He pushed his way through the group with a measure of brandy and put it to her lips. She sipped a little of the spirit, coughing and hacking as it went down her gullet. He wiped the blood from her face with a damp towel.

'Jesus, it's young Debbie Dunne. I didn't recognise her.'

'You know her?' one of the furnace men asked.

'Sure, of course. She sells fish from Ringsend when the boats come in. Along the street outside. Like her mother and all the Dunne women before her.'

'Well, it must be a bloody dangerous business, sellin' fish,' the furnace man countered. 'She's far from bein' a well woman tonight.'

There was a muttered chorus of agreement from the clientele. The barman put the brandy glass to her mouth again, but she refused it. They waited, trying awkward, soothing words around the girl, who groaned and cried for a full half-hour, until a clattering of hooves in the street outside told them that the ambulance had arrived.

Saturday November 10th, 1888

NINETEEN

'Another one in London last night.'

Pat Mossop waved the flimsy paper from the ABC telegraph. Every three hours the noisy machine spewed out crime intelligence that came in from the police forces across the United Kingdom and were collated in London at New Scotland Yard.

'Mary Jane Kelly. The Yard says she's the fifth. Found with her throat cut in Whitechapel. A lady of the night, like the others. Born in Limerick, would you believe … one of our own? About twenty-five years of age, it says here. Christ, it's barbaric.'

The Saturday-morning crime conference at Exchange Court was tense and despondent. London had the Ripper, but Dublin had its own problems.

'A week on from the Flannery girl's murder and we're nowhere. Absolutely bloody nowhere,' Mossop complained to no one in particular. 'Now we've another young girl hammered to within an inch of her life on Misery Hill,' he added. 'We're no better than the savages in the East End of London.'

None of the G-men or uniformed officers at the crime conference could summon a word to counter Mossop's pessimism on the Alice Flannery murder.

'There's nothing to say it's anything more than coincidence,' Mick Feore said. 'It's a big city with a lot of people.'

'Of course,' Swallow agreed. 'But attacks like this on women are rare. We can just hope we haven't got some lunatic trying to match what's happening across the water.'

Debbie Dunne, the young fish-woman attacked the night before, was sedated and reportedly stable at the Royal Hospital on Baggot Street. Sergeant Stephen Doolan and Detective Johnny Vizzard were by her bedside to hear what she would have to say when the laudanum the doctors had given her wore off.

'Maybe if there's a connection between the two attacks, this Dunne girl can give us something useful,' Swallow ventured. 'She might have a description at least. And she's alive, thank God.'

Any G-men who could be spared from political inquiries had been deployed across the city during the week, interviewing anyone who had knowledge of Alice Flannery's life: school-friends, acquaintances, neighbours who had moved on from Blackberry Lane. Each of her fellow workers at the New Vienna restaurant had been questioned too, but no promising lines of inquiry had presented themselves.

Each evening the G-men returned to Exchange Court to feed whatever scraps of information they had gleaned to Feore for inclusion in the murder book. Nothing of substance came in. The girl had no enemies. She was not involved in any relationship. G-men checked with the moneylenders on the south side of the city, but found only that she had never borrowed money and had no debts. By week's end there was nothing that might be construed as a motive for her killing.

On the positive side, Swallow reflected cynically to himself, the press was preoccupied elsewhere. The London murders and the terror induced by the so-called Ripper were a much juicier story. So too were the proceedings at the commission at Westminster, where government lawyers and witnesses continued desperately trying to find evidence to blacken Parnell and to link him to the outrages being committed in the land struggle.

The newspapers paid little attention to the death of a young waitress from a poor cottage in Blackberry Lane. In the ordinary course of things they would have grave editorials about police incompetence and warnings to the citizenry about monsters prowling the streets.

He reported daily to Mallon on the lack of progress. The chief of G-Division was patient, but wary.

'I've had nothing more than a routine inquiry from the commissioner about the case,' Mallon told him as they shared a midday drink on Friday at the Brazen Head on Bridge Street. 'But,' he grimaced, 'I've heard bloody plenty about what happened when Major Kelly tried to execute a perfectly legal search warrant at the detective office. Sticking a shotgun into the face of a Crown officer isn't very smart.'

'I wasn't there, chief.'

Swallow knew it sounded lame. He was the senior operational member at Exchange Court.

'That's about the only argument I can use against the fury coming from the Upper Yard,' Mallon replied. 'My line is that a relatively junior officer overreacted. And I can hardly plead that the crime inspector was above at the art college, brushing away at an easel.' He permitted himself a thin smile. 'Still and all, I'd love to have seen it myself. Mossop with the loaded Remington stuck in Kelly's snout.'

Swallow grinned and ordered another round. His was the usual Tullamore. Mallon took his customary Bushmills.

'I'll argue with the commissioner that Kelly was out of order,' Mallon mused. 'If he'd asked politely, instead of turning up with a platoon of gunmen, we'd have had to accommodate him. And that's what we'll have to do the next time they come, you know. If they want to search, and they will, we'll have to let them. And you can be sure they'll be back. Commissioner Harrel has no love for Kelly, or what he's at, but if the security fellows in the under-secretary's office are coming down on him he doesn't have much ground to stand on. He'd be dismissed as quick as a fart from a goose. That's an Armagh expression, by the way,' he added with mock seriousness.

He sipped at his Bushmills.

'The evidence coming out at the commission in London isn't great from the government's point of view though. They want anything they can get their hands on to tie Parnell in with the Fenians. Their strongest evidence is the letters *The Times* ran last year where he supposedly wrote an excuse for the Phoenix Park murders. But from what I hear from my contacts at New Scotland Yard, they're fairly obvious fakes.'

'He said so himself at the time, didn't he?' Swallow's question was rhetorical.

'He did. And most people believe him. But his word alone mightn't be enough to persuade the commission to exonerate him. Those fellows are all government appointees. They know which way the wind is blowing in terms of their own future prospects, if you understand me. The senior barristers want to be law lords. The junior ones want to be seniors. It's all to do with preferment and advancement. You know what I'm saying?'

'I do, chief. But they must all be bone stupid.' Swallow tossed back half of his Tullamore. 'Jesus, the newest recruit in G-Division knows that Parnell had nothing to do with the Phoenix Park murders.'

Mallon nodded.

'I doubt that they fail to understand. Maybe they understand it only too well. Maybe they don't really care about a few murders and arson attacks around Ireland. It might be a price they're willing to pay if they can take down the man they see as a threat to the unity of the kingdom.'

'That's a fairly cynical interpretation, chief,' Swallow said.

'Maybe. But those boys across in Westminster have a big view of their world, and the mere Irish are only a very small part of it. If they can't break Parnell at the commission then they'll try something else. They've known about his relationship with Willie O'Shea's wife all along, but they'll need some plausible proof if it's going to be put out into public knowledge. They'll want something better than a few forged letters. And that's why they want our protection logs.'

He sipped his Bushmills again.

'That is, the ones you're searching for night and day without success, unfortunately,' he said flatly.

Swallow stared straight ahead, trying not to think about Lafeyre's room in the Lower Yard. He grinned.

'Yes, chief. Night and bloody day, we're searching.'

Mallon ordered another round before Swallow went back to Exchange Court for the crime conference. He was about to call the meeting to order when Stephen Doolan arrived.

'I've just left Debbie Dunne's bedside at the hospital,' he said. 'She's poorly, but she's talking.'

'So what do we know?' Swallow asked.

'She was making her way home, she says. A man came out of the alleyway off Cardiff Lane. Came up behind her. She didn't see him, just heard heavy boots, she said. He hit her with something on the head and she started roaring. He hit her three, maybe four times. Bad lacerations to the head and a fractured nose. A broken right forearm and a few cracked ribs. She was kicked or stamped on the ground. Then he took off back down the alley. She caught a glimpse of him as he went. He was a big fellow, she said, wearing some sort of heavy coat. Not surprising given the temperature of the night.'

'No robbery? No sex assault?' Mossop commented. 'Sounds very like a repeat of what happened at Blackberry Lane.'

Doolan nodded.

'No witnesses?' Swallow asked.

'None,' Doolan grimaced. 'In that bloody cold night nobody was outdoors that didn't have to be.'

'But she'll be all right?' Swallow asked. 'She's out of danger?'

Doolan nodded.

'She should be all right, but it'll take time. She's a tough young one.'

'What's your instinct, Stephen?' Swallow asked. Doolan was a veteran of Dublin street crime. Almost a quarter of a century of pounding the beat and manning the front desk at the busy Kevin Street Station had given him what Swallow called 'a nose' for any situation.

Doolan hesitated.

'Did either of you ever hear tell of the Dollacher?' he asked after a moment.

'The what?' Swallow and Mossop responded in unison.

'The Dollacher,' Doolan repeated.

'You have me there,' Swallow shook his head.

'When I joined twenty-five years ago there was an old bobby, retired and widowed, used to live in a little house in Blackpitts. I'd be on beat at night up there and he'd ask me in for a cup of tea and a chat. He did thirty years' service in the A-Division. He told me about the Dollacher.'

'Go on,' Swallow said, 'this had better be good.'

'It was in the thirties, around '32 or '33 I think. There was a series of attacks on young women around the Liberties. Around Corn

Exchange, Thomas Street. The pattern was the same. A man would come out of an alley or a doorway, batter the woman and flee. He never actually killed anyone, but some of the victims were badly injured. Mutilated. The women said he smelled heavily, like an animal. Some said like a dog; some said he smelled like a pig. One woman said she saw him clearly and described him as having a black pig's head.'

'Jesus,' Mossop exclaimed. 'Was he ever caught?'

Doolan nodded. 'According to this old polisman, what happened was that a fellow called Olocher was due to be hanged for murder and rape in the old prison on Corn Market. But he took his own life before the hangman got him. This "Dolocher", as the locals called him, was supposed to be his ghost, prowling the streets.'

'Come on, Stephen,' Swallow laughed, 'this is bullshit. What's it got to do with what we're dealing with now? Ghosts don't batter people's heads in with fencing posts or kick them half to death with hobnailed boots.'

Doolan shrugged. 'Well, it didn't end there, Joe. On the night that Olocher took his own life, one of the soldiers on duty at the prison was found bloody and unconscious at his post. When he came around he said he'd been attacked by a monstrous black pig.'

'So this was how "the Dolocher" story came about?' Mossop said sceptically.

'Hold on. It got more complicated,' Doolan said.

Swallow raised an eyebrow. 'I can't imagine how.'

'Here's how,' Doolan resumed his narrative. 'The attacks went on over a period of a year or so. Always the same. This fellow would emerge, attack a woman in a quiet location and beat her badly. But there was no sexual assault or robbery. Then he'd scarper.'

'Doesn't say much for the beat men,' Mossop commented. 'Sure in those days didn't they have bobbies on every corner?'

Doolan grinned. 'And if my memory serves me right, a lot of them would be so addled with drink they wouldn't see Ali Baba and the forty thieves going by. Here's what happened. A miserable winter night like this. A young blacksmith has been drinking in a public house in Francis Street. It's pissing rain and he has to walk home to Pimlico. He hasn't a coat or a hat, so he spots a woman's cloak hanging behind the door. He borrows it from the landlord's wife and sets off. It's got a hood on it, so he pulls that over his head and off he goes out into the rain. Somewhere near St Catherine's, up on Thomas Street, he's jumped on by this fella who must have thought he was a woman because of the cloak and hood. But he's got his blacksmith's hammer on his belt and he lashes out and knocks this fellow to the ground.'

'Go on,' Mossop said, engrossed by the narrative.

'The blacksmith bends over his assailant. It's a man, with the blackened, hollowed-out head of a pig over his skull and face. He's knocked him out. A constable comes along and he's taken to Kevin Street. The attacker turns out to be the sentry on duty in the prison the night Olocher committed suicide and who claimed he'd been attacked by a black pig. They tried him, found him insane and that was the end of it.'

Swallow was thoughtful for a moment. Stephen Doolan was the most practical man he knew. He was not advancing a folk legend of half a century ago as a casual commentary.

'You have a theory, Stephen?'

'More speculation than anything else. There's this Ripper loose in London. Maybe some lunatic here in Dublin has decided to emulate him, drawing on this Dolocher stuff. These two assaults sound almost like a repeat from the thirties.'

Mossop shook his head. 'I doubt it, Stephen. Nobody remembers this "Olocher", or whatever you call him. I've never heard of him. You're stretching the idea.'

'Don't be so sure,' Doolan said. 'You're a Belfast man, not a Dubliner. There's still some old fellas around the city who remember their mothers warning them as kids that if they were bad the Dolocher would come and get them.'

The G-men could almost hear each other thinking. No successful policeman could ever afford to have a closed mind. Stranger things might happen. Imitative criminal behaviour was well-recognised and documented elsewhere, in Britain, France, Germany, and in the United States. There was even speculation that there was more than one hand behind the current Ripper murders in London's East End. Why not in Dublin too?

Swallow shrugged and made for the door.

'Who knows? It makes as much sense as anything else. You fellows can figure it out among yourselves for a bit. But once this conference is out of the way, I've got to be elsewhere. I'm getting married in two hours.'

TWENTY

The community chapel at the Merchants' Quay friary was smaller and more intimate than the public church that fronted onto the river. Over a century of Franciscan occupation, the monastery on the sloping ground below Christ Church had become imbued with an aura of peace and seclusion. It was a sacred place, a refuge, for many Dubliners from all strata of society.

Friar Lawrence had arranged with the Friar Superior that once the community had completed the afternoon office of None, the chapel would be swiftly prepared for the wedding. A young novice rolled out a red carpet along the short aisle. Two branched candelabras were brought to either side of the altar. They would blaze with dozens of white candles for the ceremony. Green holly boughs and winter palms were brought from the friary garden to decorate the Communion rails.

It would be a small wedding, Swallow had reckoned. But when they put the numbers together, listing the immediate relatives on both sides, it was not such a small affair after all. Both of Maria's parents were deceased, but her father's brother, her Uncle Paddy, would give her away.

Waiting for his bride to arrive, Swallow, out of professional habit, counted the numbers present. He made it twenty. Two of his uncles flanked his elderly mother, who had travelled from Kildare. John Mallon and his wife sat side by side with Pat Mossop and his wife. Mick Feore and Mrs Feore sat behind, accompanied by 'Duck' Boyle and Mrs Boyle. Maria's two immediate business neighbours from Thomas Street, Tom Fallon the butcher and George White the cabinetmaker, were there with their wives. Tom Dunne, Maria's head barman, sat with Mrs Dunne. Carrie, Maria's housekeeper and cook, was widowed, but her son, Jack, who worked as a gauger in Power's distillery on John's Lane, escorted his mother.

Father Lawrence, as the celebrant, stood at the centre of the altar, taking quiet pleasure in his precedence, for once, over the Friar Superior, who hovered behind him. Another novice who would act as Lawrence's altar attendant knelt beside him. As the bride-to-be started along the red carpet, the organist played the opening notes of the 'Halleluiah Chorus' from Handel's *Messiah*.

'It's quite profane, of course,' Lawrence later told Swallow. 'Nothing sacred about it. But it's beautiful, and sure isn't it nearly Christmas?'

When Maria arrived on her Uncle Paddy's arm she looked nervous, Swallow thought. But her wedding attire made her more beautiful than he had ever seen her. As befitted her widowed status she had eschewed the white lace dress that had been popularised by the young queen, Victoria, in her marriage to Prince Albert in 1840. Instead she had chosen a sculpted gown in cream silk, stitched with pearls. The same pearls decorated a short veil in matching lace, and she carried a small bouquet of flowering cyclamen. Her blonde hair was styled in perfect ringlets that framed her face and graceful neck.

Swallow would have liked to have a new suit for the occasion, but with the inquiries into Alice Flannery's murder there was no time for a fitting at any tailor's during the week. His best option had been for Carrie to sponge, steam and press the dark-blue three-piece he wore for court appearances. Harry Lafeyre, taking his duties as best man seriously, had volunteered to collect a new silk shirt and bow tie for him. Swallow reckoned he was passable.

Maria, naturally, had nominated her sister, Lily, to be her bridesmaid. But she had also asked Harriet to act as a second bridesmaid. They took their places in the front pew as Maria detached from her uncle to take Swallow's arm, stepping forward to kneel in front of the altar. She glanced at Swallow and smiled.

He thought the ceremony was the most moving and most joyful experience of his life. Lawrence celebrated the nuptial Mass with the Friar Superior and the acolyte echoing the Latin prayers. After the consecration of the bread and wine, Lawrence distributed the white Communion hosts to the congregation, save for Lafeyre, Pat Mossop and his wife, who were Protestant. The friar-organist played Bach's 'Jesu, joy of Man's Desiring' and Pachelbel's 'Canon in D'.

Then they pledged themselves to each other. After Catherine Greenberg's dramatic exit from Lily's painting class, Swallow had prudently decided against visiting her family business in Capel Street to procure a ring. Instead he had gone to Weir's, the recently opened jeweller's off Grafton Street. He and Maria had agreed that the ring from her first marriage would be transferred to her right hand before the ceremony. Now he placed a new gold band, inset with three small diamonds, on her left hand. He drew the equivalent of two months' salary from his savings to pay for it.

Lawrence's homily was brief. He recalled the marriage at Cana when Jesus changed the water into wine at the request of his Blessed Mother. Jesus approved of marriage, he told them. Nothing could be clearer. Otherwise he would not have performed the miracle. He wanted the couple's day to be perfect and not ruined by a shortage of wine.

'Jesus is always to hand for married couples,' he told Swallow and Maria. 'As he will always be to hand for you in your lives together. All you have to do is reach out to him.'

When the religious ceremonies were concluded, they withdrew to the sacristy to sign the register, witnessed by Lafeyre and Lily. Lawrence carefully countersigned the registry sheet, adding the letters 'OSF' for Order of Saint Francis after his name in ostentatious capitals.

'I've little time for the work of government,' he told them by way of explanation. 'When I sign the official register I'm an agent of the Crown, whether I like it or not. So that's my way of letting them know that I'm still not one of them. I belong to my order and to God, not to Dublin Castle.'

The day outside was darkening when they emerged onto Merchants' Quay. There were handshakes, congratulations and kisses. Swallow's mother was not given to shows of emotion. Her relations with her son had been distant, cold almost, over the years since the death of her husband. But she threw her arms first around her son and then around Maria.

'I couldn't be happier for you both. May you have many, many years of good life together. May God bless you in his goodness.'

Maria had arranged the wedding breakfast, as it was euphemistically termed, for seven o'clock that evening at Mr Gresham's Royal Marine Hotel in Kingstown, eight miles out from the city, along the southern shore of Dublin Bay. And Lafeyre had arranged a fleet of six closed cabs to bring the wedding party and their guests to Westland Row, where they would take the six o'clock train for the journey to Kingstown. From there a further fleet of cabs would take them the short distance from the railway station to the hotel.

It was fully dark by the time they disembarked from the train at Kingstown, and there were flecks of snow in the freezing air coming off the sea. They were glad to reach the warmth of the hotel and the private reception room on the first floor, where sherry, port and, for those who wanted it, warming tea were to be served in the interval before the start of the meal.

The room buzzed with conversation as they sat to table. Wasn't Maria beautiful beyond words? Didn't Swallow look happier than anyone had seen him before? Weren't the bridesmaids a delight? Father Lawrence's ceremony and short homily had been so uplifting, had they not?

Maria had chosen her menu with care, and Mr Gresham's hotel staff delivered superbly on their responsibilities to their guests. There was *consommé de poulet*, fortified with Madeira. Next came steamed cod with white sauce, garnished with Dublin Bay prawns. Then the chef presented his *pièce de résistance,* platters of grilled black Dover sole with a *macédoine* of fresh vegetables and creamed potatoes. After that came a sirloin of beef, carved in front of the diners according to their preference and served with fresh vegetables and brown roasted potatoes. Then there was strong blue cheese. Swallow did not particularly like it. The last course was a sponge pudding with fruit, soaked in brandy and covered with meringue and ice-cream, a specialty apparently of one of the hotel's Parisian sous-chefs, who named his creation 'diplomat pudding'.

'You have done us a great deal of damage, Mrs Swallow,' the Father Superior said, raising a half-emptied glass of sweet Hungarian Tokay wine after he had finished the sponge pudding. 'To say that we poor friars are unaccustomed to this kind of fare is an understatement. This will take months of penance.'

'Then I suggest you take the gains with the losses, Father,' Maria laughed. 'If you're going to be doing the penance, enjoy the food and the wine.'

There had been Gewürztraminer with the soup and the fish, and an excellent Burgundy with the beef. Then, when the last of the 'diplomat pudding' was done, the head waiter rolled out a three-tiered wedding cake on a trolley. Meanwhile, his acolytes were serving champagne around the room.

John Mallon stepped forward and wielded, as if from nowhere, a magnificent silver sabre. He called for silence, and then repeated the call. It took perhaps a minute for the conversations and laughter to be fully hushed.

'Now, dear friends,' he told the guests. 'The new Mr and Mrs Swallow will cut their wedding cake with the silver sword, presented to the first chief commissioner of the Dublin Metropolitan Police on the date of its inception fifty years ago. Commissioner Harrel insisted that it should be used on this occasion, and he sends his personal congratulations and warm best wishes for the occasion.'

There was cheering and clapping around the room. Swallow and Maria stepped forwards, and with hands joined across the hilt of the sword began to carve through the white icing into the rich, dark cake below.

When every guest was supplied with wedding cake, Harry Lafeyre rose to his feet and tapped his glass with a fork for silence.

'Dear friends, it is my pleasant duty as best man here to propose the toast of the bride and groom. There are no words that I can use to express my happiness and the happiness of my own future wife, Lily, Maria's sister, at being witnesses to this wonderful event.'

He raised his glass.

'Joe and Maria are to be together as one. It is their happy destiny. And everyone here wishes them long and happy lives together. I give you the toast of the bride and groom.'

The room rose as one and clinked glasses in a chorus.

'To the bride and groom. To Maria and Joe.'

Maria's Uncle Paddy, already struggling to maintain equilibrium after imbibing the wines, managed a few stammering sentences, proposing the toast of the guests. Then Swallow stood.

'I have a few things to say, as you might expect.'

There was clapping and cheering from around the room.

'First, I would like to thank you all for being here with Maria and myself on this very special day. I would like to thank Father Lawrence and the Franciscan community for doing the ceremony so wonderfully earlier today. I would like to thank Harry and Lily for being our witnesses. And I would like to thank the staff of this very fine hotel for putting on such a great banquet here for us.'

There was more clapping and calls of 'hear, hear.'

'And it is my pleasurable duty, of course, to propose the toast of the bridesmaids. To Maria's lovely sister, Lily, and to my own beautiful sister, Harriet, who have so assiduously attended my bride here today. They have added grace and beauty to the occasion.'

Lily and Harriet blushed, smiled and nodded to acknowledge the compliment. There were whistles and more clapping as the glasses were raised yet again around the room.

'But a thousand times more than anything else, I want to thank Maria for agreeing to be my wife. She is, as you all know, a wonderful woman, and I freely admit I'm not the best catch in the world. I'm well past the first flush of boyhood, and I haven't exactly trodden a straight pathway through life.'

'A classic understatement,' Lafeyre interjected, grinning.

'But that, as you will have expected, will now change,' Swallow responded humorously to Lafeyre's quip. 'With Maria and myself united today, our lives are set together for the future. It is my pledge that I will strive with all of my energies and all of my resources to make her future and our future together a happy one. Now,' he gestured to the doorway, 'in the adjoining room we can relax, enjoy a drink to help our digestion and have a little entertainment.'

The anteroom had a blazing turf fire with plenty of soft chairs and settees and a baby grand piano. Maria was insistent that there would be no requirement for the ladies to withdraw to allow the gentlemen to smoke, and the entire party moved as one from the dining room.

Harry Lafeyre was straight away at the piano as the waiters proffered drinks. There was whiskey, cognac and port wine. A waiter deposited a tray of porter and ale, ready drawn from the barrel, onto a table beside the wall.

As soon as Lafeyre tinkled the opening notes of Moore's 'The Last Rose of Summer', Pat Mossop was on his feet, singing out the lyrics in a fine baritone voice that belied his fragile frame.

Next up was Father Lawrence with a rousing rendition of 'The Minstrel Boy'. Then Maria's housekeeper, Carrie, recited six couplets from Robert Browning's 'My Last Duchess'. Elizabeth Mallon proved to have a surprisingly sweet voice as she rendered Mabel's 'Poor Wand'ring One' from *The Pirates of Penzance.*

The waiters moved around the happy party, replenishing their drinks. The turf fire blazed in the grate as the northern winter wind, funnelling up from Kingstown Harbour, blew hard against the windows.

Few of the revellers noticed the G-man who had been assigned to the hotel for John Mallon's protection slip through the door and cross the end of the room to whisper something urgently into the chief superintendent's ear as he handed him a sheet of paper. But from where he sat with Maria in the centre of the room, Swallow saw it, and he knew from his boss's expression that what it told him was not good news.

Sunday November 11th, 1888

TWENTY-ONE

It had been a short honeymoon, Swallow told himself ruefully as he boarded the nine o'clock morning train that would carry him and Maria back to the city.

It was freezing after the warmth of the hotel, with an icy coating on the carriage windows. As they boarded at Kingstown Station he could see a hoar frost on the granite piers of the great asylum harbour. Behind him, a white dusting of snow topped the peaks that ringed the city to the south, Sugar Loaf, Three Rock, Two Rock, Djouce.

Swallow's immediate instinct, when he saw the G-man bring Mallon the dispatch, had been to leave Maria's side and cross the room to get details of what it might contain. But Mallon glared at him and made a sign to stay where he was. His responsibilities as groom superseded his duties as a policeman this evening.

The party had wound down with a sense of anticlimax. The G-man's message, Swallow gathered as the news filtered out through the room, brought details of yet another attack on a woman in the city. He heard Mossop mention Gloucester Street. That was in the red-light district, just north of the river. This time, it seemed, the victim had not been as lucky as Debbie Dunne. Dr Lafeyre would be needed to examine the body of the city's second murder victim in a week.

Mallon, Mossop and Feore had abandoned the celebrations and travelled to the scene as swiftly as their cab could make it along the unlit and partly paved road that led along the coast, through Blackrock, Booterstown and Merrion, back into the city.

Lafeyre and Lily followed shortly. Lafeyre's intention was to leave Lily to her rooms at Alexandra College and then to visit the murder scene himself. 'Duck' Boyle took the view, not wholly unreasonably, that since the case did not concern his E-Division, he would stay on at the Royal Marine for a few more drinks, the cost of which could be added to the wedding party account.

Rooms had been reserved for the bride and groom and some of the elderly guests, including the friars, Maria's uncle, Swallow's mother and her brothers.

'You and Maria should take the night here in the hotel,' Mallon had told Swallow. 'Whatever needs to be done, we can do it. We'll see you at Exchange Court in the morning.'

'What details do we have, chief?' Swallow asked. He had temporarily detached himself from his bride to accompany Mallon and the others down the staircase to the waiting cab at the hotel door.

Mallon glanced at the flimsy sheet, torn from the ABC telegraph machine at Kingstown DMP Station a few minutes earlier.

'This isn't your business tonight, Joe,' Mallon said firmly. 'But if you must know, the victim is one Ellen Byrne, twenty-two years old, plying her trade as a lady of the night under the name Nellie Sweet, battered in a kip in Monto. Gloucester Street, to be precise. There's an inspector from Store Street at the scene, and Shanahan and Collins are gone over from the Castle.'

Swallow knew the dead woman's name from the files. Like many of the girls working in the brothels around Montgomery Street she would have adopted a working name that disguised her true identity. Many of them were occasional informants for G-Division, passing on snippets of information picked up from clients. Someone had a gun. Somebody else seemed to have unexplained money. A known criminal had changed his habits. It all fed into the G-Division intelligence machine.

Ellen or Nellie Byrne was a country girl, Swallow recalled. From County Wicklow, as well as his memory served him. And unusually among working girls in Monto, she was connected with various subversive groups operating in the city. As well as he could recollect she had never been connected to any incident or outrage, but she had come to his notice on a number of occasions as keeping company with men known to be involved in political violence.

'Any witnesses?' Swallow asked as Mallon stepped into the cab.

'There might be. A beat man says he was nearly knocked down by a fellow flying out of the house. We'll know a bit more as soon as we get into Exchange Court.'

Whatever G-Division knew as he and Maria stepped into the train, the morning newspapers appeared to have a good amount of detail. Swallow took a *Sunday Sketch* and an *Express* from the newsboy at the station entrance.

The *Sketch* had the story across four columns of its main news page.

'ANOTHER DUBLIN MURDER'
'VICTIM A WOMAN OF THE UNFORTUNATE CLASS'
'CONSTABLE'S VALIANT EFFORTS IN VAIN'

There is consternation in the city with the death of yet another young woman in violent circumstances last night. The victim is Ellen Byrne, aged about 22 years and understood to be a native of County Wicklow.

The unfortunate woman had lodgings at Chapel Court, Gloucester Street. Her head had received severe lacerations. It was discovered by a neighbour shortly after eleven o'clock last night.

Police Constable C35 who was on duty in Gloucester Street saw a tall man who is suspected as the assailant leave Chapel Court. The constable sought to restrain him but was incapacitated by a blow to the body and the attacker made good his escape. There was fog in the streets at the hour.

Police from Store Street attended at the scene, as did officers from Exchange Court at Dublin Castle. The city Medical Examiner, Dr Henry Lafeyre, visited the scene, as did a police photographic expert.

The *Express* had less detail about the murder, but, probably to compensate for dearth of knowledge, Swallow reckoned, reminded its readers in the first paragraph that this was the third assault on women in the city in little more than a week.

It will be recalled that on Friday night November 2nd last, Miss Alice Flannery, a waitress, was attacked near her home at Blackberry Lane, Rathmines, and sustained injuries which claimed her life some hours later.

On Friday night, Miss Deborah Dunne, a fishmonger, was attacked near Cardiff Lane on Misery Hill. Although she was badly injured and remains gravely ill in hospital it does not appear that her life is in danger.

These outrages confirm that the streets of Dublin are no safer than those of London where the so-called 'Jack the Ripper' cases, the latest also on Friday, have spread widespread terror among the populace.

It does not appear that the Dublin Metropolitan Police is any more effective in keeping the streets of the Hibernian capital safe than are their counterparts in London. Nor is the G-Division at Exchange Court, Dublin Castle, any more successful in detecting the perpetrator or perpetrators of these outrages than their vaunted detective colleagues at New Scotland Yard.

There would be a lot more of the same in the newspapers over coming days, Swallow knew. One murder in Dublin was a news story. Two and an attempted third within a week were sensational, particularly with the East End of London in terror over the Whitechapel murders.

When the train arrived at the Westland Row terminus they had taken a cab that dropped Swallow at the Castle before bringing Maria home to Thomas Street. The city was quiet with few pedestrians other than those going to or coming from Sunday morning religious services. The bells of Christ Church started to toll the hour of ten o'clock as the cab halted outside Exchange Court.

'You're rightly in time for the conference,' the duty man at the public office told him. 'Commissioner Harrel and Chief Mallon are just gone in.'

Swallow tried to remember when last he had seen the commissioner attend a crime conference at Exchange Court.

The parade room was full. Every seat was occupied. G-men sat on desks and in window alcoves while uniformed constables lined the walls. The air was heavy with the smell of sweat and tobacco and tired men. Mallon took the rostrum at the end of the room, flanked by Commissioner Harrel in full uniform. The chief's face showed strain and tension. And Harrel seemed impatient, tapping his right hand repeatedly on his knee. The divisional superintendents, A to F, sat in the front row before the rostrum. 'Duck' Boyle, red-eyed and bleary from the night before, looked as if he might slip from his chair.

Mallon saw Swallow enter the parade room and gestured to him to come forward to the front. Harrel moved to the rostrum. The room fell silent. Swallow let his gaze rove across the rows of faces. There were veteran sergeants and young beat men, hardened crime detectives and buckshee volunteers—uniformed men willing to work in plain clothes on lower pay in the hope of promotion to permanent detective duties.

'Good morning, men,' Harrel began. 'I'm not here to direct this investigation. I'm not a detective. You have officers much more skilled than I in this kind of thing. Like Chief Superintendent Mallon here.'

The commissioner was an accomplished speaker, pitching his words so they could be heard even at the back of the room.

'I do not need to tell you that we are now faced with a situation of the utmost gravity, and that the Dublin Metropolitan Police now faces a considerable challenge. Two women are dead, brutally murdered. A third has escaped with her life but has suffered severe injuries. My message to you comes from the chief secretary himself. No effort is to be spared to keep the streets of the city safe. And the pursuit of the person or persons responsible for these outrages will not abate until they are made amenable.'

A murmur of agreement rippled across the room.

'I am afraid that this will require very considerable sacrifices from members of the force at all levels,' Harrel continued. 'With immediate effect, all leave is cancelled other than compassionate leave for the death or grave illness of an immediate family member. Patrols are to be increased in the hours of darkness. I am instructing all superintendents to release members from clerical and other duties in order to get the greatest numbers out on the streets. Officers on duty will exercise stop and search powers under the Dublin Police Act to the maximum. I will personally make random checks on selected patrol books to ensure that this instruction is being complied with. If there are those who believe they can prowl the streets with impunity, wreaking violence on the population, we will make them think otherwise.' He paused. 'I shall now ask Detective Chief Superintendent Mallon to bring you up to date on the latest developments and to outline further steps to be taken in these investigations.'

Mallon's voice was heavy with exhaustion. Swallow guessed that he had no sleep after leaving the wedding celebration.

'Men, a lot of you are tired, like myself, after a long night. You've heard what the commissioner has said. I'd like to stress that this job is going to be based on the fullest co-operation between uniformed and detective branches. We need every man in uniform we can get on the streets at night until we crack this case. And we need every detective working flat out, following every clue we have. As to those clues, we have a few. Constable C35 Pat Cummins encountered a tall, well-built man hurriedly leaving Chapel Court at around the time we believe that Ellen Byrne was beaten to death. He endeavoured to restrain him but was unable to keep up with him in the fog. We don't know if we're dealing here with one assailant or with a number, or if there's any connection between the three attacks on women in the past week. But for what it's worth, Debbie Dunne also describes her attacker as a big man. Now I know that's not very precise, but it does narrow the field somewhat.

'So,' he gestured to a file on the rostrum, 'we've got a list of every known violent offender against women in the city, compiled during the week by G-Division. We're going to take each and every one of these characters and we're going to bring them in for questioning as to their whereabouts on the three dates and times of the attacks. We'll allocate the jobs as soon as this conference is ended. Now, are there any questions?'

A young, red-haired constable, his back to the parade room wall, raised a hand.

'Sir, if you please. 22C, Constable Edwards, Store Street. The word is that Cummins says there was somethin' very unusual about the man he encountered. Is that for public knowledge?'

Mallon shook his head.

'No. I know what you're talking about, but for the moment we're keeping that confidential. I don't want it going to the press.'

He glared across the room.

'And that goes for everyone here. Whatever you may have heard about whatever Constable Cummins saw, or thought he saw, it's not to pass your lips. If it appears in any newspaper, believe me, I know every editor and reporter in this city and I'll find out who's been talking. He'll be out on his ear before nightfall, I promise you.'

One of Mallon's clerks started to allocate the jobs from the file of frequent offenders. Mallon nodded to Swallow.

'We'll use your room. Bring Mossop, Feore and Doolan.'

'What's all that about, chief?' Swallow asked when they had climbed the stairway to the first-floor quiet of the crime inspector's office.

Mallon threw himself wearily into a chair.

'Lafeyre will be here in a while to fill us in. He's had Nellie Byrne down to the morgue for a post-mortem. The room was like a wreck. Apart from the blood on the floor, on the walls, on the inside of the door, everywhere, it was clear the place had been tossed. Whoever killed Ellen Byrne seems to have been searching for something in particular. I'd have said she put up a mighty struggle around the room.'

'What was the young bobby from Store Street saying back there?' Swallow asked.

Mallon gestured to Stephen Doolan.

'You tell Inspector Swallow about it. You seem to know the story.'

Doolan sighed.

Swallow nodded a silent good morning to Harry Lafeyre as he entered the room.

'35C Pat Cummins isn't the fittest man in the force,' Doolan went on. 'He's within an ace of retirement, overweight, drinks and eats too much, and he's as slow as Findlater's clock.'

'I talked to him at the scene,' Lafeyre said. 'I think he's probably suffering from diabetes. He shouldn't be on outdoor duties at all in my view.'

'Whatever the case,' Doolan went on, 'he says he tried to catch up with this individual but he lost him in the fog. Didn't get much sight of him for most of the way, but he got one good look at him under the street lamp at the Gloucester Diamond.'

Mallon shrugged.

'Tell Inspector Swallow what Cummins 35C says about this fellow.'

Doolan looked momentarily embarrassed.

'He said he thought he'd seen him before. He couldn't say where or when. But he's got a notion that he might be a policeman.'

Monday November 12th, 1888

TWENTY-TWO

The superintendents of the DMP's six uniformed divisions worked their men hard in the weeks that followed the murder of Ellen Byrne, alias Nellie Sweet, in her room at Chapel Court.

Hundreds of individuals were stopped, searched and questioned in the hours of darkness under the provisions of the Dublin Police Act in the winter hunt across the city. Most of them were known to the constables and the sergeants as petty criminals, vagrants, beggars or layabouts. All were questioned closely. Some, who were unable to give a full account of themselves, or who aroused suspicion for some other reason, were arrested and handed over to G-Division detectives for further interrogation. But the interviews yielded nothing more than a few tip-offs about stolen property and petty crimes in the planning.

The policemen worked double shifts, putting in four hours of day duty before or after the eight-hour night shift. Then the workload started to take its toll in the bitter weather. Older men went down first, with chills and chest colds. Then some of the less robust younger men started to succumb. Two cases of frostbite were reported from the C-district, where the freezing east wind whipped across the streets from the bay. The depot hospital at Kevin Street quickly filled with the sick and the exhausted.

There were some gains. Larcenies and housebreaking were reduced with the extra policing presence on the streets. Criminals stayed at home at night or drank in the public houses, unwilling to risk being grabbed none-too-gently out of the darkness by ill-tempered DMP

163

men, only too glad to have an excuse to return with a prisoner to the warmth of their station.

Teams of G-men and buckshees interviewed all of Ellen Byrne's known associates and clients. None of the working girls on Gloucester Street had seen anyone who might match the description given by Constable 35C of a tall man, much less one who looked like a policeman. None of her regular clients could be placed anywhere near her address on the night she died.

Pat Cummins, the C-Division constable who had encountered the man fleeing from the scene of Ellen Byrne's murder, had been admitted to the hospital at the Kevin Street depot on Lafeyre's recommendation. Swallow and Mossop went to interview him in his hospital bed.

'So you think the man you saw was a policeman?' Swallow said. 'But you didn't recognise him.'

Cummins's face twisted in anguish.

'I know I've seen him before. I just can't say where or when. Just for some reason I thought to myself, he's a "polisman." But don't ask me for a name.'

'Describe him, then,' Mossop prompted him.

'He was big, athletic. Maybe thirty, maybe thirty-five years. Very agile.'

'Clean-shaven?' Swallow asked. 'Or bearded?'

'Hard to say in the darkness. It was more an impression.'

'Fair enough,' Swallow said doubtfully. 'Look, when you're rested and feeling better we'll ask you to visit the various divisions around the city. It might be that you'll spot your man.'

Swallow and Mossop were present for Ellen Byrne's funeral Mass on the Tuesday at St Mary's Pro-Cathedral on Marlborough Street. It was well attended by working girls from the brothels around Montgomery Street and Gloucester Street, perhaps a score in all. There was no sign of any family. The other girls told detectives that her parents were dead, but that she sometimes spoke about a sister who lived in Wicklow.

Later in the day, after that information had been passed to the RIC, who policed the countryside out of Dublin, the sergeant at Roundwood, a small village in rural County Wicklow, made the connection, identifying the sister. A constable had been despatched to the smallholding in the Wicklow Mountains, where she lived with her sheep-farmer husband and a string of children. When the constable stated his business and disclosed his grim news she told him that she did not want to know about her sister and showed him the door.

The funeral Mass was swift and without trimmings. The elderly celebrant mumbled his way through the Latin prayers. There was no distribution of Communion and no homily. Swallow surmised that the decision not to distribute Communion was dictated by the assumption that many among the congregation, and certainly all of the working girls, were sinners and not in the state of grace. At the end of the Mass the priest descended from the altar, hurriedly sprinkled the coffin with holy water and retreated to the sacristy.

The only funeral attendee of professional interest to Swallow was Charlie Vanucchi, the acknowledged leader of the Dublin criminal fraternity since the death of Ces 'Pisspot' Downes, who had run her crime ring from her house on Francis Street. She had earned the unflattering soubriquet from her lethal use of a chamber pot on her mistress's skull when the lady discovered her stealing silverware from her fine house on Merrion Square.

In the custom of policemen who need to see and note any significant attendees, the G-men took a vantage point from where they could survey the entire church. Vanucchi nodded agreeably as he passed their pew. The unmistakably Neapolitan features of the young man by his side marked him as being another family member. He wore the same fine woollen coat as the older man. Swallow noted that they wore similar, finely crafted shoes.

'The youngest of the brood,' Mossop whispered unnecessarily in Swallow's ear. 'Tony's supposed to be the best pickpocket west of Liverpool.'

The working girls from around Montgomery Street and Gloucester Street had collected enough money to give Nellie a decent burial at Mount Prospect cemetery at Glasnevin, sparing her the indignity of a pauper's grave. The day was cold but dry. After the elderly priest had concluded the graveside obsequies, which were as perfunctory as the requiem Mass earlier, Charlie Vanucchi and his son walked across to where Swallow and Mossop stood on the gravel pathway. There were no unnecessary introductions.

'What brings you here, Charlie?' Swallow asked. 'I didn't know you were connected.'

'I'm not, Mr Swallow. Nellie was good to Ces.'

'Nellie? Good to Ces?'

Vanucchi shrugged.

'She stayed with her over in Francis Street when she was close to the end. Ces couldn't have had better care if she was her own daughter. I'd have set her up, looked after her, like. But she was too proud. So ... here's where she ended. I'm just here out of respect to Ces.'

'This girl didn't work for Ces in Francis Street using the name Nellie Byrne,' Mossop said knowledgeably. 'We knew everyone in that house. No Byrnes.'

Vanucchi grinned.

'Very thorough on the detail as usual, Mr Mossop. You're right. She was Helena Moyles when she came into the city from Wicklow. She started callin' herself Mrs Byrne after she took up with a soldier of that name out of the Royal Barracks. They weren't married, and he cleared off to India leavin' her in the family way. The child died anyway.'

Swallow nodded. He could fit scores of young women's names to the same story.

'Helena Moyles,' Mossop said thoughtfully. 'I remember that name all right. She must have been the only person ever in that house without a criminal record. Any word out on the streets who might have done it?'

Vanucchi shrugged again.

'Some disgruntled client. A maniac. Maybe some fellow who's imitatin' this Jack the Ripper character across the water.'

'You making any inquiries, Charlie?' Swallow asked. Not infrequently in his experience, the city's criminal network was ahead of the police intelligence system.

'Sure. First thing I did when I heard. But it's got nothin' to do with any o' my lads. She was just a poor girl makin' a livin'.'

'If you hear anything, you'll let us know.'

'Of course, Mr Swallow. Apart from likin' the girl, it's a terrible thing for Dublin to have this sort of thing happen. God knows, there's enough trouble down on this poor country as it is.'

Vanucchi was an occasional informant for Swallow. His criminal motivation being purely financial, he viewed all Fenians, Land Leaguers, Home Rulers, Gaelic revivalists and the like with something between bafflement and contempt. When information came his way, as it frequently did, on their activities, he considered it a commodity readily tradable for favours from G-Division. A blind eye turned here. A charge overlooked there. Charlie Vanucchi's runners and bagmen sometimes wondered how he seemed to be able to get them out of difficulties with the police, at least on occasion, and generally on less serious charges.

'You're absolutely right, Charlie,' Swallow agreed. 'We have enough troubles as it is.'

TWENTY-THREE

The investigation into the murder of Alice Flannery had ground to a halt. Geoffrey Bradley, the teacher from Synge Street School named by Dan Flannery as the witness who had met him on Huband Bridge, was questioned by Mossop and Vizzard. He confirmed Flannery's claim that he was a mile away from the murder scene shortly before midnight.

It was not impossible that he might have managed to be back at Blackberry Lane at the time his sister was attacked, but he would have had to sprint or take a cab. Every driver who had been working that night was questioned. None remembered picking up a fare around Huband Bridge. Residents of the houses that fronted the canal between Portobello and Huband Bridge were visited. Nobody recalled seeing a running man.

Father Cavendish's sick-call alibi was persuasive, if not watertight. But a second thundering letter to Commissioner Harrel from Archbishop Walsh ruled out further questioning of the young curate without first securing new evidence and clearing it through the commissioner's office. The affront to one of God's anointed would be raised in the Dublin City Council and at Westminster by Catholic representatives, Walsh threatened.

Swallow, Mossop and Feore re-interviewed the male employees of the New Vienna restaurant. Apart from Werner, the head chef, the sommelier and the professional waiters, they were either recent arrivals from the continent or casual workers doing menial jobs in the still-room or the wash-up. Those who knew Alice Flannery described her as quiet, private and keeping to herself. It seemed she had no friends among them, but no enemies either. None of them knew anything of her personal life. If she had a beau, or any relationship, they never heard it mentioned.

Meanwhile, Debbie Dunne, though small and slight, was proving herself strong and resilient. She made a slow but steady recovery from her injuries in the Dublin Infirmary at Jervis Street. Within a week she was well enough to be released. But she was required to attend every second day to have the dressings on her wounds changed. It was going to be a while before she would be well enough to get back to work selling fish.

Swallow and Pat Mossop questioned her after her discharge from hospital.

'Any detail at all that you can remember, anything that's come back to your mind since, might be a help,' Mossop told her in the bare room where she lived with her younger sister at Ringsend.

'Jesus … didn't I tell the other bobbies … everythin' I remember,' she groaned through split lips. 'I was fightin' for me life and the few shillin's I'd earned in the day.'

Her face was still a mass of bruising, yellow and blue. Her left arm was encased in plaster, the ulna having been badly fractured. It would be months before she would have the strength again to push a barrow. Swallow felt something between anger at what had happened to the girl and admiration for her grit.

'You said he had a smell. You told the other detectives it was a "musty" smell,' Swallow said gently. 'Would you say it was smell like a horse, or a dog, or what?'

'I don't know,' she said wearily. 'Who knows what any horse smells like? Ask me about fish. I can tell yez about smells offa different fish.'

'But he didn't smell of fish,' Swallow pressed her. 'You said "musty" to the other policemen.'

She shook her head.

'I don't know. Like I said, I was fightin' for me life, wasn't I?'

'I think you were, Debbie. And fair enough, you saw him off.'

'There's nothin' fair about it,' she muttered. 'Be the time I'm back on me feet, me stand will be gone. There's a dozen other wans who'll be sellin' fish down Cardiff Lane and Misery Hill.'

'We could help you on that,' Mossop suggested. 'Have you anyone else who could operate your barrow for a while?'

'There's me little sister, Lizzie. But them wans would run her off the street.'

'Not if we told them they'd be fined for trading without a street licence,' Mossop said. 'They'd be very nice to her, I'd say, in those circumstances.'

'Street licence?' Debbie Dunne managed a croaky laugh. 'Sure, none of us ever had them.'

'Well, that isn't a great surprise, Debbie. There wouldn't be much chit-chat among the girls about the Dublin Street Trading Act. But maybe it's time to enforce the law,' Mossop ventured.

She hesitated for a moment.

'Could yez do that … what you're sayin' like? It'd be great if I knew I could go back to me stand when I'm better.'

'We could,' Swallow said simply, 'and we will, if you like.'

When they returned to the Castle late in the afternoon, Swallow went to report to Mallon at his office in the Lower Yard.

Crossing the yard, he saw Harry Lafeyre's brougham standing outside the medical examiner's storeroom. As Swallow passed the building, Lafeyre's driver, Scollan, emerged through the door, struggling with a large cardboard box that he deposited onto the carriage floor. Scollan glowered at him.

'Bringin' these files up to Harcourt Street for the doctor. You'd not think paper could be so bloody heavy.'

Swallow hoped that Lafeyre's instructions to his assistant were simply to fetch and deliver. Any further exploration within the medical examiner's room carried the risk that the protection logs could be uncovered from behind the storage cupboard.

'Ah go on, you big horse of a Limerick man,' he cajoled Scollan. 'If it was a crate of stout you were carrying away for yourself, you'd say it was as light as a feather.'

Scollan muttered something unintelligible as he locked the storeroom door. Then he hoisted himself to the brougham's driving seat, flicked the reins over the horse's back and started to trundle across the yard towards the Palace Street gate. Swallow breathed a quiet sigh of relief.

John Mallon was in foul humour. As the day ended, the air in his office had become thick with fumes from the coal fire, overlaid with tobacco smoke. As Swallow went to sit, a blast of northerly wind coming across the rooftops sent a ball of sulphur-laden smoke back down the chimney. Mallon waved a newspaper to disperse the fumes.

'Jesus, if we've asked the maintenance men once, we must have asked them ten times to put a new cowl on that chimney pot up on the blasted roof. You've a choice in here between freezing to death and suffocating.'

He took his seat behind the desk.

'Any developments?'

Swallow shook his head.

'None worth talking about, chief. Debbie Dunne can't tell us any more than she has. She's worried about losing her trade, so we told her we'd come down on anyone who tries to take her pitch. None of them have trader's licences.'

'That's a Christian thought.'

'It was Pat Mossop's more than mine. She's a plucky little one. You'd want to help if you could.'

Mallon smiled.

'Would I be right in thinking there might be more than that? Does Mossop see a return on his effort?'

Swallow shrugged.

'Just a sense that maybe she might be helpful. No harm for a G-man to be owed a small favour. But otherwise no, sir, there's no news.'

Mallon seemed resigned.

'Well, all we can do is our best. All fairness to Commissioner Harrel, he understands and he's staying off my back. In other circumstances he'd be gone demented with the press roaring on about murder in the streets. But he's got other things on his mind.'

Mallon tapped his copy of the day's *Irish Times*.

'Have you been following the proceedings of the Parnell Commission in London?'

'Not with particular attention, chief. What's happening there?'

'Our old friend Pigott is being called in as a witness. Nobody's quite sure why. But it seems that the leader of Parnell's legal team, Sir Charles Russell, has something on him. There are very long faces on the gentlemen representing the government, and indeed *The Times*.

Of all the legions of scribblers that populated the Dublin newspapers and printing-houses, Swallow rated Richard Pigott as the most duplicitous. He held himself out as a Home Rule sympathiser, but when Upper Yard officials wanted an inflammatory tract planted in some publication, or sought intelligence on the intentions of Land Leaguers or Home Rulers, Pigott could be relied upon, for the right fee, to come up with the goods.

Pigott lived well, renting an elegant house at De Vesci Terrace in the salubrious suburb of Monkstown, where he lived with his two young sons, his wife having died some years previously. He moved in influential circles. Swallow had encountered him dining one evening with Smith Berry in the expensive Burlington Restaurant on Trinity Street, and on another while visiting the United Services Club on St Stephen's Green with Harry Lafeyre.

'Pigott? Nobody'd believe the Lord's Prayer out of him.'

'I agree,' Mallon said. 'They're pretty desperate if Pigott's their strongest card. I would anticipate that Russell is going to pick him asunder on the witness stand. So when the commission collapses or finds that Parnell has no case to answer, that's when they'll want G-Division's protection logs.'

Swallow's tone was mock-earnest.

'We've searched everywhere, sir. You know that.'

Mallon grinned.

'Of course. But I should tell you I've had to agree to let them do a search. They'll start in the public office. You'll have to arrange to have every room open. The same goes for cupboards, lockers, and of course the safes.'

'The men won't like it, chief. Tempers are still high over what happened before.'

'I know. And I'm going to have to rely on you to keep them cool. We don't need any hot-head stuff. I'll make it my business to be present myself throughout. So will Kelly. We've agreed it will be a joint operation. We'll have someone with each of their search teams. It shouldn't take more than a couple of hours if we're co-operative. If we're not, it means it'll take that much longer.'

'What do you think they really believe, chief?' Swallow asked.

'I'm not sure. Kelly's no fool, and he's out to cover his own backside. He has to show that he's taken every possible step to locate the logs. Whether he thinks the stupid Irish can't find the blasted things, or whether he thinks we're not co-operating, I don't really know. And I'm not sure it matters that much. He'll do what a soldier does anyway— secure the objective he's been ordered to. Whether it's worth it, that isn't his problem.'

Mallon nodded to the wall clock.

'Time to wind down the day, such as it is.'

He reached into one of the cavernous drawers of the oak desk and produced a half-full bottle of Bushmills along with two tumblers. He poured heavy measures and pushed one across the desk to Swallow.

Swallow crossed the room to fetch the water jug that Mallon's clerk, Jack Burton, always left, freshly filled during the afternoon. Without asking, he added an equal volume of water to each of the tumblers. It was akin to a liturgical process, repeated and perfected between them over years of working together. Mallon raised his glass.

'Good luck.'

Swallow did likewise.

'Good luck, chief.'

Mallon threw back half of his drink in a great swallow. He put another shot in his tumbler and did the same with Swallow's.

'So,' he grinned, 'tell me how married life is treating you.'

'Ah, much the same as unmarried life, I suppose,' Swallow laughed. 'You've possibly guessed, Maria and I are going to be … blessed … very quickly. You know what I mean, sir.'

'Aha,' Mallon said. He raised his tumbler of Bushmills again. 'Now I know I'm not losing my touch as a detective. I should have guessed that. Congratulations. When's the big event due?'

'I'm no expert,' Swallow chuckled, 'but I did my stint in medical school, as you know. It'll be August. Early August.'

'Then you'll call him Augustus or Augustine, if it's a boy,' Mallon grinned. 'I don't know the female equivalent.'

'It would be Augustina, I suppose,' Swallow reflected. 'Bloody awful name though.'

'I agree,' Mallon said gravely. 'Forget I mentioned it.'

He threw back the rest of his Bushmills.

'I think I'll call it a day, chief. Thanks for the drink. I'll be down in the morning for the reception committee. We'll astonish Major Kelly and his *amadáns* with our courtesy and co-operation.'

He left the Castle via the Palace Street gate and turned in to Dame Street. A perfect half-moon had risen behind the Chapel Royal, shimmering in the clear, cold sky.

The walk to Thomas Street through the sharp air cleared his head and dispersed the effects of Mallon's Bushmills. Two greatcoated constables watching from the shadowed corner of Meath Street nodded as they recognised him. In spite of the chill of the evening, Swallow envied them the uncomplicated simplicity of their task.

As the night went by, he knew, they would be checking and questioning those moving about on the streets. They would be noting names, times and destinations, as would scores of their colleagues, singly or in pairs across the city. Pages in notebooks would be filled with seemingly pointless detail. And yet, in there amongst the scrawls and the scribbles, there might be a clue or a connection that could solve a murder.

Although it was still a few weeks to Christmas, many of the shops along High Street and Thomas Street were already displaying their festive offerings. Dempsey's, the butcher's on High Street, had fine hams in their window adorned with sprigs of green holly. Naughton's, the grocer's, displayed bowls of raisins and sultanas along with a shining pyramid of fat, bright oranges. Donnelly's, the fishmonger's on Thomas Street, displayed a notice offering smoked cod and salted herrings up to Christmas Eve. For many, they would be an affordable alternative to goose or beef for Christmas dinner.

The night was quiet at Grant's. Tom, the head barman, had the evening off. Two young curates served a few customers in the public area and even fewer in the select bar. Maria, as ever, moved gracefully between the two sectors, greeting customers, watching the service, directing the curates with sharp eyes so that empty glasses were taken in, dirty tabletops were polished and ashtrays were promptly emptied, cleaned and replaced.

The Monday night trade was slow. Swallow went upstairs first to the private quarters. He unstrapped the shoulder-holster with the heavy Webley Bulldog and placed the weapon in the bedside locker. He washed, changed to a fresh collar and shirt and went downstairs.

Maria saw him take up his stance beside but not behind the bar. He would not serve or tend. If that were to be reported to the Castle authorities, there was no plausible explanation he could offer for engaging in a 'prohibited occupation'.

Rather, he would simply be a presence, as Maria's other half, as the man of the house. She felt more secure with him there, visible, strong, commanding. The clientele knew him for a bobby. Not just a bobby but a G-man. Not just a G-man but a detective inspector. A man of rank, of substance. It was good, in a city where murder walked the streets, where the winter darkness closed in earlier each day, to know that a man like Joe Swallow was at hand. M & M Grant's was an oasis of warmth and safety for its patrons in a perilous time.

Swallow and Maria retired early to the parlour above the bar to sit by the turf fire, leaving the bar to the curates below. Swallow had two Tullamores and Maria drank some hot chocolate that Carrie had prepared and left in the kitchen. Later they heard the last of the departing customers and the downstairs noises of the curates washing up and locking the doors. When all was silent they went to the big bedroom on the top floor with its sash windows facing St Catherine's Church across the street.

They made love silently and slowly. When they had finished Maria fell into a deep and contented sleep. Swallow watched the waxing half-moon moving across the sky behind the squat spire of St Catherine's. He had not felt so safe and contented since childhood days in Newcroft. The world they inhabited, with all its challenges and ugliness, was a good one. He and Maria were right for each other. And he knew that the arrival of new life, life of their making, would open horizons of understanding and happiness such as he had not known before.

Tuesday December 18th, 1888

TWENTY-FOUR

Kelly and his men came back, as Mallon said they would, in a more civil mode, but no less determined, after an interval of almost five weeks. As the days passed, Swallow had started to wonder if perhaps Mallon was wrong. Maybe Kelly's masters had overruled him. Or perhaps he had simply given up. But Mallon was not wrong. The search time, Mallon told him the previous evening, had been fixed for ten o'clock. When they arrived, precisely on the hour, there were no threats, no guns; just a look of cold insinuation on Kelly's face as he led his posse into Exchange Court.

There were six of them this time. Swallow recognised two from the RIC crime office in the Lower Yard. The others were strangers. Military, he guessed, or former military. They carried themselves with the air of rank. Stern, tough-looking characters. Officers, he knew. Men accustomed to taking orders and, in turn, being obeyed. But they did not have the ceaselessly searching eyes that characterise the experienced police detective.

Mallon was good on his promise that he would be on hand to ensure that the search was conducted with propriety. This was going to be done by the book. Comparisons in rank between police and military were an imprecise science, but the chief superintendent of G-Division certainly outranked an army major. So protocol required that the process should start by Kelly presenting himself at Mallon's office. Mallon reciprocated the gesture of respect by arranging for his visitor to be offered tea.

Swallow sat on a window ledge in the corridor until they emerged perhaps ten minutes later.

'The major and his men are ready to start now, Detective Inspector,' Mallon said curtly. 'Please start with the public office. I've assured Major Kelly that we will extend every co-operation. Our men will work side by side with his throughout the search.'

'We will operate in teams of two,' Kelly announced. 'I want one team to start where the logs are normally filed and then to check other regular storage places. I want another team to start in the detective inspector's and the crime sergeants' offices. The third team will search the sleeping and recreation quarters.'

Swallow gritted his teeth. Kelly had done his homework very thoroughly. He knew the layout of the Exchange Court building in detail and the functions of every room and office. In all probability someone within the G-Division had been rewarded for the information.

'I'll accompany the team searching the storage and public areas,' he told Kelly. 'Detective Sergeant Mossop will go with the team searching the offices. Detective Feore will go with those searching the dormitory and the recreation area.'

Kelly nodded to the two that Swallow had identified as police.

'You go with Mr Swallow.'

He led them down the stairway to the public office. Earlier, he had ensured that every filing cabinet and drawer in the office was unlocked and ready for inspection. He jerked his head to the G-man on duty.

'We need to close the front door for a while. You can divert any callers down the Lower Yard to the back entrance while this is going on.'

He gestured around the room.

'There you go. Everything is unlocked. Any questions, just ask me.'

The older of the two men gestured apologetically.

'Look, you should understand that we don't like doing this one little bit.'

The accent was English. London.

'We're coppers, like you. Special Irish Branch, New Scotland Yard. Seconded to work with Kelly. We're in this together, you know. The name's Tom Evans. This is Denis Coombes.'

'You're not together with me in anything, Mr Evans,' Swallow replied coldly. 'You're English. I'm Irish. And the only reason I'm in your company is because you have a warrant.'

'Come on, Swallow,' Evans said impatiently. 'Kelly's our guv'nor while we're here. He told us, "Swallow knows where they are, these bloody logs." So let's stop wasting time. We're not going to start rummaging in these cupboards because we know the damned things aren't here. But we'll get them in the end. So save yourself and us a lot of trouble.'

'So Major Kelly is a clairvoyant as well as all his other talents,' Swallow sneered. 'You're fortunate to work for such a remarkable individual.'

Evans shrugged.

'Have it your own way, Swallow. But you might be interested to know that Major Kelly has put up a reward of a hundred quid for whoever turns in these bloody books. Imagine, a hundred quid. Half a year's pay. Up front. Denis and me, we'd be happy to split that three ways with somebody who'd be helpful, if you get my drift.'

Swallow felt his anger rising.

'Offering an inducement to a police officer is a serious offence, Mr Evans. Maybe they don't think so at New Scotland Yard?'

He saw anger rise in Evans's eyes.

'You wouldn't know how we think at New Scotland Yard, Swallow. We've got a proper police force there. Not like this backwater. But let me tell you, we've got men there who'd be ashamed to admit they shared your nationality. True Irishmen, loyal to their Queen and their empire.'

Swallow shook his head.

'You don't understand a bit of it, do you?'

He nodded towards Evans's silent companion.

'Neither do you, I suspect. You've no idea why you're here. You've no clue about what's at stake. And you really don't want to, do you?'

Evans's eyes flashed with anger. He crossed the office and flung open the doors of a double-fronted tallboy cabinet.

'Right. We've tried to do this the friendly way. We've put out the hand of co-operation, but you're not interested. So be it. But we've got a job to do. Come on, Denis. Pitch in here.'

They started to pull manila files from the shelves, scattering papers and records. When the floor was littered, Evans went to the duty officer's desk, drew out the drawers and emptied their contents onto the floor. Coombes riffled through the sheets and forms, tossing them to left and right after cursorily glancing through them. When every drawer had been emptied, Evans joined in.

After a few minutes, they gave up.

'Now,' Evans wiped his hands together, 'let's see how we get on in the rest of this dump.'

Swallow stayed with them as they went at random from one department to the next. Over his head he could hear the crash of iron bedsteads on the floor above as another team searched the dormitory where the single G-men slept. It was clear from the cursory examination of each cupboard and drawer that they did not expect to locate the logs in any of the obvious places. This was simple provocation; a display of power for its own sake designed to humiliate and to show who was top dog.

At one point, as they crossed the landing to the stationery stores, they encountered Kelly and Mallon standing side by side. There was no conversation. The expressions on both men's faces made it plain that neither was pleased to be in the other's company.

The operation at Exchange Court took less than two hours to complete. By then, each office, storage space and utility room had been searched. Every cupboard and drawer had been opened. Every series of records had been examined. Each G-man's personal locker had been opened and checked.

Kelly dismissed his team and waited with Mallon and Swallow in the public office as his men filed out. He glared at Mallon.

'What angers me more than anything else, Detective Chief Superintendent, is the absolute transparency of what has happened here. You have complete records and logs up to three years ago. After that, they simply disappear. You haven't even made an effort to pretend that this is a lack of organisation. You've simply taken away the ones that you've been ordered by your authorities to provide.'

'I can only tell you I don't know where they are,' Mallon replied sharply.

Kelly nodded.

'Words very carefully chosen, Mr Mallon. And indeed, you may not know where they are.'

He turned to stare at Swallow.

'But somebody here does. And I suspect I wouldn't have to search very far to find out who that is. I'm not going to let it end at this. There are other places we have yet to look. And getting warrants won't be a problem, I can assure you.'

Swallow returned his stare and held it. Mallon gestured to the door, smiling coldly.

'And I wish you a very merry Christmas too, Major Kelly.'

Wednesday December 26th, 1888

TWENTY-FIVE

It was 'Duck' Boyle, a week later, at Christmas, who got the first significant lead in the murder of the prostitute Helena Moyles, alias Ellen Byrne, alias Nellie Sweet, at Chapel Court. It was ironic, Swallow reflected when the information came through, that the corpulent Boyle, wholly unaccustomed to any exertion in the discharge of his duties, should from time to time come up with information that could make the difference between solving a crime and failure. But in reality, he had to acknowledge to himself that Boyle had a talent for being in the right place with the wrong type of people. That was what a policeman had to do sometimes. Usually it was no hardship for 'Duck' Boyle because it involved drink or food for which somebody else was paying. And occasionally it yielded dividends.

Christmas had brought a welcome respite from the bitterness of the winter. Christmas Eve saw temperatures rise to a balmy thirty degrees Fahrenheit, with thin sunshine filling the streets and courts across the city centre. It dropped, naturally, in the afternoon, once the sun went down and darkness had fallen. But Christmas morning was again pleasantly mild. Thousands of people took to the city parks to stroll in the unseasonal sunshine. Crocuses and snowdrops had started appear in St Stephen's Green in the heart of the city. A report from the Zoological Gardens in the Phoenix Park had it that hibernating animals had started to stir, sensing the spring-like warmth.

Swallow worked hard through the week. In spite of the heavy patrolling on the streets, there had been a spike in the petty crime figures as the poorer classes sought to provide some Christmas comfort for their families in the only way that many of them could. G-Division's detectives had to operate flat out to deal with house-breakings, purse-snatching and thefts from shops and businesses, but thankfully there were no instances of violence. By six o'clock on Christmas Eve the typewriters in Exchange Court had fallen silent, the crime files had been put away, the paperwork had been shelved and most of the denizens of the detective office had adjourned to their favoured public houses in the environs of the Castle.

Swallow broke with seasonal tradition, confining himself to one quick drink at the Brazen Head with Mossop, Feore and a few of the others. There had been a great many Christmas Eves when he had no idea how he got home or at what hour, but now he was a married man and an expectant father. His wife was engaged in operating a business while carrying his child to term. His place on one of the busiest nights of the year was in Grant's, by Maria's side.

The public house was filled all evening. Tom and the junior barmen toiled ceaselessly, drawing porter from the taps and filling and refilling measures of whiskey, gin and brandy for the merry-makers. There were seasonal drinks on the house, of course: two for full-time regulars, one for occasional patrons. The barmen knew which was which. But in the event of doubt, Maria's instruction to the barmen was to err on the side of generosity. Closing time came as a relief. By half past eleven the house was empty, the last stragglers having downed their drinks before heading to the Midnight Masses at the churches of St Nicholas of Myra on Francis Street, St Catherine's on Meath Street, or the Franciscan monastery on Merchants' Quay.

On Christmas morning he and Maria went to the ten o'clock Mass at Merchants' Quay. Later, Lafeyre and Lily came to Thomas Street for a quiet Christmas dinner, prepared and served by Carrie before she went off to join her son and his family in the Coombe to enjoy the rest of the day.

Maria had employed Tom to decorate the hall and parlour in the private quarters. He had hung tinsel stars and gaily coloured paper chains along the walls. Maria had never bothered to put up a Christmas tree, even though the practice, introduced in England by the Queen's late husband, Albert, had become common in most comfortable households. But now she instructed Tom to procure a six-foot fir from the traders who brought them in from the mountains to sell by St Audoen's. He brought three big bunches of holly too, and when he had finished the hall and stairs, the parlour and the dining room, were shining with rich green sprigs.

'We're going to have to take Christmas a lot more seriously when this baby arrives,' she told Swallow happily. 'There has to be a place for us to put out the presents, and we'll have to light up the tree with candles on Christmas Eve for him—or her.'

Swallow's mind went back to childhood and Christmas traditions in rural Kildare.

'And it's the youngest one in the house that lights the Christmas candle in the window. He'll have to do that too,' he said, 'or she—of course.'

Maria smiled.

'Things will be so different, Joe. We'll have our own lives and our little one to raise.'

The day after Christmas—Boxing Day to the English but St Stephen's Day to the Irish—was always busy in Grant's. Many employers now gave their workers the day off in addition to Christmas Day, so both bars did a brisk trade from late morning. Swallow put in a short day at Exchange Court. The crime reports from around the city were mercifully few, and he was back at Thomas Street by late afternoon to provide a supportive presence to Maria and the staff.

Shortly before closing time he was surprised to see the portly figure of 'Duck' Boyle enter the select bar in plain clothes, his overcoat and bowler spotted from the light rain that had brought the spell of dry, balmy weather to a close. He pushed his way through the crowded, noisy room to where Swallow stood beside the door that connected to the even noisier public bar. It was his customary sentry point, allowing him to monitor activities in both areas simultaneously.

Boyle had never been in Grant's before, at least not to Swallow's knowledge. Even at a distance he could see the signs of drink. The superintendent's jowly features glowed a mottled red, and he seemed to be having some difficulty maintaining focus.

'Season's greetings, superintendent. It's a pleasant surprise to see you here at Grant's.'

He thought it best to be formal, but not unwelcoming.

'You'll have something ... for the night that's in it?'

Boyle nodded appreciatively.

'I could manage a Power's ... for the night that's in it.'

Swallow nodded to Tom behind the bar.

'Large Power's,' he mouthed.

'Can we talk somewhere quietly for a minute?' Boyle inquired, a pudgy hand reaching for the golden glass proffered from behind the counter by Tom.

Swallow led the way up the stairs to the parlour. Away from the hubbub and smoke of the bar, Boyle seemed to deflate. He lowered himself into an armchair and gulped at his whiskey.

'Somethin' I came across, Swalla'. Information that could be good on yer case. The murder of Nellie Byrne, or Moyles, or whatever she called herself.'

Swallow nodded.

'It'll be very welcome, superintendent, if you have something. What can you tell me?'

Boyle gulped again at his whiskey.

'This is solid, Swalla'. I'm tellin' you. I was down in Mulligan's of Poolbeg Street earlier, at the invitation of certain friends, as you'll understand. It bein' Stephen's Night, there was a fair bit o' drink goin' down. Tongues loosened a bit. An' as you know, I'm skilled at gettin' important information outta otherwise unwillin' subjects. Wan o' the company, I won't say who, told me that Nellie Byrne or Moyles had a bank book, or a post office book, I don't know which, givin' her access to a bit o' money that Ces Downes left behind to her, be way of thanks for lookin' after her in her closin' days. That's why she was killed. Nothin' to do with clients in her trade. Somewan wanted the book. Somewan who knew the story and wanted to get their paws on the cash, believin' they had a claim to it.'

'Jesus,' Swallow exclaimed. 'It'd make sense all right. None of her regular clients was anywhere near the murder scene. And her room was tossed in a complete mess.'

'That's what I'm tellin' ye, Swallow.' Boyle drained the last of his Power's. 'It musta been someone in Ces's organisation. I don't know who. I can only tell ye what I was told tonight.'

190

He eyed his empty glass ruefully. Swallow went to the sideboard and produced a bottle of Tullamore.

'Try this, superintendent.' He poured a generous measure for Boyle and another for himself.

'Good luck.' He raised his glass. 'Fair dues to you. Leave it to me. And here's to the night that's in it.'

Thursday December 27th, 1888

TWENTY-SIX

'I need to have another talk with Charlie Vanucchi, throw everything we have at him, and tell him that unless he can give us the killer of Nellie Byrne, he's in the shit—if you'll pardon my expression, chief.'

Mallon nodded at Swallow's suggestion. Swallow had told him about his conversation with Vanucchi after the girl's funeral in Glasnevin and the intelligence picked up by 'Duck' Boyle about the money she had supposedly inherited from Ces Downes.

'The ladies of the night over in Monto aren't usually good at holding on to money,' Mallon mused. 'God help them; it's hard earned and easily spent.'

'That's true, chief,' Swallow agreed. 'But Nellie Byrne was a bit different. We know that she was associated with some of the Fenian lads. She'd turn up at Land League meetings. Mostly the ladies over there don't give a toss for politics.'

'Fair point,' Mallon conceded.

'She was close to Ces, so she'd have been known to all of Vanucchi's gang going in and out of Ces's house. So which of them might have known that Ces left her a bit of money? That's the question,' Swallow said.

'Boyle's got a dangerously high opinion of himself as a detective, but he isn't often wrong in his information,' Mallon said. 'If he's got a whisper that one of Vanucchi's men killed her, it's likely to be on the mark. So if we take Vanucchi in, what do we have on him to concentrate his mind, so to speak?'

'I wouldn't propose to take him in, at least not now.'

'What then?'

'I'd get more out of him in a quiet conversation with a bit of threat behind it. We tolerate a lot of his carry-on because we get a good flow of information from him. But I can tie him in to a score of burglaries in Rathmines and Rathgar where he fenced the proceeds. I can link him to the gang that robbed Morrison's jeweller's in Exchequer Street in September. I can line him up with a whole series of thefts down on the docks—furs, Scotch whisky, a consignment of Swiss watches bound for a jeweller's in Grafton Street. So I think an informal discussion, if I can use the term, would be likely to concentrate his mind, to use your own phrase.'

'But could you get convictions for him on any of those?'

'With respect, chief, that's beside the point. We might never get enough evidence before a court. But we could shift him out of his rather comfortable living arrangements and have him remanded to Mountjoy Prison for a year while his case is being prepared. He wouldn't like that. Not one little bit.'

'He'd try for bail,' Mallon countered.

'He could. But he wouldn't get it with the character reference I'd put before the judge.'

Mallon smiled.

'I could probably add a few lines to it myself. I agree. So go ahead and do it.'

Swallow stood to go.

'Any follow up from the powers that be after our visit from Major Kelly and his merry men, sir?'

Mallon shook his head.

'Not a word. But I wouldn't expect it over Christmas. The chief secretary and the under-secretary are gone to England and won't be back until next week. Kelly might be gone himself. I think London is home for him. But we haven't heard the last of them, you can be sure.'

'You kept a very cool head with Kelly, if you'll allow me to pay you a compliment, chief,' Swallow said.

'I have to,' Mallon said simply. 'It's open warfare now between us. The English are determined to find some way of taking Parnell down, even if it means bloodshed and mayhem here. They can't understand why people like you and me are reluctant to go along with that.' He sighed. 'So there aren't any marks for past efficiency, or loyalty, or even an acknowledgement that Irishmen might know more about how to manage Ireland's affairs than wealthy blow-ins from Scotland.'

It was a tacit reference to Chief Secretary Balfour, Swallow knew. Balfour's family owned famously rich estates in Scotland. That John Mallon would utter such sentiments, even in private, was a measure of his frustration and anger.

Later that evening a chambermaid from the Dolphin Hotel on Essex Street, a minute's walk from Exchange Court, dropped a plain envelope into the letterbox of Charlie Vanucchi's house in Pimlico. Because she too lived in Pimlico she was an ideal secret courier between Swallow and his informant. The envelope contained a single sheet of paper upon which Swallow had written the letter 'H' and the number '21'. When Charlie Vanucchi read the sheet, he knew that Swallow wanted him to come to Hanrahan's of Stoneybatter at nine o'clock.

When Swallow arrived he found Vanucchi waiting in the public bar at Hanrahan's, impeccably groomed, as usual, and wearing his fine worsted overcoat. He joined him in a casual manner that to any observer would have suggested nothing more than a coincidental encounter.

'Mr Swallow, I didn't expect to meet you here,' Vanucchi called aloud. 'What will you have?'

'A Tullamore would be grand, Charlie.'

'A large Tullamore here,' Vanucchi called to the barman. 'And another large Power's for myself.'

Swallow waited until the drinks were served. He raised his glass to Vanucchi.

'Cheers, Charlie. Your good health.'

Vanucchi raised his glass.

'And yours, Mr Swallow. And a happy New Year to you.'

Swallow came directly to the point.

'We've got good information that someone in your outfit was responsible for the murder of Nellie Byrne, or Helena Moyles as you might know her better, in Chapel Court in November. We know she had money left to her by Ces Downes. Someone went to try to get hold of it. We know it's in a bank book or a post office book. You can probably tell me who that person is.'

Vanucchi sipped at his Power's. His expression seemed to be one of genuine surprise, Swallow reckoned.

'I don't know what you're talking about, Mr Swallow. I told you, Nellie was good to Ces. But I don't know anythin' about money bein' left to her. I swear it.'

Swallow grimaced.

'Well, Charlie, someone took the view that they were entitled to whatever Ces had left behind. So you'd best come up pretty fast with a candidate. I'm under pressure from Chief Mallon to present a result on this. So go and find out. Then let me know.'

Vanucchi shook his head.

'I don't know. I can only do me best, Mr Swallow. But it'll take a bit o' time. If you're tellin' me that one of our lads did for Nellie, I'd be very upset. Angry, like. I wouldn't let it pass. Gimme a couple a days to get to the bottom of it.'

Swallow threw back what remained of his Tullamore.

'Right, Charlie. That's your job now. And let me be very direct with you. In the ordinary course I wouldn't want to inconvenience you. We've been very useful to each other in the past. But I need an answer on this one. And if you don't come up with it, you're going to find yourself quick as a wink in the Bridewell, then into Mountjoy. I can put you down for ten years without the slightest bother at all, Charlie. Are we clear then?'

Vanucchi winced visibly.

'Mr Swallow, you've absolutely no call to start takin' that sort of attitude with me. I'll do what I can. I always do. You know that. But I can't say I'll come back with what you want on this one. Will you give me a couple of weeks?'

Swallow patted the back of the gang leader's hand.

'I'll give you one week, Charlie. And I know you'll do your best with that. I just hope for your own sake that it's good enough now.'

Friday December 28th, 1888

TWENTY-SEVEN

More than once in his career, Swallow would concede, sheer coincidence of events in time, happenstance or good luck, as distinct from good police work, had impacted dramatically upon the course of important investigations.

A wholly fortuitous sighting by an off-duty policeman of the Phoenix Park assassins had given G-Division an early start in their pursuit of the 'Invincibles' in May 1882. Similarly, two years later, a G-man travelling from the North Wall to Liverpool to attend a family funeral had found himself by random chance sharing a third-class cabin with a Fenian gun-runner that Swallow had been pursuing for a year. The man was arrested by Liverpool police once the vessel docked in Merseyside.

Late on the Friday evening, one of those formless, fallow days that run between Christmas and New Year, Swallow made his way through the gloom from Exchange Court to the ABC telegraph office in the Lower Yard. Had he not done so, he later reflected, had he sent a clerk to discharge a routine task, it was likely that he would never have known about the telegram from Berlin.

Earlier he had recounted his conversation with Charlie Vanucchi to Mallon.

'You gave him a week?' Mallon was incredulous.

'Yes, chief. I'd say he genuinely knows nothing. So I think he needs the time.'

'Sounds as if you're going a bit soft, Swallow,' Mallon said.

Swallow could not be sure how seriously the quip was intended to be taken.

Mossop wanted to make good on his promise to young Debbie Dunne that her fishmonger's stand would be protected from predators until she was strong enough to go back to her trade at Misery Hill and Cardiff Lane. Would-be usurpers were to be threatened with prosecution for failure to hold or display street-trading licences unless they allowed her young sister to do business in her place.

'You'd be best advised to have the divisions put out warnings first,' Mallon had counselled. 'If you start issuing summonses without notice there'll be a lot of stink. The beat men will start getting hell from the fish-ladies and God knows what might happen.'

'The plan would be that there wouldn't be any summonses, chief,' Mossop explained. 'It's just a threat. Sure, if we locked up a fraction of the unlicensed street traders in the city there'd be standing room only in Mountjoy and Kilmainham.'

'Even so,' Mallon countered, 'do it by the book. Get a notice out on the routes and let the beat men start issuing the warnings. That way nobody can say we're not playing fair.'

And so it was that on Friday afternoon Swallow spent an hour drafting an instruction in Mallon's name for distribution to all stations on the ABC. It would be included in the daily and nightly charges delivered by the shift sergeants before their sections went out on their beats. All street traders were to be cautioned that their licences needed to be in order and that there would be consequences for any who did not comply with the law's requirements.

He stepped into the telegraph office a few minutes after six o'clock. Reports from all thirty-five police stations across the city were transmitted promptly on the hour, so the room was filled with the chattering noise of printer machines, spewing out details of petty crime, property both stolen and recovered, missing animals and snatches of what was supposed to be criminal intelligence: a known housebreaker seen in a suburban street and a pickpocket spotted boarding a tram that would take him to Sackville Street to ply his trade.

An icy gust came through the door with him. A heavy-set constable, in the act of tearing a sheaf of telegraph paper off a printer, shouted above the din without turning around.

'Shut the bloody door.'

Swallow grinned tolerantly. The men who worked the ABC office were notoriously ill-tempered. Virtually without exception they had been taken off the regular roster and allocated to telegraph duty because they were unfit for outdoor work.

When the constable did turn around, Swallow recognised Pat Cummins, the C-Division constable who had encountered the man running from Chapel Court on the night that Helena Moyles was murdered.

'I didn't know you'd got off the regular, Cummins. When did you start here?'

'Sorry, Inspector, I didn't realise it was yourself,' he began apologetically.

Swallow raised a hand.

'Don't worry about it. I'd say you're glad to be indoors. Diabetes is a tough condition.'

Cummins shrugged resignedly.

'It knocks th' energy outta you. You're no good on the street then. You're only a danger to yerself. But no use complainin'. Dr Lafeyre put in a word with the surgeon at the Kevin Street hospital right away after Nellie Byrne was murdered, and he got me back in here.'

'Got you back? Did you work here before?'

Cummins nodded.

'I've not been well for maybe three years. So I had more than a year of light duties here. Then the surgeon said I was fit for outdoors again. I was only back on the regular a few weeks before that night.'

'Still no name for the fellow you saw at Nellie Byrne's?' Swallow asked.

Cummins shook his head.

'No, sir. Sergeant Mossop took me around all the big stations to see if I could recognise any of the "polismen". Ah, sure maybe it was only in me imagination that I thought I knew him. You know, th'oul diabetes can muddle the thinkin' a bit on top of everythin' else.'

He reefed a sheet of flimsy off one of the clanking telegraph machines.

'Now, what can I do for you, Inspector?'

Swallow handed him the circular he had drafted earlier.

'A routine notice from Chief Mallon. He wants the divisions to start tightening up on street traders' licences.'

Cummins chuckled.

'I'd wish him well. Them ladies don't take too readily to payin' out for that kinda thing. Can't say I blame them. But sure, I'll get it off within the half hour.'

He reached for a wire tray piled with telegraph paper tear-offs.

'By the way, there's an unusual wan in here for G-Division. I suppose you might as well take it back with ye.'

He rummaged in the tray.

'It's down here somewhere. From Berlin no less. Th' English is good though. Near enough word perfect. It's for the attention of the *Kriminalpolizei*. That's you lads, I suppose.'

Swallow nodded.

'I suppose so. Is it anything serious?'

'Not for us, I think. They have an Irish fella in custody there. Name of Carmody. He's up for a serious assault on a chef in a hotel where he's workin' in Berlin. The Berlin police want a check on his background here.'

He pulled a length of flimsy from the pile and handed it to Swallow.

'Here it is. That'll keep wan o' your lads busy for a while.'

For a moment Swallow toyed with the idea of handing the paper back to Cummins with an instruction to put it in the file that would go to the duty officer at G-Division later in the evening anyway. Then he decided that since he had to pass Exchange Court to make his way home to Thomas Street, he might as well take it with him.

He climbed the stairs to his office, and when he had wrapped himself in his overcoat he smoothed the sheet on his desk in order to read the message.

Königliche Schutzmannschaft
Kriminal Directorat
Berlin Waterstraße 11

To

Direktor von Detektiven
Polizei Kriminal
Dublin
Vereinigtes Königreich von Großbritannien und Irland

Herr Direktor,

In the matter of an injurious assault in the Hotel Oslo, the Berlin police hold in its custody a British citizen, Michael James Carmody. Prisoner states to be born in Dublin, United Kingdom in 1865.

Prisoner Carmody has been in Berlin since November. Prisoner by trade is assistant kitchen chef. He states he was employed at Dublin at the Dolphin Hotel and at New Vienna Hotel. States there are no criminal convictions in United Kingdom.

This department would thank you to confirm records for Prisoner Carmody for return quickly please. If necessary fotograph likeness may be sent to you through international postal.

Trusting yours cordially

Johann Pfaus
(Hauptmann/Kapitän)

Swallow read the message a second time with gathering excitement. Michael James Carmody might be spinning a false yarn to the Berlin *Kriminalpolizei*. But if he was telling the truth about working at the New Vienna, there was a gap in the details that Stefan Werner had given to him and Pat Mossop in November. There was no Carmody on the list of employees at his restaurant that he had furnished to G-Division.

And if this Kapitän Pfaus was right about the timing of Carmody's arrival in Berlin, it was just days after the murder of Alice Flannery.

Saturday December 29th, 1888

TWENTY-EIGHT

The Dublin Criminal Registry was housed in two cavernous brick-faced buildings on Great Ship Street, just outside the back gate to the Castle's Lower Yard. Something in excess of 100,000 files had accumulated in its storerooms and corridors over the half-century since its establishment.

The clerk-constable on duty took less than five minutes to locate three files under the name of Michael James Carmody. DCR was acknowledged as a model of its kind, and police forces from across the kingdom had visited Dublin to see and learn from its operation. Latterly it had been organised on the decimal system of library classification, devised more than a decade previously by one Melvil Dewey of New York.

'Take yer pick there, Inspector.' The clerk dropped the three bulky folders onto the counter in front of Swallow. 'There's another score of Carmodys there too. There's a couple of Michael Johns and Michael Josephs. There's even a Michael Marmeduke, if you don't mind. Sure, you know yerself, a lotta them fellas drop names and pick up new ones to suit themselves.'

Swallow knew that too well. It was little more than twenty years since the authorities had introduced the compulsory registration of births. Anyone born before 1836 could change identity more or less at will since there were no central records, and local baptismal records were notoriously unreliable and inadequate. But according to Pfaus's telegram, Michael James Carmody was born in 1865. If he had a criminal record it was less likely that he could succeed in leaving his past behind.

Nor did he. The topmost file showed a birth date of June 2nd 1865 for Michael James Carmody, born at the vast workhouse known as the South Dublin Union, to Mary Anne Carmody, aged eighteen years. Father: unknown. Mother's occupation: none stated. She was probably a street-girl, on the bottom rung of Dublin prostitution. Hardly the best start in life, Swallow reflected, for baby Michael James.

Yet remarkably, he had just two convictions. Petty theft at twelve years of age. And then, at sixteen years, a conviction for assault that drew a sentence of eighteen months' imprisonment at Mountjoy. The file showed his last known address in Dublin as a tenement house in Gardiner Street. His last recorded employment stated him to be a kitchen porter at the Dolphin Hotel, Essex Street, Dublin.

If, as the Berlin police appeared to have been told, Carmody had been employed at the New Vienna in South Great George's Street, it was not recorded in the Criminal Registry. That was not necessarily surprising, Swallow knew. The filing system was superb; information could be retrieved within minutes, but details were frequently out of date. The system could only give out what had at one stage or another been put into it. It was simply impossible to keep every file up to date with the most recent information. The full facts about anyone who figured in the files at DCR almost always had to be established by the time-tested methodology of knocking on doors and asking hard questions.

It was time to put a few of those questions to Stefan Werner.

TWENTY-NINE

The New Vienna was bustling. The lobby's glowing gas lights created an inviting space to welcome diners in from the gloom of the wintry midday. There was a noisy hubbub from the bar. When the doors opened a heavy cloud of cigar smoke wafted into the lobby. Swallow could nearly feel it, like a green film, on his face and hands. It was distinctly unpleasant, sickening almost, but Mossop sniffed it appreciatively. Swallow grinned in spite of his distaste.

'I'd say that Cuban tobacco's a bit out of your price range, Pat. You'll have to stick to the Navy Plug.'

Stefan Werner was not pleased to be called from the dining room to meet the two G-men.

'Gentlemen, may we please be very brief. I have been very co-operative, ver*y gewesen*. You must realise that this is one of the busiest days of the year. Every businessman in the city wants to take lunch with his friends.'

As he spoke, the bar doors swung outwards to disgorge a noisy, already inebriated band of half a dozen gentlemen making their way across to the dining room. Swallow recognised one or two of the florid faces from routine inquiries at banks or businesses around Dame Street.

'Ye've a full house all right,' Mossop observed when they had passed. 'There won't be much work got outta them lads for the rest of the day.'

Werner permitted himself a thin smile.

'It is a tradition in Dublin, as you understand, I'm sure. Men of commerce use the days between Christmas and New Year to engage in a little *Gastfreundschaft*, hospitality, with business acquaintances and friends. For us it is very important business.'

'I don't doubt it,' Swallow said. 'And we won't keep you from it. But something has emerged in routine inquiries that we need to clarify with you.'

'And what is that?'

'The Berlin police have an Irishman in custody on serious charges. He claims to have been an employee of yours.'

Werner shrugged.

'This is possible, I suppose. But why do you tell me this? He is in Berlin. It is a matter for the authorities there.'

'Don't you want to know his name?' Swallow asked.

'Not particularly. But you will tell me, I imagine.'

'Yes,' Swallow said. 'He gives the name of Michael James Carmody. Thirty-three years of age. He claims he worked here at the New Vienna and previously at the Dolphin Hotel.'

'Yes, I believe I remember him,' Werner nodded slowly. 'Carmody. He was here for a short time. He left some weeks ago. He was quite difficult. Quite aggressive. He had difficulties with other employees.'

'Difficulties?'

'He threatened a kitchen porter with a knife. He said he would kill him after they had finished work. The kitchen porter did not want to come back after that.'

'Why didn't you tell us this before?' Swallow asked.

'It didn't seem important. What could it have to do with the matter you came to inquire about? The death of … that poor girl.'

Swallow wondered if Stefan Werner had genuinely forgotten Alice Flannery's name or if he was affecting amnesia.

'It's no trivial thing when one man threatens to kill another, Mr Werner. In fact it's a crime, and a very serious one. And the girl's name was Alice Flannery, by the way.'

'Mr Swallow,' Werner's smile was condescending, 'thank you for reminding me. My lapse of memory was very temporary, I assure you. As to that kind of language, it will be heard every day in a busy kitchen. Nobody takes it literally. Certainly nobody would regard it as a crime.'

Mossop was scribbling in his notebook.

'Did Carmody have any dealings with Alice Flannery?'

'I might have seen them speaking on one or two occasions.'

'Any idea what they might have been speaking about?' Mossop asked.

Werner shook his head.

'Not in the slightest. How could I?'

'But their work wouldn't have required conversation between them?'

'That is probably so,' Werner agreed.

For a moment Swallow thought the restaurateur seemed somewhat distracted.

'Yes, that is so,' he repeated as if something had just occurred to him.

Swallow struck a deliberately grave tone.

'Mr Werner, when I asked you for details of your employees here you did not mention the name of Michael James Carmody. You furnished my colleagues with a list of employees that did not include his name. Yet now you tell me he threatened violence against another member of your staff. That is, in spite of what you say, a crime. And I have to tell you that he has been convicted in the courts for a serious assault. This could have a bearing on a murder inquiry. Your omission may have serious consequences.'

Werner's face darkened.

'I hope you're not threatening me, Detective Inspector. I am, as I say, being co-operative with you, at the expense of my responsibilities here on what you can see is a very busy day. This Carmody had left our employment when you visited me. If I were to give you the names of every kitchen porter and still-room worker who worked here in the past it would be a very long list, I assure you. I gave you a full and complete list of those employed here when Miss Flannery was killed.'

Swallow acknowledged silently that he might have a point. But he was not prepared to concede it.

'With respect, Mr Werner, that doesn't fully address my point. We are investigating the murder of one of your employees. I'm sure you can understand the potential significance in the fact that she worked with a man who has a record of violence.'

'What can I do?' Werner raised his eyebrows in a gesture of helplessness. 'It never occurred to me. I'm sorry.'

He hesitated.

'There is one other matter concerning Carmody,' he said.

'Go on please.'

'He stole some cash, maybe as much as fifty pounds from my office. I found him in here one afternoon. He said he wanted to talk to me about a rise in his wages. Later that evening I realised the money was missing from a drawer in my desk.'

'Did you challenge him, accuse him?' Swallow asked.

'Of course. But he denied it. What was I to do? If I reported it to the police I'd have the likes of you tramping around in here night and day. That would be bad for business. One simply carries the loss as a hazard of business life. And one takes better precautions.'

'Have you any details on Carmody?' Mossop asked. 'Address? Family? Acquaintances?'

'As I explained before, we do not keep records for our casual workers. They come to work, and if they do it satisfactorily I pay them. They don't come to work or they do not work properly, I do not pay them. It is as simple as that.'

The door to the dining room opened and a bald, middle-aged waiter poked his head anxiously into the lobby.

'Yes, Hans,' Werner called to him, 'I'll be with you immediately. These gentlemen will be leaving shortly.'

He made a slight bow to Swallow.

'As you will gather, I am required in the restaurant, Detective Inspector. I'm afraid I cannot help you any further. Please excuse me.'

He turned on his heel and vanished through the frosted-glass door into the noisy mayhem of the restaurant.

Monday December 31st , 1888

THIRTY

'You want to go where?'

John Mallon rose from his chair as if propelled by an unseen, counter-gravitational force.

'Berlin, chief. This fellow Carmody could be our man for the Alice Flannery murder. The only way to be certain is to question him ourselves.'

Mallon came from behind his desk and stood, gazing into the Lower Castle Yard, white in the grip of a heavy frost that would not yield to the weak December sunlight and which was likely to endure until New Year's Day.

'How much?' he asked over his shoulder.

'Boat and train fares about £30,' Swallow told him. 'Kingstown to Holyhead and London. Overnight in London. Dover to Calais and on to Paris. Then Paris to Cologne, overnight on the train. Cologne to Berlin. Another £30 for subsistence for ten nights. £10 for contingencies. I'd say £70 would cover it, chief.'

Mallon turned to face him and grimaced.

'If it was to track some drunken Fenians there'd be no problem. We both know that. You could go to Timbuktu if it was political. But since it's only a waitress from Blackberry Lane, there'll be objections. A G-man skiting off to London and Paris? Oh, they'll make a big thing of that. You'll have to leave it with me, Swallow.'

'Of course, chief. But you might remind the powers that be that this is one of a series of crimes that includes two murders and one attempted murder. There's talk in London that the government might even fall over the Ripper murders.'

'You're reading the wrong newspapers, Swallow,' Mallon answered curtly. 'There's no likelihood of that, although it's more than a little embarrassing for the Home Secretary. Tell me, how'll you manage for language there? You don't speak German, I suppose?'

'No, chief. But this Kapitän Pfaus seems to have enough English to write a fairly long telegram. We'll manage.'

Mallon sighed.

'You can take it that I'll manage the money. Do a minute for Jack Burton outside in my office to let him know the details of when you're travelling. He'll make the bookings and he'll have the cash. You'll need travel documents, a Home Office letter … a passport, as they call it. He'll take care of that too. I suppose you'll have Mossop act up for you on the murders while you're away?'

'He knows most about the files, chief.'

Mallon nodded.

'I agree.'

The unspoken understanding was that in having Pat Mossop undertake an inspector's duties for a few days he would garner an extra pound or two to meet the costs of maintaining his large family.

'And what about Charlie Vanucchi?' Mallon asked. 'You're due to hear back from him on the Ellen Byrne murder. What arrangements will you make to keep the pressure on Charlie?'

'I'll brief Mossop on that too, chief. It's always been understood that when Vanucchi can't reach me for whatever reason, he talks to Pat.'

Mallon nodded unenthusiastically.

'Fair enough. Just make sure that Mossop keeps me informed of any developments.'

'Right, chief. All that will be done. Now, I'll go and do some homework on the train timetables. And I'll have to fix things with the Berlin people so they're prepared to assist.'

Harry Lafeyre had invited Swallow and Maria to ring in the New Year with himself and Lily over dinner at the United Services Club on St Stephen's Green. It was always a good night, and Swallow and Maria had enjoyed Lafeyre's hospitality there on many occasions before.

But by the time he had researched the boat and train timetables and prepared instructions for Mallon's clerk, he was running late. Maria would be anxious, he knew. He had assured her he would be at Thomas Street in plenty of time to change and make sure he was looking he was looking smart.

He was barely in time for the cab that Maria had summoned for half past seven from the stand outside St Catherine's Church. He had hurriedly flung on his suit and run a comb through his hair while Maria sat impatiently in the hallway, her heavy woollen coat wrapped tightly around her in anticipation of the chilly journey to St Stephen's Green.

The warmth of the club was welcoming. Lafeyre was, as usual, a perfectly attentive host, paying particular attention to Maria, ensuring that she was seated comfortably where she could receive the heat from the turf fire in the dining room. The elegant room was filled to capacity with a lively hum of conversation and laughter from the diners while a string quartet played in the background.

'Ever been to Berlin, Harry?' Swallow asked, as the waiter served a steaming turtle soup at the table. Lafeyre sipped approvingly at the accompanying Amontillado.

'Berlin? No. What's your interest in Berlin?'

'I might have to travel there. The Berlin police are holding a likely suspect in the Alice Flannery murder.'

Maria's face clouded with anxiety.

'You never told me anything about this,' she said. 'Nothing at all.'

Swallow grimaced an apology.

'Sorry, I should have. It's not certain, just a possibility. It's up to Mallon. I'm not even sure he can come up with the money.'

'How long would you be gone?'

'Oh, just a matter of days. If it happens.'

Maria's smile was rueful.

'I know you, Joe Swallow. You wouldn't mention it if it wasn't going to happen. You're telling me this gently, aren't you?'

'What's the journey? How long does it take?' Lafeyre intervened, sensing the tension between them.

'London and on to Paris,' Swallow said. 'Then a further train journey through Cologne. That takes about a day. Travel shouldn't be more than two days each way. Then say two days to interview the suspect. I'd be back within the week, give or take a day or two.'

Lily smiled protectively at Maria.

'I'll mind my sister if you're away, Joe. She'll be well looked after. But don't you dally over there. You're needed here.' She laughed. 'And we've all heard stories of the night entertainments in Paris.'

'Oh, you needn't fear,' Swallow grinned. 'I doubt I'd even be allowed to stay a night there. Jack Burton, Mallon's clerk, is a notorious skinflint. He'll pare down costs to the bone.'

At midnight, the quartet played 'Auld Lang Syne'. There was a champagne toast to the New Year. Lafeyre and Lily kissed, as did Swallow and Maria.

When they sat into the cab to travel home, he put his arm around her and drew her closely in so that she could take warmth from him.

'Summer,' she said, as the cab rounded the corner into Grafton Street.

'Summer?'

'Summer. This baby will arrive in July or August, you know. A summer baby. Won't that be wonderful?'

Thursday January 3rd, 1889

THIRTY-ONE

Swallow had never experienced anything like the cold as he disembarked at the Hook of Holland. It penetrated his greatcoat and the heavy tweed suit underneath, chilling his limbs and torso. It seeped through his fleece-lined gloves to numb his fingers. The freezing dry air from the North Sea cut into his face and neck and ears.

There had been no Paris. And he had not stopped in London, hurrying instead by cab from the Holyhead train terminus at Euston to Paddington, from where the night express to Harwich departed. He had been travelling for eighteen hours when he boarded the packet for the Hook. But at least there was a decent dining mess, and he was glad of a hot stew and two pints of ale.

Mallon's clerk, Jack Burton, had been brutally direct when he went to collect his tickets, his travel letters and his cash advance.

'I'm saving the ratepayers nearly two quid on your estimate,' he told Swallow with unconcealed satisfaction. 'I made some inquiries and this way is a lot cheaper. And it's faster, so I'm doing better on accommodation as well. You can forget about Paris and Cologne I'm afraid. It's straight across to the Low Countries, and then a train to Hamburg and another to Berlin. Less than seventy-two hours in all from Dublin. Bloody amazing, when you think about it.'

Swallow was prepared to acknowledge that Burton's research was impressive. He did not particularly care about missing London. He had seen most of the sights a year ago when he had escorted the East End criminal Teddy Shaftoe there on his way to the Tower. But he was disappointed about not going to Paris. The new wonder of modern engineering, Gustave Eiffel's tower, was to open in the springtime, so it was still off limits to visitors. But to view it soaring skywards over the city would have been something.

The train from the Hook to Hamburg was warm at least. Steam pipes carrying heat from the engine were set down low along the carriage walls, favouring passengers seated next to the windows. To his considerable satisfaction, Swallow had persuaded Mallon's parsimonious clerk to place him in first class for this section of the journey, so the seating was comfortable.

There was just one other passenger in the carriage: a man, perhaps in his thirties, with a black moustache, swaddled in a heavy frieze coat with a dark wide-brimmed hat. Swallow reckoned him for a business type, perhaps a commercial traveller, but since he never spoke, declining to respond to Swallow's 'good morning,' he could hazard no guess as to his nationality. As the train rattled and swayed across the darkened flat countryside, he nodded off into a fitful sleep.

At the frontier he was shaken to wakefulness by a diminutive Prussian customs inspector, accompanied by a uniformed and helmeted policeman. Swallow reckoned they both smelled of drink.

'Papers *bitte*.'

He opened the Home Office travel letter with which Mallon's clerk had provided him. He had requested that it should not detail his occupation or the reason for his travel. He held it up to the inspector.

'Ah, Englander. *Auf geschäft*? On business?'

Swallow nodded.

'Yes. On business.'

'Your destination?'

'Berlin.'

The official cocked his head to one side.

'The nature of your business? Your exact destination?'

The tone was hostile. Swallow could smell the alcohol distinctly now.

'I'd rather not say. Private business.'

He could see the inspector's face redden angrily in the dawn light.

'You will answer,' the man barked, jabbing a finger towards his uniformed companion, 'or it becomes a matter for the police.'

'I have shown you my travel letter,' Swallow answered quietly. 'It is quite in order.'

'I will not ask again,' the inspector hissed. The policeman's right hand moved towards his holstered pistol.

Suddenly, the man who had been sitting silently opposite since the train had departed the Hook rose from his seat to place himself between Swallow and the pair.

He thrust a black, leather-covered wallet in front of the inspector's face.

'Ja, das ist eine Sache für die Polizei. Ich bin ein Offizier der Kriminalpolizei.'

Swallow had not understood the language, but it was clear enough what was going on. The inspector took a step back and bowed slightly.

'Apologies, mein herr. *Ich wusste nicht.* I did not realise....'

Swallow's rescuer winked at him under his brimmed hat as the two moved awkwardly to the door, bowing again in unison. He held his hand out, smiling.

'Pfaus. Berlin *Kriminalpolizei.* I'm sorry you were bothered by those two stupid drunks.'

He resumed his seat across the carriage. Swallow could not conceal his surprise.

'You're Pfaus? Then you know who I am.'

'Of course, Mr Joseph Swallow. You may call me Johann. I believe that is not inappropriate given the equivalence in our ranks. Or we can address each other by rank.'

His English was perfect. The accent, Swallow thought, had an American trace.

'Well, Johann, or Kapitän Pfaus, this is a bit of a surprise.'

Pfaus grinned again. He removed his hat and stretched his legs as if he had decided to relax, his identity having been revealed.

'My superiors decided we couldn't have a senior British police officer coming to make a visit without taking care of him on his journey.'

Swallow smiled back.

'So are you travelling with me to protect me or to keep me under observation?'

Pfaus grinned again. He drew a flat pewter flask from the pocket of his greatcoat, unscrewed the top and held it out.

'Here, have some good Prussian schnapps as a welcome. Protection or observation? Both, of course. We can't allow an English detective to wander across the country as he pleases, can we?'

Swallow drank from the flask. The fiery schnapps caught at the back of his throat.

'I'm not English; I'm Irish.'

Pfaus downed a long swallow from the schnapps and handed the flask to Swallow again.

'English, Irish … no difference.' He chuckled. 'My colonel distrusts all foreigners. When he knew that I had invited you to come to Berlin he told me you would be my responsibility. Anyway, you work for the Queen of England, yes?'

'Actually she's the Queen of a united kingdom. Ireland is one of four countries in that kingdom,' Swallow explained patiently. 'She's also Empress of India, although I suppose that isn't very relevant to my business here.'

Pfaus chuckled again as Swallow knocked back another draught of schnapps.

'You could be a spy, my colonel thinks, so I was not to reveal myself any sooner than was necessary. Are you a spy, Mr Swallow?'

Now Swallow grinned.

'I'd be called worse by some of my own countrymen. No, Johann, Kapitän Pfaus, I'm just a policeman trying to solve a brutal crime that took place in my city. And I'm hoping that your … guest, as you call him, Mr Michael James Carmody, the man you told me about in your telegram, might be able to help me.'

'Tell me about the crime.'

'Murder. A young girl of eighteen years named Alice Flannery, beaten to death as she walked home at night from her place of employment two months ago. She was a waitress in a restaurant called the New Vienna. Owned and operated by a countryman of yours, as it happens.'

'You take very seriously the murder of a waitress? Is that usual in your country?'

It was an extraordinary question, Swallow thought. Yet, he realised, the murder of Alice Flannery was not a matter of great import to his own masters in the Upper Yard of Dublin Castle. Perhaps in Germany there was more honesty about what was important and what was not.

'Well,' he answered slowly, 'it may not be important to everyone. But it's important to me and to my colleagues in the police. And it may be linked to other crimes as well.'

'I think I understand,' Pfaus said. 'And this man, Carmody, is he a suspect? He has a record of violence.'

'Let me put it this way … he's not off the list of possible suspects. He left Dublin immediately after the murder. And as I told you, he worked in the same restaurant as the murder victim.'

Pfaus nodded.

'It's far from conclusive, but professionally I'd take the same view. He must at least be a suspect.'

He paused.

'I appreciate that you may not want to share all your information with me since the murder is in your jurisdiction and not mine. But if you can tell me more about these cases I may be able to help you.'

'There's no reason why I shouldn't tell you what I know. You've been generous enough to offer your assistance. Dublin is generally a safe city for women. It's well policed, and it's very rare for any female to be molested or troubled. But there's been a series of attacks in the past two months. Two women are dead, and another has been badly injured.'

'I have heard, of course, about these so-called Ripper murders in London,' Pfaus said. 'They appear to have baffled even the famous detectives of Scotland Yard. I did not realise there were similar cases in other British cities.'

'I'm not suggesting there's any similarity between our cases in Dublin and those in London,' Swallow said. 'Dublin is a very different kind of place from London. And it's not British, like I told you; it's Irish.'

Pfaus shrugged.

'Very well. But you believe there is a link between these attacks in Dublin?'

'We don't know. We haven't got very far in identifying a definite suspect. There are a number of possibilities, but nothing that one could bring a charge on.'

'So where does the *Kriminalpolizei*'s guest, Mr Michael James Carmody, fit into your inquiries?'

Swallow took another shot of Schnapps.

'I don't have any reason to connect him to any crime other than the case I've described, the murder of the young waitress called Alice Flannery. She was the first to be attacked. I've told you her employer is a man who is from Berlin. His name is Stefan Werner. Does that name mean anything to you?'

Pfaus shook his head.

'The name is not familiar to me. Of course, Werner is not an unusual name. There are probably thousands of them in Berlin. What happened to the young woman?'

'She walked home from the restaurant late at night, and some person or persons attacked her in a dark laneway not far from her home. She was badly beaten, but it seems that she fought back as best she could. She was found by two soldiers returning to barracks nearby. They brought her to the hospital, but she died a few hours later. The cause of death was injuries to the head, possibly inflicted by a heavy wooden stake that was found nearby.'

'I presume you're satisfied the soldiers weren't involved?' Pfaus said. 'They'd be on my list of suspects.'

'Naturally it was one of our first lines of inquiry,' Swallow told him. 'But it was clear very quickly that they were telling the truth when they said they came upon her as they returned to their barracks.'

'So is Carmody a suspect? What's his connection?'

'That's what I'm here to find out. We checked out all the listed employees at the New Vienna. There was the possibility that some of her fellow workers might have been involved. Carmody's name was not included in the list of employees given to us by the restaurant. But after I received your telegram I revisited the place and they confirmed that he did in fact work there for a time. He was a troublemaker. He threatened to kill another kitchen worker, and according to Werner he stole money from the office.'

228

Pfaus nodded.

'Ah, I see. I think I understand a little more now. Did the owners of the restaurant tell you why they did not have his name on the list of employees?'

'They said they don't keep details of casual workers. And in reality, it seems, that's the practice in the hotels and restaurants in Dublin.'

Pfaus grinned.

'They wouldn't get away with that in Berlin, I promise you. The German Empire is strong and prosperous. One of the reasons is that our administration systems are very thorough. Your Mr Carmody had to be registered to work. That is how we knew who he is and where he came from.'

'Your intelligence system must be very thorough,' Swallow said.

Pfaus nodded.

'So,' he said, 'will you tell me about the other cases?'

'A young girl of about the same age, in this instance a fishmonger, was attacked and very badly injured in what looks like a similar attack a few nights later in another part of the city, perhaps twenty to thirty minutes' walk from the first crime. She has survived, but she can tell us little beyond saying that her attacker was a big man. Again, we can't identify any motive.'

'And the other crime?' Pfaus asked.

'Somewhat different. A young prostitute was killed in the city centre in her room. A policeman saw a tall, well-built fellow running from the scene. And we may have identified a motive. It seems she had come into possession of some money, and some petty criminals may have known about it. As I said, random violence against women is rare in Dublin, so we're keeping an open mind about possible connections.'

'But you've got no connection for this Carmody to any of these crimes except the murder of the waitress?'

'That's true,' Swallow conceded. 'So tell me, Johann, what sort of man is he?'

'Uneducated but not unintelligent, I would think. I've interrogated him myself. He gives very little away. He doesn't frighten easily. Now it seems he thinks he has some information to trade, so he is, how would you say, a bit cocksure of himself.'

Swallow smiled again.

'Your English is excellent, Kapitän Pfaus. Learned in America, I think?'

'Thank you,' Pfaus nodded. 'Yes, you have a good ear, Detective Inspector Swallow. I was raised in the Bronx, New York City. My wife, Elena, she is American but of German parentage also. My parents had emigrated from Prussia. Then when my father inherited a small business from his uncle, the family returned to Berlin. I was a United States citizen until I became a policeman, when I had to choose to be a German.'

'Do you think you made the right choice in that?' Swallow asked.

Pfaus smiled.

'I understand your question. You English think that your systems of government and law are superior to everywhere else. You think of your police as servants of the community rather than the instrument through which government keeps order. Well, that's just one viewpoint you know.'

He proffered the flask again.

'There's a little left,' he grinned. 'You finish it.'

Swallow drained the last of the schnapps.

'I've already told you. I'm not English. I'm Irish. And the Irish people certainly don't think of the police as the servants of the community, or whatever phrase you've used. They actually are the means by which the government keeps order. If you can call it order. The police are not popular in Ireland.'

Pfaus looked puzzled.

'But in New York all the police are Irish. Sure, they have to deal with troublemakers. But they're respected, and it's considered an honour to have a son or a brother in the police department. In truth, the New York police department wouldn't function without the Irish.'

Swallow smiled ruefully.

'It's a bit more complicated than that in Ireland, Johann. In fact, it's a lot more complicated.'

Friday January 4th, 1889

THIRTY-TWO

It was mid morning by the time they reached Hamburg. Through the windows Swallow saw a dull, dark city with a few thin spires reaching skywards. They switched to the train for Berlin that stood on the next platform at the *bahnhof*, the red-and-black engine belching steam. Frost glistened on the brass plate fastened to the boiler, displaying the imperial arms of the Hohenzollern dynasty.

Pfaus selected seats in a first-class carriage. Swallow's travel arrangements, priced and booked by Mallon's parsimonious clerk, Jack Burton, relegated him to second class for this part of his journey. He could see that the second-class carriages were already crowded, but first class was almost empty. As if sensing his doubt, Pfaus waved a hand airily around the compartment.

'Officers of the *Kriminalpolizei* have the privilege of first-class travel without charge while on duty,' he grinned, 'as do their guests.'

Shortly after the train got under way they went to lunch in the first-class dining carriage. A good ham terrine was followed by veal in pastry. Pfaus ordered a bottle of Riesling, crisp and white, to wash it down. Swallow settled back in the plush banquette seat and watched the countryside roll past the window.

Snow lay here and there, piled in drifts along the railway embankment. The countryside was as flat and featureless as his native Kildare, but the layout of the farmland was different. At home, fields were generally bounded by high ditches. Here, longer and wider strips of land were divided by straight, shallow gullies. The farmhouses were different too. The larger ones were squat and solid with wooden trusses at the gable ends. He thought they lacked the simple Georgian elegance of the two-storeyed dwellings favoured by strong farming families in rural Ireland, but, he reflected, had he been travelling on his own he would have liked to attempt a simple sketch of the structure.

They reached Berlin shortly before five o'clock. Through the frosting windows Swallow could see lines of carriages and cabs, oil lanterns flaring in the early evening darkness, jostling on the cobbled forecourt of the *bahnhof.*

Two uniformed policemen sprang to a perfectly synchronised salute as they emerged past the ticket barrier. One reached to take Swallow's suitcase.

'*Guten Abend, Herr Hauptmann. Ihre Anweisungen bitte.*'

'I have arranged accommodation for you at Hotel Bremen, off Wilhelmstrasse,' Pfaus told Swallow. 'It's a good hotel, and it's just one minute from our headquarters. My men will bring you there now, so you can wash, rest for a while or whatever you wish. Would you like to start your interrogation of the prisoner this evening, or would you prefer to leave it until the morning when you will have slept?'

It would not be clever, Swallow knew, to go straight into an important interrogation directly after a tiring two-day journey. But it might be useful in forming an opinion of his man to see Carmody briefly, perhaps get something of his measure and maybe discomfit him, softening him up for later questioning.

'I'd be glad to freshen up and rest briefly. Perhaps I might see the prisoner then later in the evening. For perhaps half an hour?'

'Very well,' Pfaus nodded. 'I have to report to my superiors, and I shall meet you at the Hotel Bremen, shall we say at seven o'clock this evening in the lobby, and I will take you to our headquarters. Then afterwards perhaps you would do me the honour of having supper with me and my family at our home. My wife does the best Wiener Schnitzel in Berlin.'

That sounded good, Swallow reckoned.

'Thank you, Johann; I'll accept that offer with great pleasure.'

The room on the second floor of the Bremen was small but comfortable, with a high bed on a solid iron frame. But the sheets were fresh linen and the blankets solid, comforting wool. Swallow used the adjacent bathroom with its running water supply to wash the grime of the journey from his body and put on a fresh shirt. He lay down on the narrow bed, closed his eyes and rested until it was time to go downstairs.

Pfaus was on time and waiting in the hotel lobby. He led the way into the street and across two blocks to the main doorway of the Berlin *Kriminalpolizei*, a featureless grey building that might have housed any government department. It was distinguished only by the presence of a uniformed police officer at the door with a spiked helmet and a heavy rifle on his shoulder.

'We have a room with a special one-way window that we can use for your questioning tomorrow,' Pfaus told him as he led the way down steps to the basement and then along a corridor, bright with electrical globes. 'So if you wish I can monitor your interview without the prisoner's knowledge. It can be helpful.'

There were perhaps twenty cells along the corridor. Most of the heavy wooden doors, reinforced with steel spars, were ajar. Swallow could see that the cells were surprisingly spacious and adequately furnished, in contrast with the dungeon-like spaces in which prisoners were held at Exchange Court.

'A quiet night,' Pfaus said ruefully. 'Not too many customers, as you can see.'

He stopped outside one of the few closed doors, drew a brass key from his pocket and inserted it into the lock.

'Your man is in here. I'll be waiting here until you are finished. Leave the door open and call if you need me.'

He turned the key, pushed the door and gestured Swallow to step inside.

The cell was pleasantly warm. The man sitting at the wooden table reading a newspaper looked older than his twenty-four years, but he seemed relaxed. An empty dinner plate with the bones of what looked like a couple of lamb chops lay on the table. He looked up with surprise when Swallow entered.

'Michael James Carmody?' Swallow asked unnecessarily.

The prisoner nodded.

'I'm Carmody. And who are you? You sound Irish?'

Stepping closer, Swallow could see that the newspaper was the *London Daily Sketch*. Carmody was clean-shaven apart from a thin moustache and neatly tended side-locks. He seemed well nourished, and was of average height and build. His hair was dark, oiled and perfectly parted. Michael James Carmody presented himself well, Swallow noted silently.

'You're right. I'm Swallow. Detective Inspector, G-Division at Dublin Castle.'

Carmody's eyes widened. He rose slowly from the chair, dropping the newspaper to the table.

'From Dublin? Are you serious? Did you say your name is Swalla'?'

'Sure. Don't doubt me. Do you want to see my warrant card?'

Carmody shook his head. His expression remained fixed in astonishment.

'No need, mister Swalla'. I'd know a bleedin' G-man anywhere.' He grimaced. 'Sorry. I didn't mean any offence. But what are you doin' here? What d'you want wi' me?'

'Sit down there.'

Swallow gestured to the bunk at the wall. Carmody moved across the cell as Swallow took the vacant chair.

'You're a long way from home, Michael. And you're in a bit of trouble.'

Carmody attempted a weak grin.

'Yeah, you might say that, sir. I was gettin' trouble from wan o' the chef's lads at the Hotel Oslo where I was workin'. He wen' to clock me. So I had to defend meself. It's what any Irishman would do, isn't it? It was pure self-defence. That's God's truth, sir. But these Germans won't believe anythin' I say, and the other lad's tellin' lies.'

Swallow nodded gravely.

'Well, it's not just that, Michael. The fight at work is one thing. I hear you have a habit of fighting with employees in kitchens. But it seems you weren't truthful to the police here about your record. You claimed you had no convictions. They checked with us, and we had to tell them what we

236

had in our files. So now you're in for a long sentence for trying to mislead the police and the courts. It could be ten years before you see daylight.'

Swallow was exaggerating wildly. He hoped that Carmody had no great knowledge of German criminal law.

There was a long silence. The prisoner shifted uneasily on the bunk. He squinted inquisitively at his visitor.

'I don't think it'd be that bad, Mr Swalla'. They might put me away for a bit, but ten years? Nah, I doubt that. So, why are you here?'

Swallow smiled. Michael Carmody was no fool and he didn't frighten easily, even if he was locked up in a foreign police cell.

'I can tell you that I'm here to investigate certain serious crimes in Dublin. But I think I can help you if you're smart enough to help yourself. I need you to think back to when you worked in the New Vienna in Dublin.'

Carmody looked up sharply.

'The New Vienna? The bloody New Vienna? That bastard Werner? What do ye want to know about that place and that bastard?'

'For a start I want to know about the cash you stole from the office there. More than £50 was taken off the desk when you got his back turned, I believe.'

'Me? Steal money from Werner? From his office? You can't be serious. Anyway, there's no witness to anythin'.'

'Don't be so sure,' Swallow bluffed. 'Maybe someone saw you.'

Carmody's eyes narrowed. Swallow knew he had him worried.

'Look,' he said, 'I'm not forgetting about the money. But I want to know about Alice Flannery.'

'What about her?'

'How well did you know her?'

'Not very well. She has notions about herself. All high an' mighty. You know. She wouldn't want anythin' to do with the likes o' me.'

'You were trying to make her sweet on you, weren't you?'

Carmody shrugged.

'She's a pretty thing. A lad can only try his luck.'

Swallow noted Carmody's use of the present tense when referring to Alice Flannery. Either he did not realise she was dead, or he was even smarter than he thought. It was impossible to tell.

'But she wasn't interested.'

'Nah. All she wants is book readin' and the like. Straight away home after work. I asked her to come for a walk down be the canal, and she nearly took me head off. Fiery and all that. That's Miss Flannery for ye.'

'But you wouldn't take no for an answer, Michael. Wasn't that it?'

Carmody shook his head.

'I wasn't goin' to waste me time or go knockin' on a door where I wasn't wanted. I didn't bother.'

He was giving his version of events effortlessly. In all probability, Swallow guessed, the young man was telling the truth. But he decided to press on.

'I don't think that's so, Michael. I think you wanted Alice to be your girl. And when she said no and no again, you decided to punish her.'

'Punish her?' Carmody seemed genuinely puzzled. 'Wha' de ya mean?'

'I mean that you waited for her on the way home from work and killed her. And that's why you cleared off out of Dublin and ended up here.'

Carmody shook his head violently.

'Ah Jesus, no. Are you tellin' me that somewan killed Alice? Sure she wouldn't hurt a fly. Why would anywan want to do tha'?'

Swallow put on his angriest tone.

'Don't give me that sort of bullshit. You know damned well that she's dead. That's why you left Dublin so bloody fast. You weren't happy about being given the push. She put you down, insulted your pride, so you decided to teach her a lesson. Isn't that what happened?'

Carmody made the sign of the cross on himself.

'I swear, Misther Swalla', you're wrong, wrong, wrong entirely. I didn't know about anythin' happenin' to Alice. I went on the batter after leavin' work with the few quid I had. Drank me way aroun' Dublin for the best part of a week, and the next I knew I was on the packet on me way to Liverpool. I have a brother there. I swear it. I'm not proud to say it, but I'm a bit doubtful how I ended up on that boat or who put me there.'

Either he really was telling the truth or he was a world-class actor, Swallow reckoned. A little more pressure might tell him which.

'That's very convenient, Michael. You just got mouldy drunk and you can't remember anything. The judge won't be impressed with that story. He's heard it too often before.'

'No, wait. I can tell ye this,' Carmody wagged a finger. 'It's comin' back. There was bobbies. Two o' them. Two big fellas. They picked me up at Sackville Street, took me to the station for a bit and then they marched me to the North Wall to the boat. I remember that. I remember tellin' them I had a brother in Liverpool and I had the fare in me pocket. He's workin' on the docks there. Got a missus and a child, he has. I kipped in wi' them for a few days, but the missus didn't want me aroun' and I had to go. The brother loaned me the cash to get on through England to come here.'

If it was true that Carmody had been in police custody, even briefly, before leaving Dublin, there was nothing in the DCR file about it, Swallow knew. But that would not necessarily be surprising. Beat men were notoriously careless about paperwork. And what Carmody had described was commonplace in the C-Division around the docks. Young country men, bound for England and hoping to find employment there, frequently fell victim to drink, or the ladies of 'Monto', or both, as they tried to make their way to the steam-packet wharf on the North Wall. If they came to the attention of the police, the simple solution was often to assist them on their way.

'So why come all the way here?' Swallow asked. 'Why not just move down to Birmingham or Manchester or even London? You'd have found work somewhere.'

Carmody shrugged.

'I've got a bit of a wanderin' spirit, Mr Swalla'. I started off for Manchester, sure enough. There's a lotta Irish there too and work in the fact'ries, they say. But I met a German fella on the train. A waiter, he was. He told me there was plenty o' jobs here in Berlin and that speakin' English would be okay. I told him I was workin' in a restaurant in Dublin, an' he said that was what they'd like to hear in Berlin. So I just kept goin'. I'd be lyin' if I told you I paid me fares on the trains to get here. But it's easy enough to dodge the ticket collectors.'

'Okay, so tell me about Alice Flannery.' Swallow softened his tone. 'What kind of girl was she? Who'd want to harm her?'

Carmody smiled weakly.

'You're after givin' me a fair shock tellin' me she's dead, ye know. Ah, she's … was … a lovely girl. Right, she didn't like me and I wasn't gettin' anywhere with her. She was all right. Just a bit full of airs and graces, thinkin' she was better 'n the rest of us workin' there.'

'Did she have any falling out with anyone? Any difficulties?'

'Nah, apart from the accident with the boilin' soup. There was a big pot where the chef used to boil the vegetable soup. It was too heavy. She tried to carry it from the range and she fell. It went all down her leg and burned her. She screamed somethin' terrible. Then after that she started havin' trouble with Werner.'

That explained the disfigurement of Alice's skin that Lafeyre had noted in his post-mortem examination of her body, Swallow noted silently.

'Tell me about that. What happened?'

'She was off work for maybe a month, in and out to the infirmary there on Jervis Street to get the burns dressed and that. Then she comes back to her job. She says she's entitled to have it back. Werner's gone and taken on another girl, someone from the country, and he doesn't want Alice back. He says he doesn't need her and her job is filled. But she says she knows her rights and she's entitled to her job so she's stayin' on.'

'How do you know about this?'

'Well, first they were havin' this argument for all to hear in the kitchen. Then he said she was disturbin' things and he took her to th' office. But sure, when she came out an hour later she said she had the job back an' she told a few of us abou' it. Said she knew her rights and she knew the law. So in th' end Werner gave in. He told her she could stay if didn't make any more mistakes. Like, he was makin' out that it was a mistake, her fault, when the big pot o' boilin' soup kem down on her.'

'So there was trouble between them?'

'Bloody sure. She got back to work, which was what she wanted. But she must have been fierce unhappy at it. He criticised her all the time, makin' out she was doin' things wrong. She told him she was a good worker, and then she said she wanted compensation for th' accident.'

'Compensation?'

Carmody grimaced.

'Yeh. I told her it was a stupid idea. If somethin' happens at work, that's your problem, isn't it?'

'But she didn't agree?'

'Nah, she thought she could get money outta Werner because o' wha' happened.'

'So how did Werner deal with that?'

Carmody shrugged.

'She told me he offered her a few quid to just clear off and go somewhere else. But she said she wouldn't be bought off so easy.'

It was just possible, Swallow reasoned, that Carmody was close to the truth of the matter. Alice Flannery was an assertive young woman, insistent on her rights. If she became an irritant to Werner it might not be beyond the bounds of imagination to think that he could have arranged to have her taken out of circulation. Or perhaps to have her taught a lesson, which then went too far.

He needed time to think, to reflect on what Carmody had told him. He had got far more in this preliminary questioning than he had expected. And he was tired after the journey. Suddenly the idea of a hot meal at Pfaus's home seemed especially attractive. And he needed a good night's sleep. Michael Joseph Carmody would still be here in the morning, when he would be back to question him again.

Carmody spread his hands in a gesture of openness.

'Look, mister Swalla', I don't know what way your mind is goin' here. But I can tell ye again, I got nuthin' to do with Alice Flannery's killin'. Now, if I figure you right, you think that Werner might have done it or got someone to do it for him. I can give you a lot of evidence on the trouble between them. I'll go into the witness box, no bother. But I'll want somethin' in return.'

It was the psychological moment to break off, Swallow reckoned. Carmody had showed his hand. Best now to make no response and to let him sweat.

He stood and banged on the cell door.

'Kapitän Pfaus, can you open the door please? I'm sure it's past your supper time and I'm done here.'

He turned back to Carmody.

'Get a good night's sleep, Michael. I don't know if there's anything I can do for you. But I'll come back tomorrow, very likely. If I don't, sure I might see you back in Dublin in a few years after they let you out of here.'

THIRTY-THREE

The Pfaus family lived in a third-floor apartment just fifteen minutes' walk from the headquarters of the *Kriminalpolizei*. Swallow formed the impression that Berlin was not a big city like London, but perhaps closer in scale to Dublin. The streets were busy with carriages and tramcars. And the coffee houses they passed, well-lit in the gloom of the January evening, seemed full. But there was none of the surging crowdedness he had experienced in London during his visit to New Scotland Yard the previous year.

The apartment was spacious, with wooden block flooring, high ceilings and tall windows giving out onto a quiet street. A delicious aroma of cooking had greeted them as Pfaus led him through the main door into a small vestibule or entrance hallway.

'Elena, my love,' Pfaus laughed as he greeted his wife, kissing her on the forehead. 'This is Detective Inspector Swallow. I have told him about your wonderful cooking, and I promise you he is very hungry.'

Elena was small and dark, with a happy smile. Her well-rounded proportions suggested that she did not just like cooking for the sake of it, but also enjoyed the fruits of her endeavours. She held out a hand in welcome.

'It's very nice to meet you, Mr Swallow. You are an honoured guest in our home.'

Her English had a distinctive American pronunciation.

'I understand from Johann that you are here on police business, so I hope that this evening may be a pleasant distraction for you. Come, sit and have a glass of wine and tell me what it is that brings you to Berlin.'

There was a hint of reprimand in Johann Pfaus's tone.

'Oh, Mr Swallow is investigating a brutal murder case. You have no need to be upset by any details.'

Elena smiled knowingly, but did not answer. Swallow sensed that there were two strong spirits in the Pfaus household.

Three places were set for dinner at a circular table by the window, with good china and heavy crystal glassware, set on a lace-trimmed tablecloth. Pfaus poured them a dry Riesling.

'You have a very nice home, Mrs Pfaus,' Swallow said.

Elena smiled contentedly.

'Thank you, Mr Swallow. We don't have many guests because Johann works so hard. For me it is a very special evening when we have a visitor from England.'

Swallow was not going to bother explaining that he was not from England. But Pfaus anticipated the point.

'Inspector Swallow is not from England but from Ireland, my dear. From Dublin. He has reminded me more than once since we met that the Irish and the English are not the same race. You remember there were many Irish people in New York?'

Swallow thought he detected something close to momentary disappointment in Elena Pfaus's expression.

Before she could respond, two small voices came in unison from behind him.

'Good night, Papa. Good night, Mama.'

He turned to see two little girls, dark-haired like their mother, in their night attire standing in the doorway. Swallow guessed the slightly taller child might be seven, with her sister perhaps two years younger.

'Ah,' Pfaus beamed. 'Meet our two precious jewels, Anna and Louise. They are just on their way to bed.'

He stood from the table and took them, one in each hand, to meet the visitor. They shook hands gravely and said something in German that Swallow could not understand, so he nodded and smiled.

'It's a pleasure to meet you,' he said as warmly as he could. He realised how little he knew about dealing with young children. He had hardly ever spoken to one since his own childhood, other than on special occasions when he brought sweets or perhaps chocolate to Pat

Mossop's brood. He nodded and smiled again and tried to summon the few words of German that he knew.

'*Danke schön … danke schön.*'

The children first giggled, then nodded solemnly and smiled as they backed towards the door to go to their beds.

'Do you have children, Mr Swallow?' Elena Pfaus asked.

'Regrettably, no, Mrs Pfaus. I married rather late in life. Just very recently in fact. But I am happy to say that my wife, Maria, is due to be delivered of our first child later this year.'

'Oh, that is exciting news,' Elena clapped her hands. 'The joy of children is a gift like no other. I am sure you will be an excellent father, Mr Swallow. Your wife is keeping well, I trust?'

'Yes, thank you. She is in good health, and everything appears to be going well. Her doctor is very happy about that.'

Pfaus poured more of the Riesling.

'I recall reading somewhere that Dublin has one of the most advanced maternity hospitals in the world,' Pfaus observed. 'Our maternity services here in Berlin are good, but I believe that Dublin's reputation is unmatched. Curious in a relatively small city.'

'That's true,' Swallow acknowledged. 'The Rotunda Lying-In Hospital is perhaps 150 years old. I'm told that women who give birth there are more likely to be healthy along with their babies than in any other institution in the United Kingdom. Dublin is, as you say, a small city, but it has a strong tradition in medical discovery. I studied medicine myself for a number of years before becoming a policeman.'

His thoughts went momentarily to Maria. Grant's would be starting to get busy with its night-time trade by now. He hoped that she was being prudent, as she promised, resting at this time in the parlour or in the bedroom rather than spending long hours supervising in the bar downstairs.

'That's a rather unusual career path,' Pfaus said. 'Why did you not complete your studies?'

'It's a long story,' Swallow said ruefully. 'Let's just say that I didn't concentrate on them as I should have.'

'Would you have been happy as a doctor?'

'The best answer I can give you is that I don't know,' Swallow said. 'I sometimes regret that I didn't qualify.'

Pfaus did not press the issue. Swallow sensed his understanding that it was best not to probe further.

Elena Pfaus's Wiener Schnitzel was as good as her husband had promised it would be. The veal was thick and tender and the breadcrumb coating was crisp and golden.

'And so, Mr Swallow,' Elena asked, 'what are the fashions in Dublin this year? It must be an elegant city. I am always interested to know about other cities and other countries. Berlin is rather a dull place, you know, especially after New York. And the wife of a police captain is rather constrained in her social life.'

'I'm afraid you're asking the wrong man about fashion,' Swallow laughed. 'As I told you, I'm only recently married myself, so I haven't had much experience with that kind of thing. And the social life of a police inspector in Dublin isn't exactly adventurous either.'

'Dublin is a troubled city, is it not, Inspector?' Pfaus said, slicing into his veal.

'Ireland is a troubled country, Johann,' Swallow answered. 'And the countryside is more troubled than the city. A struggle continues between rich landowners and small tenant farmers who want to have the security of ownership of their farms. And the country's political fate is in the balance. You may know of the Irish parliamentary leader, Charles Stewart Parnell. He is trying to secure Home Rule for Ireland, to give it an independent parliament rather than having it simply represented at Westminster as a region of the United Kingdom.'

Pfaus laughed quietly.

'That's an ironic contrast with Germany. Almost twenty years ago the peoples of these states of central Europe united to form the German Empire, centred here in Prussia. Our great statesman Prince Otto Von Bismarck saw that the future lies in unity. And of course, the United States is the great example of strength through unity. How curious that your Mr Parnell sees a future in separateness. So where do you stand on that issue, Joseph?'

'Policemen are not allowed to take part in politics in my country, Johann,' Swallow said cautiously. 'We enforce the law as best we can.'

Pfaus grinned.

'Ah, yes. It's the same in Germany. But it doesn't prevent one having views, does it?'

'No,' Swallow admitted. 'I don't mind saying that I would like to see Parnell succeed in his objective. Ireland is a different country from England. It has a different culture, a different language, even though I must confess I don't speak the Irish language. And I believe if Mr Parnell doesn't succeed, people who are prepared to resort to violence will take over the argument. I'd also like to see the land of Ireland belong to the ordinary farming people, not to landowners who live in another country on the rents they extract from their tenants.'

'I know that women are not supposed to be involved in political issues,' Elena said quietly, laying her knife and fork on her plate, 'but if the Irish are a different race from the English I think it makes perfect sense for them to be allowed to have their own parliament and to own the land their ancestors held.'

'That is an argument, my dear, that appeals to emotions,' Pfaus said.

Swallow detected a hint of irritation in his voice.

'Prince Bismarck's vision is based on reason, and it has been proven,' Pfaus went on. 'There is strength and prosperity in unity. Look at the great advantages that the people of Germany have now compared to how it was in their parents' day. There is universal education, good hospitals for all, pensions for the elderly, support for the infirm and even legal protections for those who suffer injury in the course of employment.'

Elena shrugged.

'Yes, I understand that people now are much better off. But there are other things that make people happy too.'

'Consider the conditions in which we live here,' Pfaus resumed enthusiastically. 'You see no fire in this apartment, Joseph, yet it is beautifully warm, is it not, on this cold January night?'

Swallow had been aware of the pleasant, even temperature of the apartment from the moment he had arrived.

'Yes, indeed.'

'Central heating,' Pfaus said. 'Many of the new buildings in the city have it. Coal from the Ruhr is burned in the basement furnace, driving heated water through the whole system.'

When they had finished their Wiener Schnitzel, Elena served a fruit tart with a warm raspberry syrup. Then she excused herself from the table.

'I'm going to retire to allow you gentlemen to converse. Good night, Mr Swallow. It's been a great pleasure to meet you.'

Swallow noted that as the evening had progressed, Elena Pfaus's American pronunciation had become more accentuated. He had the sense that she was more than a little happy to connect to things that brought her back to the life she had left behind in the United States.

He stood and shook her hand politely.

'Thank you, Mrs Pfaus, for a fine dinner and lovely company. Good night.'

Pfaus poured a peach brandy for each of them when Elena had gone. Then he opened a small wooden box, decorated with images of fierce-looking military men in helmets with impressive moustaches. Swallow declined the offered cigar.

'So,' Pfaus said, striking a match and drawing deeply on his own cigar, 'tell me what progress you made with our young Mr Carmody.'

Swallow sipped at the peach brandy. It was sticky and too sweet for his taste.

'He says he had nothing to do with the murder. And I'm inclined to believe him. He'd have liked to develop some romantic interest with the girl, but she rejected him, he says. I think he could be a helpful witness about the circumstances leading to the death, and he wants to do a deal with me.'

'What sort of deal?'

'I didn't want to start negotiations with him tonight. Better to let him sweat for a bit. But I imagine he'll want to be freed from any charges here and allowed to go free in return for his assistance.'

Pfaus shrugged.

'That's not a problem as far as the *Kriminalpolizei* are concerned, Joseph. We don't want him here. He's costing the German Empire money, so you're welcome to have him if you think he can be of help to you.'

Swallow sipped again at the peach brandy. It was definitely too sweet for his taste, but he felt he might give offence if he left it unfinished.

'I think he can, Johann. You mentioned something earlier that might actually have a bearing on this case. Tell me more about the law here in Germany about compensation for people who are injured at work.'

Pfaus tilted his head to blow cigar smoke towards the ceiling and smiled. Swallow saw something between smugness and pride in his host's expression.

'Ah, yes. It is a very advanced measure, one of many that reflect the personal thinking of Chancellor Prince Von Bismarck. He devised this particular piece of legislation himself for Prussia, and now it applies across the empire. Essentially, it means that if anyone is injured in the course of their employment, and if it can be shown that this is due to some neglect or failure to provide safe conditions, then the employer is obliged to compensate them.'

'Are there many cases in which this has happened?' Swallow asked.

Pfaus rapped on the table to emphasise his point.

'That is the very success of the measure. Because employers know that they can face financial penalties, factories and other places of employment are now much safer. The numbers of accidents have come down, even in dangerous work like mining and heavy industry. It means work for the city police forces, of course: they have to inspect factories and other premises to ensure that there are safety measure in place.'

He threw back the last of his peach brandy. Swallow did likewise. He was grateful that Pfaus did not offer a refill.

'In fact,' Pfaus said, 'I read in the newspaper recently that the increases in our industrial output have more than met the additional costs of policing and inspection. So the exchequer and the empire are actually better off as a result.'

He blew more smoke to the ceiling and smiled again. Definitely smugness this time, Swallow reckoned.

'I understand the concept may be difficult for you to grasp, Joseph. Industry in England does not think progressively as it does here.'

Swallow resisted the temptation of yet again explaining that Ireland was not England. But it would have been beside the point. No such provisions had even been thought of in Ireland or England, as far as he knew.

'Perhaps you are right, Johann. But what I'm interested to know is if this compensation scheme would apply to someone who is injured while working in a restaurant?'

'Of course. One or two of the earliest cases involved accidents in hotels and restaurants here in Berlin. A kitchen worker lost an arm in a machine used for grinding meat at one of Berlin's finest hotels. There should have been a protective shield, but it had been removed for some reason. He was unable to work again. So the hotel had to pay his medical costs and give him a lot of money. I think it was the equivalent of a year's wages.'

Swallow felt the surge of energy that he always experienced when the elements of a mystery started to come together to form a coherent picture. The evasive arrogance of Stefan Werner on the two occasions when he had questioned him at the New Vienna now started to make sense. What Pfaus had just told him fitted in with what he had learned earlier in the cell from Michael James Carmody. His every instinct as a detective, developed over more than twenty years probing the criminal mind, was telling him that Werner was the man who had ended Alice Flannery's life.

'I think perhaps, Johann,' he said cautiously, 'that even though we don't have these laws in Ireland or England, Mr Werner didn't realise that. When Alice Flannery was injured in the kitchens of the New Vienna he may have seen himself facing an action for damages.'

Pfaus frowned.

'Are you saying this man murdered the young woman, or had somebody murder her, simply to avoid an injury claim?'

'Murders have been committed with much less compelling motives, Johann. You know that as a policeman.'

Pfaus shook his head in disbelief.

'Most of my work has been on political crime. My experience with criminal investigation of this kind has been very limited. I have difficulty with the idea that a young woman's life can be taken so lightly. But I defer to your knowledge.'

'There is some information that might make my theory stronger,' Swallow said. 'Could I ask you to have someone make an inquiry for me?'

Pfaus nodded.

'If it relates to this crime in any way, it is perfectly in order for the *Kriminalpolizei* to inquire into any matter. What do you need to know?'

'I need to know about this man, Stefan Werner, who owns the New Vienna restaurant. He is a native of Berlin, or so he says. He claims that his family is well known in the restaurant business here. And he says he worked as a restaurant manager in London. He knows his business, and I imagine that he would have been well established in it here before he went to Dublin. I want to know what he did here, where he worked and when. And anything else that might be significant about his past.'

Pfaus had taken a small notebook from his pocket, and scribbled the details as Swallow spoke.

'Werner. Stefan Werner. The name does not mean anything to me. On a police captain's pay I am not a frequent patron of Berlin's expensive restaurants or hotels. But by tomorrow afternoon, Joseph, you will know everything that is known to the Berlin police about this Mr Werner.'

Saturday January 5th, 1889

THIRTY-FOUR

Swallow decided on a lie-in in the morning. The Bremen Hotel served breakfast from seven o'clock to half past eight, but he was well fed from Elena Pfaus's dinner of the night before. So he luxuriated in his warm bed until after nine. Then he rose, washed, shaved and dressed.

It would be midday before Pfaus would have collated whatever intelligence there might be in the files on Stefan Werner. It might yield something that could offer a line of approach in his resumed questioning of Carmody at the *Kriminalpolizei* headquarters. So he decided he would defer that task until the afternoon and spend the morning sightseeing.

The day was sharp and dry, with the sky a clear blue canopy over the German capital. Hard snow was compacted where the pavements met the walls of the buildings. But the walkways were swept clear and well gritted, offering the pedestrian a better foothold. He took coffee, a bread roll with butter and some spicy sausage at a café close by the hotel, and set off towards the government quarter. The official buildings were not particularly remarkable and seemed rather austere and functional compared to London or Dublin. But Bismarck's new parliament building, the *Reichstag*, still under construction, was already impressive.

Pfaus had told him how to find the Imperial Art Gallery, just a short walk from the *Reichstag*. Remarkably, and to his delight, they had guidebooks available at the entrance in several languages, including English. But the collections were a disappointment. Not surprisingly, the work of the German school predominated. He advanced through long galleries hung with gloomy portraits of princes, bishops and sour Teutonic ladies, sometimes with fat children by their side. But the Italian, French and English collections were quite limited. The Italian displays at Foulks's national gallery in Dublin were far richer and more varied. Only the sense that he should not waste an opportunity that would be unlikely to come again kept him moving through the poorly lit rooms.

He was relieved when his watch told him it was almost noon and time to rendezvous with Pfaus. He was familiar with the streets now, and he walked briskly to the offices of the *Kriminalpolizei*.

Pfaus was waiting for him with the satisfied look of a man who has discovered something he believes to be significant.

'Now, Joseph,' he grinned, 'you will be able to tell your superiors in Dublin of the efficiency of the policing system of Berlin, of Germany, indeed.'

He turned the cover on the green cardboard file that sat before him on his desk.

'Here we have the details of one Wilhelm Stefan Werner, born on 6 November 1845, now aged forty-four years. His place of birth is stated to be Hamburg. His father's occupation is given as "restaurant porter". But far from having any great success or reputation in the restaurant business here in Berlin, we find young Wilhelm Stefan at twenty years of age following in his father's footsteps and working also as a restaurant porter here in the Hotel Imperial in Freidrichstrasse.

'Now,' he flicked to the next page of the file, 'nothing wrong with that. Honest work, you might think. But this is where it starts to get interesting.'

Swallow could see that Pfaus was relishing his role as narrator of whatever drama was about to unfold.

'He has a few offences on the record committed in Hamburg. Two charges of assault, one serious, on a street girl near the port. She died a few days later, probably as a result of the beating he gave her. But the post-mortem showed she had liver disease and a bad heart, and there was not enough evidence upon which to mount a charge of murder. He did a year in prison. Then another assault on a police officer. He spent a month in jail for that. Then he moved to Berlin and somehow got a job at the Imperial, apparently helping to manage supplies coming into the kitchens. Then in February 1879 the manager of the hotel lodges a complaint with the *Kriminalpolizei*, alleging that Werner, along with another employee, had been systematically defrauding the place over three years, charging for goods that had never been supplied and lodging the proceeds in a false bank account.'

'If they had a free run for three years, they must have creamed off a bit of money,' Swallow ventured.

'Indeed. They got away with an amount that might equate to several hundred of your British pounds.'

Swallow did not attempt to conceal his incredulity.

'What do you mean "got away with"? Are you saying they didn't get jail?'

'That's precisely what I'm saying, Joseph. They were never charged. The owners of the hotel had already decided it was time to sell out. They had agreed a price with new investors, underwritten by one of Berlin's leading banks. They didn't want any scandal around the running of the business. In fact, they gave Wilhelm Stefan Werner a fine letter of commendation to his new prospective employers in London.'

'Do I have to guess?' Swallow asked. 'The Savoy Hotel in the Strand?'

Pfaus grinned.

'Indeed. And he did very well there. He was not the restaurant manager, but he rose to be a senior waiter. It was probably not too difficult from that to pass himself off in Dublin as being more accomplished in his trade. So it seems that the respectable Herr Werner who moved from London to establish his fine restaurant in your city is not everything he seems or claims to be. He's able to pass himself off in the restaurant trade, but he's also got a record for violent crime. He's a thief. A very successful one. A skilled fraudster. And, it seems, not just a career criminal but a very clever man.'

It was as if something like a child's jigsaw had been rearranged and fallen into place in Swallow's head. Carmody was less likely to be Alice Flannery's murderer than a potential witness. Werner was the more likely perpetrator of the crime. He had motive, means and opportunity. And he was no stranger to violence.

'I think, Johann, that I'll need to take a formal statement from Carmody. His price will be that you release him. I'll take him off your hands and bring him back to Dublin. Would you be willing to witness and countersign his statement this afternoon? I'd like to depart as soon as possible.'

'Happy to do that, Joseph. But first we'll have lunch. You haven't experienced the delights of the *Kriminalpolizei* canteen.'

They lunched on the canteen dish of the day, thick stew, washed down with Bavarian Hofbräu. The stew was good, with hot spices and cubed chunks of lean meat. The beer was sharp and zesty.

'It's called goulash,' Pfaus said. 'The Hungarians make it with beef, or whatever they can get, but the canteen cook is Austrian, so he uses veal.'

Swallow's eyes watered as the spices hit his palate. Pfaus chuckled.

'That's paprika pepper. Very cleansing.'

Swallow took a mouthful of Hofbräu to quench the fire in his throat.

'So,' Pfaus said, forking veal into his mouth, 'you believe you are moving closer to solving one of your murders. But there have been other crimes, as you told me. Do you still believe they are connected?'

'I don't know,' Swallow answered. 'If your countryman Stefan Werner is responsible for the death of Alice Flannery, I can't see how or why he'd have any involvement in the other cases.'

'Then that is good news,' Pfaus said. 'You're not dealing with what our English colleagues refer to as a multiple or mass killer; your murders are separate, individual crimes.'

Swallow shrugged.

'You're probably right. I don't have all the answers my superiors would like to have. Maybe I can just clear up one problem at a time.'

Pfaus nodded.

'That's what we do as policemen, Joseph. We can't put the world to rights, much as we'd want to. We learn that, even if we're good at what we do, we can solve only one small problem at a time. That's why policemen don't get into the history books but soldiers do. Maybe that's unfair. But if you can bring the guilty person to account for the violence you have described in this case it will be work well done.'

They finished their goulash, drained the last of the Hofbräu, and made their way to the custody cells in the basement of the *Kriminalpolizei*. Pfaus collected foolscap paper, inkwell and pen as they passed his office on the ground floor.

Carmody was finishing his own midday meal, seated at the deal table in his cell. Swallow noted that he was dining on the same fare that he had just consumed in the canteen upstairs, including a tankard of beer. Not bad, he thought.

Pfaus smiled coldly at the prisoner.

'I hope you enjoyed your refreshments, Mr Carmody. Because when you are transferred to the state prison shortly you will find that the standard of the food is very different. You are in police custody here with all the privileges and comforts it offers. Prison is another story.'

Carmody glanced nervously at Swallow.

'I gave you the information you needed, Mr Swallow, didn't I? You told me I'd not be stoppin' here. We had a deal, hadn't we?'

'Not exactly,' Swallow said. 'I didn't promise you anything. I want you to repeat what you told me in a formal statement. I'm going to write it down and you're going to sign it, and Kapitän Pfaus here is going to witness it. Then if it's satisfactory and complete, and if it's helpful, I'll see about you going back to Dublin with me.'

'An' I'll be a free man ... if I do that?'

'No. You'll be charged with theft of money from the New Vienna restaurant and lodged in Mountjoy on remand. You'll give your evidence in court in Stefan Werner's trial for the murder of Alice Flannery. When that's over, you'll be released. You'll do six months, a year at most.'

Carmody pushed the tankard away and stared at the ground.

'Can I trust you, Mr Swallow?'

'You haven't much choice, Carmody,' Pfaus said sharply. 'You're here in comfort because Inspector Swallow asked me not to have you taken off to the state prison. So either you co-operate with him as he wishes, or you're on your way to a penal institution and for a long time. I don't give a damn where you go as long as you're out of our cells here.'

'Your choice, Michael,' Swallow said quietly. 'Just don't waste my time. There's an evening train I'm going to catch, either on my own or with you. Make your mind up.'

Carmody grinned mirthlessly.

'Like this bloody sausage-eater says, I don't have much bloody choice do I?'

He shot a glare at Pfaus.

'All right, Inspector. Lay out yer writin' paper. I'll make me statement, like you want.'

The hammering on the cell door was hard and urgent.

Carmody had just signed the fourth and final sheet of his four-page witness statement. Swallow signed as chief witness and handed the steel pen to Pfaus for his countersignature.

The statement had been remarkably coherent, Swallow reflected. He guessed that Carmody had rehearsed it well in his head during the night and in the hours before he and Pfaus had returned to the cell. It set out succinctly what Carmody claimed to have seen and heard after Alice Flannery sustained her injuries in the kitchen of the New Vienna restaurant a year previously. It described Stefan Werner's anger. It recounted her conversation with Carmody in which she spoke of her intention to take Werner to law in order to secure compensation. Perhaps most significantly of all, Swallow estimated, it recounted Werner asking Alice for her home address and his departure from the restaurant almost immediately after she had finished work.

The witness had required a little prompting here and there, but not much. Swallow was careful to allow Carmody's bad grammar to stand so the statement spoke the words of an uneducated man rather than a stenographer concerned with making the right impression in court. When Michael Carmody would give evidence in the Dublin Criminal Court, his statement and his evidence would complement each other.

'If he is returning to Dublin as a witness, that makes things very simple,' Pfaus had said earlier. 'There is no need to have any extradition warrant if he is going with you voluntarily. What happens when you return to your own jurisdiction is not of concern to us. If he is then charged with a crime, what is the German Empire to do about that?'

'Apologies, Kapitän Pfaus, I have an important message.'

The uniformed officer who had hammered on the door now hovered on the threshold. Pfaus crossed the cell and stepped out into the corridor, closing the door behind him. When he stepped in again, perhaps a minute later, Swallow knew instantly by his expression that something was terribly wrong.

THIRTY-FIVE

The train journey through the dark of the freezing Prussian night was like a bad dream from which there was no escape. Swallow sat, transfixed, staring through the window into the blackness that hurtled by, broken occasionally by showers of orange sparks from the locomotive.

Sitting opposite him in the carriage, Michael Carmody slumbered uneasily beside the impassive, helmeted policeman whose left wrist was chained to his right. Even if he was returning to Dublin voluntarily and as a witness, neither Swallow nor Pfaus were taking any chances that he might simply vanish off the train at some point on the journey.

There would be a railway police escort at the Hamburg *Hauptbahnhof* to see them onto the train for the Hook of Holland. A Dutch escort would take over at the border, Pfaus had explained, and would accompany them as the packet crossed the North Sea to Harwich.

Half a dozen times, as the train plunged through the darkness, Swallow reread the telegram in the weak light, as if somehow he might discover a different, more hopeful interpretation of its stark, ungrammatical wording.

MARIA ADMITTED ROTUNDA
+ CONDITION SERIOUS
+ ESSENTIAL RETURN IMMEDIATELY
+ LAFEYRE

What could possibly have gone wrong, he asked himself repeatedly. Maria was in the Rotunda Lying-In Hospital. That had to mean there was some problem with the baby. Or with Maria. But the specialist at the hospital had said that everything was in order, Maria was healthy, and he could hear the baby's heart in his stethoscope. 'Condition serious', Lafeyre had said. What did that mean? Did 'serious' imply a threat to her life? Or the baby's? Or both? It had to be grave. He would not be recalled from an important investigation for any trivial reason. The only word in the telegram from which he could take comfort was the signoff: 'Lafeyre'. With Harry engaged, Swallow knew, Maria would get the best possible care and attention.

Pfaus had hurriedly arranged transport from the *Kriminalpolizei* building when Swallow, now ashen-faced, had handed him the opened telegram in Carmody's cell. The police sidecar had sped to the Berlin *Hauptbahnhof* to catch the next train for Hamburg.

'I shall telegraph your Doctor Lafeyre in Dublin, Joseph,' Pfaus assured Swallow as he climbed aboard the sidecar. 'I'll try to find out what I can and communicate what I learn to my colleagues at Hamburg. When you change trains, be sure to check if there is a message from *Kriminalpolizei* Berlin.'

But there was no message at Hamburg. The railway policeman shrugged and offered a puzzled apology when the escorting officer queried him. And there was no message at the police post on the wharf at the Hook of Holland. But there were two Dutch police officers to take custody of Swallow's prisoner from the Prussians.

It was dawn when the packet sailed from the Hook into a calm, sunless sea. A mile from the Dutch coast the vessel was enveloped in a freezing yellow fog that persisted throughout the twelve-hour crossing. The policemen took turns guarding Carmody in a cabin on the upper deck. After a couple of drinks in the miserable saloon bar, Swallow retired to his own cabin. But sleep was impossible. He tossed and turned, marking every hour with his watch. When he rose to have supper in the ship's dining room, the darkness of the January evening had already blacked out whatever visibility there had been. And when the captain eased the vessel alongside the quay at Harwich, even the strong carbide marker lights were hardly visible through the gloom.

Two uniformed constables of the Essex Constabulary stood, faintly illuminated below the gangway, to take Carmody into custody from the Dutchmen. Frost gleamed on their helmets and greatcoats. A man in plain clothes standing beside them nodded to Swallow as he stepped ashore. He extended a hand in greeting.

'Essex CID. Detective Inspector Swallow?'

Swallow nodded.

'Yes. Have you information for me?'

The detective handed him an envelope stamped with the royal crest. 'There's a telegram here for you from Dublin. Two, in fact. You'd best read them yourself. Come into the waiting room. It's warm and there's good lighting. You've half an hour before the London train.'

A warming coal fire glowed in the waiting room. Swallow opened the first telegram. The transmission address was 'POLICEDUBLIN'.

PFAUS DETAILS OF FLANNERY INQUIRY TO HAND
+COMPLIMENTS
+REGRETS FAMILY NEWS
+CONFIRMING COMPASSIONATE LEAVE
+MALLON

It was if something hard, metallic almost, had clutched his heart. Compassionate leave was rare in G-Division. John Mallon's resources were stretched to the degree that he needed every G-man he could have on duty and available at all times.

He tore hurriedly at the second telegram. It bore the transmission stamp of the General Post Office in Sackville Street. It was dated twenty-four hours previously. He glanced at the sender's name. It was Lafeyre.

MARIA STABLE
+HOSPITAL DOING ALL POSSIBLE OTHERWISE
+NEXT 48 HOURS IMPORTANT
+ROTUNDA IMMEDIATELY YOU ARRIVE
+LAFEYRE

Stable is good, he told himself. Stable means Maria is alive. Stable means that even if she is ill, she isn't getting any worse. Lafeyre used medical terms precisely, so words meant what they said. But 'doing all possible otherwise'? That had to refer to the unborn baby. 'All possible' did not read well. 'All possible' was a medical term too. It was an excuse. It meant that something or some things could not be done. But surely in a hospital like the Rotunda, with its surgeons and doctors, with its skills and reputation, anything was possible? Within reason.

But what had happened? Why in the name of Jesus could Lafeyre not have told him straight out what had gone wrong? As far as he knew he had left a perfectly healthy wife less than a week earlier when he departed for Berlin. What was being kept from him?

He parsed and analysed the telegram over and again as the night train chugged slowly on the two-hour journey from Harwich to its London terminus at Liverpool Street. The two Essex constables, he learned, were regulars on escort duty, bringing prisoners from the North Sea port to the capital. They dozed with Carmody seated between them, one or the other opening a lazy eye to mutter the name of a station to his companion as the train slowed, marking their slow progress across the darkened countryside.

At Liverpool Street the uniformed Essex men handed their prisoner over to the three Scotland Yard CID officers waiting on the platform. Swallow recognised one of them from a visit to London a year ago when he investigated the murder of pawnbroker Ambrose Pollock at Lamb Alley in the Dublin Liberties. It took him only a moment to recall his name. It was Montgomery. Special Irish Branch. Family background in Donegal.

The CID man stepped forward, unsmiling.

'Sorry to meet you again in these circumstances, Swallow.'

He held out a hand.

'I gather the doctors in Dublin have done their best.'

Swallow wanted to shout at the man, but he forced himself to be very calm.

'Thank you. Your men are in order there with my prisoner?'

The other two CID men had already handcuffed Carmody between them.

'Of course. We've a car outside to take us to Euston. The boat train leaves there at midnight. The escort will travel with you to Holyhead and cross with you to Kingstown.'

He nodded to the platform clock.

'You'll be in good time.'

'Look,' Swallow took him by the arm, stepping aside from the others, 'I need someone to tell me what's happened to my wife. All I've got since I left Berlin thirty-six hours ago is evasion and silence. Can you tell me what's going on?'

Montgomery grimaced sympathetically.

'I'm sorry. I just know there was some sort of incident. An accident … I don't know much more than that. Your wife was injured. But as far as I know she's not in any mortal danger….' He stammered. 'I … I … just don't know any more….'

'An incident? Or an accident?' Swallow heard himself raising his voice. 'So which was it? Where was it?'

Montgomery spread his hands, palms downward, in a calming gesture.

'Please, Swallow. If I knew more, I'd tell you more. Your own people will know more, I'm sure.'

He gestured towards the barrier at the end of the platform.

'Come on. Let me get you to the car. You've a long journey ahead.'

Monday January 7th, 1889

THIRTY-SIX

He could see Harry Lafeyre in the morning half-light as the steam packet edged into the wharf at Kingstown. The city medical examiner stood where the gangway would be run out from the passenger shed once the vessel was docked. Swallow silently cursed the time lost to the captain's caution, his engines at near standstill, slowly closing the last few feet to the wall.

Pat Mossop was there too, his slight frame lost in his greatcoat, his chin tucked down into its heavy folds against the morning chill. Even from where he stood on the deck he could see that they both looked serious and strained. Two other G-men stood behind Mossop, waiting to take Michael Carmody into custody from his Scotland Yard escort. Their instructions were to charge him with larceny from the New Vienna and to convey him to Mountjoy Prison.

The vessel's hull bumped against the wharf. Heavy ropes were thrown out and looped around the steel bollards to make it fast against the wall. The gangway was rattled out on noisy iron wheels. Swallow was the first person off the vessel.

Lafeyre stepped forwards to grasp his hand. He gestured silently to the harbour offices behind. When he did speak, his tone was slow and measured.

'Maria will be fine, Joe. I'm going to take you to her shortly in the hospital and you'll see that for yourself.'

The harbourmaster had made a small anteroom available to them beside his office. A coal fire burned in the grate, and there was a steaming urn of tea on the table. Mossop poured three full mugs. Swallow was silent.

'Unfortunately, she lost the baby. The haemorrhage was very heavy,' Lafeyre said, using the same deliberate, slow delivery. 'Do you understand what I'm saying, Joe?'

'Yes. I understand,' Swallow snapped. 'I've understood what you're telling me pretty well for two days and two nights now. But nobody's told me what happened.'

Mossop cleared his throat.

'I'll explain, boss. But first I have a message—it's an order—from Mr Mallon. When I tell you about this, you're not to take any action on your own. Once you've seen your missus you're to go straight to the Castle. He'll be waiting for you.'

He glanced nervously at Lafeyre. Swallow saw Lafeyre nod.

'Well this is how it happened, boss. You were gone away on the Monday just after New Year. The week was quiet. Nothing out of the ordinary. Then Friday morning, just after eight o'clock or so, Martin Shanahan was duty man at Exchange Court and in comes Carrie, the cook from your missus's place. She's in a hysterical state, saying that Maria—your missus—has had an accident above in the house and they wouldn't let her get the doctor.'

'They?' Swallow said sharply. 'Who are we talking about?'

'Well, that's the point, boss,' Mossop grimaced. 'That … bastard Kelly … Major Kelly and his gang arrived an hour earlier with a warrant to search the public house and your private quarters, looking for the protection logs that you were supposed to find for them.'

Swallow felt his rage start to spill over.

'What are you telling me?' He realised he was shouting. 'Are you saying that Kelly got a warrant to raid my house, Maria's house, while I wasn't there? Is that what happened to her?'

Mossop's face contorted.

'I'm sorry, boss. That's the truth of it.'

'Jesus,' Swallow exclaimed. 'Was there nobody there from G-Division to look after my wife? Didn't anybody try to stop them? We're supposed to be the police, the bloody detective division, aren't we? Aren't we supposed to look out for each other?'

'I understand.... I'd prefer to be at the gates of Hell myself than bringing this news to you, boss,' Mossop groaned. 'But we didn't know. Nobody in G-Division knew. They said they'd got a warrant from the assistant under-secretary. He's a magistrate, as you know yourself.'

'And what happened? What bloody well happened?'

'They broke in the side door, probably around seven o'clock, and they made straight up the stairs to the private quarters. It seems that Mrs Swallow came out of her room and confronted them, told them to get out of her house. According to what Mr Mallon was told, Kelly showed her the warrant and told her to read it. There was some sort of an altercation then and ... well ... she fell on the stairs.'

Mossop turned his face imploringly to Lafeyre.

'Maybe Dr Lafeyre can explain the ... medical details ... from that point, boss.'

'Kelly says she tripped,' Lafeyre said, grimacing. 'I've spoken with Maria myself, and she says that she was manhandled down the stairs when she tried to prevent them searching the bedrooms. She says she fell heavily about halfway down, and the next thing she remembers was Carrie kneeling beside her on the floor.' Lafeyre paused. 'Carrie came in to work around half past seven, so it seems Maria was lying there for maybe half an hour. Carrie knew there was something very wrong. Maria told her she was in pain, and Carrie wanted to send for the doctor, but Kelly wouldn't permit it until after the search was completed. It would have been a breach of security, he told Mallon later, if she left the premises.' He laughed bitterly. 'But he wasn't entirely without humanity. He let Carrie move Maria into the lower parlour and get her onto the settee. He even ticked off one of his men to help. Carrie was smart enough though. As soon as Maria was resting on the settee and she was on her own she slipped out through the window, went across the back yard, out into the laneway and made straight for Exchange Court.'

'Martin Shanahan was fast too,' Mossop interjected. 'As soon as he got the picture from Carrie he sent Eddie Cussen up to Harcourt Street for Dr Lafeyre and dispatched Mick Feore and Johnny Vizzard up to Grant's on the double. Carrie said she'd go down to Francis Street and get Dr Morrow too.'

'I got there as quickly as I could,' Lafeyre resumed. 'I was about to depart for Marlborough Street, and Scollan had the carriage ready outside my door. Detective Cussen came with me, and I was there in ten minutes. Kelly and his men were still in the house, but they didn't obstruct us.' Lafeyre paused. 'You know, I think if they had I'd have asked Cussen for his revolver and gone in there at gunpoint.'

'And Feore and Vizzard would have been with the doctor. They'd have done the same,' Mossop added, nodding vigorously. 'They were there just ahead of him. You know,' he added, 'I should have let fly at that bastard when I had the Remington up against his gob in the public office.'

'Maria was in a lot of pain and she was bleeding,' Lafeyre continued. 'In my view she needed to get to the Rotunda where they have the specialised knowledge and the right equipment for that sort of thing. She knew herself that something had gone seriously wrong. Dr Morrow arrived then, and he agreed with me that she had to go to hospital. We managed to get her to the carriage and make her as comfortable as we could. Scollan had us at the Rotunda inside a few minutes. They managed to stop the bleeding after a while. She was very weak, but I don't think she was ever in mortal danger.'

'Was she … in pain?' Swallow asked.

'Initially, yes, I'm afraid,' Lafeyre said cautiously. 'I know this is a difficult thing to accept, Joe, but pain is often helpful in these situations. It enables the doctors to identify and locate the problem. And they eased it for her with laudanum as soon as they could.'

Mossop pushed Swallow's mug of tea an inch closer.

'Will you not take a drop of scald there, boss? It'll do you good,' he said softly.

Swallow took the mug and raised it mechanically to his mouth. He sipped the hot brew without tasting it.

'Could they do … nothing?' he asked Lafeyre.

'You have to understand, Joe, at that early stage of pregnancy the baby is very fragile. A lot of women lose their babies in the early weeks and months. A lot can go wrong, even where there isn't an accident….'

'This wasn't an accident!' Swallow said coldly. 'This was a killing. They murdered my child, Maria's child. The bloody cowards. The bloody cowards came into our home while I was away and there was nobody there to stop them.'

'I'm sorry, Joe,' Lafeyre said quietly. 'I'm truly sorry ... for you and for Maria.'

He drank from his own mug.

'In a situation like that, where the foetus suffers a trauma, even an indirect one, it's really ... dislocated ... and there isn't any way of putting it right again. The emphasis has to be on saving the mother, and that's what they did. They did it very successfully, praise the Lord. The baby is gone, unhappily, but Maria is fine.'

All three men were silent. The sounds of the harbour came faintly through the windows. Voices on the wharf. The rattle of cartwheels on granite paving. Gulls calling.

Swallow started to feel a strange ease, very gently at first. It did not displace his sorrow or his anger, but he could sense the strength and the support and the friendship of the two men sitting with him as they narrated the tragedy. His tragedy and Maria's tragedy and their lost child's tragedy. Nothing could be done to change what had happened. He could not alter the past. Not a whit of it could be changed. What was important now was what would happen next. And he could influence that.

Mossop broke the silence.

'You'll remember now, boss, what I told you about Mr Mallon's orders. You're to do nothing ... nothing at all. You're to talk to him straight away after you've been to visit your missus.'

Swallow did not answer.

He stood.

'I think I should go to see Maria now. Will you take me to her please?'

THIRTY-SEVEN

There was a sense of unreality about the short train journey from Kingstown Harbour into the city. It was impossible, Swallow told himself, that only a few days previously he had travelled outward along this railway line, past these same houses and villages, full of joy and celebration with Maria and their guests, making for their wedding celebration at the Royal Marine Hotel. The waters of the bay were a dark foreboding grey this morning, with the tops of the waves flecked white by the wind. The city itself seemed threatening.

At the Westland Row terminus they took a cab to the Dublin Lying-In Hospital, the Rotunda, above Sackville Street, and forming the southern side of Rutland Square.

Maria was in a quiet ward of twelve beds, close to the hospital chapel. In contrast with the noisy wards on the ground floor, filled with the squalling sounds of new life, there were no babies here. The patients here were women whose babies had been stillborn or whose pregnancies had been lost. Swallow could sense the atmosphere of emptiness, sadness almost, once he walked through the door with Harry Lafeyre.

Lafeyre spoke to the nurse on duty and led Swallow to the end of the ward.

Maria was half-asleep, half-awake. The first thing that struck Swallow was the paleness of her complexion. Even in the morning light he could see that her face was waxen white, her eyes sunken into dark sockets under her forehead.

'She's been asking for you all the time, Joe,' Lafeyre had told him as they travelled. 'She's been very agitated, so don't be surprised if she

274

becomes upset. It's not because she doesn't want to see you. Quite the opposite.'

Her eyes opened wide when he touched her hand. Lafeyre stepped back to afford them privacy.

'Maria, dearest. It's me. Joe,' he told her quietly. 'I'm here and you're safe now. All is well.'

She said nothing at first. Her eyes searched his face as if disbelieving his presence.

'I'm sorry, Joe,' she whispered then. 'I'm very sorry.'

'Oh, hush now, my love,' he told her. 'It's fine. All is well. And there isn't any need to be sorry. I'm here. I'm with you and I'll take care of you.'

'Dr Morrow says … he says … he thinks it will be all right. That I can … have other children … he says there's no reason….'

Swallow realised that he had not even addressed that question in his own head. It had not seemed to be in any way important when set against the immediate circumstances.

'You mustn't worry about that either,' he told her. 'If that happens, it will be fine. If it doesn't, it will be fine too. We have each other, Maria.'

She closed her eyes and smiled for the first time.

'We have each other,' she said. 'We have each other.'

Lafeyre came forward and touched Swallow's shoulder.

'I think we should leave Maria to sleep for a while. She'll rest a lot more peacefully now that she knows you're here. Sleep and rest are what she needs now in order to build her strength back up.'

They stepped into the corridor outside.

'How is she?' Swallow asked. 'She looks very pale and she seems very weak.'

'She'll be fine, Joe,' Lafeyre told him. 'She's weak and she's tired. That's very much to be expected. She's a strong woman, but there's also the emotional shock of what's happened. Losing a pregnancy can have all sorts of mental effects on a woman, so what she needs is reassurance, calm and certainty. And of course affection. So that's your first duty now over the next little while.'

Swallow nodded.

'I understand, Harry. Thank you for all your care and support. You're a true friend.'

Lafeyre smiled.

'You're not a bad fellow yourself, you know. And you mustn't start blaming yourself for any of this. It could have happened whether or not you were here or in Berlin or wherever. What's important now is that you take care of Maria. And that you take care of yourself. If anything happens to you it will hurt Maria and slow her recovery.'

'How long will she have to stay in hospital?' Swallow asked.

'A few more days, maybe a week,' Lafeyre said. 'I'd advise that. She's well looked after here, but when she goes home she'll have to rest for a long time. She can't go back to the business straight away. You'll have to stand firm on that, Joe.'

'Of course,' Swallow nodded. 'Will she need nursing care when she's home? I could make arrangements.'

'I doubt it. Dr Morrow can see her there, and she has Carrie and Tess. Lily can spend time with her too. But we can see how it works out. After a few days' rest she should be up and about. That would be best from a medical point of view. She needs to get her body back to doing usual, normal things. And her mind too.'

Swallow felt a small twinge of comfort in Lafeyre's words. Things would be as they were. He and Maria could resume their lives in their home above M & M Grant's.

But now there was police business to be done. He realised that he had no idea what progress if any had been made in the murder inquiries while had been away. They had not entered his head since he had received word in Berlin about Maria. Had Charlie Vanucchi come back to Pat Mossop with any information on the identity of Ellen Byrne's killer? Had any suspects emerged for the assault on Debbie Dunne, the young fish-seller? Had anything turned up on the murder of Alice Flannery?

He needed to get to Exchange Court. And he needed to talk to John Mallon.

THIRTY-EIGHT

It was a coincidence of the clock that just around the time that Swallow was stepping off the Holyhead steam packet at Kingstown, a party of policemen, comprising plain-clothes G-Division officers and uniformed constables, was moving into position around a house at Mount Pleasant, just beyond the Grand Canal bridge at Portobello.

And it was fortuitous for Superintendent 'Duck' Boyle that the operation to arrest the chief suspect in the murder of the young prostitute Helena Moyles, alias Ellen Byrne, alias Nellie Sweet, was taking place within his area of jurisdiction, the E-Division. The division stretched from the canal to Rathmines in one direction and to the southern shore of Dublin Bay in the other. It was, after all, Boyle's unnamed informant who had first intimated that Nellie's killer might be an associate of criminal boss Charlie Vanucchi. Yet, in the event, it turned out that the information was unsound.

When Vanucchi had sent a message on the previous day asking to meet Detective Sergeant Mossop, Mossop anticipated that he was going to be told the name of that associate. He had been sceptical at first when Swallow told him to expect Vanucchi to give him a name. Why would Charlie want to inform on one of his own?

'You've heard the expression "there's no honour among thieves", Pat,' Swallow had grinned. 'Well, it's not quite true. There are rules even among Dublin criminals. There's live and let live. And if some thief has broken the rules and raised the stakes by murdering a working girl up in Monto, the rest of the tribe aren't going to shelter him.'

And moreover, Swallow had continued, if Vanucchi didn't deliver, he was going to face more trouble and grief than he could handle, including a long spell behind bars. He explained the ultimatum he had delivered to the crime boss at their meeting in Hanrahan's of Stoneybatter. But when Mossop had met Vanucchi later in the evening at the Long Hall public house on South Great George's Street, what the criminal told him was not what he had expected to hear.

'Your boss, Mr Swallow, and that fat super out in Rathmines, Boyle, got it wrong this time, Pat,' Vanucchi told him as their drinks came up in the snug. 'Nellie wasn't killed by any of my lads. I didn't think she was, and I told Mr Swallow that. But he said he had good information. Well, it wasn't so good.'

Mossop still doubted. In all likelihood Vanucchi simply wasn't prepared to squeal on one of his own men. He was trying to pin it on somebody else. But what the crime boss told him next shook him out of any such belief.

'The story about Nellie having money left to her by Ces Downes is true enough,' Vanucchi told him. 'And it's true that she had it in a post office book. But there was a lot more money in Nellie's account than Ces ever left to her. And it wasn't any of my boys who went after it.'

'So who was it then?' Mossop asked, downing a double gulp of his porter.

'You know that she was involved with some of the dynamite crowd, the patriots, the Fenians?'

'Sure, but she wasn't active in anything.'

'Don't be so sure about that. Your young G-men working down in Monto didn't ask all the right questions of the other girls in Gloucester Street. There's one of them, and I won't say who, was a close friend of Nellie's. She told our lads when we talked to her that the Fenian crowd were using her post office account to pay off people for guns and dynamite.'

Mossop did his best not to appear taken aback. If what Vanucchi was saying was true, it was a serious lapse in G-Division intelligence. But, he acknowledged silently to himself, the young G-men assigned to monitor the red-light district were novices, still learning their trade. With their more senior colleagues stretched on security duties, they had little mentoring or guidance from more experienced officers. They could easily miss the obvious.

'Go on.'

'That stuff isn't cheap. They get it bit by bit from soldiers and quarrymen and sailors, and even from the odd peeler.'

'So,' Mossop said cautiously, 'how did this work?'

'Simple enough. The Americans gather dollars, convert them into pounds and send them over here. The Fenians are all known to the police, and they know that your fellows have agents watching transactions in all the banks. It's too risky for them to shift any money about. So the money gets lodged into Nellie's post office account and she draws it out to pay these fellows who come to her pretending to be clients. Well, maybe some of them are clients for all we know. But basically, Nellie was passing on money to pay for guns and dynamite for the Fenians. She was a sort of banker.'

Mossop tried not to sound impressed.

'All right, that's not especially significant information, Charlie. But I'll see that you get looked after with a nice few quid if it turns out to be solid. It still doesn't tell me what I came to find out, and that's who killed Nellie?'

'Ah, but there's more, Mr Mossop. A lot more. Nellie told her friend that she believed she'd been rumbled by some of your friends in the Castle. This English officer, she said, seemed to have twigged the thing, and he was seeing a lot of her, pumping her for details of the transactions. He told her he loved her. He'd take her away to England and all that. Of course, she didn't believe him. But she liked to hear him say it.'

Vanucchi sipped at his whiskey.

'Now, on the night Nellie was killed her friend saw that English officer visiting her. And she knows his name.'

'You'll give me that name, I suppose, Charlie.'

'I will, Mr Mossop.' Vanucchi tapped his whiskey glass. 'But first, you'll need to buy me another.'

THIRTY-NINE

'I want an interview with Smith Berry,' Swallow said. 'I'll have it. After that I want to talk to the chief secretary. If it comes to it I'll go to the lord lieutenant, or I'll go to London to the bloody prime minister.'

'Will you please sit down and stop pacing up and down like a wild animal above in the Zoological Gardens?' Mallon said firmly. 'I'll ask Smith Berry for a meeting, but he may not want to agree to it. I've already asked him to see me and he's put me off twice so far.'

'He'll see me if I have to knock down the blasted door,' Swallow snarled. 'I want Kelly's head. I want him out of his job, out of the Castle, out of bloody Ireland. They can send him to Africa or China. With any luck he'll get skewered by the natives or boiled alive in a pot.'

'I understand how you feel,' Mallon said. 'If it was me I'd feel just the same. I'm really very sorry for you and Maria. It's a shocking thing to have happened. Every man in G-Division is outraged about it. There might be other ways of dealing with Major Kelly though. I'm going to tell you something important in a little while.'

'With respect, chief, that's not nearly good enough. My wife is lying above in the Rotunda hospital. Our dead child will never see the light of day. Maria might have died herself if it wasn't for getting good medical care so quickly. Somebody's going to pay for it all, one way or another.'

Mallon groaned.

'I can only say again how sorry I am. And Elizabeth too. She's asked me to express her particular sympathy to you both. It's a hard thing to lose an unborn child.'

280

'We didn't "lose" the child, chief,' Swallow snapped. 'A gang of blackguards broke into our home and killed it. This was murder, except we can't charge anybody for it.'

'I'll put in another request to see Smith Berry,' Mallon said. 'But if he agrees to it we'll go together. You've got to control yourself on this. We'll need to agree on what you say and what you want from him. And you've got to be prepared for a very hard response. He'll stand behind his people.'

'Then he'd better know that I'll stand for myself and my wife and our lost child. Either he deals with Kelly or they can have my resignation. And I won't go quietly. I've got my own contacts in the newspapers too, and I'll use them. These bloody people count on us to hold the country for them. We do a bloody good job of it, and this is the thanks we get. I'll want every policeman and their families the length and breadth of Ireland to know how they'll be treated if it suits the Smith Berrys and his like.'

Mallon raised a restraining hand.

'Enough, Joe. You'll say things you could regret. If you decided to hand in your papers, nobody could blame you, and I certainly wouldn't. But if that's your plan, stay quiet about it. They'll find some way of sacking you instead. You'll be out. No pension, and your name blackened. If you'll be patient, as I said, there's very likely to be another way of dealing with it.'

'The hell with their pension,' Swallow answered. 'I don't need their pension. There's a business to be run in Thomas Street. The truth is I should have pulled out of this bloody job long ago like Maria asked me to.'

'Look,' Mallon said, 'I feel a degree of responsibility for this. Now, I'm picking my words carefully here. I was the one who asked you to … shall we say … "locate" the protection logs. If I hadn't done that there never would have been any search at your home.' He paused. 'You're exhausted and you're angry. If you could see the cut of yourself, you'd believe me. You need to go home, get them to fill a hot bath for you, take a few hours' sleep and then come down to my house later. We'll have a drink and you'll eat supper with us. You'll feel a lot better.'

Under his anger, Swallow knew that Mallon was right. He had not slept properly for three nights. His mind was racing to cope with too many issues. He needed rest in order to restore his judgement.

'I'll do that, chief,' he said more calmly. 'And I hear what you're saying about the protection logs. There's no fault on your part in any of what happened. You couldn't have known they'd break into my home or threaten my wife. Civilised Englishmen aren't supposed to do that sort of thing to senior officers of their own police force.'

Mallon nodded.

'Thank you. I appreciate what you say.'

'I'd just like to fill you in on what happened in Berlin,' Swallow said. 'I think we're nearly home and dry on the Alice Flannery murder.'

'I got the gist of it from your messages,' Mallon answered. 'Mossop kept me up to date on it. You've brought this fellow Carmody back, I know.'

'Carmody's in the Bridewell now, or in Mountjoy. I've enough to keep him in custody for as long as it takes. I'll do a full written report of course, but in summary Carmody will give evidence of Stefan Werner threatening the girl because she wanted to claim compensation for the accident in the restaurant.'

'It's circumstantial,' Mallon said. 'You'll need more.'

'There's more, chief. Werner left the restaurant early on the night Alice Flannery was murdered, and he made her tell him her address. And it turns out that Werner has a record of violence.'

Mallon nodded.

'Well, that's more persuasive. So what do you intend to do next?'

'I'll do like you said, chief. I'll get some sleep and then I'll bring Mr Werner in as a suspect for murder.'

'Fair enough,' Mallon said. 'I'll get the warrant organised. There's two magistrates sitting in the police courts all day.'

'There's one other thing to tell you, Joe.' Mallon attempted a humourless smile. 'There's some news in that could please you in the light of what we've been talking about.'

'It'll be a change to hear something good,' Swallow said.

'I thought about telling you this at the start of our conversation,' Mallon said, 'but I knew you'd want to get things off your chest about

Kelly and Smith Berry, so I decided to hold back a little bit until you'd had your say.' He paused. 'Charlie Vanucchi came back on the Nellie Byrne murder with a name for Pat Mossop.'

'So which of his fellows is it?'

'It's none of them. But Vanucchi told Mossop the identity of the man who was with Nellie before she was killed. Now he's our prime suspect.'

'So who is it?' Swallow asked, professional interest asserting itself in spite of his exhaustion.

'You're not going to believe this, but it might change your plans a bit. It's a fellow we both know. It's Kelly.'

'Kelly?' Swallow could not believe his ears. 'Kelly? Nigel Kelly? Major Nigel Kelly? So what are we doing about that information?'

Mallon looked at the wall clock.

'Right now he should be in the Bridewell, I imagine. "Duck" Boyle and Mick Feore and half a dozen men in backup collected him from his bed, or more accurately from the bed of one of his lady friends in Mount Pleasant, a little earlier this morning.'

His smile broadened just a fraction.

'So I imagine that we'll get our interview with Mr Smith Berry very soon. Very soon indeed.'

FORTY

It was a rarity for two suspects to be held separately but simultaneously in the city in two parallel murder investigations. Nobody in G-Division could recall such a thing happening before.

Swallow had got four hours of passable sleep, a hot bath and a change of clothes at home in Thomas Street before returning to the Castle in the early afternoon.

'You look a bit better all right,' Mallon commented drily. 'I've got your warrant for Werner. I've put a few men across at the Bridewell in case any of the crowd from the Upper Yard try to do anything dramatic about Kelly. But Johnny Vizzard is waiting in Exchange Court to go with you to the New Vienna.'

Vizzard was the newest recruit to G-Division. He would be a good G-man in time, Swallow reckoned, but he was still raw. Assisting in an arrest for a murder case would be a learning experience for him.

'What's happening with Kelly over at the Bridewell, chief?' Swallow asked.

He chided himself silently as he asked the question. The uppermost thought in his head was more to do with nailing the secret service man than bringing the Alice Flannery murder investigation to a successful conclusion. He was allowing emotional distress to cloud his professional judgement.

'It's peculiar,' Mallon said. 'I thought he'd be screaming blue murder. He wants word to be sent to the Upper Yard for his people to come and get him out, of course. Mossop is playing for time and doing nothing. But Kelly's sitting there calmly, it seems, answering Mossop's questions, being very reasonable and denying everything.'

'Did he come quietly when they lifted him?'

'There was a bit of excitement when they arrived at his lady friend's house at Mount Pleasant. The two of them were still in bed, it seems. The E-Division lads managed to slip the lock on the back door and in they went. Quick as flash, Kelly was out of bed, naked as the day he was born, out on the landing with a bloody big Mauser pistol in his hand. The two lads on the stairs thought their last moment had come. He told Mossop it was the uniform that saved them. If they were in plain clothes he'd have concluded they were Fenians out to do for him and he'd have blazed away.'

'And you've heard nothing from Smith Berry or anyone about their man being dragged off to the Bridewell?'

'Not a word. I don't know what to make of it. They probably don't even know yet that we have him. I'm expecting Mossop here at around five o'clock with a report on the interview. And I'm calling a full crime conference at six. I think you should sit in if you can.'

'I'll do that, chief. I'd hate to miss hearing about how that bastard likes it over there staring at the walls of a cell.'

Mallon's mouth formed a wintry smile.

'There's one other thing you'll be interested to hear. And it pretty well cooks Kelly's goose, I believe.'

'Yes, sir?'

'Mick Feore found Nellie Byrne's post office book in his jacket pocket.'

'Jesus,' Swallow exclaimed. 'How does he explain that?'

'Well, as I said, he doesn't. He's just saying nothing, insists he hasn't done anything, and says he's happy to co-operate if his people in the Upper Yard are sent for.'

Mallon stood.

'All we can do is see what develops. You go and do what you have to do with Werner.'

He crossed the Lower Yard to Exchange Court and found Johnny Vizzard waiting for him in the crime inspector's office.

'This won't be difficult and it won't take too long,' Swallow told him. 'I've a warrant to take this fellow Werner into custody on suspicion of Alice Flannery's murder. He'll be no great problem. He's not expecting us, and he'll protest that he's busy running his restaurant. We may need to persuade him that he hasn't any choice about coming back here with us. And I should tell you that behind the veneer he has convictions for assault and violence on the continent. He's unlikely to cause a row at the restaurant, but we'd need to be on our toes all the same.'

'I'm your man, Inspector,' Vizzard said eagerly. 'First time I've had anything to do with an arrest for murder. Anything I need to watch out for?'

'Watch out for yourself,' Swallow answered. 'It's a bit different with murder all right. You know that when you take someone into custody it's not like any other offence. When it's murder, you're very likely bringing them on their first steps to the gallows. You've got to be sure you've got the right man.'

'I know you'd be sure you've got the right man, Inspector,' Vizzard said confidently. 'That's your reputation. Everyone in the force knows that.'

It was ironic, Swallow thought. He had a reputation, he knew, as a man who didn't make mistakes. He was not just good at his job. He was a first-class detective. Thorough, focused and committed. But none of that counted in the minds of the masters of his fate in the Upper Yard. They thought nothing of his loyalty or his service. He was just a cog in their machine. When it suited their purpose, the privacy of his home, the welfare of his wife or the life of his unborn child could all be set aside.

They exited Exchange Court onto Dame Street. The afternoon light was starting to fade and the gas lamps were already burning in Dan Lowrey's Music Hall opposite the Palace Street gate. In a few hours the theatre would be buzzing as patrons flocked in for the evening show. Tonight's performance was Dion Boucicault's melodrama of murder, innocence and love, *The Colleen Bawn*. It always drew packed houses. Swallow sometimes reflected on the paradoxical juxtaposition of one of Dublin's leading entertainment venues with the grim granite gateway to the Castle across the street.

It was a short walk up South Great George's Street to the New Vienna. The lobby, with its mahogany panelling and brass fittings, was warm and enticing, as always. A young man in a waiter's dress suit looked up from the desk when Swallow and Vizzard walked in.

'I'm sorry, gents, lunch is finished. Would yiz like to put yer name down for a table for dinner later? Startin' at seven o'clock.'

Swallow showed his warrant card.

'We're not for dining, son, I'm afraid. Detective Inspector Swallow and Detective Officer Vizzard. We'd like to see Mr Werner please.'

The young man rose from the desk.

'I'll tell him yiz are here. Yiz can take a seat.'

Swallow and Vizzard stayed standing as the young man went into the dining room. A minute later he was back.

'Mr Werner said to tell yiz he has someone wit' him and yiz are to wait. He won't be long.'

He resumed his place at the desk. Swallow watched him laboriously copying out menu cards for the evening dinner. But there was no sign of Stefan Werner. After a couple of minutes, Swallow called to the waiter at the desk.

'Will you go and see if Mr Werner is ready? It's police business and we haven't got all day.'

The young man looked embarrassed.

'I can't do that, sir. He said he wasn't to be disturbed.'

Swallow knew instantly. He would have twigged it earlier, he later reflected, were he not so tired from his travels and emotionally astray. He snapped at Vizzard. 'Get around the back, quick. You might just get him in the laneway.'

Swallow sprinted across the lobby into the dining room, along the short corridor and down to the office where he had previously interviewed Werner. He flung the door open. The room was empty. He spun on his heel. A man in a chef's uniform emerged from the kitchen door opposite.

'Police,' Swallow told him. 'Where's Werner?'

'Mr Werner? Sure, he's just gone,' the man answered, a puzzled look on his face. 'He went out the back way.'

Swallow pushed past him into the lobby and onto the street. South Great George's street was busy. He scanned the pavements. There was no sign of Stefan Werner.

Across the street, a steam tram bound for Rathmines was pulling away from its stop outside Pim's department store. On instinct he sprinted across the street, stretching his speed to its limits as the vehicle gathered momentum. Its next stop would be at Aungier Street, beyond the intersection with Stephen Street. His wind would not bring him that far in time to catch it, he knew.

Then the double-decked vehicle jerked to a halt with a hiss of steam and a squeal of its metal brakes. Pedestrians turned to see what was happening. From where he stood, Swallow could see that a messenger delivering groceries or packages of some kind had tumbled from his bicycle, momentarily bringing the traffic to a halt. He started to run again. He jumped as the vehicle moved off and grabbed the rail above the open platform at the back.

Stefan Werner was sitting on the side bench in the lower saloon, his coat wrapped tightly around him, a black bowler hat jammed forwards in an effort to conceal his face.

Swallow hauled himself into the saloon. He drew his Webley with one hand and held his warrant card aloft with the other. There were gasps from passengers as he made his way along the saloon. A woman screamed.

'Police!' he shouted. 'I'm a police officer. There's no danger.'

He reached towards where Werner sat and pointed the Webley at his chest.

'Stefan Werner,' he said loudly, 'I am arresting you on suspicion of the murder of Alice Flannery.'

FORTY-ONE

There was an air of something close to elation as John Mallon stepped up to chair the crime conference at Exchange Court. Every member of G-Division had known since the morning that Major Nigel Kelly, the detested chief of the Upper Yard's secret service office, was in custody in the Bridewell. When word spread that Swallow had Stefan Werner in the cells at Exchange Court for the Alice Flannery murder, the atmosphere became almost exuberant.

'As you know, men, we've got suspects in custody for the two murders,' Mallon told the score of G-men and uniformed constables who had gathered.

'A senior member of the secret service department has been identified as having been at the scene of Nellie Byrne's murder at Chapel Court, Gloucester Street. And the late Alice Flannery's former employer, Stefan Werner, was arrested in connection with her death this afternoon by Detective Inspector Swallow.'

A quiet murmur of approval ran around the room. Stephen Doolan whispered to Swallow, 'Well done.'

Tired constables nodded in quiet satisfaction. The weeks that had followed the murders, with no progress of any kind, had challenged morale and dampened spirits. Every man would feel better with things looking up.

'But we still need all the evidence we can get on these two cases,' Mallon said. 'Neither of the suspects has made a confession. We're relying on circumstantial evidence and any additional witness testimony we can get. On the positive side, it doesn't seem that there's any connection between the two deaths, so we're not dealing with some sort of a madman.'

Another murmur of satisfaction susurrated around the parade room.

'So,' Mallon continued, 'first we'll review what we have on the Nellie Byrne murder. Detective Collins, if you please.'

Martin Collins was the book man on the case. He was not the best book man in Exchange Court. That distinction was held by Pat Mossop, followed by Mick Feore. The really good book men not only recorded every item of information on an investigation, but also had a gift for spotting connections or patterns. It wasn't Collins's strongest point, but his murder book, the ledger in which every detail of the progress of the investigation was recorded, was invariably accurate and complete.

'Murder of Helena Moyles, alias Ellen Byrne, alias Nellie Sweet, aged twenty-two years, Chapel Court, Gloucester Street, Dublin on Saturday 9 November last.'

Swallow saw Mallon wince as Collins started his report with a ponderous and unnecessary recitation of the facts already known to every policeman in the room.

'The deceased was a member of the unfortunate class that frequent this district,' Collins intoned. 'The remains were examined at the scene by the city medical examiner, Dr Lafeyre, before removal to the morgue at Marlborough Street. The post-mortem examination revealed that she had suffered multiple blows to the head and upper body.'

He paused to draw breath before resuming his narrative from the murder book.

'As a result of confidential information, a party led by Superintendent Boyle, E-Division, this morning executed a search warrant at an address at Mount Pleasant. A gentleman, identified as Major Nigel Kelly, was taken into custody. Detective Sergeant Feore found an item relating to the murder in his jacket pocket, to wit, one post office savings book held in the name of Helena Moyles. Constable Patrick Cummins C35 was on duty in the vicinity of the crime on the night in question. He encountered a man running from the deceased's place of residence. The description matches that of Major Kelly.'

That was stretching it a bit, Swallow told himself. Cummins's description of the man fleeing the scene was so vague as to be almost useless. Yet he was not far wrong when he said that he thought the fugitive might have been a policeman. It was highly likely that he would have seen Kelly in or around the Castle on occasion.

He flicked the next page of the murder book.

'G-Division intelligence indicates that the deceased was a known associate of members of the Irish Republican Brotherhood, better known as the Fenians. She was also known to keep company with members of the Hibernian Brotherhood.'

'Thank you. Thank you, Detective.' Mallon waved an impatient hand, silencing Collins. 'The case is strong. I have a report from Detective Sergeant Mossop, who has been questioning the suspect in the Bridewell during the day. Cummins will visit the Bridewell shortly and will be asked to identify the suspect. If his identification is positive, I intend to have Major Kelly charged with murder right away.'

Another murmur of approval went around the parade room.

'Now, Sergeant Feore, would you please tell the conference about the state of play in the Alice Flannery investigation?'

Feore would be brief, Swallow knew. He would speak from his notes rather than reading laboriously from the murder book.

'The evidence to date is a bit circumstantial if you ask me, chief,' he said, shrugging. 'The principal suspect is Stefan Werner, a native of Berlin, proprietor and operator of the New Vienna restaurant on South Great George's Street. He was seen leaving the restaurant shortly after Alice Flannery on the night she was murdered and after he had asked her for her address. His shoes match the size of the footprint left in the mud at the crime scene.'

He glanced, perhaps apologetically, at Swallow. Every man in the room had tensed at Feore's implicit distancing of himself from Swallow's identification of Werner as the chief suspect. If the evidence against Werner was merely circumstantial, the case might not be as strong as they had been given to understand. Feore cast his eyes down unnecessarily, pretending to scan his notes.

'As a result of information received from Kapitän Pfaus of Berlin CID, Detective Inspector Swallow travelled to Berlin to interview a witness, Michael Carmody, who has returned with him to Dublin. Carmody is on file here in DCR, but is willing to give evidence of hostility and threats from Werner towards the deceased. Details from Berlin police records confirm that Werner has convictions for violence in Germany and Holland.

'Carmody is now lodged in Mountjoy Prison on a charge of larceny from the premises of his former employer. Earlier today Detective Inspector Swallow and Detective Vizzard visited the New Vienna to detain Mr Werner under a magistrate's warrant. He fled the restaurant and attempted to escape. He was apprehended and arrested by Detective Inspector Swallow on a tram leaving South Great George's Street, and he is at present in custody here at Exchange Court.'

Mallon turned to Swallow.

'Inspector?'

'There's not a lot to add, chief,' Swallow said. 'Werner has been questioned, and I'll resume that questioning shortly. In summary, he admits nothing. He hasn't got an alibi for where he was at the time of the murder, but he says that Alice Flannery was a troublesome employee. He also denies that he has any criminal convictions on the continent, but I have copies of the records from the Berlin CID, *Kriminalpolizei*, and they're very specific.'

'So what do you intend?' Mallon asked.

'I intend to charge him with murder,' Swallow said.

FORTY-TWO

Supper at Mallon's house might have been, in other circumstances, what Swallow needed. Elizabeth Mallon was a wise and motherly woman who had already raised a large family. He would have liked to have her counsel on Maria's condition and how he might best care for her once she had been discharged from hospital. Instead, the evening was disrupted and overlaid with apprehension.

The meal was late, for a start. Mallon had been at the Bridewell to check on the questioning of Major Kelly. Swallow had spent two hours interrogating Stefan Werner in his cell at Exchange Court on the murder of Alice Flannery. Ordinarily, John Mallon and his family would aim to dine not later than seven o'clock, but it was almost nine when Mallon, his wife and Swallow sat to table.

Swallow had finished his interview with Werner and had been making his way to his office on the first floor, passing the duty man's desk in the public office.

'There's a few pressmen outside waiting for you, Inspector,' the G-man on duty told him, nodding to the swing doors that led to the lobby and the street. 'They want to know about that German fella in the cells.'

Swallow cursed silently. He was not surprised that word of Werner's arrest on the tram in South Great George's Street had reached the newspaper offices, or that the reporters had been able to identify the man dramatically taken away at gunpoint from the scene. Other business people on the busy street would have identified their restaurateur neighbour being taken in handcuffs down the street to the Castle by Swallow and Vizzard. But he had always made a point of co-operating with the gentlemen of the press. It was a policy that generally worked well for him. One never knew when one might need their support or co-operation.

There were three of them: Dunlop from *The Irish Times*, Sheehan from *The Freeman's Journal* and Hamilton, a freelance who serviced the needs of a number of London publications. They stood as one from the wooden bench on which they had been waiting when Swallow came out.

'Has Werner been charged, Joe?'

'Did he confess?'

'Can you tell us why he did it?'

'Don't get too far ahead of yourselves,' he told them. 'You know there's a man in custody. And yes, it's to do with the murder of Alice Flannery. But he hasn't been charged.'

'But he's the right man, Inspector, isn't he?' It was Dunlop from *The Irish Times*. 'It's the German. Isn't that why you went to Berlin?'

Some friendly G-man had marked Dunlop's cards about his travels. Swallow nodded. He had long since learned that it was foolish to lie to the press, but it was not always necessary to tell them all of the truth.

'Draw your own conclusions. You seem to know a fair bit.'

The pressmen scribbled hurriedly in their notebooks.

'You're sure you've got the right man, Joe?' Sheehan asked. 'Can we say that?'

'Say what you think,' Swallow answered. 'Just don't put words in my mouth.'

Questioning Stefan Werner had been more difficult than he had anticipated. He steadfastly denied that he had any criminal record in Germany or anywhere else. He agreed, though, that he had clashed with Alice Flannery when she worked at the New Vienna restaurant, and described her as troublesome and disruptive. And he confirmed that she had injured herself lifting a heavy pot of boiling soup in the kitchen. He believed it was her own fault. She wanted to work with the chef in order to learn from him. The chef had tolerated her intrusion into his work area, but she should not have attempted to lift the heavy vessel.

Had she threatened to take legal action to secure damages, Swallow asked. Werner shook his head. He had no knowledge of any such thing. It had never been mentioned. And he had never heard of such a thing in Irish law.

'You left the restaurant around the same time that she did on the night she was attacked,' Swallow insisted. 'And you asked her for her home address. Isn't that so?'

'Yes, I probably did leave around the same time,' Werner answered. 'I leave at that time each night. I work a long and arduous day and I have a good head waiter and a trusted cashier to see the last of the customers finish their meals and pay their accounts.'

'So why did you want Alice Flannery's home address? Why did you want to know where she lived?'

'I had decided finally to terminate her services. I paid her wages for the week, and I was going to write her a formal notice, ending her employment.'

'So where did you go that evening, Stefan?' Swallow asked. 'Can you account for your movements?'

'I will not answer that, Mr Swallow. The fact is that I had an assignation with a lady who is someone else's wife, and I will not embarrass her by giving you any details about her. That is my private business and I intend to keep it that way.'

It was one of the oldest dodges in the book, Swallow reflected. He had encountered it on more than a few occasions in the course of his inquiries. Any married woman would be ruined in her reputation, and very likely banished to poverty if it were to be revealed that she had an involvement or attachment in contravention of her matrimonial vows. And no man with a vestige of decency about him would be forgiven for compromising a lady, even if the consequences were to be serious.

'You know and I know, Stefan, that if you stick to that position it will turn against you. If you have an alibi for the night when Alice Flannery was attacked, and if it stands up, you'll walk out of here a free man. But if you haven't an alibi, if you can't give me evidence that you were elsewhere, it will add very greatly to the case against you. I can assure you that if you give me the lady's name I will make my inquiries very discreetly. Nobody but she, you and me will know.'

Werner shook his head.

'No. I do not trust you. I would not trust the word of any policeman. I don't doubt that by now you have gathered a lot of information about me and about my life. Some of it will show that I am not a man without blemish, and that I have, how do you say, created a false face to the world. That would be true also of very many of the respectable businessmen in this city. But I insist that I am totally innocent of this crime.'

'I'm certain that he's prevaricating,' Swallow told Mallon as they eventually sat to supper. 'He's got smooth answers for all the questions, but I'm sure he's hiding something. And he can't come up with an alibi as to where he went when he left the restaurant on the night of the murder.'

'Isn't it possible that what he says is true? Maybe he's involved with some married lady, as he says,' Mallon said.

'He wouldn't accept my offer of a discreet inquiry, chief. If he won't even give us this supposed lady's name we can't check his story. Personally, I think it's a fiction.'

Elizabeth Mallon smiled.

'But if it were true, that would be honourable, in a way, wouldn't it? I'm not condoning that kind of behaviour, of course.'

Swallow shrugged.

'You could say that, Mrs Mallon.'

'But you've not charged him. Why?' Mallon asked.

'He just might decide to make a statement, tell us a bit more after a long night in the cells. I'll charge him in the morning one way or another.'

Mallon had opened a bottle of some sort of white Bordeaux. It was not sufficiently chilled, but Swallow sipped it out of politeness.

'What's happening with Kelly over at the Bridewell?' he asked.

Mallon shrugged.

'He's sticking to his guns. He denies everything, refuses to answer any questions. He says he answers to the assistant under-secretary for security, Mr Smith Berry, and he'll talk to nobody else.'

Swallow felt his anger beginning to rise again.

'By God, if I was over there I'd find a way to make him talk. That's where I should be now.'

'Don't let your anger get the better of you, Joe,' Elizabeth Mallon said quietly. 'You'll be no good to Maria when she comes home from hospital if you're like that.'

Mallon grunted.

'Elizabeth's right, Swallow. Everyone understands your anger and how you want to see Kelly pay for what's done. And you've just demonstrated the reason you're not over in the Bridewell. This is too personal for you. You're too close to it. Leave it to Pat Mossop and the others.'

He poured more wine.

'Cummins should be at the Bridewell around now. If he identifies Kelly as the man he saw at Chapel Court when Nellie Byrne was murdered that'll be more than enough to have him charged.'

'Cummins is a fairly good witness,' Swallow said. 'He keeps on saying that he knew the man and thought he was a policeman. He said he'd know him again if he saw him.'

'That's true,' Mallon agreed. 'But even if Cummins doesn't identify Kelly, the fact that he had the dead woman's post office book in his pocket is damning.'

'Sure,' Swallow nodded. 'What do we know from the details in the book? Was Nellie deeply involved in the Fenian business?'

'Oh indeed she was,' Mallon said. 'The book was in the name of Helena Moyles, and that name meant nothing to the post office people in their routine spot checks. Upwards of £2,000 has been moved in and out of the account over the past two years. That kind of money can buy a lot of revolvers from soldiers or sailors looking to make a few quid. Or from quarry workers who can put a few sticks of dynamite away every month.'

'Maybe you should stop talking about work, John,' Elizabeth Mallon said.

There was a hint of sharpness in her voice.

'The hour is late. You should take your own advice perhaps and leave this Major Kelly to the men in the Bridewell. I'd like to hear from Joe about how Maria is doing and when she will be coming home from hospital.'

Swallow saw a fleeting look of resentment or annoyance in John Mallon's face. But the chief of detectives was outranked in this domestic setting.

'Very well, Elizabeth. We'll speak no more of police business until we've finished our supper.'

Swallow felt a tinge of resentment too. He wanted to hear more of what had transpired in Kelly's arrest and questioning. But he had to take his lead from Mallon.

'Thank you, Mrs Mallon,' Swallow told her. 'Maria is weak and tired, but out of any danger, thank God. I saw her first thing this morning and she's deeply upset, naturally. But she's strong and she's determined to be back to her usual routine as soon as possible. Dr Morrow says that it's for the best, both in her physical well-being and for her emotional state.'

'It's far from an easy thing for a woman,' Elizabeth Mallon said gently. 'And I know it's not easy for the husband, the father, either. But thank God she's not in any danger, and who knows, there may be other blessings, other children, in your life ahead.'

Swallow nodded.

'You're right, Mrs Mallon. We try to count our blessings.'

'And forgive our enemies,' she said.

Swallow saw the flash of annoyance again in Mallon's eyes. And he saw Mallon watching him, reading his own mood. He recalled what his boss had once told him after a clash with a particularly obnoxious civil servant: 'Forgive thine enemies … but bloody well remember their names and addresses.'

The maid had started to clear away the dinner plates when a bell jangled on the wall beside the mantle. Mallon came to alert.

'Front door,' he said unnecessarily, rising from his chair. 'I'll see who it is.'

Swallow could hear the short, muffled exchange from the hallway before Mallon came back into the room. He did not resume his seat at the dining table.

'You'll have to excuse us, dear,' he told his wife. 'The assistant under-secretary for security wants to see me with Detective Inspector Swallow in his office immediately.'

FORTY-THREE

The man sitting beside Howard Smith Berry reminded Swallow of nothing as much as a lean hunting dog. Deep, cold eyes were set in a long, cavernous face. He was perhaps forty years of age. A heavy moustache framed thin, unsmiling lips. His sandy hair, turning to grey, was neatly parted in the middle. He wore the standard well-cut dark suit of the senior bureaucrat, with starched white collar and cuffs and a neat bow-tie in dark silk.

Swallow had never met him. But he knew the chief secretary for Ireland, Arthur Balfour, by sight. He had worked on his protection detail on a number of occasions since his appointment as the head of the British administration in Ireland almost two years previously.

'Bloody Balfour,' as he was commonly referred to by Irish nationalists, was no ordinary civil servant. His uncle, Lord Salisbury, was prime minister. He was reputed to be the wealthiest minister in the government. The Balfour family fortunes were grounded in the lucrative business of provisioning the forces holding the empire in India. He had earned his unflattering soubriquet through his zealous promulgation of stern measures to suppress agrarian unrest and by his implacable opposition to Home Rule for Ireland. His Coercion Act, passed into law a year previously, had given the Crown extraordinary powers to suppress opposition and dissent, including the suspension of trial by jury.

It was evident from the moment that Swallow and Mallon crossed the Upper Yard to Smith Berry's office that this was not to be a routine briefing or anything such. Two of Kelly's secret service men, swaddled in heavy winter coats that bulged with concealed firearms, guarded the doorway. Two others were posted on the landing outside the under-secretary's office.

Smith Berry sat behind his desk with the chief secretary to his right. Waters, the former RIC man whom Swallow had previously encountered at Mallon's house, sat to his left. Unusually, there were no clerks or secretaries present to take notes. The turf fires that normally blazed in the two grates were out. Swallow surmised that the trio had not been in the office very long, but that they had held earlier conversations elsewhere.

'Sit down,' Smith Berry commanded.

Swallow and Mallon took the two chairs indicated in front of the desk.

'Mr Mallon, you know the chief secretary, Sir Arthur Balfour, of course,' Smith Berry said.

'Of course. Good evening, sir.'

Balfour nodded in recognition, almost imperceptibly. Swallow was not introduced. A mere detective inspector was the beneath the notice of Her Majesty's Chief Secretary for Ireland, he knew.

'Mr Mallon,' Smith Berry said icily, 'you have utterly overstepped your authority in detaining Major Nigel Kelly, a senior officer of my department, and a gentleman I should add, personally selected for his duties in Ireland by the chief secretary himself. Mr Balfour's presence here is earnest, as I would hope you understand, of the gravity of the situation in which you have placed yourself.'

Mallon looked oddly relaxed, Swallow thought. He had observed this technique before in challenging encounters. It involved absolute discipline and a refusal to respond emotionally to whatever might transpire. When the chief of detectives spoke, his voice was even and calm.

'Mr Smith Berry, Major Kelly is in lawful custody and is to be charged with murder of Helena Moyles, alias Helen or Ellen Byrne, alias Nellie Sweet. I'm sure the chief secretary understands that it is my duty to investigate serious crimes, of which murder is, of course, the most serious, and to bring to justice those towards whom the evidence of responsibility is pointing.'

Smith Berry snorted in annoyance.

'Major Kelly is not guilty of any murder, Mr Mallon. And if you had any sense of your wider duty you would have reported to me before taking any action against a senior and valued officer of my department.'

'You will be aware that I sought twice to meet with you over the past two days, sir,' Mallon countered, 'and on both occasions the message came back that you were otherwise engaged.'

Swallow saw Smith Berry wince slightly. He believed he saw Balfour's eyes flicker briefly as the riposte was delivered.

'Do not be disingenuous with me, Mr Mallon,' Smith Berry said. 'I do not believe, even if I had been able to make time to see you, that you would have informed me of this ... proposed outrage.'

'It is true I wanted to discuss a number of things, sir, but I would never fail to inform you fully on matters within your purview.'

It was a skilful answer.

Balfour spoke for the first time.

'I had not understood that you sought to speak with the assistant under-secretary, Mr Mallon. What was it that you wished to discuss with him, please?'

Swallow felt a surge of elation. The conversation was playing right into Mallon's hands.

'Thank you, sir,' Mallon nodded to the chief secretary. 'I would have briefed Mr Smith Berry, as I always do, on the progress of criminal investigations and on matters pertaining to security. I would also have wished to register my dismay and concern at sending armed men under Major Kelly's command to raid the dwelling accommodation occupied by Detective Inspector Swallow and his wife.'

'It was perfectly legal, and made necessary by your failure and his to produce official records under your control,' Smith Berry shot back.

'Legal, perhaps,' Mallon said. 'Necessary or appropriate, not at all. Inspector Swallow and his men have done all in their power to locate these documents. He and I have co-operated in every way possible with your officers. But you, sir, might equally well have consulted me before undertaking any such action against a senior member of G-Division who is also one of your most loyal and diligent servants in the struggle against subversion and crime.'

This time Swallow was sure he saw a flicker in Balfour's eyes.

'May I speak, sir?' he asked.

Balfour nodded.

'Sir, you are with us here in Ireland, I know, something less than two years. But you will know that Mr Mallon and the men he leads, of whom I have the honour to be one, are untiring in the discharge of their duties. It was nothing less than a betrayal of my loyalty, when I was absent on duty, out of the country, that Major Kelly and a group of his men should violate the sanctity of my home and manhandle my wife, causing her injuries that have led to the loss of the child she was carrying in her womb. Every man in G-Division is appalled and angered at this action.'

Balfour leaned forward.

'I am aware of what happened, Swallow. And I regret it. But as I understand it your wife sought to obstruct Major Kelly in his search. What happened was an accident. Unintended and regrettable, but an accident nonetheless. Major Kelly was seeking to locate certain files which, I understand, you had been requested to produce.'

Swallow started to answer, but Mallon raised a silencing hand.

'Sir, if I may,' he addressed the chief secretary. 'I am sure that Detective Inspector Swallow appreciates your expression of regret. And I am sure that you can understand his distress. His wife is yet in hospital and will require ongoing medical care and rest. I would prefer to return to the matter of Major Kelly's detention, if I may.'

'You may, Mr Mallon,' Balfour's tone hardened. 'But nothing I have said should be construed as dissenting from Mr Smith Berry's sense of outrage at the major's arrest.'

'Thank you, sir. But I believe it is important to state that the evidence against Major Kelly in respect of this particularly brutal crime is strong. He was identified at the scene by one witness, and I expect that identification to be confirmed by a constable on duty nearby on the night that the girl was killed. Moreover, the dead girl's post office account book was found in Major Kelly's pocket by one of my officers in the arrest party. Finally, we have evidence that Major Kelly had been a visitor to the dead girl's accommodation on a number of occasions.'

'Is that all, Mallon?' Balfour asked.

'I should add perhaps that the Dublin police have been the target of criticism from various quarters because of a number of murders and violent attacks on women in recent times. No doubt you're aware of some of the comment in the press, sir. In the difficult times we live in, it is more important than ever, I suggest, that the police are shown to be capable and efficient in the discharge of their duties on behalf of the population.'

Balfour nodded.

'Well said, Mr Mallon. And insofar as I can go, I agree with your sentiments. But there are wider considerations, and there are aspects to this matter of which you may not be aware.'

He gestured to Smith Berry.

'Would you be kind enough to explain to the gentlemen what you have told me about Major Kelly's excellent work?'

Smith Berry's face showed a satisfied smile.

'Certainly, sir. The facts are, gentlemen, that Major Kelly had recruited the deceased woman as a paid agent, an informer if you like. She was deeply involved with members of the so-called Irish Republican Brotherhood, the Fenians. She acted as an agent in the financing of guns and explosives. Major Kelly had, shall we say, socialised with her. He worked his way into her confidence and had accumulated a great amount of valuable intelligence on the Fenian organisation, its personnel, its structures and its intentions. This is information, I might add, that had not come in through G-Division's intelligence system. Or, if it had, no action was taken about it.'

'With respect, sir,' Mallon said, 'G-Division was well aware of the girl's association with members of violent organisations. My judgement was that it was better to watch, to wait and to build information rather than rushing in to arrest a relatively minor individual.'

Mallon was gilding the lily, Swallow knew. What G-Division knew about Helena Moyles, alias Nellie Byrne, was that she kept bad company with Fenians and other subversives. The fact was that they had no knowledge of her role as an intermediary in the procuring of guns and explosives for the insurrectionaries. Kelly and his agents had somehow procured intelligence that G-Division had not. Mallon was on thin ice.

Waters spoke for the first time.

'The amount of money that passed through the hands of this "relatively minor individual", as you describe her, bought a great number of guns for the Fenians, Mr Mallon. How long would you have allowed that to continue?'

It was a skilful, tricky question, Swallow knew, put by a senior policeman with a lifetime's knowledge of his subject.

'I don't know, Mr Waters,' Mallon answered. 'But I would say that if we had taken the girl out of circulation, it would only be a matter of days before the Fenians would have replaced her. And it might take some time for us to identify her replacement. I'd also say that what is really important is to know the Fenians' intentions in regard to the weapons they have. And nothing in my intelligence reports suggests that they have any imminent intention of using them.'

Waters nodded thoughtfully. He understood that Mallon had a point, Swallow reckoned.

Balfour raised a hand.

'There's a lot of speculation here, and I haven't all night to sit listening.'

He jabbed a finger towards Mallon.

'I'm not going to waste time, Mr Mallon, and I'm not at all required to set out any reasons to you to justify my decisions. But I have heard much about you, and I have a high regard for the work you do. I believe it is better that I persuade you to my way of thinking rather than simply issuing a directive.'

He looked to Smith Berry.

'The assistant under-secretary has taken the matter of Miss Byrne's or Miss Moyles's death very seriously. Notwithstanding her unfortunate station in life and her involvement with violent elements, she was entitled to live out her natural span of years, however long or short that might have been. Major Kelly has furnished Mr Smith Berry with a fully convincing account of the circumstances that led to Miss Byrne's death. And while her demise was unfortunate, I have absolutely no doubt that she was the instrument of her own fate and that no blame whatsoever can attach to Major Kelly.'

Swallow could not contain himself any longer.

'This girl was attacked savagely. Beaten to death, sir. She didn't do it to herself.'

'Do not be impertinent, Inspector,' Smith Berry snapped. 'Remember who you are addressing.'

Mallon raised a pacifying hand.

'You'll forgive Inspector Swallow's distress, I know. He has been deeply affected by what happened to his wife when Major Kelly searched his dwelling place. But I would be grateful if you could set out the reasons why Major Kelly is to be exonerated. I cannot see any circumstances in which he can be considered blameless.'

'That may be a failure on your part, Mallon,' Smith Berry replied. 'Perhaps you have not approached this matter with a sufficiently open mind. The fact is that Major Kelly was violently assaulted by the now deceased Miss Byrne when he went to visit her in pursuit of his intelligence-gathering duties. She was frequently inebriated, as you may know. When Major Kelly arrived at Chapel Court on the evening of her death, she told him that she believed he was a spy, and she made to stab him with a knife that she had concealed in her clothing. He pushed her away, but she rushed at him in a fury. He pushed her away a second time and endeavoured to take the knife from her. When she attempted to stab him again, he grabbed the knife by the blade, sustaining a deep cut. He struck her on the head with his revolver and she fell, striking her skull on the fire grate. Major Kelly attempted to revive her, but she had expired. Concerned that his security could be compromised, he departed rapidly and reported the incident in full at this office.'

Mallon was silent.

'Mr Smith Berry,' he said quietly after an interval, 'I have no doubt that these are the facts as you have been told. But the medical examiner, Dr Lafeyre, has reported that the dead woman had at least eight wounds to her head. She was beaten repeatedly. She did not simply fall against the fire grate as Major Kelly has claimed. The version of events that has evidently been given to you is a one-sided and self-serving account by the chief suspect. And it is utterly contradicted by the medical facts as established by the city medical examiner.'

'Enough,' Balfour said sharply. 'This is not a cross-examination in a criminal court. The issue is not how many times this woman was struck.

The reality is that a valued agent of this department, a distinguished officer from one of the finest regiments in the army, found himself in a situation that was not of his choosing while endeavouring to discharge his duties. I will not have him placed in jeopardy as a result of this woman's death.'

He pointed his finger at Mallon again.

'I am giving you a direct instruction, chief superintendent. You will arrange the immediate release of Major Kelly from police custody. And you will have all statements, files or any other papers relating to his arrest and detention delivered here to this office forthwith. Are you clear on this?'

'I understand your instruction, Mr Balfour,' Mallon said evenly. 'But it goes against my every instinct as a police officer and as a Christian who believes that man's justice should seek to emulate that of the creator. A great wrong has been done here.'

Balfour put his hand wearyingly to his forehead.

'Chief superintendent, I do not have the luxury of being able to think like a policeman, or to indulge in abstract morality propositions. If I did my life would be a lot simpler. And if I could, I would arrange the world—or this country at least—in the shape that the creator probably intended it to be. But I cannot do that either. So I repeat my instruction. Release Major Kelly or by midnight there will be a new chief superintendent in charge of G-Division.'

Tuesday January 8th, 1889

FORTY-FOUR

'Dan Flannery's done what?'

If the G-man on orderly duty at the public office in Exchange Court had told him that Queen Victoria was having breakfast in the police canteen, Swallow could not have been more incredulous.

'I'm telling you, Inspector. He walked in here not ten minutes ago asking for yourself, and telling me he wants to confess to the murder of his sister.'

'You can't be serious?'

'I wouldn't make jokes about something like that, sir.'

'Where is he then?'

'Johnny Vizzard took him up to your office, sir. He's above there with him now. Martin Shanahan's there too. Vizzard said to tell you the second you showed your face here.'

Swallow took the stairs two at a time and flung open the door to the crime inspector's office.

Vizzard was standing beside his desk. Dan Flannery was sitting on a bentwood chair in front of the desk. Martin Shanahan was seated between Flannery and the door. Vizzard looked distraught. He leaped to his feet when Swallow entered the room.

'Can I have a word, sir? Outside, that is.' The young G-man was struggling to keep his voice steady.

They stepped into the corridor. Vizzard strode rapidly to the landing to ensure they were out of earshot.

'Did I hear right from the duty man downstairs?' Swallow asked.

Vizzard nodded vigorously.

'Yes, sir. I think so, sir. I was just in the door myself. Flannery came into the public office just ahead of me. He had a copy of *The Freeman's Journal* and he flung it down on the desk. "Let me see Inspector Swallow," he says. God, but it was strange, sir. There was tears coming down his face, but he was laughing. A sort of bitter, mad laugh, sir.'

'What did you do?'

'We told him you weren't in yet but that you'd be here in a while. So he opened the newspaper and showed us the report about Werner being in custody and going to be charged for the Alice Flannery murder. "The German didn't do it," he says. "I did it. I killed her, God forgive me. But I won't see an innocent man hang for something he didn't do." That's what he said, sir.'

He showed Swallow his notebook.

'I wrote it down, sir. Exactly like he said.'

Swallow's brain was spinning. It made no sense. Dan Flannery's alibi had held up, or so it seemed. The witness he named had placed him at Huband Bridge, well away from Blackberry Lane at the time his sister had been attacked. In contrast, Werner had no alibi, he had a motive, and he had a record of violence.

'Of course,' he said. 'Yes, writing it down is important. Well done.'

'He says he'll sign a statement,' Vizzard said. 'But he wants you to witness it.'

'Is he fantasising?' Swallow asked. 'Does he seem rational? Coherent? It may all be in his imagination, a story he's making up for some reason.'

'I don't know, sir. He seems a bit distracted all right, but he doesn't sound like a man out of his mind.'

'Right,' Swallow nodded. 'I'll take it from here. Would you get one of the lads to slip down the yard and tell Chief Mallon what's happened? But not a syllable to anyone else. And tell that fella down on the desk in the public office to keep his mouth shut too.'

Dan Flannery attempted a weak laugh when Swallow re-entered the crime inspector's office with Johnny Vizzard.

'Well, Mr Swallow, it turns out yer not so smart after all, are you?'

Swallow pulled up a chair and sat.

'Will you tell me what all this is about, Dan?'

310

'I killed her. I killed Alice, Mr Swallow. It's as simple as that.'

'You'd want to be very careful now, Dan.' Swallow put a hand on his shoulder. 'I need to tell you that anything more that you say will be taken down in writing here by Detective Vizzard, and it may be used in evidence. Do you understand that?'

'Of course I do. I'm not a fool.'

Swallow nodded to Vizzard to take out his notebook.

'Before you say anything else, I'd remind you that you already made a statement denying anything to do with Alice's death and saying that you weren't anywhere near home when she was killed. You gave us an alibi that you were at Huband Bridge and you told us that a man called Geoffrey Bradley, a former teacher of yours from Synge Street Christian Brothers School, met you there. And you told me to look to the priest as her killer.'

Flannery made a little laugh.

'Ah, that's true. I did. And I'd have been happy if you'd blamed him. He's the cause o' me sister's death even if it was me own hand that ended her life.'

'Would you explain that to me?' Swallow asked.

'I waited for her comin' home up the laneway. I knew where she'd pass, and I waited in the gateway. I was goin' to use a big stone. There's lots of them on the roadway there. But I found that post, a big heavy wooden thing, and I just swung it at her. I hit her a few times.'

'Why did you want to do that to your sister?' Swallow asked, watching Vizzard's pencil flying across the pages of his notebook.

'I didn't tell you the full truth about her and the priest. Well, a lot of what I said was true, about him botherin' her and makin' to get close to her and all that. But I didn't want to say what was really goin' on.'

He hesitated. Swallow saw that he was blushing deeply.

'Tell me, Dan.'

'Well, truth is that she was leadin' him on. Oh, I could see it, and I said to her, "You shouldn't be makin' free with him. He's a priest. He's God's anointed. If you put temptation in his way, it's a terrible sin." '

'What did she say to that?'

'She told me that it didn't matter. She said that Protestant ministers get married, and that he said he'd turn Protestant and marry her. But I knew that was just her imagination. A priest can't leave the priesthood.'

'You're not telling me you killed her because she had developed some sort of an idea about Father Cavendish?'

'I am so.'

'But why in God's name?' Swallow asked. 'How could that justify doing what you did to her?'

Flannery frowned.

'You're a Catholic yourself, aren't you?'

'Not that it's any of your business, but yes.'

'Then you should understand the shame and the sin that would be involved. My poor mother would rather die, and my father would turn in his grave. The idea that their daughter would descend to the level of a prostitute, throwin' herself at a priest!'

Swallow struggled for words. In his years as a crime detective he had encountered many strange motives. This was beyond his experience, or indeed his imagination.

'If I said I didn't believe you, Dan, it would be because I can't conceive of anyone choosing to do violence to a young woman, much less your own sister, whatever you might think about her behaviour.'

'Well, Mr Swallow, your standards and mine are probably very different. You don't have any difficulty it seems workin' for England against your own people, your own country and your own faith. So I don't imagine you'd understand how someone like me could want to stand by their principles.'

Swallow shook his head.

'I'm sorry, Dan. You've got a very warped sense of values if you think murder can be justified like that. You know it was more than likely that any foolish notions Alice had would probably have just faded away in time.'

'I don't think God would see what I did as murder.'

'You're able to read the mind of God, then?' Swallow said.

'I know what's right and what's wrong,' Flannery answered. 'Just as I knew when I saw that you'd taken in an innocent man that I couldn't let him go to the hangman. So I'm willin' and prepared to pay the price.'

Swallow stood.

'It's not for me to say, but I think you will pay the price, Dan. You'll pay it in a court of law, and you'll pay it before God in time.'

'I know that,' Flannery said simply.

'Will you sign the statement that Detective Vizzard will draft up now from his notes?'

'I will.'

'Then I'm charging you formally now with the murder of Alice Flannery on or about 8 November 1888 at a place within the city of Dublin.'

He turned to Shanahan.

'Martin, would you go down to the cells and release Mr Stefan Werner? Tell him he's free to go. And send a message up to the governor at Mountjoy. There'll be no charges against Michael Joseph Carmody. They can open the gate and let him out.'

FORTY-FIVE

'Thus conscience doth make cowards of us all.'

John Mallon filled a third of Swallow's tumbler from a newly opened bottle of Tullamore. He pushed the water jug across the desk.

'That's Shakespeare, you know. *Hamlet*. He'd have made a good detective, Shakespeare. Great insight into the criminal mind. It's all about conscience, that *Hamlet*. That's what made young Flannery admit what he'd done. I wonder if anyone's ever counted the numbers of cases in this city when fellows have walked into police stations and said "I did it"? There's something to be said for the Catholic sense of guilt.'

'Are you shifting your loyalties, chief?' Swallow gestured to Mallon's whiskey glass. 'Abandoning your beloved Bushmills for the vines of the King's County?'

Mallon managed a thin smile.

'Ah no, I thought you deserved something special. You've been through a rough passage. And I know you only drink the Bushmills out of politeness and to humour me.'

Swallow added water to his whiskey.

'I appreciate the thought, chief. But it wasn't necessary. Bushmills is no hardship. I nearly sunk the whole bloody ship, chief,' he said quietly. 'I nearly walked the wrong man into court on a murder charge.'

A blast of January wind rattled the windows of Mallon's front parlour. Elizabeth Mallon had drawn the curtains before retiring, but the black of the winter night seeped through from the Lower Yard outside.

'Don't let it worry you, Joe,' Mallon said. 'Sometimes one's instincts get knocked off course too. That's all that happened. I'd have probably gone for Werner as the most likely suspect myself. Though you've got to give credit to Feore. He had doubts where both of us believed the evidence pointed in one direction.' He laughed. 'And we managed to get the misers in the Upper Yard to fund your visit to Berlin. That's an achievement, even if it led nowhere.'

'I know, chief.' Swallow threw back a mouthful of the whiskey. 'But I'd have put money on Werner as our man. He's a slimy, slippery bastard. And if he's not guilty of Alice Flannery's murder, I'll wager he's guilty of something else. I didn't believe his story about being with someone else's wife when he spun it, and I don't believe it now.'

'It's not relevant now, at any event,' Mallon said. 'He wouldn't be the first suspect to come up with that sort of thing. And you wouldn't be the first policeman whose instincts told him it was all bull. Did he say why he fled from the New Vienna when you and Vizzard went to arrest him? If he had nothing to hide, he wouldn't have run.'

'I think in Germany when the police come calling for you, most people try to make themselves scarce,' Swallow said. 'But there might be a more specific reason. Pat Mossop got word from a pal of his in the excise office that Mr Werner owes a lot of money to the Crown, built up over the years for imported wines and spirits at the New Vienna. Maybe he thought we were coming to collect it.'

'If that's the case, the excise people will get their due. They always do,' Mallon mused. 'Right now, just be thankful that you held back and didn't charge him. That was good judgement too. So be thankful that we don't have to explain our way out of that.'

Swallow knew he was right.

'I shouldn't have been taken in by Dan Flannery either,' he said ruefully. 'Mossop has checked out that alibi. Flannery said he'd been seen at Huband Bridge by this fellow Geoffrey Bradley, his teacher from Synge Street. But it turns out that Geoffrey Bradley is also Seathrún Ó Brolcháin. It's the Irish version of the name. And he's a member, along with young Flannery, of the Hibernian League. These patriot fellows will swear a hole in a tin bucket to protect each other. Giving a brother-member an alibi in a police investigation wouldn't be a big thing.'

'It should have been checked earlier,' Mallon said. 'Did we have him on our books?'

'In the Irish form only. Ó Brolcháin's been known to G-Division for at least a year. He was in teacher training with my sister. But these fellows slip from an Irish name to an English one and we lose track of them.'

'We should be ahead of that game,' Mallon said testily. 'The first thing you do when you go back to the office is to put out an instruction that subjects under surveillance or investigation should be recorded under both English and Irish forms.'

'I'll do that that, chief,' Swallow said. 'And we'll deal with Bradley. At very least we'll do him for giving false information and wasting police time.'

Mallon grunted.

'Put him away if you can. Another bloody liar.'

'Right, chief, we'll do our best.'

Mallon frowned.

'I want to say that I'm sorry about Kelly. It's shameful.'

'You had no choice, chief, I know that,' Swallow said. 'But it's bloody hard to think of him out somewhere tonight laughing at us, while my Maria is lying above in the Rotunda.'

Mallon poured himself another shot of Tullamore.

'No, Joe. I didn't have a choice. No bloody choice at all. Did you do any Latin at school?'

'I did.'

'Then you'll know the phrase, "*salus populi suprema lex est*", I'm sure.'

'The safety of the people is the supreme law.'

'Absolutely,' Mallon said.

There was bitterness in the one-word sentence.

'The safety of the people, as defined by our lords in Westminster, overrules every other consideration. So Major Nigel Kelly may be a killer and a brute, but as long as he's doing the dirty work of the powers that be, they'll stand behind him and give him cover.'

He drank from his tumbler of Tullamore.

'I'm truly sorry, Joe. For you, for Maria, for your baby. I wish there was a way for me to say that we could nail him.'

'It's not your fault, chief,' Swallow said. 'I understand the rules of the game at this stage. We're just the gravel on the road. Small cogs in a big wheel … and so on. I know that if you didn't release Kelly you'd be gone from your job within the hour, and some time-serving arse-lick from England would be in your place.'

Mallon thought silently for a moment.

'Maybe there's a case for stripping away all this pretence. Maybe it would be better to have all those bloodless Englishmen in charge rather than the likes of you and me. We're as Irish as any of the characters we chase and trace, sometimes arrest, sometimes see on their way to jail and sometimes see to the gallows, like the Invincibles.'

'D'ye think so, chief?' Swallow asked.

'Ah, not really. We can keep some sort of grip on things. Maybe save Ireland from the foolishness of the English. That's why we stay with this job, I often think.' He laughed. 'Apart from the great wages, that is.'

Swallow echoed the laugh.

'All for the empire upon which the sun will never set.'

'Indeed,' Mallon smiled. 'And you know why that is?'

'Tell me.'

'Because God couldn't trust the English for what they'd likely do in the dark.'

'I'll drink to that, chief.'

Maybe, Swallow thought to himself. Maybe Mallon was right. It was a whole rotten mess. Nigel Kelly should be in a prison cell awaiting trial and then facing the rope for the murder of Nellie Byrne. He and Maria should be facing into the light of spring and then the warmth of summer, anticipating the arrival of their first-born child. A young woman called Alice Flannery should be building her dream of being a cook in a restaurant or a great house. Instead, she lay in a cold grave in Mount Jerome.

It would be so easy to walk away from it all.

'By the way,' Mallon said, 'there's developments in the Debbie Dunne case too. The bobbies in Irishtown had a walk-in. A lunatic navy deserter, living down by the Grand Canal Dock in a shed, just rolled in to them and confessed to it. He says he thought she was a lady of the night. God gave him an order to do it, he says. Harry Lafeyre has sent him for a mental examination at the Richmond Asylum.'

Strange, Swallow thought. Two murders and one near-murder, all in one small city over a few short weeks. A terrifying pattern of violence, it seemed. And now, when it was all broken down, it was no more than a series of unconnected criminal acts, committed by unconnected perpetrators, motivated by the basest instincts. Such was the nature of his work, he reflected. Individual human crises and tragedies would arise to be dealt with every day. A policeman's lot.

'All part of the rich tapestry of life,' Mallon said, as if reading his thoughts. 'Wouldn't you be thankful to Jesus that we're not dealing with anything like that Ripper business in London?'

Swallow took a sizeable draught from his whiskey.

'You're right, chief. But maybe Stephen Doolan wasn't totally off the mark talking about that "Dolocher" fellow attacking women around Dublin forty years ago. There's always characters living on the edge of sanity. They can be set off by anything. Even a newspaper report of a killing somewhere else.'

Mallon shrugged.

'Who knows? Maybe the doctors in the Richmond will get inside the mind of this navy deserter fellow.'

He rose from his chair and walked to the window, drew back the curtain and stared out into darkness of the Lower Yard.

'I've got to stay with it, Joe. I could understand it if you wanted to throw it all to hell and leave the job. But I can tell you, I won't let the bastards drive me out. And if you want to stay with me in holding the line, I'll be glad to have you on my flank. No obligation, but you know what I'm saying.'

'I do, chief.'

Swallow checked his watch. It was coming to eleven o'clock. Maria would want him to be at M & M Grant's to oversee last drinks and to see the last of the night's clientele off the premises. Time to be on his way.

He drained the last of his Tullamore and stood to go.

'I'll go home, chief. Thanks for the drink. I enjoyed it. And I appreciate the words. I need to do a lot of thinking about all this.'

Mallon nodded.

'I understand. You need to get some sleep and get ready to welcome Maria home. You'll be needed for a while there. Let me know whatever you want in terms of leave and I'll make sure it's all right.'

'Thanks, chief. Good night.'

Mallon crossed to the door.

'There's been big developments in London, by the way. Parnell's lawyer, Russell, has exposed the *Times* letters as forgeries, put together by that chancer, Pigott. The word is that Pigott has gone on the run. They say he's gone to Spain.'

Swallow grinned.

'They're welcome to him out there. It's one less reptile around Dublin.'

'Tell me,' Mallon pulled a mock-serious grin, 'is there any sign of those protection logs that you've been searching for at Exchange Court? I'm sure the lads been going at it with all the resources they have.'

He opened the door to allow Swallow to step out into the icy air of the Lower Castle Yard.

'Not a sign, sir, not a sign. But you can be certain, in a matter so important, I'll ensure that not a minute is wasted.'

Friday January 11th, 1889

FORTY-SIX

Harry Lafeyre offered to make his brougham available to bring Maria home. Swallow was more than happy to accept the offer.

He had met Dr Morrow, her physician, at the hospital on the evening before her discharge. Morrow was confident about Maria's recovery, but he was at pains that she would follow a strict regime of rest and take a nourishing diet for at least a month after returning home.

'No watching over the business until all hours,' he admonished. 'She should have at least eight hours' sleep each night and a long rest in the afternoons. And she needs to eat well. Regularity is important too. Meals at the same time each day. And plenty of nutrition. I understand you have a good cook, so get her to put up food that's restorative but easily digestible … stews, chicken, fresh vegetables and fruit.'

Lafeyre's driver, Scollan, displayed a surprising gentleness in assisting Maria from the hospital doorway to the carriage, taking one arm as Swallow took the other. She stood for a moment at the door, taking in the strange sights and sounds of the outside world after the quiet confinement of the recovery ward. At first, the thin January light was hard on her eyes. Swallow saw faint, dark half-circles above her fine cheekbones.

Scollan took them home to Thomas Street at a gentle pace, along Capel Street, up Ormond Quay and across the river to Winetavern Street. Swallow had told him to avoid the route that would take them past the Castle and Exchange Court. Anything or any place that could be associated with his work and the events of the past week was best avoided.

A pale sun was setting to the west, bringing the city's short day to a close. For a brief minute as they made their way past Cornmarket it threw a weak, yellow light across the roofs of the houses.

Swallow squeezed Maria's hand gently as they turned into Thomas Street.

'You know, we're nearly halfway through January. A couple of weeks and it'll be February, the first month of spring.'

She smiled for the first time since they had left the Rotunda.

'Ah, go on. That's only an idea. Spring is a long way off.'

'No,' he countered, 'St Brigid's Day is the 1st of February. That's the day the birds start looking for mates to build their nests with. They know the winter's over.'

'They make a fresh start, I suppose,' she said. 'There's new life isn't there? It's well for them,' she added after a moment.

Scollan drew the carriage to a halt at the side door of M & M Grant's. Carrie, the housekeeper, was out to greet them, followed by Tess the maid and Tom, the head man from the bar.

'You're welcome home, ma'am. A thousand times welcome,' Carrie called out.

Tess could find no words. She clutched her apron to her face in silent emotion.

'God bless you, missus,' said Tom quietly.

When Scollan had departed and the others had gone back to their work, Swallow and Maria settled into their usual places in the parlour over the public house. Tess had left a strong turf fire going in the grate and the lamps had been lit. Outside on the street, darkness had overtaken the failing day.

This was their citadel, their redoubt, where they always sat to settle the issues of the day, to support each other in whatever challenges it had thrown up, and increasingly, as time went on, to exchange words of tenderness and love.

And sometimes they said nothing at all. It wasn't always necessary. All that they needed to feel complete was to sit quietly together, listening to the sounds of the street below and the occasional whisper of the ash falling in the turf fire.

– The End –